Dead Parrot

Dead Parrot

John Huxley

Walla Walla Press

Published by Walla Walla Press
P.O. Box 717
Petersham, New South Wales 2049
Webpage: *www.asc.zipworld.com.au*

ISBN 1 876718 66 8

Edited, designed and formatted by Ed 'n' Art, Newport, Sydney
Printed by Ligare Pty Ltd

Front cover illustration
Night Parrots painted by William Cooper

DISCLAIMER: Though some of the scenes, many of the police
procedures and all of the birds, including the night parrot, are
meant to be realistic, the characters in this book are entirely
fictitious, and any resemblance to actual persons living or dead,
is purely coincidental.

If at all, then fringe dwellers
                    of the centre.
Ghosts of samphire, navigators
of the star-clustered tussocks.
Of salty marsh, limestone niches,
                    and acrid airs.

If at all, then flitting obscurely
The rims of water tanks, the outlands
of spotlights and filaments of powerlines…
in brief nocturnal flight, with *long
drawn out mournful whistle*

If at all, then moths in a paper lantern.

～ John Kinsella, *Night Parrots*

ACKNOWLEDGMENTS

Thanks to John Kinsella and Fremantle Art Centre Press for allowing me to quote from *Night Parrots* and to the National Library of Australia for permission to reproduce William Cooper's painting. Both are exquisite works of art.

Details about the real-life search for the night parrot were drawn from the author's own extensive research, including field visits and interviews, and several other sources. Foremost among these was *The Flight of the Emu: A Hundred Years of Australian Ornithology 1901–2001*, by Libby Robin, for whose encouragement I am most grateful. Some of the chapter quotes came from the anthology *An Exhilaration of Birds*, edited by Jen Hill. Reference was made to *The Field Guide to Australian Birds* by Graham Pizzey and Frank Knight, among other bird guides.

Specialist information on birds was supplied by members of Birding NSW, including Alan K. Morris, its records officer. Impressions of Botany Bay, on which the fictional Moreton Bay is loosely based, were picked up on visits in the company of Phil Straw, respected leader of the NSW Wader Group.

The NSW Police Service, and especially Superintendent Nick Kaldas, kindly provided advice on procedures about the *e@gle.i* system.

Examples of recent advances in forensics were taken from Deborah Smith's article 'Body of Evidence' (*Sydney Morning Herald*, 23 March 2002).

I also want to thank Mac and Libby Jacob, Nigel and Sandra Marsh,

Garrett and Frannie Jones, Sam North, Andrew Keenan and Sandra Harvey for their encouragement, Selwa Anthony for her advice and patience, and Richard Cashman, John O'Hara and Margaret Gallogly of Walla Walla Press for their assistance in the publication of *Dead Parrot*.

Finally, I want to thank Carol Floyd — not just for her meticulous editing, but also for resolving several inconsistencies in the plot and suggesting many more improvements.

All the mistakes, obviously, are my own.

To my wife, Marianne, our families and friends, and
to birders everywhere

1

One man may take a walk and scarcely see a bird; another with him, sees or hears, perhaps five and twenty species.
— A.J.R. Roberts, *The Bird Book*

It was going to be the most wonderful day. Madelaine Warnock just knew it. A whole day birdwatching. Well, several hours' birdwatching: ticking off species, perhaps spotting one or two new ones. The time would be broken by a pleasant picnic overlooking the harbour, chatting with friends — again, some old, some new, she hoped — and relaxing.

What a pleasant change from all that sex and violence and crime and corruption that she saw whenever she opened a newspaper or turned on the television news. She looked at her watch. Coming up to 8 o'clock. I wonder when he'll turn up, she wondered, unpacking her binoculars and walking across the car park at the narrow, north end of Moreton Bay, to a boat ramp. This was the place they were supposed to meet, wasn't it? For weeks, Maddy, as she much preferred to be called, had been looking forward to once again joining this exclusive celebrity birding expedition along the Sydney harbour foreshores, led by Phillip Clarkson, known to millions as television's 'Mr Birdman'. Numbers were strictly limited to just ten. While no doubt a larger group would have been more lucrative, it would also have been far less manageable. More noisy, more like a 'bloody circus', as Clarkson would have put it.

The $50 charge would be money well spent, thought Maddy, as she trained her binoculars across the bay at a sand bank exposed by the retreating tide, looking for wading birds. She'd discovered birding relatively late in life, in her mid 50s, after her husband had died a few years back. Now, she never tired of it. Well, she'd explain to non-birders, who she knew had begun to regard her as an 'odd bird', it offered almost everything she wanted: intellectual stimulation (what was that 'little brown job'?), physical exercise (a long, stop-start walk) and companionship (with other odd birds).

'Hello, there. Maddy isn't it?' a voice suddenly boomed behind her. 'Fat chance you've got of spotting anything interesting there, you know.' She cringed and turned to see a youngish man, in his 30s she guessed, pausing to point a key ring alarm back towards a big, sleek BMW, which he had somehow squeezed in between her own little car and the boat ramp.

She'd met the man before, on a bird club outing only a few weeks earlier. Now, what was his name? Oh, dear, how could she forget so soon? Finch. That was it.

Simon Finch. A flash Harry. A bit of a show-off. A know-all. How, Maddy wondered, would Finch get on with Clarkson. Unlike Finch, she suspected, he was a proper expert, a high-paid, high-profile performer who really did know it all — and wasn't afraid to let paying customers know it, too. As she knew from a recent newspaper article, even in an industry crowded with big egos, he had a certain reputation. On-camera he oozed charisma and charm. 'The man who succeeded in making ornithology awfully sexy,' one TV columnist had put it. Off-screen, he could be snippy. All right, arrogant.

One of Maddy's friends who'd signed up for one of his 'celebrity-guided' rainforest walks still giggled at the great man's frustration with people in the party who couldn't pick up and instantly identify a small, anonymous-looking bird. 'After all, it was 200 metres away up the top of a blue-gum,' explained her friend. 'And we were looking into the sun.'

Clarkson had quickly lost patience. 'Up there, up there,' he'd ended up shouting, before stomping away to look for the next invisible rarity. And woe betide anyone who turned up late. 'Car park. 8 am. PROMPT. Latecomers will be left behind,' said the voucher supplied by Clarkson Bird Tours.

Maddy resumed staring fixedly through her trusty old East German 8 x 30 binoculars at the dunes across the bay. Maybe it was mistiness on her lenses, but even at this early hour they seemed to shimmer, to dance, in the heat haze. It was going to be a hot, sticky day.

Behind her, Finch continued his lecture. 'Nah. Only thing you're likely to get here these days is rubbish birds. A few scruffy miner birds. "Rats with wings", I call them. Some mouldy old pigeons. And maybe a couple of one-legged gulls that've got lost on their way to the local council dump. Anyway, we're wasting our time here unless we can wait a few thousand years for evolution to come up with a bird that can eat crap.'

Maddy turned round and frowned.

Finch apologised. 'Oops, sorry. But you know. All those cigarette ends. Fast-food cartons. Plastic bags. Industrial waste. Probably even a few syringes.'

Maddy sighed. He was probably right. Not so long ago, this tail-end of Moreton Bay had been a top spot for waders attracted by its extensive mudflats, a favourite fast-food stop for migrating birds. Now, it was little more than a dirty, litter-strewn backwater, hemmed in and gummed up by an ever-advancing army of oil refiners, plastics makers and metal bashers.

Worse, it seemed even the little patch that remained would soon disappear. There were plans to expand the nearby industrial estate. It had been in all the newspapers. More concrete. More glass. And a new name. Pelican Business Park.

How ironic!

Maddy wished her friend Libby Griffiths would get back from the toilets and save her from Finch. Libby would also be able to tell him how, only a couple of weekends ago, they'd come to this very spot and seen lots of birds. Not just pelicans, but bar-tailed godwit. Scores of them. They ran across the foreshore, kak-kak-kakking loudly, obsessively prodding the mudflats with long, slightly upturned beaks, having a final feed before embarking on their long flight — several thousand kilometres — northwards and southwards each year.

At last, here came Libby. She was as tall and stringy as Maddy was short and dumpy, but they'd quickly become friends. They were about the same age. They had both lost husbands (though Libby's had not died, he'd run off) and they were both hooked on birding.

Libby was talking to a man, obviously another birder. Maddy turned to study him, as she might an unfamiliar bird. A balding, bespectacled, middle-aged man, closer in age to her than to Finch, he looked vaguely familiar. Like a country grocer, a small-time embezzler or one of those colourless politicians she so disliked.

He'd detached himself from what must be other members of today's group, who were now standing around, chatting, peering through binoculars, looking at watches, wondering what had happened to their famous guide, wondering indeed whether they were going to get their money's worth.

'I do, err, apologise. My name is Derek. Derek Morris,' the man said in a plummy accent. English, probably Home Counties, thought Maddy. The man moved forward, bowing slightly, preparing to introduce himself with old-world courtesy, except his right hand appeared to have become entangled in his gear.

For a few seconds he fumbled to disengage himself from a tangle of straps. Somehow, his rucksack, his heavy spotting 'scope, his binoculars, bottle-holder and plastic wallet, no doubt containing bird checklist and pen, had become hopelessly tied. Mr Morris, Maddy and Libby would later agree, looked a bit odd. Eccentric, even for a birder. He wore open-toed sandals and grey socks, voluminous, knee-length shorts and a cheap, canvas jacket. From its many pockets, other pieces of equipment — those not hanging in confusion round his neck — seemed to be trying to escape. A polite man. A timid man. A man who, they felt sure, would benefit from some feminine organization.

'Dreadful about the development plans, eh?' Libby was saying. 'Is there nothing we can do?'

Morris shrugged apologetically, as if he bore personal responsibility for the failure to save yet another piece of foreshore. 'I know. Awfully sorry. But I think you'll find the council's already approved the development plans.'

He paused, awkwardly, before pressing on. 'I'm, err, retired now — well, to be honest, my, umm, company "let me go", as I think they say these days.'

'Oh dear,' said Maddy.

'Thanks. But I still do a spot of consultancy. Well, more like b-b-ook-keeping, it is. The thing is I-I, err, was with Berwick Council for a while. The officials, they're not a bad bunch, but the councillors, mmm, not the brightest, I'm afraid.'

'But surely, they understand the importance of the bay?' said Maddy, angry at the prospect of another local habitat being lost. It was already being squeezed by the large international airport, local light and heavy industry and big concrete roads being built here and there.

'Sadly no,' said Morris. After a timid start he seemed to be showing unexpected passion. 'The place has been allowed to become a dump. I mean, look over there.'

The little group, joined now by a young couple, followed his raised arm to the right. They could see a large, concrete pipe protruding obscenely, like a drunken giant taking a leak over the bay, thought Maddy with a shudder.

At the pipe's mouth, wide enough for a person to stand up in, some toxic-looking, blue-green sludge had formed a semi-solid after slowing from a spew to a trickle and then to a virtual stop. A wide area of water and reeds was stained. Elsewhere, the bay was littered with garish plastic bottles, lumps of white polystyrene packaging and, predictably, a couple of supermarket trolleys, dumped in shallow water at an angle that reminded Maddy of the Titanic, 20 minutes after its encounter with the iceberg.

Morris spoke again. 'And, of course, there's the other problem with the dunes.' He paused. He coughed.

'And what's that?' asked the two older women, almost in unison. Morris cleared his throat: an old-fashioned warning that what followed was of a somewhat indelicate, distressing nature. 'Men. Umm, meeting each other. Of course, I-I-I wouldn't know, but according to the councillors the bayside's become notorious as an area at night for men, umm, meeting each other. You know, for...'

Do get on with it man, thought Maddy impatiently.

'Sex?' prompted a no-nonsense young woman, one half of the young couple who introduced themselves as Jane Clifford and Chris Workman.

'Yes,' said Morris staring fixedly into the distance. 'I'm afraid they sometimes leave the evidence behind.'

It was then, as she tried to clear this unpleasant revelation from her mind, that Maddy spotted something. 'Well I never!' she exclaimed. 'How unusual!'

'What is, my dear?' Finch asked her.

Several answers flashed through several heads. A rare kelp-gull, wondered Libby Griffith, hopefully. A council clean-up squad, wondered Derek Morris, despairingly. Two men clocking on for the early shift, thought Chris Workman. As he was later to boast to Maddy, he was a 'man of the world, a former national newspaperman', though he'd recently 'sold his soul' to the public relations industry.

'It looks like...'

With a slow twist of the middle finger of her right hand, Maddy adjusted the fine tuning on her binoculars and focused on a patch of desolate, dirty sand. Nearby, a crooked line of wire fencing recalled the council's long-lost battle to stabilise the shifting dunes.

'It is. It's a pair of boots.'

'Fascinating,' said Finch, with growing irritation. 'No birds, but a flock of old welly boots. Tick off welly boot, yellow, lesser spotted. Not exactly a rarity hereabouts, I suspect.'

'No,' said Maddy, undeterred. 'Look for yourself. There's two boots.' She paused. 'Together. A pair. What's odd is they seem to have been turned up. Towards the sky. And...I may be wrong, but at this distance it looks as though they're still attached.' Simultaneously, she and Libby glanced up and at each other, nervously.

'What? Let me have a look,' said Finch, grabbing his binoculars.

'It must be some sort of joke.' As Finch was to tell the police later, the boots were, indeed, protruding from the soft sand, like a piece of avant-garde sculpture.

'Goodness me, I think she's right,' confirmed Jane Clifford, as the rest of the party decided to take the sighting seriously and homed in on what appeared, at least from 50 metres away, to be two bright, orange stumps. Surely they couldn't literally be stumps?

'Bloody hell,' said Workman, temporarily lost for a facetious comment.

Libby shivered. 'This is horrible. Perhaps we ought to phone the police.' Maddy nodded.

Even before she had completed the sentence, Finch had offered the use of a mobile. 'It's in the car.'

Jane Clifford remained unconvinced. 'Don't you think we should check it out first? I mean, a pair of feet. Not very likely, is it? Anyway, what if someone comes back and collects the boots in a few minutes?'

'But who?' said Maddy. 'I mean, I've not seen a soul over there this morning.'

Workman interrupted. 'OK, so, someone's dropped their boots...laced together, I suppose, off a boat or...worst case,' he went on, brightening, 'someone's fallen out of a boat, been drowned and got washed up. That'd be it.'

He paused, and darkened again. 'More likely, we've got it wrong. You know how, like with birds, the light can play tricks, make things look all sorts of funny shapes and colours. We should check them out.'

He turned to his girlfriend for support. 'Yes,' she replied. 'We don't want to make fools of ourselves.'

Maddy shrugged. Despite a growing feeling of foreboding, she felt a typical birdwatcher's sense of proprietorship over something she, after all, had spotted first. But she agreed. 'All right, then. Let's walk round. No point in driving round in convoy. It'll only take 15 minutes or so.'

'You go. I'll stay here,' said Libby. 'I don't want to come. It's too grisly.'

Leaving her behind wondering how to explain to Clarkson that the rest of his party had wandered off to check out a potential corpse — Maddy took charge of the foreshore tour group.

It was not quite what she had expected. But one way or another, what an adventure it was turning out to be!

Solemnly, as though on some perilous expedition, the group backtracked across the car park, now slowly beginning to fill with cars, four-wheel-drive vehicles and boats.

They picked up the road that ran along the perimeter of the sprawling industrial estate and joined Bayside Drive, which clung to the sand-covered sides of clearway as it swept noisily beneath the soft, moonscape line of dunes into the city.

There was no footpath and Maddy was soon overtaken by Workman, who seemed now to be vying with Simon Finch — who was 'something in finance' she now recalled with distaste — for unofficial command of the group.

After several minutes, they turned into the first sizeable gap in the dunes, indicated by a scruffy patch of roadside ground, criss-crossed by tracks and clearly used for illicit parking.

To one side, Maddy noted, a narrow path led away through some scrubby, scorched trees, and a scattering of still more rubbish. A disembowelled television set. A discarded condom. She shuddered. A couple of car batteries. A pile of broken house bricks, no doubt dumped by a builder too lazy, or too mean, to go to the council tip and pay for their disposal.

Struggling to stay up with the younger birders, Maddy now found herself overtaken by three more latecomers. 'Exciting, eh?' said a bulky, intense-looking man, a woman, presumably his wife, and a teenage girl, presumably their daughter. Certainly, they were plump enough to be part of the same family.

The big man halted for a moment to regain his breath: as well as all his birding gear, he was carrying a bigger haversack than any of his companions had. Probably full of food, thought Maddy.

'Wouldn't want to miss, this. Whatdya reckon?' Far from fearing his day might be ruined by a dead body, the man had enthusiastically joined the charge, even dissuading his wife and daughter from waiting by the car.

'What d'you think? Accident? Suicide? Murder, maybe?'

You wish, thought Maddy, frowning again. 'More likely, nothing at all.'

She caught up with the rest on the top of dune, where they stood, as if assembled for a group photograph, sweating — as much from apprehension as exhaustion, Maddy expected — in the heat of the mid-summer morning. As the police noted when they arrived later, they did not look much like a line-up of suspects in a murder case.

'There,' shouted the portly patriarch of what Chris Workman had already secretly decided to call the Fat Family. 'Over there.'

'Well, come on, we can't just stand here,' said Workman, excitedly. Several years covering police rounds for the local newspaper was about to pay off with the biggest exclusive story of his life. He prayed.

Already, he was looking round for detail with which to spice a narrative that that was taking shape in his head. The sand, he pointed out to Maddy, was undisturbed. 'See, no footprints. Except for the birds'.'

True. It hardly looked like the crime scene of the century.

'Let's go and have a closer look,' said Workman, turning from Maddy to the big man. 'Sorry, don't know your name.'

'Waddell. Gordon Waddell,' the man replied curtly, before remembering his family, standing meekly behind him. 'Geraldine. And Emma.' The two nodded glumly in his direction.

Workman nodded back and gave Maddy a conspiratorial wink. 'Waddell?' he whispered. 'More like "waddle". Most appropriate.'

As they trudged the last few metres, not over soft dunes, as it had appeared from a distance, but across still damp, slow-hardening sand, they grew close enough to see not just boots, but what looked horribly like legs. Like passers-by who arrive at the scene of a pedestrian accident and stand awaiting the doctor who asks to be let through, or like worshippers observing some, strange pagan ritual, they gathered in a neat circle round the upturned boots.

Maddy could now see she had been wrong, at least in some minor details. The boots — which seemed to rise out of the sand like quotation marks at the end of a completed sentence — were not orange, but a light, man-made olive material. Orange socks had been turned neatly down over them.

She was correct, however, about the bits that filled the space between socks and sand. Not sticks, not discarded bottles, not exactly stumps, but definitely a pair of legs. Hairy, bleached, sand-coated legs. Almost certainly, adult, male legs.

'You know, I have a horrible feeling I know who those belong to,' she whispered to no one in particular. Close-by, cars roared past on the freeway, clickety-clack, clickety-clack, over ill-joined concrete sections. Elsewhere in the distance an airplane was coming in to land, an outboard motor was being tugged into life, and noisy miners were mobbing an errant magpie.

For several seconds no one spoke, as the birders paused. To observe a minute's respectful silence? Or simply to imagine the grisly possibilities presented by their find? Maddy wondered.

Like most people, she suspected, they read the papers and watched the television news bulletins that gleefully showcased the latest Sydney mayhem and murder. But, with one or two notable exceptions, members of this group probably had no experience of dealing with unexpected dead bodies. Human bodies, at least.

Most could be moved to tears by the sight of, say, a dead tawny frogmouth, killed in a collision with a power line, or of a dead little tern, strangled by some carelessly discarded fishing line, but the macabre discovery of a pair of human feet seemed to prompt an uncomfortable mix of horror, pity and prurient speculation.

Had the legs, socks and shoes been separated from their owner and placed upside down in the sand? After all, if the newspapers were to be believed, body parts often turned up in Sydney's waterways: only the previous night, two arms had floated ashore at Pittwater. Police were now looking for the remaining parts.

Or was their owner still attached? 'It looks just as if someone has dived headfirst into the sand,' suggested Simon Finch, with a rush of imagination.

'Dived,' murmured Derek Morris, looking round guiltily to see whether, perhaps, the group was being observed, before adding, in an ominous, almost theatrical aside. 'Or was pushed.'

Jane Clifford grimaced. 'For God's sake,' she cried. 'We can't stand here staring at this all day. Someone ring the police.' She was not in the mood for playing amateur detectives. If this was, indeed, a piece of skulduggery, then the birders shouldn't be standing around, making a parlour game of a mystery. 'One way or another,' she reminded the others, 'some mother's son, some wife's husband, or possibly some child's father has died a violent death. Whoever he is, he was a human being.'

Even as she spoke, and the plump man's wife and daughter started to sob, Finch was detaching himself from the group, turning his back and, beep, beep, beep, jabbing out the emergency services numbers on his mobile.

2

The courage of this little bird is singular...he pursues and puts to flight all kinds of birds that come near his station, from the smallest to the largest, none escaping his fury...
— Mark Catesby, *The Natural History of Carolina, Florida, and the Bahama Islands*

Friends and family members were always teasing him gently about it. Mario Palmeira simply did not look like a 'proper' policeman, still less a detective inspector whose excellent crime clearance rate while stationed at Berwick had earned him a rapid transfer to the crack homicide agency in the city centre.

Certainly, he did not appear to match any of the stereotypes they had come across through whodunnit paperbacks, action flicks and TV cop shows.

'Real' cops were meant to be scruffy, unkempt. But Palmeira was short, dapper, dandyish even, usually appearing at work in a lightweight suit, business shirt and patterned tie or, when duty took him slumming, clean, pressed pants and open-necked shirt. The product of a love match between a Brazilian father and Australian mother, both of whom had died before sharing his hard-won success, Palmeira was dark without being swarthy.

He always seemed to find time to shave and his curly black hair was kept at average length, neither fashionably cropped nor flamboyantly long. To his more burly, more obviously bulky, Australian colleagues, he looked slightly effeminate. Hence his nickname: 'Pamela'. It was a tag he laughed off. Or just ignored.

So neat was his normal appearance that he could easily have been mistaken for an accountant, a taxman, or some kind of salesman, such as one of those earnest, clean-cut men who market eternal salvation on behalf of American churches.

Indeed, on one memorable occasion, colleagues would gleefully recount, a woman suspected of having information about a stabbing in country New South Wales — where they don't see too many men in suits — fled through a back window when she saw DI Palmeira approaching her home. She explained later that she had fled not because she thought he was a policeman, but because she feared he might be a Jehovah's Witness.

'Real' cops were meant to be fat, flabby and unfit, the result of too much fast food and free beer, too many late nights and lost weekends. They were meant to start dying of neglect by their mid-thirties. At 40, Palmeira was in glowing good health, the result of keeping his body, like his emotions, for the most part, under strict control. He was a fitness enthusiast, attending his local gym to lift some light weights, run on the treadmill and, if time permitted, do aerobic classes. After each visit, he meticulously filled in a card, recording weights lifted, kilometres travelled, repetitions completed. To his more easy-going wife, it appeared a fairly harmless form of vanity.

He did not smoke, and he drank — red wine — only on rare occasions. He resisted the canteen fry-ups, preferring instead homemade salads, sandwiches and pastas, brought in plastic boxes and heated in the office microwave.

'Real' cops were meant to have chaotic personal lives, wrecked by unsocial hours, unsavoury experiences and unhinged emotions. Palmeira's private life was more orderly. He could not honestly claim never to have looked at other women. Indeed, as he grew older and became increasingly aware of time slipping away, he found he looked at them more often and with more interest. But he had been — by and large happily — married for about ten years to Jenny, who had been a successful interior design consultant before she and Mario started a family.

Now, there were two girls, Claire, seven, and Preya, five. They lived in a three-bedroom bungalow in Leichhardt, a lively, inner-city suburb that had undergone rapid gentrification and, inevitably, a house-price explosion. Most Sundays they went to St Michael's Catholic Church.

'Real' cops were meant to be rough and rude, often sexist, and occasionally even racist. Palmeira, by contrast, was urbane, educated —

he had a degree in psychology — seemed able to control his temper better than most, and apparently left any unavoidable rough stuff to others.

As far as any colleagues could tell, he didn't fiddle his expenses, he wrote up his reports punctually, and he certainly did not take backhanders.

Indeed, to family and friends, the only respect in which DI Palmeira appeared to resemble 'real' cops — such as Morse, Dalgleish and Banks, say — was in his liking of classical music. But, then, he also liked folk, rock, country and, most of all, 'middle of the road' music, as well as walks in the bush, books about European history and, not surprisingly, films made in foreign languages.

At times his habits seemed positively unAustralian. But the eccentricities of DI Palmeira were regarded with a mixture of affectionate amusement and suspicion by colleagues at the Homicide & Serial Violent Crime Agency, who were more likely to be found propping up the bar at the local Flinders Hotel than pushing up bars at the nearby Sweat Factory.

Even his immediate junior, his self-styled 'dogsbody', DS Wayne Danniher, who rather prided himself on being the biggest slob in Crime Agencies, had grudgingly learned to forgive him his squeaky cleanliness. As he told his mates, 'Say what you like about him. He's fussy. He doesn't know one end of a football — not a real football — from the other. He can be a real pain at times. But he gets results.' And, as most cops had to admit, that was what ultimately counted.

Now, as the one still lay in bed sleeping off a huge hangover and the other emerged from a typically gruelling 45-minute sermon by Father Meagher at morning communion, little could DS Danniher and DI Palmeira have imagined that Sunday lunchtime that their lifestyles were about to be turned upside down.

ಲ಼ಲ಼ಲ಼

The process by which the worlds of these two men — one a top crime-buster, the other a downwardly mobile gut-builder — were about to be re-ordered began, as serious police business so often does, with a telephone ringing. Or more, precisely — because he'd considerately switched his phone from 'ring' to 'vibrate' when he entered church —

with a tingle in Mario Palmeira's groin.

An increasingly unfamiliar sensation, reflected Palmeira, as he pulled the phone from the side pocket of his Sunday-best pants. Far from improving, his sex life had suffered since little Preya had joined her sister at school and Jenny had resumed part-time work.

Though the extra income helped to pay the girls' private school fees, his wife was frequently 'too tired' — wretched cliché — at the end of a day spent trying to balance the demands of family and fresh clients.

He spoke quietly into the phone. 'Palmeira.'

Officially, he was rostered off, but he wasn't exactly surprised to discover it was homicide operations room. Moving out of earshot of fellow worshippers walking back to their cars, he listened silently as the duty officer, an incorrigibly cheerful young man called Kevin Smith, set about ruining the rest of his weekend.

Palmeira and Jenny had planned a late brunch and a lazy afternoon round the plastic pool, watching the girls play and reading the Sunday newspapers. So far, he'd only managed to take in the biggest, most breathless of the tabloid headlines. Four intoxicated teens killed in a motorway pile-up. The previous day's Sydney air show disrupted by a snap stopwork meeting by traffic controllers. Politicians promising to crack down on inner-city curb crawlers. Two high-profile footballers, so far unnamed, tested positive to 'recreational' drugs. The police commissioner, poor man, under attack again. Nothing much new there, then, he noted.

Ho, hum. He knew he shouldn't but he increasingly preferred the supposedly lighter sections of the papers devoted to social events, showbiz and sports — though it was a sign of just how seriously sport was now taken that, sadly, these pages now seemed to be dominated by high finance, medical matters, legal wrangles and global politics.

Anyway, such diversions would now have to be postponed as duty called in the matey voice of Senior Constable Smith, who was speaking from Homicide HQ at Strawberry Hills in the city centre.

'Smithie, here, sir,' he announced unnecessarily. 'Sorry to get you on your weekend off. But Danniher hasn't arrived yet and we can't seem to raise him.'

That'd be right, thought Palmeira. 'Cut to the chase, Smith.'

'Right. Well, the super thought your team would like this one, sir. Bit of a mystery. Likely, a lot of media interest. And back on your old patch. Beautiful Berwick by the sea. Moreton Bay to be exact. Chance to top up your suntan.'

'Smith!' Palmeira shouted in exasperation, turning heads among the departing churchgoers. Sure, his experience of working in Berwick made him a suitable choice, but the prospect of returning there to run a case didn't particularly appeal to him.

Racily, rapidly, in a staccato style pinched from a TV show, the constable now passed on the detail Palmeira needed.

A body found. About three hours ago. On — 'well, more like, in' — the sand. Near the dunes that run alongside Bayside Drive. Uniformed officers on the scene. Legs poking out of the sand. No signs of life. So no need for ambos. Looked like a drowning, but boys 'did the proper thing', assuming suspicious circumstances until proved otherwise.

Berwick duty officer, Inspector Clive Leyton — 'an old mate of yours, I expect, sir' — went out, took a look, straightway called in Crime Scene. Government pathologist on way. DC Koslowski, three crime scene officers, and other 'assorted odds and sods' already on the spot.

'Waiting for you, no doubt, sir,' added Smith finally.

Palmeira winced. 'OK. I've got to pop home first. Let them know I'm on my way,' he said wearily. He'd worked with Koslowski, a New Zealander predictably nicknamed 'Kiwi', before. Good bloke. But Leyton, he recalled, was a plodder, a fussy old man. And then there was the local commander, Jonathon 'Jonno' Sedgwick, who could be counted on to make life difficult.

It was just after noon when Palmeira, brunch quickly folded into a sandwich and packaged in a polythene box, bottled water in a cool-bag, arrived at the scene. It was unmissable. A 200-metre stretch of Bayside Drive had been transformed into what now resembled a linear car park. More than a dozen cars, paddy wagons and two trucks were parked haphazardly, half-on, half-off the clearway.

One lane had been cordoned off to avert accidents likely to be caused by stickybeak motorists slowing for a look at all the activity. A kilometre or more of blue-and-white police tape tacked on to wooden poles ran for about 100 metres along the road before zigzagging at either end across the dunes for another 100 metres.

At the entrance to the narrow track through the dunes, a young constable stood, sweating profusely in the mid-day sunbake.

'Here, sir,' he said, surprised to see Palmeira, who'd changed out of his church clothes while dropping Jenny and the kids at home. Light blue polo shirt and bright, white slacks. It didn't look much like he intended getting his hands dirty, thought the constable.

'Any news yet, inspector?' yelled a young woman, rushing forward, thrusting a mini-recorder under his nose. Others formed a quick ruck around him, rephrasing the same question. Media. Sharks, already circling after picking out the call on the police radio, no doubt. 'Give us a chance,' he smiled, through gritted teeth.

Another truck pulled up. It was carrying several lengths of inflatable plastic boom and a hydraulically operated back-hoe, of the sort used by builders to scoop out trenches or pile up earth. Serious stuff.

'You're a bit big to be building sandcastles, aren't you?' Palmeira shouted, trying to distract the media with a joke, as the driver approached, shaking his head in dismay at the challenge of driving his machine over the dunes.

Slipping past the journalists, Palmeira headed down the track, crossing a couple of sparsely and spikily grassed sandhills that overlooked the bay. From the top, he could see that booms, reinforced with sandbags, were already being laid along a stretch of shore, three metres above the present waterline, by some bare-footed, bare-chested workmen.

Between the boom and the dunes, six constables, heads down, hands encased in dispo-gloves, were moving like wading birds in a slow line, evidently engaged in a sweep search of the sand exposed by the morning's outgoing tide and now dried and hardened by the sun. A police launch was been drawn up to the water's edge.

'Nice day for messing about in boats, is it, constable?' Palmeira shouted at a dishevelled, disinterested-looking young officer, who was dangling his bare feet over the side. 'Nothing to do?'

'Sorry, sir. Just having a smoko,' he said, jerking to attention. 'They thought I might be needed for a water search, sir. I've had a poke about, but most of the time I've been keeping people out the way.'

'Should've brought your fishing rod, son. Tie up, get out, and start helping the others before the whole area is washed away.'

Satisfied the site was secured and safe from disturbance by either elements or idiots and that the search team was not actually burying possible forensic evidence with their big feet, Palmeira turned to what was clearly the focus of intense police activity.

In what he reckoned must be the centre — the dead centre — of the beach area cordoned off by boom and tape, Palmeira could see a tableau of some ten or so people, some standing, some bending over, in a circle, around which waist-high canvas sheeting had been erected. To protect the site? Or perhaps to provide privacy? he wondered, automatically looking round to scan the surrounding dunes for the prying telephoto lenses of the media.

As he moved closer, he now realised why the tableau struck him as familiar: it reminded him of him the Nativity scene which had been on display at St Michael's Church until only a few weeks ago.

For Virgin Birth read violent death, though. For shepherds and wise men, read…well, some averagely intelligent blokes and, good, one bright woman. Government pathologist Sandra Prior. Palmeira's mood improved when he sighted her.

He liked 'Pathological Prior,' as she'd been christened by colleagues at the Glebe morgue. She was intelligent and attractive: tall, striking rather than drop-dead gorgeous, mid-thirties and, as far as he knew, still single. Now, he could see, she was bent over a man, a dead man, whose partly clothed body had been laid face-down on blue, plastic sheeting. A rectal thermometer protruded unattractively from his buttocks.

Prior turned, exchanged nods with Palmeira and went back to work. She moved quickly, removed and checked the thermometer, which would help fix approximate time of death, made a note, then gently brushed sand off the man's face and into one of several bags that stood to the side awaiting collection and analysis.

Lovely lady, thought Palmeira, switching to one of his wise men, DC Koslowski. With two crime-scene officers, he was already examining the hole from which the body and three piles of sand, also waiting to be bagged up, had been recently dug.

Palmeira leant forward on one of three spades standing in the sand and peered into the hole. He was relieved to see that, instead of blundering in like pirates rushing to dig up buried treasure, the 'uniforms' had assumed the worst — a suspicious death — and sent for the crime-scene experts.

Good. Even before tackling the body they'd done a thorough search of the immediate area, which would have been marked out and combed by officers methodically closing on the body. Evidence would already have been bagged and tagged, measurements, photographs and video pictures taken, sketches made.

Only then would they have tackled the body. Correctly, he observed, they'd used the standard, 'pedestal technique', carefully excavating a doughnut-shaped trench round the body, leaving it on top of a block of sand in the middle. Again, they would have taken photographs and collected sand samples. With any luck, the samples would yield clues on how and when the shallow grave had been created. Naturally or by human hands.

In some cases, he knew, their final report on physical — as opposed to testimonial — evidence could take several weeks to complete and could run to tens, occasionally hundreds, of pages. But like real cops, Palmeira was in a hurry. He wanted help, now.

'What do you reckon, then?'

'Oh, g'day, sir,' said Koslowski, looking up. 'Thought we'd get Danniher, but they told us you were coming. Good to see you.' Palmeira wondered if the man was being facetious, decided he wasn't and asked, 'So?'

'Murder she wrote,' Koslowski said, nodding at the pathologist. 'OK to take a look now, Sandy?' The officer seemed to be on friendly terms with the desirable Ms Prior. Palmeira felt a momentary pang of envy.

'Be my guests, guys. I'm finished here anyway.' She spoke, for the first time in several months, to Palmeira. 'Hi. Nice to see you again, inspector.'

'We really can't go on meeting like this, Sandra.'

'Seems the only time we get to meet these days is over dead bodies, Mario,' replied Prior. Was she flirting? Suggesting a meeting over dinner elsewhere? wondered Palmeira hopefully. Dream on, he thought, quickly re-focusing on other things: his box of sandwiches toasting on the back seat of the car, the dishevelled state of DC Koslowski's clothes, and unavoidably, the sorry and suspicious state of the body now lying, on its side in front of him.

He'd seen worse: far worse, he thought, as a picture of Gemma Smith flashed unwanted across his mind. Little Gemma. The same age as his darling Claire. Her mutilated corpse had been found by charity workers, dumped in a car park clothing bin. So small, so fragile, so broken, she was. By contrast, this body looked big and bloated and, well, almost comical.

Its feet — until the body had been given a name it was still an 'it' — were still encased in garish socks and shoes. Its hands now wore plastic bags, tied round the wrist by crime-scene officers, hopeful of finding something — possibly evidence of a struggle, beneath the fingernails. The upper torso, he could see, was still swathed in khaki shirt and expensive-looking safari jacket. The lower torso remained unflatteringly white and bare. Not that its owner any longer cared.

'No pants?' motioned Palmeira pointing out the blindingly obvious.

'No. Wasn't wearing any, sir,' confirmed Koslowski.

'Had a look around for them?'

'Yes. Nothing so far, sir.'

'Odd.'

Palmeira peered more closely into the man's discoloured face. It stared back lifelessly at him through a thin coating of sand, caked blood and goodness knows what else. Like that of an ill-fated Antarctic explorer covered by snow. Palmeira judged him to have been in his early thirties, a good-looking, well-built man — until recently, at least.

'Looks familiar.'

'He is,' replied Koslowski, opening another plastic bag and gently pulling out a leather wallet. 'This was still in his jacket.'

Palmeira opened it and the man's driver's licence fell out.

'Phillip Charles Clarkson,' he read.

'He's that guy who does the nature programs on telly,' prompted Koslowski. 'Docos and things. Always having a fiddle with wombats and possums and birds. Especially birds. That's who he is. The Birdman. You must have heard of him.'

'Yes, thanks,' replied Palmeira, curtly. Clarkson, he recalled, had evolved from being a cult-figure 'anorak', to being a quirky television personality. He'd done for birding what other larger-than-life characters had done for other chores such as cooking, gardening and house-decoration.

'Believe it or not, I do watch the ABC, occasionally, you know. Australia's answer to David Attenborough? Yes, I know. So, any idea yet what's happened to him?'

Koslowski hesitated. 'Well, obviously, dead as a parrot. Deceased. Extinct. No more. Joined the choir invisible,' he ventured, thinking some humour might lighten what looked increasingly like stretching into another long, hard day. His Pythonesque humour prompted nervous laughter from the two other officers and Path Prior, but Palmeira winced uneasily. 'Very funny, Kiwi,' he said sternly.

'Sorry, sir.'

A sense of awkwardness descended once more over the scene as Palmeira once more studied the corpse. Though there were no obvious signs of prolonged exposure to the sea, parts of the upper body were already discoloured and livid.

The silence was broken by Sandra Prior. She knelt down once more and, with a gloved hand, gently turned Clarkson's head, to what those who worked with the man would later confirm he believed to be his 'good side'. It wasn't now.

'Look, here, sir. And here. And, here.'

Behind the ear, close to the hairline, he could see there were a number of dark, reddish-purple contusions and what looked like a mash of broken skin, soggy with sand. Also, there were what looked horribly like bone fragments. Higher up the head, a flap of scalp appeared to have unfolded, revealing a sizeable gash, say ten centimetres long.

'I suppose it's out of the question that he could have, say, lost balance…hit his head? Bounced? Fallen off a boat or something? I mean… 'Palmeira was anxious to rule out innocent explanations before confronting more brutal, criminal and infinitely more time-consuming theories.

'Mmm, sorry, 'fraid not. Hitting your head that hard — and several times twice in the same area — no, most unlikely,' said Prior.

'No sign of a weapon yet, I suppose?' asked Palmeira, knowing it was wishful thinking.

'Still looking, sir. On the beach. In the sea,' one of the crime-scene officers assured him, adding brightly, 'We've collected a few things for examination, though — you know, lumps of wood, bricks, lengths of pipe — but so far nothing that looks like it fits.'

Silence again. Just when Koslowski was wondering whether Palmeira was more interested in Prior's body than Clarkson's, his boss spoke again.

'Any indication of how he got here?'

The officers looked at one another. 'Not yet.'

Palmeira tried again. 'In the absence of a black box flight recorder, I think we can safely assume our Birdman did not drop from the sky. So the immediate question is: was he killed here or brought through the dunes and dumped here?'

'We've started checking around for witnesses, but this isn't exactly a very busy part of the beach, sir,' explained Koslowski. 'And there's no houses to canvass.'

'Right.' Palmeira seemed disappointed. 'How about time of death, then?'

'I'm sorry I really can't say yet, sir.' Prior said. 'Obviously I'll know more when I do the post-mortem. I'm pretty much tied up tomorrow, I'm afraid. So we're probably talking late afternoon.'

'Ttch.'

'Perhaps you and crime-scene can talk, say, first thing Tuesday. Should have something fairly precise by then.'

'OK. I'll just have to be patient.' That was not in Palmeira's nature, but he had plenty of other inquiries to make and plenty of other things to think about, including the media. Assuming the worst-case scenario, they'd love this. A vicious attack. A semi-naked man. A shallow grave. A celebrity murder. Big headlines. Palmeira was not a callous man, but like the media he could not help himself. The prospect of what was shaping as a high-profile, highly successful case cheered him too.

His train of thought was interrupted by the arrival of a woman he recognised as being from police media.

'Carol, good to see you. Koslowski here will bring you up to speed. You can tell our media friends a body's been found. Suspicious circumstances. Nothing else, just yet, please.'

'I think they know that already.'

'I'm sure you're right, but they haven't got a name. And I don't want them given one this big right now. It'd only set off even more of a feeding frenzy. Tell them the name is being withheld until identity is established, family informed et cetera, et cetera. Give us a chance to think how we're going to handle things.'

With reluctance, Carol Symonds agreed. 'But I'll need to have a proper briefing soon.'

'Don't worry. You'll get it.'

Koslowski had a question. 'You'll be talking to the man's family, then, sir?' he asked hopefully.

'I'll leave that to you, Koslowski. No doubt you can get the address from his driver's licence. Not too much detail at this stage, but tell them they'll have to make a formal ID at some point. Sooner the better, I suppose.'

'OK,' replied Koslowski, grumpy at the prospect of another few hours' work while the DI, at least, appeared to be heading home to enjoy what was left of his ruined weekend.

⁝⁝⁝

In fact, he wasn't. For a couple more hours, Palmeira prowled the scene, getting a feel for this unattractive fag-end of 'the world's most beautiful harbour', pausing now and then — to wave goodbye to Prior, to study the incoming tide and to wonder what, if anything, the police might have already missed as the crime scene was slowly dismantled.

Finally, he returned to where Koslowski was still 'doing a bit of tidying up' before heading off to Clarkson's home, which he'd been pleased to learn was in Paddington, not too far out of his way home.

'Almost forgot. Is the woman who found the body still around?'

'Doubt it. There were a few of them, actually, sir. A group. Birders. Apparently, they'd paid to go on a guided tour with Clarkson. I checked they were all OK — no shock or anything — but there didn't see any point keeping them baking on the beach here.'

'Right.' It was obvious Palmeira was not altogether pleased.

'Well, they'd only have got in the way,' Koslowski explained. 'And, anyway, some of them wanted the toilet, stuff from their cars… you know what people are like — so I sent them back 'round the other side of the bay.

DC Park may still be there with them.'

'I think I'll just drop by. Good job here, Kos.'

'Thanks,' said a surprised Koslowski. You never quite knew with Pamela, he thought. Could be matey, could be moody.

Palmeira marched back across the dunes, silently cursing the heat and the heavy sand clogging his shoes, to find his unmarked Holden Commodore one of only three vehicles remaining. With a screech of tyres, he executed a flashy U-turn and took the short drive back round the bay. When he arrived at the car park, he found that of the birdwatchers, only two older women remained and were still talking to DC Park.

Palmeira was introduced to Maddy Warnock and Libby Griffiths. 'I understand it was one of you who found the body,' he said, courteously.

'Me,' said Maddy. She did not seem too distressed by her close encounter with violent death and was happy to repeat the details for Palmeira. He listened intently, thanked the women, said he'd want to talk to them again, and turned to the officer. 'All done, then?'

'Yes, sir. Didn't seem any point keeping people here. Names, addresses, preliminary statements will be on your desk first thing.'

'Good.'

'I've told everyone they'll have to come in and make proper statements, but to be honest they didn't seem to know much more.'

I'll be the judge of that, thought Palmeira turning again to the two women. 'Nasty business, I'm afraid, ladies.'

'An appalling accident. Most upsetting. He was a remarkable man, you know,' said Maddy. 'How do you think it cou…'

Palmeira interrupted. 'Who was?'

'Who was what?'

'A remarkable man?'

'Mr Clarkson, of course.'

'You know?'

'Oh yes. We thought we recognised the socks and boots. They're his own — what do you call it — brand, you know?'

'They're advertised on television,' Libby elaborated.

'And then we heard two of the policeman talking. "That chap who does the programs on TV," one of them said. "Clarkson".'

'It all fits, I suppose,' added Libby, solemnly. Like her friend she hadn't seen any rare birds, but the day had been far too exciting to have been entirely wasted. What a tale to tell her workmates at the library.

'Look, I'd be really grateful if you keep all this to yourselves for the time being,' said Palmeira, in a tone that he hoped conveyed polite intimacy as well as implied threat.

'Of course, inspector,' replied Maddy, as the two women walked away to their car. 'You can trust us.'

3

Our birds are like our men of genius. As in the literary world there is a description of talent that must be discovered and pointed out by an observing few, before the great mass can understand it or even know its existence...so the sweetest songsters of the wood are unknown to the mass of the community, while many very ordinary performers whose talents are conspicuous, are universally known and admired.

— T.W. Higginson, *The Birds of the Pasture and Forest*

Detective Sergeant Wayne Danniher had woken on Sunday clutching his head. 'Oooh,' he moaned. Even before he checked his missed telephone messages — which, he was alarmed to discover, included one demanding his immediate presence at a suspicious death in Berwick — he felt lousy. Saturday had been his 32nd birthday. Still, that had been no excuse for embarking on yet another bender, he reflected guiltily and somewhat confusedly.

The session had begun around lunchtime with what were intended to be 'just a couple of cool ones' with some mates from his previous posting at Brighton-le-Sands, south of Sydney. But it had kicked on, with higher-octane shots, at watering holes in Bondi, Bronte and Coogee before a prolonged session in Kings Cross at the famous Bourbon & Beefsteak bar.

It was not until three or four o'clock in the morning — he couldn't recall quite which — that he'd stumbled out of the taxi into which he had been poured by persons unknown, had climbed the stairs of his two-bedroom unit in Kogarah and had fallen, fully clothed, asleep on the lounge.

At some point, he must have switched the television on, for he was woken by the screaming voice of a commentator trying to generate some excitement in a late afternoon replay of an overseas rugby league match.

Danniher, a burly man who'd inherited the red hair, ruddy complexion and a weakness for the grog from his Irish-born father, had been a promising footballer himself once. He'd seemed destined for first-grade until a snapped cruciate ligament forced him out of the game and, in the footsteps of several mates, into the police force.

Though it was his second-choice, policing proved a smart career move, at least for the first ten years. A strong, gregarious, generous man, gifted with both common sense and common touch, Danniher was popular both with his peers and his superiors who first made him a detective and, not long after, promoted him to sergeant. Then, a few years ago, things had started to go wrong. During investigations into a drugs cartel, he became too closely — some thought corruptly — involved with an informant. She turned out to be seriously bad company. He had also aggravated his old knee injury during a chase and was forced to take time off. Time which he'd spent drinking.

And, most traumatically, his marriage to childhood sweetheart Kylie had come to a bad-tempered conclusion. Insults were yelled, dishes thrown, lawyers engaged. Disentanglement had been painful and expensive.

These days, Danniher wallowed not in self-pity so much as self-denigration. Looking back, he blamed himself for most of what had happened. Because of the demands of the job, because of the amount of time he spent with his mates, perhaps simply because he was a selfish bloke who did not understand his wife. Too often, he'd not been there for her.

Since the break-up, Danniher had enjoyed — though that probably wasn't the word he would have used — several brief relationships with unsuitable women and spent far too many long nights with his drinking buddies. He suspected they now saw him as a sad case, whose career was on the skids.

Hell, it was probably true. Far from being in his prime he was now overweight and unfit. Nothing really wrong with that if he was happy. But he wasn't. He'd tried often to mend his ways. In theory, at least, he permitted himself no more than five cigarettes a day, ten at weekends if he wasn't working. And, most radically, he'd promised not to get on the drink if he was on duty the following day. But, jeez, birthdays didn't count, did they?

They did: Sunday was a wipe-out. After a long alcoholic lie-in, Danniher dried out, went for a long walk, watched some television, and after promising to do better, went to bed before midnight. The result was that he woke early and surprisingly refreshed on Monday for the delayed start to his working week. Of course, he'd have some awkward explaining to do about his whereabouts on Sunday. 'In bed, touch of food poisoning, boss,' he'd say. Or had he used that excuse recently?

Whatever. He could still expect to receive an almighty bollocking from the superintendent and whichever poor sod had been sent to cover for him at Berwick. On the whole, though, he felt confident that he could talk his way out of another tight spot. The feeling lasted as long as it took him to go to the ground floor and pick up the morning paper. He took a quick glance at the front page.

'Jes-us!' he exclaimed, before suddenly running back upstairs, switching off the kettle, and dashing back into the bedroom, where he stripped off his board shorts, pulled some work clothes out from a week's worth of dirty washing piled up in the corner and threw them on. 'This time, they're going to nail me,' he thought.

৪৩৪৩৪৩

In fact, at that moment, as he studied a complete set of morning newspapers, spread on his desk at police HQ Berwick, Mario Palmeira was wondering whom he wanted to kill first: the cretinous journalists who'd written the stories, Danniher, or the two old ladies who'd clearly betrayed his trust and given them the information.

He hadn't needed a call from HQ to remind him that public disclosure of the dead man's name before relatives had been informed was a serious breach of procedure.

The previous night, Palmeira had not arrived home until after eight o'clock. Not only had he missed the final part of an English history documentary he'd been looking forward to watching, but he'd also been cold-shouldered by Jenny, who was annoyed at losing him for the afternoon, and forced to heat up his uneaten brunch for dinner.

At least he'd gone to bed satisfied that the overnight inquiries he'd set in motion would produce some encouraging signs of progress; something with which to soften the bad news of a famous man's apparent murder to the media and to placate his own boss.

Instead, he was confronted by this! Unlike 'real' cops who tended to regard the media as reptiles, Palmeira actively cultivated and sought to manipulate them, feeding them bits of information as and when it suited him. But it looked like he'd already lost the initiative.

Despite suicide bombings in the Middle East, dire warnings of fresh famines in Africa and some big scores in cricket matches played over the weekend, Sydney's two biggest-selling newspapers still found prominent space for the item about the body on the beach. Surprisingly, the high-circulation tabloid had been the more cautious, running only a brief report on page two, under a headline, 'New body washed up on gay beach'. By its own execrable standards, it was relatively accurate and it had not named names. Out of ignorance or caution, it was not clear.

Not so the broadsheet. Typical, thought Palmeira: it invariably adopted a high-minded literary tone of righteous indignation, but never denied its readers the sordid detail.

The 'exclusive' story, entitled 'Australia's birdman crashed to death, fear police', had been stripped across the foot of page one. Accompanying it was a double-column colour photograph of Phillip Clarkson, clad in jacket, shorts and, yes, those signature socks and shoes. He seemed to be pointing up at an invisible bird in an impossibly blue sky.

Palmeira shook his head in disbelief at the caption — 'The dead man in happier times' — before reading on. An unidentified source — he bet he knew who — was quoted as saying that the body of the Birdman looked like it'd fallen from the sky 'like that skier Eddie the Eagle'. The famously unsuccessful ski-jumper.

Palmeira had to smile. The article, he noted, was a masterpiece of the genre. It was a clever mix of facts (Clarkson found dead), errors (the reporter had erroneously re-located the body to the less pointy, less polluted end of what he incorrectly spelled as 'Mortown Bay') and damaging speculation about how Clarkson's feet came to be pushing out of the sand.

Even the local financial paper had included a one-paragraph story on its general news page, alerting readers to the 'feared death' of Mr Clarkson, 'one of the nation's highest-earning TV personalities'. Trust them to find a financial angle, he thought.

As if to remind Palmeira that Sod's Law applied even in unruly cities such as Sydney, it had been 'Jonno' Sedgwick who'd first alerted him to the news stories, personally taking the trouble to ring him at home. Palmeira had been preparing to go for his early morning run when Jenny called him back.

'Ah, Sedgwick, here. Hope I haven't got you up,' said the quiet voice of a large, fit man, in his mid-fifties, whose urbane exterior and measured diction, Palmeira knew, concealed a temper of legendary, volcanic proportions.

'Nice to have such a famous detective back with us at Berwick. If you see Ms McCrimond, I'm sure she'll show you the space we have already made available for you and your team.'

'Thank you,' mumbled Palmeira, trying to recall a McCrimond. Ms McCrimond? Good-looking girl? Irish or something?

'Meanwhile,' Sedgwick continued, 'have you, by any chance had time to look at the newspapers?' he rumbled ominously.

'No, sir.'

'Well, they inform me that you've found a body.' He paused.

'Ah, yes sir.'

'Yes sir.' Well, I'm just off with the commissioner to see the police minister and thought it might be useful if I knew what was going on.' Another pause.' Or should I perhaps wait for tomorrow's papers?'

There would be no morning jog, probably no breakfast, certainly no time to play happy families this morning, thought Palmeira as he apologised. 'Sorry,' he said, there had been a 'breakdown in communications'. No, he had not 'prematurely leaked' the details. Yes, yes, he reassured Sedgwick that investigations were proceeding along several lines and should yield something soon.

At least, he desperately hoped they would.

'Good,' said Sedgwick, adding with menace, 'Then perhaps in future you could speak to me before talking to your newspaper friends. I do have a mobile phone, you know.' Click. The line went dead and Sedgwick was gone, to discuss with the minister yet another reorganisation — or rather disorganisation— of the state police force.

Little wonder Sedgwick was in such a particularly foul mood, Palmeira had thought. Had he heard a word of his explanation? But Palmeira hadn't had time to be bitter and twisted about that. Within minutes, he'd made more excuses to his family and plunged into the morning rush-hour traffic, criss-crossing the city into work.

Predictably, he too had arrived at the station, an ugly, boxy, two-storey building located at the back of the Berwick shopping mall, in a bad mood.

He was annoyed with himself for not having been firmer with the two interfering ladies. He was annoyed with Danniher, who after going AWOL the previous day, had still not arrived at work. He was annoyed with the world this fine Sydney morning.

Already questions big and small crowded his mind. Obviously, number one: assuming Prior was right, who killed Clarkson? Suicide could probably be ruled out, but who was Clarkson behind the studiously eccentric, public, 'birdman' persona, anyway? Did he have enemies? Most public figures, most 'tall poppies', did. That's why they were chopped down.

Was he gay? And if he wasn't gay, what was he doing at night on a beach known as a rendezvous for homosexuals? How did he get there? Did he leave a car somewhere? And if so, where? Or was he taken there, perhaps? And, another thing, whatever happened to the dead man's trousers?

Palmeira needed some answers. From bitter experience he knew that murder trails went cold quickly — quicker than a cappuccino, he thought, staring into his half-empty cup. It was now 20 hours since the body was found and though Clarkson's driver's licence had been conveniently found on the body, the dead man's identity or cause of death had not even been confirmed. Forensics, he expected, would provide important clues, but nothing conclusive could be dragged from them until later that day or, more likely the following day. The thorough Ms Prior, he knew, could not, would not, be rushed

Koslowski, too, had so far drawn a blank. In a long, rambling message left on Palmeira's answering machine, he had explained that there had been no reply at Clarkson's home, which, he had described briefly with what sounded like barely concealed envy, 'as one of those smart Paddington terraces with the fancy ironwork balconies'. He'd interviewed a neighbour who told him she thought Clarkson was away on one of his trips. She'd also revealed the interesting fact that he was single and shared the house with his mother. She was also away, perhaps visiting her other son.

Koslowski suggested he go back that afternoon to tell her the bad news. Depending on how she took it, he'd ask her about the dead man's coming and goings and... Then the tape ran out.

More sitting around waiting, thought Palmeira. Still, elsewhere, the murder inquiry was beginning to gather momentum, though it seemed to be eliminating possibilities rather than highlighting them. More than a dozen officers had already been thrown at the Birdman case and their reports were already beginning to trickle in to the station where they were being collated.

Searches of the immediate area — the dunes, the roadside — were continuing, but had so far produced nothing of real significance. No murder weapon. No pair of trousers. And no unusual sightings. Crimestoppers had appealed for witnesses, but these were proving, predictably, difficult to find. There were no homes nearby, so conventional house-to-house inquiries were out of the question. Factories and offices in the area had been closed over the weekend.

Industrial security guards and local council rangers, who regularly patrolled the area had seen nothing unusual. Interviews in known gay clubs and hotels had started, but detectives who returned to the dunes area had, so far, drawn a blank.

There had been a few people about. Some had been innocently walking their dogs, taking a stroll or going fishing; others, officers reported, were clearly in the dunes on 'other business' and didn't want to give their names, let alone help in a murder inquiry. No one, it seemed, had seen the dead man, his attackers, his car, his birding equipment or his trousers — presuming he had some or all of these with him at the time of his death.

At first light, police divers had been sent back into the murky waters of the bay to look for a murder weapon, but had come up empty-handed.

What next? Palmeira picked up the list of the birders provided by DI Park, and stared at it intensely. Nine names, six addresses, seven telephone numbers, attached separately for easy reference. His eyes ran up and down the list several times, principally noting names, suburbs and occupations, seeking anything that might link the people who found the body with the murderer or murderers.

MADDY WARNOCK, 62, of Brighton Avenue, Roseville. Retired teacher. Part-time worker in St Vincent de Paul Society charity shop.

LIBBY GRIFFITHS, 60, of 14a/94 Pacific Towers, Chatswood. Librarian.

SIMON FINCH, 29, of 4/46 Gresham Gardens, Double Bay. Foreign exchange dealer.

DEREK MORRIS, 58, of 42 Balaclava Parade, Kurnell. Financial consultant.

CHRISTOPHER WORKMAN, 38, of 6 Parkes Street, Surry Hills. Press/public relations consultant.

JANE CLIFFORD, 32, of same address. Social worker.

GORDON WADDELL, 43, of Cormorant Place, Kensington. Managing director, waste-disposal company.

GERALDINE WADDELL, 40, of same address. Part-time shop assistant.

EMMA WADDELL, 14, of same address. School student.

According to brief statements, attached by DC Park on a single sheet of paper, all had arrived roughly between 7.45 and 8.15 am in cars. The Waddells, naturally, had come together, in a four-wheel drive Land Cruiser; so, too, had the two older women, in their old Daihatsu, and Mr Workman and his girlfriend, in a Mitsubishi Lancer.

Ms Warnock had described how, after spotting what looked like feet poking out of the sand across the bay, the group — minus her friend — had walked round to investigate. Then they had rung the police. Others had confirmed this. And that was about it.

'All seemed happy to help, though some — especially Finch — asked if the police could do anything to get them their money back for the trip,' Park had noted.

Palmeira frowned. Forex dealers, waste disposal directors, 'consultants' — such jobs always sounded suspicious to him. Still, so long as gossiping to the media wasn't a crime, none of the names leapt from the list, screaming 'arrest me'. Indeed, the list seemed to comprise a pretty fair cross-section of middle-class, predominantly middle-aged people, he thought.

He didn't know much about birders. An odd lot, he suspected. But killers? Well, as a psychology major he wouldn't rule it out. He'd known stamp-collectors, slot-car racers, amateur astronomers who'd come to blows: when passions became obsessions even the most mild-mannered people could turn nasty. Certainly reckless. He recalled reading about a couple of young men killed in a high-speed motor accident recently. Turned out they were birders competing in some mad 'twitchathon' thing, racing to tick as many species as they could in 24 hours.

But murderous? It seemed to him improbable that he would find the birdman's killer among a bunch of birders who had paid up and turned up, fully expecting to go on an outing with the victim. But then, again, who could tell what guilty secrets the group concealed? Just because they loved their feathered friends didn't mean they loved their fellow human beings.

Suddenly, Palmeira jumped into action. 'Bob,' he shouted.

'Yessir,' came a voice from the outer office.

'Can we get these names checked out? It's unlikely, but see if any of them's got a record. Soon, please.'

'No problem, sir,' said Sergeant Robert Adamovitch. A gaunt, grey man, he was Berwick's longest-serving officer, Palmeira recalled. Though he'd long ago given up hope of further promotion, he was proud of his local knowledge and encyclopaedic memory.

'Let's see what we've got here,' he said, scrutinising the piece of paper. 'Warnock, Griffiths... ah, both women. Getting on, too. Pretty much puts them in the clear. Waddell. Workman. Mmm, nothing seems to ring a bell... wait a minute, Morris...'

'Know him?'

'Well, fairly common name, mmm... but back in the late eighties I'm sure there was a Morris. Made a name for himself for a while. Thievings, muggings, break and enters. Nasty piece of work, if it's the same bloke. Like all of them, he got caught and put away eventually. GBH, I think.'

'Haven't heard his name for a while, but. Could've died. Or moved on. But he'd be about the right age. I'll check.'

'Anyway, quick as you can,' said Palmeira impatiently. His interest has already switched from the list of birders back to the newspapers. Rightly or wrongly, like wars and politics, policing had become a battle fought out increasingly through the media.

Now he thought about it, perhaps the rush of publicity wasn't as bad as it seemed.

For one thing, some key details — the missing trousers, for instance — had been omitted, or simply not passed on by the gossipy women. For another, the story hadn't mentioned his involvement in the case, relying instead on the unusual 'police sources say' quotes. And, for yet another, he actually knew the reporter, who'd concocted — all right, written — the Birdman story in the broadsheet. She might turn out to be useful.

౫౦౫౦౫౦

Like Palmeira, Karen Chan was an 'ethnic', as older Australians liked to call fellow citizens with funny-sounding names or funny-coloured skin. Despite or more likely because of that, she'd done well on the paper. Belatedly, newspapers had recognised the more multicultural nature of Sydney society by employing more 'ethnics'. The broadsheet, he knew, now had three, out of a staff of more than 200. Tellingly, Chan and one of the others had been given police rounds. As if crime was a largely ethnic problem.

That was how he'd come to help her before, on a story about street gangs in the south-western suburb of Bankstown. She was a smart journalist. Not to be trusted, of course. No journo could be. But hard-working and willing to trade favourable coverage for a bit of inside info.

Palmeira tapped out her number.

'Hello. You've reached Karen Chan. I'm not at my desk right now. Please leave a message and I'll get right back to you,' a thick Australian accent promised.

Damn. 'Karen, it's Mario Palmeira, Berwick police, here. You might remember that last year you...'

Suddenly, the Australian voice broke in. 'G'day, inspector. Sorry to filter you ... just working on something.'

'That's OK. How's it going?'

'Good. Guess you saw the piece today.'

'Yes. Good stuff,' he lied.

'Thanks. Bit over the top with the Birdman stuff, perhaps. But you know what the subs are like. Beat everything up. You've not rung to complain, then.'

Palmeira laughed. 'Not yet. No, I was just wondering if you could help me with something... you never know, down the track, as this thing unfolds, maybe you and I can ... well, you know.'

'Sure. Go for it. Anything to help,' she replied — also lying, he suspected. It was all part of the game.

'Thanks. I stress we haven't confirmed that it is Clarkson yet. But it certainly looks that way. Thing is we're pulling together a picture of the man. We'd be really grateful for some help. Cuttings, biogs, maybe even an obituary, if you've got one already written somewhere. You'd know the sort of thing.'

'It's a deal,' said Chan. 'Funny you should mention it, inspector. Just doing an obit now. "One of Australia's best-loved and most-respected TV personalities brutally cut down in his prime", et cetera, et cetera.'

'Sounds great.'

'Got a fax number? I'll send you what I've got.' Chan was lying again, Palmeira thought. He knew what journos were like. She'd send him a carefully chosen selection of her material. She probably feared that if she sent him everything he'd be back on the phone, nit-picking, editing her story, trying to lay down conditions.

Karen broke into his thoughts. 'The Clarkson obituary stuff. I guess we're safe to run that in tomorrow morning's paper?'

Palmeira grimaced. 'Yes, I guess so. But don't say I said so.'

'Great.'

'One more thing, Karen...'

'Sure.'

'The two women. Did you use everything they told you? Or can my boss expect more nasty surprises when he picks up the paper tomorrow?'

'What women are you talking about?'

'The ones who tipped you off about our friend the Birdman.'

'It wasn't the women. It was some guy.'

'Oh.' This was tricky. 'Now I know I couldn't persuade any of you journos ever to betray a source, but seeing as we may be working together a bit on this one, any chance of a clue?'

There was a long silence, then: 'Well, let's say I'd be looking in the PR department. But, as you'd say, don't tell anyone I said so. Keep in touch. Ciao.'

Cheeky girl, thought Palmeira, suddenly tiring of this game-playing. After all this was a murder inquiry. Perhaps he should've bullied her instead, threatened to ring her editor. Anyway, what did she mean by the 'PR department'?

Not the police media department. Carol Symonds had just sent him a memo, copied to Jonno Sedgwick, and to Homicide HQ, protesting bitterly that her department had been made to look foolish by the release of the dead man's identity, that it had still not been briefed properly. Her staff couldn't go on, she complained, saying 'no comment' to the electronic media, now frenziedly trying to catch up with the papers.

Well, tough, thought Palmeira. Whose side were police media on anyway? As ex-journalists, most of the police media still looked to their old mates for admiration and approval, he suspected.

Media relations? Public relations? What did Chan mean?

Suddenly he remembered. One of the birders was in that murky business. Now, what was his name?

'Bob, you got that list there?' he shouted, as a small forest of smudgy faxes started rolling out of his machine.

'Just finished with it, sir. You'll be interested. Quite a few surprises, there.'

'Oh?'

'Yes. First, the bad news. Wrong Morris, I'm afraid. I was thinking of Dennis Morris. Remember him? Mean, ugly bastard. Anyway, I was close, but this, here, is Derek Morris. Nothing on the computer about him.'

'Go on then. Give me the good news. I could do with some.'

'Well, Simon Finch has a couple of drink-drive convictions. No big deal, perhaps. But, this guy, number seven on your songsheet, sir. That Gordon Anthony Waddell. Different address, but same thug, I suspect. Three convictions for assault. Fair while ago, but — here's the good bit — all for bashing gays.'

'Now there's a coincidence,' said Palmeira, his mood lifting. 'I'll pay him a visit myself.'

'Be worth it. I phoned a few old mates. They hadn't come across Waddell for a while. But they thought he was still mixed up in some right-wing politics. Doesn't like gays, doesn't like Asians, doesn't like anyone much, it seems.'

'Interesting,' said Palmeira.

'One other thing, sir,' Adamavitch went on. 'Christopher James Workman. Nowhere near murder, sir, but he's been in trouble a few times before. Basically, domestic violence — bashed his wife. Damage to property. Her new boyfriend's home, it was. Given a suspended sentence.'

He checked a computer print-out. 'Oh, yes, and, before that he was done for trespass. Commonwealth property. Broke into a defence lab with a bunch of demonstrators.'

'Workman. Remind me, which one was he again?'

'Umm,' said Adamavitch checking the list. 'Youngish bloke. Newspapers. No, public relations. Not much difference, is there these days?'

So, it wasn't the two women who'd tipped off the press. It was Workman. Old habits? Old allegiances? A spot of mischief? A lucrative tip-off? Or, maybe something more sinister?

'Thanks, Bob. We'll get him checked out asap. Give him a scare if nothing else. May I'll do it myself if . . .' He glanced down at his watch. 'Hell. One o'clock already.'

Where had the morning gone? He'd have a quick bite of lunch and then go 'round to Waddell's. He looked the likeliest of the birders. Leave Workman to one of the others.

Palmeira rose, walked into the outer office and over to the mini-fridge and pulled out his plastic lunchbox. Spinach and ricotta quiche with salad and a bottle of mineral water. Obviously, Jenny had not been too angry with him.

He was just about to open the water when there was an explosion of laughter. Danniher and Koslowski, who'd no doubt popped in on his way to the Clarkson's, were obviously sharing some sort of joke.

'Danniher! Good of you to pop in. Better late than never, eh?'

'Sir,' started Danniher. 'Look, I'm really sorry but...'

Palmeira cut him off. 'Not now. We'll speak later,' he said, shaking his head gravely. It wasn't the time or the place, in front of an office full of people waiting expectantly for some theatrical confrontation between the two men, to give Danniher a well-deserved rocket.

Palmeira knew that he and Danniher didn't have much in common. But in an odd-couple way, they could complement each other. Palmeira may have considered himself well-organised, but Danniher had the common touch. For now, though, they eyed each other suspiciously.

It was Koslowski, a neutral who got on better with Danniher but respected Palmeira as a policeman, who defused the situation. 'If there's nothing else for me, I'm off to try Mrs Clarkson again, sir. Want to come?'

Palmeira thought. Usually, senior investigating officers took a strategic role: allocating tasks, supervising canvasses, reviewing physical and testimonial evidence as it became available. But already it was clear this wasn't going to be a usual case. So far, there were no weapons, no witnesses, no obvious motives. And in the absence of the pathology reports, some personal background on Phillip Clarkson seemed the best way to move the inquiry forward. Danniher, the quiche, the rest of the world, could wait.

'Sure, Kiwi. Give us a couple of minutes.'

He returned to his office, photocopied the list of birders, gathered up the thick sheaf of newspaper cuttings from his fax machine and re-emerged.

'Here, Danniher, do something useful,' he said, handing him the list. 'If you've read the papers you'll know what this is all about. There's more detail here. If you're feeling better today...'

He stopped himself. No point in taking a cheap shot at his deputy. Not in front of the others.

'... anyway, talk to them all again. No rough stuff. Be polite. You know the routine. Make sure they weren't out burying bodies on Saturday night. Find out if they'd had dealings with Clarkson before. You know the sort of stuff.'

'Pleasure, sir,' said Danniher. He seemed relieved to be off the hook, again.

'Start with this character. Christopher Workman. It was him who tipped the papers off. So you don't have to be too polite with him. If you get my meaning.'

Palmeira paused. 'Oh and another thing. Just in case the family hasn't got anything, see if you can get some mug-shots of Clarkson. Recent ones.'

'Where?' Danniher immediately regretted the question.

'Use your initiative. Try the back of one of his books. From his publisher. Or the television company that screens his films.'

Typical dogsbody stuff thought Danniher, but he bit his tongue and turned away. Clearly, it was going to be a long week, with or without the occasional drink.

4

...an entire subculture and a type of tribe, with its own rules, struc-
tures, history, customs, language, etiquette and values.
— Mark Cocker, *Birders, Tales of a Tribe*

Like most busy city-based people, Mario Palmeira had never taken more
than a fleeting interest in birds, even those that occasionally strayed into
his small backyard in Leichhardt. He could pick a kookaburra by sight
and sound. But asked to identify other common birds he couldn't tell a
currawong from a magpie, a rainbow lorikeet from an eastern rosella, an
Indian mynah from a noisy miner. To him, most birds were either parrots,
pelicans, something he would call a 'seagull' or, well, just a bird.

Now, though, he was doing a crash course on the subject. Was
birdwatching really, as one article claimed, 'Australia's fastest-growing
pastime'? Surely not. Only recently he'd read it was basketball. Or, women's
soccer. Or, perhaps, roller-blading. Still, everyone to their own taste,
whether they were amateurs who packed a pair of binoculars, 'just in
case', when they went for their weekend walk, hard-core enthusiasts, or
professionals like Clarkson, for whom it was clearly a major source of
income.

Palmeira flipped to another article. Apparently, there were several
hundred different bird species in Australia. Precisely how many, even the
experts couldn't agree. Most lists put the total for the Australian mainland,
Tasmania and the Bass Strait at about 760. But after that, well, as with
most things in life, 'it all depended'.

It depended on whether species found on islands or flying thousands of
kilometres out to sea, were included. Or on how one counted similar
species: albatrosses, it seemed were particularly tricky to pick apart. It
also depended on whether certain birds were actually present in Australia.
The fact that their pictures appeared in the big, fat guidebooks didn't
mean a thing. They could be rare visitors. Or extinct, as young Koslowski
had joked about the Birdman.

It could all get very complicated. In the material she'd faxed him, Karen Chan had included an article in which various experts — including Clarkson, he noted — argued for ages about the likelihood of spotting something called an upland sandpiper. Apparently, there'd been only one sighting of the bird. Back in 1848. Near what was now Sydney airport. Presumably, the bird had taken a wrong turn on its way from North America to South America. To Palmeira, it looked like a lot of fuss over a pretty dingy, anonymous-looking bird.

'Funny business, this birding lark,' he said, looking up. Some people, he knew, spotted trains. But this seemed a bit like spotting trains without numbers on their sides. 'I mean, you can never be sure you've seen what you think you've seen.'

'Pretty harmless, though, you'd think, sir,' said Koslowski.

'Suppose so.'

He started another article. It was all about an elite group called the '750 Club' — so called because that's how many species you had to have seen to be a member. At the last count, the club had more than 20 members on its list, topped by a man in Victoria with 770 or so.

He was obviously very keen. Once, the man had gone missing for several days and almost came to grief in the outback looking for one rare bird to boost his total, Palmeira read.

'Unbelievable.'

'What is, sir?'

'The lengths these birders'll go to.'

In Britain, which seemed to have more birders than anywhere in the world, competition to spot the most birds had actually turned ugly. Disputes over who'd seen what had ended in court or in fisticuffs. Or both. So much for the Poms' reputation for good manners, thought Palmeira.

At least in Australia competition to spot the most species remained friendly. And, for the most part, honourable. Birders even helped one another by posting details of unusual sightings on the Internet and telephone hotlines.

Still, as a member of some national records committee, whose job was to adjudicate on all these odd claims, said, 'There's a lot more at stake than just another tick. Expertise. Honour. Reputation.'

And, marketability, thought Palmeira. Authors, guides and TV experts, such as Phillip Clarkson had turned a pastime into a profession. Birding had clearly provided him with a good living. Could it, as well, have somehow been the cause of his grisly death?

Certainly, some spotters seemed prepared to go to almost any expense, any distance. But to any extreme, even to the murder of ...well, what? A rival birdwatcher? It seemed a ludicrous idea. Palmeira felt certain that Clarkson's killer would be found not in his public but his private life.

But what sort of private life did he have? He'd glanced at a few of his programs on television and may have been able to identify him if shown a picture. But what was he like behind the TV make-up? All he knew was what Koslowski had told him: that Clarkson was single and lived with his mother.

Predictably, the newspaper cuttings offered few clues, despite the inclusion of several, so-called 'in depth' profiles. The planned obituary — a 'work in progress!!' Ms Chan had scribbled across it — was basically a quick cut and paste job, but it did contain some basic facts.

Phillip Charles Clarkson, whose age was given as 34, had been born in North Sydney. Both parents were academics: his late father Charles, who encouraged the boy's early interest in birds, had been a zoologist. His mother, Margaret, had lectured in English literature, specialising in 19th century Australian women writers. He had a brother, two years younger, called Paul.

After attending the local boys' high school, Clarkson went to Sydney University, where, surprisingly, he'd done an arts degree. After graduating with honours, he'd gone into television on a graduate trainee scheme. Four years later, after working off-screen as a researcher, he'd left and joined a small independent film company, specialising in wildlife programs. There he had started to front documentaries. One of his first, a highly acclaimed film tracking the restless lives of albatrosses, had been bought by the ABC.

In recent years he had travelled all over the place to top birding destinations. The Okavango Delta in Botswana. The Galapagos Islands in Ecuador. The rainforests of Sri Lanka. Fair Isle off Scotland. He had made more films, written a couple of coffee-table books on birds, started his own company offering birding tours, become a prominent spokesman on wildlife issues and, most recently, had launched his own line of signature leisurewear, starting with the boots and shoes in which he had died.

What a waste, thought Palmeira.

As Chan noted, in a rush of purple prose, 'Phillip Clarkson was funny, sexy, energetic, good-looking... like a breath of fresh air in a field full of fuddy-duddies. He introduced a whole new generation to birding by turning it into show-business.'

From what he read, Palmeira wasn't sure he would have wholly liked Clarkson. Unlike himself, he was a blue-eyed boy, from a well-to-do family, who'd faced few obstacles in life. How effortless, how inexorable, his progress through life had been, if the obituary was to be believed. How extraordinary that it should end like this, with him dead at 34, face down, bum up, in Moreton Bay, still promoting his footwear. It was sad. Though slightly comical. Almost as if whoever killed him was playing some cruel joke.

As Koslowski neared Paddington, Palmeira quickly scanned a few more profiles. They had been cut from women's magazines clearly besotted with the boy wonder. They added little of substance. Indeed, they read more like PR handouts. Drooling over Clarkson's curly blond hair and slightly chubby, school-boyish features — if only they could see him now. Gushing over his clean-cut image. Celebrating his new age sensitivity. Here was a man who seemed to have none of the modern vices of fast food, fast cars or fast women, but was quickly moved to tears by examples of other men's inhumanity. Especially to animals.

It was near the end of the 40 minutes journey, spent speed-reading through a wad of feature articles and news stories. As Koslowski circled, looking for a parking space, Palmeira realised he hadn't even scratched the surface. He certainly hadn't improved his powers of identification. Nor had he been able to see quite what made 'tickers' — as some of the birders were called — tick.

Still, there were enough hints here and there in Clarkson's clippings to suggest the Clarkson story had not been one of unqualified success. Not even journalists feel able to speak ill of the dead, at least not in print. So these insights were encased in euphemisms.

Clarkson had 'not suffered fools gladly'. Translation: he could be difficult to work with. He was a 'perfectionist'. Correction, he was impossible to work with. He was 'respected by' his colleagues. Not 'liked by' or 'popular with', noted Palmeira.

And, he was no 'stranger to controversy'. Now, what did that mean? he was wondering when the car stopped and started to reverse. At last, Koslowski had found a place to park. This was quite an achievement. So elusive were places in this neighbourhood — one of Sydney's best — that locals told jokes about a man supposedly found lying in the roadside. Asked if he was all right, he explained that he and his wife had been walking along when they spotted the parking place. He was now waiting while his wife went home to fetch the car.

'Not far to walk from here, sir,' said Koslowski, apologetically, jumping out. Palmeira could see he looked uncomfortable. No doubt the young officer was worrying that this interview would drag on and he would miss some pressing domestic duty — a school concert or a rare night out with his wife, perhaps. As Palmeira knew all too well, it was difficult to be a good father and husband as well as a good policeman.

Palmeira pulled him back to the present. 'Remind me when we get back, Kiwi. I've got to check out something called the 750 Club. I'm sure Clarkson would've been a member.'

'No problems, sir. What is it? One of those gay places on Oxford Street?'

'Not quite.'

'This it sir,' announced Koslowski, spotting movement inside. 'Looks like we're in luck.' The pair stopped and rapped the brass door-knocker of an elegant house. Must be worth a couple of million dollars, thought Palmeira.

Clarkson's birding business must have been prospering. Or he had a very rich mother.

The door opened to reveal an attractive, elegant-looking woman. She had a deep tan and black hair, cut in pageboy style and was dressed in a black suit with white blouse. She looked tired — from her recent travel, perhaps — but could easily pass for about 50. From Clarkson's obituary, Palmeira knew she must be in her mid-sixties.

'Detective Inspector Palmeira. Detective Constable Koslowski,' said the senior man, bowing suavely.

'Margaret Clarkson. Come through. Excuse the mess. I'm just back from the airport,' she said leading the way. 'Mrs Wolff — next door — said the police had been round. I was just looking for a number to phone.'

Palmeira winced. Obviously, she'd not read the newspapers or been told about her son's lurid death. He was half-hoping she would have been. He'd done 'death knocks' plenty of times before, but they were always painful. He cleared his throat.

'It's about Phillip.'

'Yes. I thought it must be,' she said, tensing visibly round the shoulders.

There was no easy way to say it. 'Mrs Clarkson, I'm afraid a body of a man has been found. We've strong reason to believe it is your son,' Palmeira explained.

'What? That can't be true.' She paused, as the news sank in. 'What happened?'

As gently as he could, Palmeira gave a brief, sanitised description of the body's discovery, adding that, to his deep regret, the death was being treated as suspicious.

'What do you mean suspicious? I thought you said it was an accident.'

'I'm afraid not. No. We won't know for sure until tomorrow. But it doesn't look like an accident. I'm awfully sorry.'

'Oh, my god. That's terrible.' Margaret Clarkson collapsed into a chair, dropping her head into her hands. A slow, rhythmic sobbing shook her body.

For all his experience in such situations and all his studies in psychology, Palmeira never quite knew what role he was expected to play. Comforter? Inquisitor? Right now, he didn't even know quite where to look.

'Koslowski, why don't you make everyone a cup of ... err, tea? Coffee, Mrs Clarkson?' he said. God, he made it sound like a cop-show cliché.

'No, no, not now, thanks,' she murmured.

For more than a minute, Palmeira and Koslowski sat in silence. While the distraught mother fought to regain some composure, they tactfully inspected the room. Warm, cream walls. Oil paintings, mainly still lifes.

Clusters of plant pots and soft-colour, floral furnishings. All very chintzy. Very feminine. No photographs. No bird pictures. No hint that this was also the home of a 34-year-old man.

Palmeira glanced back at the woman. Was it time to risk a few questions? Or give her a few more minutes? He didn't want to have to deal with an hysterical woman. In that moment, he noticed that Margaret Clarkson must be wearing a wig.

It had been dislodged slightly as she kneaded her damp face, exposing wispy grey hair. How fragile and old she suddenly looked.

'Would you like us to come back later?' he asked. Behind him, Koslowski seem to brighten involuntarily. 'Perhaps we could talk to one of his friends, if …'

'No, no, I'll be fine. I think.' With an effort, she jerked herself upright. 'I'll see how I go. I'd really like to get this bit over with. I know you must have some questions for me.'

'If you're sure…'

'I'm sure. You know, inspector, it's funny… well, more ironic, really, I suppose. Phillip was so popular with the public. They adored him. But he didn't have any real friends.'

'Oh?' replied Palmeira, wondering whether it was an appropriate moment to ask the obvious question: was Phillip Clarkson gay? Perhaps later.

'He's always been close to his brother, of course,' Mrs Clarkson went on. 'But he lives several hours away. Coffs Harbour. You know it? Not very close, is it?'

'No.'

'Look, I'm sorry. I'm rambling.'

'No, no. Don't apologise,' murmured Palmeira. If he didn't apply some pressure, this interview would go nowhere. 'When did you last speak to Phillip, Mrs Clarkson?'

She shook her head, as if it would bring her thoughts into clearer focus. 'Of course. Friday night — mmm, about ten-thirtyish — it would've been. I rang here. Just to let him know when I'd be home.'

'How did he seem?'

'No different from usual, as far as I can remember. Bit vague. But then that was Phillip. Always got his mind on bigger things.'

'Did you ask him what he'd been up to? What he'd got planned for the weekend?'

'I guess I must have done. He said, like "oh, just the usual". Something about taking a group out to look at birds on the harbour. I don't think he was looking forward to it much.'

'Really?'

'Oh, they could be very boring people. But, as he said, they paid the bills.'

'Did he speak about anything else?'

'No, that was about it, I think.'

'I know you said Phillip didn't have friends. But what about, err, acquaintances? Do you remember anyone coming round to visit him? People from work, perhaps?'

As Margaret Clarkson considered the question, her face seemed to crumple. Oh, dear, she's going to burst into tears, thought Palmeira, looking across to Koslowski, who looked as though he wanted to escape, if only to the kitchen to make some tea.

But, with apparent difficulty, Mrs Clarkson pulled herself together again. Literally, it seemed, from somewhere deep inside she summoned the effort to raise her head again.

'Sorry, what…'

'Acquaintances?'

'No, no one special. In the early days, people from the film company used to come round, for planning meetings, to celebrate finishing a series. That sort of thing.'

'I see.'

'Actually, when I think about it there was a young chap used to come round every now and then. But then he stopped. I remember I asked Phillip about him and he didn't want to speak about it. I think he and Phillip must have had a disagreement.'

'Don't recall a name I suppose?' Palmeira prompted gently.

'Dear me. Umm. I remember thinking at the time it seemed an appropriate name. A bird of some sort. Swift? No, that wasn't it…'

Palmeira brought a neatly folded list from the inside breast pocket of his suit. He consulted it. 'Possibly, Finch. Simon Finch?'

'That's it. Is it important?'

'Could be,' Palmeira said neutrally. 'Do you know what they talked about, by any chance?'

'Birds, I imagine.'

'Right.' Palmeira nodded and let the subject rest. 'And what about girlfriends?' he asked. He tried to make the question sound casual, spontaneous. But Mrs Clarkson looked at him darkly.

'Oh, there were girls. Women. Of course. From the film crew. Clients. But never anyone serious, so far as I know. To be honest, I don't think Phillip was very interested.'

'Right.' Palmeira nodded, wondering again whether he should raise Clarkson's sexuality. He did not need to. His reply had dropped into the silence so leadenly that Margaret Clarkson felt obliged to elaborate.

'Look, inspector. The thing is... Phillip was... he was... very, how can I put it, self-sufficient. He was always engrossed in his work. His documentaries. His trips. His books. His schemes. He was always full of ideas, but never very gregarious, I'm afraid. As I said, he got on well with Paul. That's his brother. Most of the time, anyway. But he seemed, you know, happiest in this own company. "Away with the birds", Paul used to joke. Phillip liked that. Even when he was in Sydney, living in the same house, we'd go several days at a time not seeing each other.'

'How so?'

'Well, I still do part-time work at the uni. He was often out in the evenings, eating — neither of us is fond of cooking — giving talks to bird groups and that. We get on... sorry, got on, fine... but we had separate lives, as well. We both liked our space.'

'I see.'

'And, anyway, when Charles...my husband...died, what, eight years ago, we divided the house. I live downstairs, Phillip upstairs. It's pretty much self-contained.'

'Any chance we'd could take a quick look?' Koslowski, who'd been quiet, taking notes, was clearly beginning to think the DI would never ask.

Wearily, Margaret Clarkson took the two men upstairs to a large, square landing, decorated with images of birds. Not photographs but artwork in an eclectic mix of styles.

The landing led to what was obviously a bedroom, and through swing doors inlaid with stained glass, into a living room, which seemed to occupy almost all of the first floor. It was well-lit by a wide picture window and was large enough to be sub-divided. Dazzling white walls, polished pine flooring, ingenious planning and minimal furniture created an illusion of space. An absence of clutter.

There was also a small dining area enclosed by low bookshelves, a study space equipped with desk-top computer, printer and fax machine, and a place for doing whatever Phillip did: relaxing, watching television and videos and listening to music, Palmeira supposed, looking at the expensive-looking equipment.

Koslowski seemed envious, probably comparing it to his own home. But Palmeira thought it appeared rather sterile, like something out of a catalogue. To his eye, this looked like the working and living space of a lonely man, a well-organised man. More, an obsessive man.

Indeed, the only thing out of place, he noted, was a Birds Australia mug, still half-full of milky coffee that had formed a cold, brown tide mark.

That hardly turned the living room into the poop deck of the Marie Celeste, but it did suggest to Palmeira that Phillip Clarkson had made a hurried final exit.

'May we?' asked Palmeira, pointing to the bedroom. Mrs Clarkson nodded.

The door opened to reveal another pleasant, airy room. It contained a double bed, a set of drawers and two full-length mirrors on opposite walls. It adjoined an ensuite bathroom and a walk-in wardrobe. One of its sliding doors had been pushed open.

Someone — presumably Clarkson, though he'd get fingerprinting round to confirm — had been rummaging around inside. Looking not for the expensive, designer-label clothes, neatly hanging or lying folded in racks, but for some old cardboard boxes of papers.

One of these had been left, its lid off, its contents spread in no discernible order, over the navy blue and white doona. Palmeira nodded and Koslowski walked over and examined them. Bank statements, invoices, schedules and costings for forthcoming trips.

'I'm afraid we may have to take these away for a closer look, Mrs

Clarkson,' Palmeira said.

'I quite understand.' She slumped forward. 'Poor Phillip. How he hated the paperwork. He was a good organiser, but paying bills, send out invoices, dealing with banks…it seemed such a waste of his creative skills.'

'Surprised he didn't get a full-time secretary or, what do you call them, personal assistant.'

'Oh, for a long time he did. Christine Withers. But she left. Must be a few months ago now.'

'Oh?'

'Yes. Phillip asked her to go. He didn't think she was very good. A bit too young and dizzy, I think. Said she'd messed things up once too often. A double-booking, or something, I expect.'

'Shame.'

'Yes. Actually, it all got a bit unpleasant for a while.'

'How's that?'

Mrs Clarkson hesitated, as if suddenly wondering whether she was saying too much. She probably just wanted to get these policemen out of her house. To be left alone. 'One night some man came round, looking for Phillip. Luckily, he was out.'

She looked at Palmeira. He was listening intently.

'I wouldn't let the man in and he got very angry. Said he was Christine's boyfriend and that he'd come to collect her entitlements…Except he couldn't say it properly. Kept stumbling, and calling them "entitled-ties". No, "entitled-ments". That was it.'

She giggled. Now, she's becoming hysterical, thought Palmeira, noting that Koslowski was sneaking a look at his watch.

'Phillip and I laughed about it afterwards. But at the time it was really scary.'

'So what happened?'

'Oh, nothing. I imagine he must have sorted things out. As far as I know we didn't hear from them again.'

'Perhaps you could find Withers' contact number for us. Just in case,' said Palmeira, turning now to leave.

'You don't think she…? Or he?' she started.

Here it comes, thought Palmeira. The inevitable 'whodunnit' question asked by every bereaved parent, spouse, friend, who finds it incomprehensible that a loved one has been killed. And, worse, that the police have not already arrested those responsible.

'I'm sorry, I really can't say at this stage,' he said, adding lamely, 'Right now, we're following a number of lines of inquiry.' A number that's just increased by two or three, thought Palmeira, preparing to leave.

But not quite yet. Most real cops, Palmeira had noticed, liked to catch interviewees unawares by springing on them one, last, killer question. For the life of him he couldn't think of one — though he did suddenly remember a couple of important pieces of detail.

'Did Phillip have a mobile phone?'

'Yes.' She recited the number.

'Any idea where it is now?'

'No. It wasn't found with his... body?'

'No, not yet. How about a car?'

Yes. Of course he had a car,' replied Mrs Clarkson. Her tone suggested she considered non-ownership of private transport as evidence of a deviant personality.

'Where's it kept?'

'Outside...oh dear. Gone?

'Looks like it. Do you know the make?'

Mrs Clarkson did: a newish, green Volkswagen Beetle. How appropriate. Somehow, it matched Clarkson's public persona as a man more interested in conservation than conspicuous consumption. She also knew the registration number.

'Thanks. That'll do for now.'

Satisfied with their afternoon's work, and with reassurances that Margaret Clarkson would call on her neighbour Mrs Wolff if she needed help, the two men left.

ೞೞೞ

Koslowski had other priorities. He just wanted to drop off his passenger and to meet his wife and son, as planned. God, look how late it was! Still, they were now only ten minutes or so away from Berwick, he calculated, looking again at his watch as he accelerated out of a roundabout.

Suddenly there was a scream. 'Look out, man!' Koslowski looked up and saw a car coming towards him, cutting the corner. He reacted immediately, braking, and, with the same hand, sounding the horn and wrenching the steering wheel hard to the left. In an instant, the driver in the other car seemed to do the same.

There was a shriek of rubber, a puff of smoke but, miraculously, as Koslowski and Palmeira braced themselves, no sudden clang of metal sheet scraping and bouncing against sheet metal. Just as quickly as they had converged, the two cars resumed course.

Koslowski's heart was thumping, but he tried not to show it. 'Sorry, sir,' he tried to say calmly, acting like he'd been in total control throughout the incident.

'A close call,' said Palmeira, shaking his head. He looked back over his shoulder at the other vehicle, already disappearing round a bend. 'I don't believe it. You know who that was?'

'No.'

'That idiot Danniher. Dashing off to the pub, I bet. Could have got us all killed.' The thought jolted Koslowski. What about his family? He hadn't even had time to say goodbye properly to them that morning.

೮೨೮೨೮೨

Not far behind them, Danniher pulled up. Turned off the ignition. Took a deep breath. And pulled out a cigarette. Just the one. To calm him down.

He considered. What an idiotic thing to do. Now he was in real trouble with the DI, who must have recognised him. Then again, perhaps the narrow miss was a good omen. They'd all escaped without a scratch to either body or bodywork. The gods seemed to be taking pity on him. Maybe even smiling on him. About bloody time.

In fact, he could honestly say he'd not been on his way to the pub — though if asked he would have admitted to his mates that his lapse in concentration occurred while he wrestled with the temptation to drop in for a quick one.

No, sir, he'd been going home, for a record second consecutive early night after a bloody good day's work, if he did say so himself. All right, five or six hours' of hard detective work. But it felt like a fresh start.

He'd been unable to talk to Christopher Workman — 'out, seeing prospective clients all afternoon', according to his woman — but had fixed a meeting for first thing next morning. Meanwhile, he'd found some recent pix of the dead man. In fact, he'd even driven across town to the TV studios to pick them up personally.

Smart move. Instead of finding Mr Birdman's television colleagues deep in sorrow, they seemed to have got over his death very quickly. Of course, it was 'an awful thing to have happened', 'all very sad', and him 'so young', etc., etc., but less than devastating.

Danniher had chatted up a young girl from the publicity team. He prided himself on being a smooth talker. Anyway, she'd let slip, while looking for the PR pictures, that Clarkson wasn't exactly everyone's pin-up boy. 'You should ask his film crew about him,' she suggested.

Good idea, thought Danniher.

ରୟରୟରୟ

This suggestion — along with several mug-shots of the dead man — were on Palmeira's desk, with several other reports, when he got back to his office. As he read through the pile, Palmeira reflected hungrily how, in only 36 hours, he'd been completely sucked into the Birdman Case. He'd barely had time to eat and sleep, let alone get to a gym or go for a run, or read a book or watch some television. If he didn't watch out his home-life would become non-existent.

Since returning from the Clarkson home he'd defused Sedgwick, who'd preferred to vent his wrath on politicians meddling with his beloved police force. He'd read Danniher's report on his trip to the studio. And he'd given the police media some grains of truth, including a photograph of the dead man and details of his car, to feed to the chooks. The journalists.

Now, he badly wanted to go home. But there was something else he was supposed to do. What was that? Something to do with the forensics? No. Something to do with HQ? No. Thankfully, they were leaving him alone to get on with things. So far.

After a few seconds, it came to him. The 750 Club. Koslowski had gone off without reminding him. He wandered from his desk into the corridor and spotted a familiar, attractive face. Helen McCrimond. He remembered her now. The very officer who had set him up with a desk, whiteboard, and other bits and pieces. 'Hello, you still here, then?' he called out.

'Oh, it's you sir,' the woman said, glancing up. 'A few more hours to go yet,' she replied in an attractive Scots voice. 'We should have your incident room up and running by tomorrow.'

'Good, good. There was something else, though...'

'Ask and it shall be done, sir.'

He smiled. 'Do you know much about the Internet?' he asked. Most officers these days did.

'Of course. Absolutely invaluable, I'd say. Investigations, research, that sort of stuff.' He remembered how young and bright and enthusiastic, she was. Wouldn't take Berwick's grumpy old men long to knock that out of her.

'I was wondering if you could give me a hand with some research.'

'Sure.'

'When you've got a quiet moment, log on and see if you can find anything on something called the 750 Club. It's an elite group of birders, twitchers they call themselves. See what you can find out. See if our body Phillip Clarkson was a member.'

'Will do. Oh, by the way, sir, your wife rang again.'

Palmeira swallowed hard. What did she mean 'again'? Had someone failed to pass on a message? Why had Jenny rung the first time? Why had she rung again? He looked at his watch. If he rang now, he'd only wake the girls.

He began tidying away for the night. The last thing to go into the tray for filing was the colour photograph of Clarkson supplied by the TV station. He looked at it carefully, as if seeing the face for the first time, and noticed that Clarkson was not, in fact, a 'blue-eyed boy'. He had one blue eye, one brown eye. How odd. Just like Alexander the Great, Palmeira recalled from a documentary he'd seen on the History Channel.

Perhaps he could discuss it with McCrimond over a cup of coffee later.

5

It is amusing to find pieces of newspapers bedizening the house of wood-thrushes so frequently, though it cannot be said that they showed the highest literary taste in their selections; for one or two of the fragments contained accounts of political cause.

— Leander S. Keyser, *In Bird Land*

There was still thunder and lightning about — the final special 'boom, crash opera' effects of a typical late-summer Sydney storm — as Wayne Danniher drove north for his interview with Chris Workman early the next morning. Explosions, flashes of light, sudden bursts of torrential rain — they all reminded him of that frightening evening back in April, 1999. What a night that had been! In barely 30 minutes, the storm had caused $1 billion damage — $10,000 of it to his old Ford Escort.

Hundreds of cars had been trashed, trees blown over, and roof tiles smashed. Danniher had stopped to help a young bloke who'd been hit by a lump of ice. As 'big as a basketball', his girlfriend swore.

Don't know about that, Danniher had thought. But it had been big enough to come through the soft-top on the man's sports car and fracture his skull.

The storm had spooked the city. Ever since, distant rumbles, lightning bolts, even odd changes in the colour of the sky were enough to send Sydneysiders running to the windows, where they'd stand oohing and aahing at the light show, or running to protect person and property.

It was a ridiculous over-reaction, thought Danniher. Anyway, everyone knew lightning didn't strike twice in the same place. No point constantly looking for the black cloud lurking behind the silver lining.

For a change, he felt good. No hangover. He'd risen early, read a thin file on Workman over breakfast, and still found time to do a quick check of the Bayside Drive dunes to familiarise himself with the crime scene. He wasn't surprised to find that — at least from the road — there was now no sign of anything out of the ordinary ever having happened there. The blue and white crime scene tape had been removed. Commuter traffic was moving normally.

Even though it was raining heavily, a man was dragging a reluctant-looking dog for a walk along the roadside. Or possibly even a swim. He knew blokes, trainers, who'd take their greyhounds for a morning swim.

He wondered if the dunes were still attracting the after-hours crowd. Or whether media talk of a 'gay-basher' on the loose had scared them away. Personally, he hoped not. Bet someone down here must have seen something. Or done something, he reckoned.

To his way of thinking, this Workman interview was a waste of time. He'd be better off chasing this other bloke. Waddell. Or scaring up a few witnesses in the dunes later on. Bit more of a hands-on approach. Still, he didn't mind helping Palmeira go through the motions and, hey, he certainly had no objections to leaning on a journo or two. To be honest, he didn't much like the type. In his experience, they were nosey, pushy, untrustworthy and always getting in the way. And Workman was a birder to boot. A bit of a weirdo? Possibly.

Only the other weekend, Danniher had been attacked by a bird. Not the usual magpie, but an, aggressive brown and white thing, with long legs and drooping yellow jowls. Seemed to be protecting a yellow tennis ball in the mistaken idea it was an egg. Must remember to ask this birder what all that was about.

The rain was easing and the skies lightening, as he pulled into Parkes Street, and started looking for number six. The neighbourhood was an odd mix of little businesses, cottages and corner-shops. A friendly looking place that the developers had missed, just a drop kick away from the Sydney Cricket Ground. Nice and handy.

The house was even odder. A plain, single-storey, rectangular building of whitewashed-brick on a long, narrow block at the junction of a lane, from which a back gate provided entry to a small yard. At one time it must have been a shop, or more likely, a workshop, Danniher imagined.

He checked his watch. Just gone 7.50 am. Bit early, but he could see a light on inside. He knocked. Almost instantly the door was opened, not by Workman but a slim, willowy woman, with wet, blond hair. Very tasty.

She was dressed casually in a skimpy black T-shirt decorated with an Aboriginal flag and black denim jeans. Jane Clifford, he presumed, checking his crib sheet. '32, same address, social worker'.

'Oh hello, I'm Jane,' she said before he could even get a word in. 'You're Danniher. Right? Come in. I'm just finishing breakfast.'

Righto. Walking in, he was able to take in virtually the whole house in a single sweeping glance. It comprised just one extra large room, apart from a kitchen, which was sectioned off by a low breakfast-bar, and a bathroom, which he'd already passed on the way in. Across the angle of the right-hand, far corner stood a large, iron bed. It was still unmade: as if the recent occupants had hopped out of it directly into the shower or, possibly, the rain.

The bed pointed diagonally across the room towards a wide-screen television set, the most expensive item in the house, by the looks of it. It was switched on, but muted. The only other substantial piece of furniture was a desk, piled with papers, which almost concealed a cheap laptop computer, and a matching chair.

Journalism — correction PR — did not look very lucrative. Or, perhaps, Danniher hoped, Workman was paying money to an ex-wife. Still, the overall effect was cheap and cheerful and cosy. Lucky bastard.

'Coffee?'

'Thanks. I'd kill for one. Black. Two sugars, please,' said Danniher, listening to the rain dance on the tin roof. Quite romantic, that. He sat at a stool at the bar and stretched out his legs, making himself at home. It'd been a long time since he'd joined an attractive woman for breakfast.

'Chris won't be long. He's just popped out to get the papers.'

'No rush.' He smiled. 'Must be keen? Going for the papers in this.'

'More like completely addicted, actually,' she said with an exaggerated frown. 'But, no, the shop's only about 50 metres away.'

'Handy.'

'I suppose so.' Almost as an afterthought, she seemed to remember the reason for Danniher's visit. 'Any news on Clarkson? Accident? Suicide?'

'Fraid not. We're pursuing lines of inquiry, as they say in the trade,' he said, providing the textbook answer.

'Good.' Jane Clifford didn't seem to care one way or another. Or perhaps she simply had more important things to worry about. Either way, Danniher thought, he ought to return and ask her a few questions.

Had she had any previous dealings with the dead man? Where was she in the hours before his death? Did she fancy going for a drink? That sort of thing.

ೞೞೞ

At that moment, though, the door flew open, followed by a podgy, unshaven man, with a pasty complexion. He was wearing a voluminous surf-label T-shirt, boardshorts and thongs.

Shaking himself off like a dog after a swim in the sea, Workman removed a thick chest-plate of newsprint. Most people would have used it as a temporary umbrella. Clearly he'd shielded it from the rain.

'Oh. Danniher, I presume. You're early.'

'Sorry.' Why, despite his best intentions, had he taken an instant dislike to Workman? Envy? Prejudice? No, he concluded, it was probably because it would save time in the long run.

'Anyway, I see you've made yourself at home.'

Danniher did his best to ignore the remark. 'This shouldn't take long, sir.'

Looking past Workman, he could see the muted television news was now reporting on the Clarkson murder. A reporter, a sleek, young man in a tight suit, was speaking to camera. He could just imagine what the man was saying as he looked around meaningfully, across the sand hills.

'It was here, among these notorious dunes, that police believe TV personality Phillip Clarkson, known to millions of viewers as the Birdman, was savagely attacked, his body thrown in a shallow grave…'

'Sorry, I'll leave you two to it,' announced Jane Clifford, standing up. Apparently, she was already wearing her work clothes.

'Social work, isn't it?' asked Danniher.

'Yeah.'

'Anything special?'

'Homeless single women, actually.'

'What, bashed wives, junkies, that sort of thing?' Danniher regretted the words almost before they left his lips.

'Not just them,' replied Clifford, tolerantly. 'Like women with post-natal depression, for example. Anyway, must be going…'

As she gathered her things and left, it struck Danniher that she probably didn't know about her partner's marital record.

'So, Jane doesn't get to be interviewed, eh?' There was aggression in Workman's voice.

'What do you mean?'

'Well, she was there as well. How about a bit of sexual equality? Or perhaps you think one interview, with the man of the house, fits all.'

Despite his rush to give Workman a work-over, he'd not forgotten his partner was also on the birders' list, nor Palmeira's advice not to allow himself to be provoked. 'Not at all. One at a time, sir,' said Danniher.

Workman let it go. Obviously, his own work could wait, for he seemed in no hurry. Rather, he deliberately laid out the three newspapers he had bought on his desk and studied them.

'Great story,' he said, at length.

Danniher sneered. Personally, he objected to the way that in the grubby hands of the media, real-life events were transformed into a 'story' — as though they were parts of a piece of fiction, worked up for the entertainment of readers, listeners, viewers. Then again…

The Clarkson inquiry, he saw, now filled the complete front page of the tabloid newspaper, though the words were almost squeezed off by a full-face shot of the dead man and a headline. BIRDER MURDER. Oh my god, thought Danniher, Sedgwick will go troppo if he sees the sort of sensationalist treatment the story was getting. And he could hardly fail to.

The self-styled 'quality broadsheet' also had a report on its front-page, beneath a very boring story about interest rate rises.

Inside was Karen Chan's sober obituary and a background feature article that revisited stalking cases and other crimes against celebrities, from American aviator Charles Lindbergh, whose infant son had been kidnapped and murdered, to the English TV personality Jill Dando.

From what Danniher could make out, the newspaper had already decided that Clarkson's murder had not been random — a matter of being in the wrong place at the wrong time — but that he had been killed because of who or what he was. Obviously, they knew better than the police or the pathologists!

Even the financial newspaper had a follow-up story: a short feature on the Birdman's business empire. It was illustrated with a graphic showing the value of different income streams. The paper estimated his annual earnings to be about $1.2 million.

A rich man, then, thought Danniher. How long would a policeman have to work to make as much? A quarter of a century?

The funny thing was that, according to Palmeira, Clarkson's wallet had been found with his found with his body. Cash and credit cards still intact. So theft could surely be ruled out as a motive. Then again, maybe he had enough money in the bank and enough skeletons in his cupboard to make him a blackmail target.

Especially if he'd been looking for some rough trade in the dunes. Even in these enlightened times, some gay men didn't want to go public. It could ruin the image, for one thing. Danniher made a mental note to mention it to Pamela, though. He was pleased, at least, to see that two out of the three newspapers had included a map of the Bayside Drive crime scene and descriptions of the dead man's clothing and car.

They'd also carried the Crimestoppers appeal for anyone who had seen anything suspicious that night to come forward. Suspicious, like a semi-naked man being bashed on the head, dragged off through the dunes and buried head first in the sand.

'Unless it's our coffee, I take it you don't approve of all this?' Workman asked, waving one of the papers, smiling.

'Irrelevant whether I do or I don't,' Danniher replied. He didn't want to get into a bloody debate on the subject.

'Please yourself. Personally, I believe in the public's right to know.'

Danniher couldn't help himself. 'At any cost, I presume?' he snapped, nodding in the direction of the 'fridge. It was plastered with photographs of Workman and or Clifford fighting for that right: on picket lines, outside a petrochemicals plant, inside what looked like the perimeter walls of detention centres.

'Almost,' said Workman, unabashed.

'So what is it the public has a right to know about Phillip Clarkson —

who he's been screwing and where, I suppose?'

Workman let the words circulate for a moment before replying. 'Now, there's two very interesting questions.' He paused again before continuing.

'I'd say people like Clarkson — high-profile people on television, in sport, business, even in politics — have some right to privacy. But in some cases, yes, I believe the public has a right to know things they'd rather keep private. Part of the price of fame.'

'What sort of things?'

Workman again paused. 'I don't know how much homework you've done already, but it's no secret I've had several dealings with Clarkson in the past.'

'Oh?'

'Yes. In fact, it was through Clarkson that I first got interested in this whole birding business. And, at his level, I assure you that's what it is. A business. Pretty big business.'

'Like the second-hand car business? Or the advertising business, I suppose?'

'Not at all. I actually did get hooked on the feathery things as well.'

'Money in it, is there?'

'Not really. It was a few years back. I was still full-time, feature writing, on the newspaper. I was sent off to do this profile — for the TV guide of all things — on this new local documentary-maker.'

'Before he hatched out as TV's Mr Birdman?'

'Correct. I must admit I was impressed by the guy... yes, officer, I am capable of being impressed. He was young and good-looking in an eccentric, young, outdoor sort of way. You know: masses of curly, blond hair, wildly enthusiastic eyes. Looked terribly good in a pair of shorts. He really seemed to know his stuff. And, unlike a lot of those old buggers Clarkson could still get people revved up about the subject, get them interested with a few jokes.'

'Oh.'

'Yeah. Even used to give the birds odd names.'

'Really?'

'Yes, I can't think... oh, on a radio interview once he started talking about the Glamorous Claude Reebler. Like it was some sort of character.'

'I don't get it.'

'It's a joke. There's this cute little bird called a clamorous reed warbler.' Danniher still didn't get it.

'Anyway... I did this interview with him. Went out with him and a photographer to get pictures. Long Reef, up the coast, I think it was. Wrote the piece. Straight up and down. No problems. Everyone happy.

'Then — it must have been, what, a year or so later — a package arrives at the office. Inside, there's all this stuff about what someone called "your friend Clarkson".'

'What sort of stuff?'

'A lot of it was just crazy stuff. You can always pick it: capital letters, underlinings, exclamation marks. They're always a dead giveaway. Might just as well sign off "yours sincerely, a nutter".'

'But in there was a lot of personal stuff — how Clarkson wasn't as smart as he thought he was, how he was a bully, a liar, a hypocrite, how he was heading for a fall and so on.'

'Who sent this?'

'No idea, I'm afraid. Anonymous. It often is in cases like this. Someone is making serious allegations, but hasn't got the guts to put their name to them.'

'So what sort of allegations?' On the television, Danniher noted, a woman was showing how to make a cake of some sort.

'Mainly dealings with local councils. And, what did come as a bit of shock, with developers. I guess, the idea was — in journalistic terms — how Phillip's image was a sham. In public Clarkson was popular Mr Birdman, but in private he was, well, feathering his own nest...'

'Very funny.'

'Yes. I even had the headline written. But, yeah, feathering his nest by taking money to advise councils and big businesses on how to beat the dreaded greenies.'

'Sounds a great piece of investigative journalism.'

Much to Danniher's disappointment, Workman failed to notice, or chose to ignore, his irony. 'Yes. But any story's got to be cost-effective. You know? How much effort am I going to have to put in? To get what sort of story?'

'So what happened?'

'I had a go at it, but the councils and the developers stonewalled, Clarkson got stroppy, first being outraged and uncooperative, and then threatening injunctions and the rest. The paper's lawyers started getting nervous.'

'Not surprising.'

'Still, I had a go at writing something. Hard-going.' He frowned. 'Anyway, then I was sent off round Australia, mainly WA and Northern Territory, to do a big series on land rights. And, to be honest, I got a bit sidetracked by domestic problems.'

'Marriage?'

'You know all about that, then?'

That's wiped the smile off your face, mate, thought Danniher. 'The results of your attempts to deal with those domestic problems are in the police computer.'

'I see.'

'Anyway, so what happened to the big story?'

'Nothing. It didn't get written. Not yet anyway.'

'We'll need to see that material, please, sir.'

'Not possible.'

'Why?'

'Blame my ball-breaker of a wife.'

'Oh?'

'When I got back from Darwin, the house was empty. She'd shot through. Moved in with some new man. A real creep. But not before she'd made a bonfire of my clothes, my books and the files of all the stories I'd been working on at home.'

'Fabulous!'

'Not really. Now I've got myself sorted out here I thought I'd have another go at Clarkson. I don't think I'm really suited to public relations: smarming around, being nice to people, saying positive things about clients' products.'

'Would've thought you'd be good at that.'

'Very funny. In any case, it would've made a nice piece, say for one of the colour mags. It still could. "Revealed: the amazing truth about TV's Mr Birdman".'

'I can hardly wait,' said Danniher, making a note in his book to check out possible connections between Clarkson and both Berwick Council and whoever was developing Moreton Bay. Pelican, was it? Not for the first time Danniher was struck by how often bird names cropped up.

He went on. 'I'm sure you've a perfectly good explanation, sir, but why if you and Clarkson didn't get on did you pay good money — what was it, 50 bucks? — to go on a guided tour with him?'

'Oh, I don't know. Mischief. Give him a bit of a scare. Show him I was still on his tail. Get some colour for a possible story. You know, see the great man in action.' And blackmail him, wondered Danniher.

'Instead, you turn up and discover he's got himself killed.'

'Yes,' said Workman, grinning. 'Wonderful piece of timing, that. I particularly liked the way the legs poked out of the sand. Just as if the Birdman had fallen from the sky. Nice touch. Very symbolic. He was heading for a fall anyway.'

'Any ideas who might want to push him?'

'None. You're the detective. I didn't even know he was gay. If he was gay. He could have been, but I met him two or three times and would never have guessed. But I would have said he had plenty of enemies.'

'Including you?'

'In a way. He would have seen me as a threat. I hope. But of course I didn't kill him.'

'You've got an alibi, I suppose.'

'I'm sure if you tell me when he was killed, I'll be able tell you where I was at the time,' said Workman. 'And it certainly wasn't anywhere near the dunes on Bayside Drive. Saturday night, for instance, I stayed in and watched television. Never miss *The Bill*. Essential viewing for anyone interested in serious police work. You should watch it.'

'Anyone here with you?'

'There certainly was. All night,' Workman replied with a meaningful smirk. 'You know who. Ask her yourself.'

Smug bastard, thought Danniher. Workman was older than him, but acted younger and seemed more attractive to women. 'Don't go wandering off. We'll probably want to speak to you again.'

'That's fine. You know us media types. Always happy to talk about the seamier side of life.'

'So we noticed. That tip-off to your journo friends.'

Workman beamed. 'No crime in that. Anyway, I'm always speaking to my birding friends and passing on bits and pieces.'

'Oh?'

'It's small world. If we're not in the same clubs, we're probably sharing the same Internet sites, swapping info on the same chat lines. I don't quite know where the Fat Family, the Waddells, fit in, but the rest of us will be keeping in touch. They'll be interested to know I was first on the interview list. We're all suspects then, are we, officer?'

'For the time being, yes,' said Danniher. Well, why not? With no other strong leads, they had to be.

'How exciting. It'll give us something to talk about at our next meeting.'

'When's that, then?'

'Oh, nothing's fixed. But all those on…on Clarkson's Last Trip have already been talking about getting together again soon. For another trip. Or some sort of reunion.'

'Well, perhaps you could keep me informed, too,' said Danniher. He handed over his card, giving phone and fax contact details.

'If you think of anything else, give us a call,' he said, turning back just in time to see Workman toss the card on to the pile of papers.

Danniher slammed the door behind him and emerged from the cottage to find the storm clouds had died away. The sun was shining. Well, that hadn't gone badly, he thought as he strode back to the car.

He had resisted the temptation to thump Workman. On the contrary, he had skilfully extracted from him a few new leads. In footballing terms, he'd come away from his 90-minute encounter with an honourable draw. In short, Danniher had made a good start to the day.

ಐಐಐ

So too had Palmeira. The previous night he hadn't left the office until after 9 pm. Three times, it turned out, Jenny had telephoned in asking when he was coming home and left messages that he'd missed. Not surprisingly, the detective had found his dinner half-congealed, awaiting warm-up in the microwave, his two daughters already asleep in bed and his wife in a sulk. His apologies and his explanation that he was involved in a top celebrity murder case — 'you must have seen it on the news' — failed to placate her. These days, she complained, he was always working on a big murder case that took priority over domestic duties.

A real cop might have demanded a little more understanding. After all, he was under a lot of pressure. Police chiefs, the media, the public — all demanded a quick result. It wasn't as if he'd spent the evening out drinking with Danniher, or McCrimond, or his favourite pathologist, Sandy Prior.

Though come to think of it, it wasn't such a bad idea.

Instead, Palmeira had resolved to do better. He'd coped with periods of pressure before and knew that he shouldn't allow them to ruin his personal life. For one thing, working round the clock, missing meals, and losing his temper with colleagues only reduced his efficiency. This was a time for clear thinking.

Methodically, he had heated and eaten his pasta supper, laid out his running gear in the hope he might fit in a jog the next day, kissed the faces of his sleeping girls and, before turning off the bedroom light, mumbled another apology to the back of his wife. If she heard it, she didn't say so.

With the late meal lying heavy in his stomach, Palmeira had found sleep difficult. When it did come, it was accompanied by nightmares. In one he was ploughing with leaden feet through sand dunes planted every few metres with body parts, fleeing a series of grinning faces — Sedgwick, Danniher, Clarkson, and others he could not recognise. In another he was being assailed with rolled-up newspapers. The newspapers were critical of his handling of the case. One, he was horrified to see, had a full-page picture of him, looking like some hapless Inspector Clouseau of Pink Panther fame, under the headline BIRDBRAIN.

In the morning, he'd been relieved to discover that none of his dreams had come true. No more body parts had been found and, so far, no one appeared to be demanding his head over the Birdman affair. But it wouldn't be long before they did. He had — what? — 72 hours to make a breakthrough, better still an arrest. Or Mount Sedgwick would erupt. Palmeira shuddered at the thought.

Keep calm, don't panic, he'd told himself, as he devoted some quality — if not quantity — time to his family. Relations with Jenny had thawed slightly and he had spent more than a hour eating breakfast, seeing the girls off to school and chatting. Like a proper family.

Now he learned why Jenny had been upset. Apart from not knowing where he was the previous evening, she had some news of her own: she'd been offered a job. A full-time job as a design consultant to a city-centre development company.

'Really? That's great,' he replied, trying hard to sound pleased by the news.

'Thanks. I've been trying to tell you.'

'Sorry. Anyway, congratulations.'

'It's a great opportunity. Not just the work, but the pay, the super, the paid holidays. I can virtually pick my own hours.' She stopped. He knew why. She was preparing, after this burst of good news, to hit him with the bad. He braced himself.

'Of course, it would mean rearranging one or two things.'

'Like what?'

'It might mean you'd have to pick up the girls once or twice a week. Things like that. Or we could pay for a nanny.'

Oh, no. Palmeira didn't know how to reply. 'I'm sure we can work something out for the best,' he had started unconvincingly, before being saved by the telephone bell.

It was Danniher. Jenny had sighed deeply and moved off, clattering the breakfast things melodramatically. Not pleased, thought Palmeira gloomily, as he tried to ignore the noise and concentrate on Danniher's brief account of his meeting with Workman.

'Really…Yeah…That's interesting,' Palmeira muttered every few sentences, encouraging his junior officer to continue. Soon enough, he knew, Jenny would lose patience and leave the room. He needed time to think about her plan.

Danniher now wanted to go out and find Waddell. He was a man with a record. A bad temper. A thing about gays. Surely, that made him a prime suspect. All Danniher needed was a few hours with him.

'Sorry, Wayne.' It was the obvious thing to do, but Palmeira didn't want his junior charging through the list of birders like a wounded bull. 'I know you're on a roll. But I want you back at Berwick ASAP. Bill Argent from Crime Scene's coming in to give us a quick run-down on the pathology. Then I want to get everyone round the whiteboard for a few minutes and go through a few things. See where we're up to. I want you there. OK. Thanks.'

He put down the telephone. Damn, he'd forgotten. He'd meant to ask Danniher what the hell he thought he was doing trying to kill them in his car. And letting them down on Sunday.

'Jen? Sorry. I'm going to have to rush.' Silence. Palmeira shrugged, checked his appearance — fresh, light-blue sports shirt, blue slacks — in the mirror, grabbed his running gear and headed for the door.

'I'm off then,' he had shouted breezily. Still no reply. He gently closed the door. Not until he was half-way to the station did he remember that he'd forgotten his lunch.

𝕰𝕺𝕰𝕺𝕰𝕺

It was just before 10 o'clock when Palmeira arrived at the station. Argent had not yet turned up, but Koslowski and Park were already waiting. Almost immediately, he was interrupted by a call. It was from McCrimond, telephoning from home to tell him about the 750 Club.

'The what? Oh, yeah, that.' He'd half-forgotten that he'd asked her to help. 'Can it wait? OK, fire away. But make it quick. I've got this meeting in a couple of minutes.'

'I got on the computer as soon as I got home, sir. And, well…I'll give you a full report when I come in later, but basically, in answer to your question, no, Clarkson wasn't a member of the 750 Club.'

'Surprising.' Palmeira mumbled, as he was distracted by Argent's arrival.

'Sort of. He's on the big list of birders. But the last time it was posted on the website, he was still about 20 short of getting into the club.'

Interesting, thought Palmeira. 'OK. Thanks for that, then.' He was about to replace the receiver when the lilting Scots voice came again.

'One more thing, sir.'

'Be quick.'

'Well, when I typed "Phillip Clarkson and 750 club" in the search window I came up with several matches. Three of them pointed to stories about a wee spot of bother he had with another bird fancier, or whatever you call them.'

'Oh.'

'It's probably something and nothing but a few years back he had this row with a fellow by the name of… it's in my notes here, somewhere… Ellis Enderby.' She spelled the name out.

'Now he — guess it's a he — is a member of this 750 Club. Though it seems he caused a big sensation when he claimed he'd just spotted some rare parrot or other. Never heard of it myself.'

'And?' Palmeira prompted.

'Huge row. Clarkson got stuck into this Enderby character. Basically said he couldn't possibly have seen this parrot in this place at this time. Enderby got right upset, sir. Threatened Clarkson with all sorts of things…then it all seems to have died down again. It was only in, like, bird fanciers' newsletters. Never got in the proper papers as far as I could see.'

'Thanks, McCrimond. Sounds like a bit of a, you know, storm in a teacup. But you never know. Put it in a report, anyway, please. Sorry, got to rush.'

'Right,' said McCrimond. 'Seem a weird lot these birders, don't they, sir?'

'Yes. Bye.' Suddenly, Palmeira yearned for one of those good, old-fashioned Aussie murder cases. One in which people were whacked for their loot or for sleeping with someone else's sheila. Or bloke.

6

The first law of fieldwork is exact observation, but not only are you more likely to observe accurately if what you see is put in black and white, but you will find it much easier to identify the birds from your notes than from memory.
— Florence Mirriam, *Birds Through an Opera Glass*

Some cops he knew still preferred gut feelings to forensics. But Mario Palmeira, being the methodical rather than emotional hit-and-miss type, firmly believed the crime-scene scientists were a detective's best friends. He hadn't always thought like that. In the early days he'd shared the average policeman's scepticism of technology's 'black arts'. Successful sleuthing, he recalled being told by an old hand, was 90 per cent hard work, 10 per cent hunch. And 10 per cent good fortune!

However, one weekend he attended an international conference organised by police medical officers in Sydney. He went in a sceptic and emerged a true believer. Palmeira was amazed to learn how technology had been used to cracked tough cases.

Take the grisly case involving the death of a baby whose dismembered body was found scattered over a small town in Queensland. More than a dozen forensic specialists had combed through DNA traces, dog bites, dental records and blood samples for months.

It had been horrendously expensive. But it produced the evidence that sent a local butcher and the baby's young mother to jail. As Palmeira told Jenny over supper one night, one team of scientists had even spent several days analysing 'three bags of dog vomit' only to discover that it contained not human remains, but dog food.

Good story, bad timing. 'Oh thank you very much for sharing that with me,' Jenny had said, stomping off with her unfinished food.

It was difficult to keep up with innovations. New chip technology would soon allow DNA to be tested at crime scenes and samples to be swiftly checked against a national database. Right now, Palmeira often complained, it took ages.

Miniature infra-red spectrometers were being developed to analyse and identify paint chips at the scene of hit-and-run accidents. Portable vapour analysers would soon be able tell immediately if fires had been deliberately lit.

All very exciting, but what could the eggheads tell him about a body buried in the sand last Saturday? Quite a bit, Palmeira was pleased to hear.

'Good morning, gentlemen… and, sorry, ladies,' said Bill Argent, looking round the small team gathered in the temporary incident room. 'I've got one or two things of interest for you.'

Though he hadn't worked with him before, Palmeira had recognised Argent immediately: he had reportedly been one of the first people on the Birdman crime scene. He seemed like a bright guy. A young, slim, floppy-haired man, who wore glasses that made him look like a grown-up Harry Potter. Neat and well-organised. Qualities Palmeira admired.

Argent had already photocopied and distributed a short list of 'principal findings', based on notes he'd taken as Path Prior conducted the previous evening's post mortem.

Palmeira glanced round the room. Danniher, typically, had phoned in on his mobile to say he was stuck in traffic near the airport and was running a few minutes late. Other officers were either seated or draped over desks and window ledges: Koslowski, Park, and a couple of other on-loan local detectives, DC Melissa Holmes and DC Jim Munro. Also, Jonno Sedgwick.

Blast, thought Palmeira. He had been happy to invite the boss, but only on the mistaken assumption he wouldn't have time to attend.

Never mind. He was pleased to see the team come together. During his previous posting at Berwick, he knew, he'd earned a reputation for being a reluctant team player, following his own leads, hoarding informants and information and for being a loner.

At one point, he recalled, an anonymous note had been pushed under his door. 'Dear Sir,' it read, 'Other officers in the team would just like you to know that if you ever need to talk, their door is always open.'

Fair enough. But success, promotion and transfer had given him greater confidence. While he wouldn't ever be one of the boys, he thought he could earn respect as a good team leader. What with things turning chilly at home, he could do with a few warm friends at work.

'Just ask if you've got questions,' Argent began, shuffling his papers. 'But I'll try to keep it simple.'

'You'll be OK, then,' Koslowski whispered to Holmes. Palmeira smiled.

'The deceased. Now positively identified, I think I'm right in saying ...' Several heads nodded.

'... by his mother, was Phillip Charles Clarkson. Age 34. Height: 179 cm. Weight: 91 kg. Appendectomy scar, one or two old broken bones, extensive dental work. Mostly cosmetic. Slightly overweight, but otherwise appears to have been in good health when he died.'

'Cause of death...' He paused. 'Well, I hate to disappoint our friends in the media, but the Birdman did not fall to his death. A flight of journalistic fancy, I'm afraid. If he had dropped from the sky, we'd be looking at far more damage.'

There was scattered laughter. Palmeira had never thought Clarkson had fallen from the sky, but the media had clung tenaciously to the romantic notion. At least now he could put Carol Symonds' mind at rest. The media office was still receiving calls asking if the police were checking for unusual helicopter or light aircraft movements about the time of Clarkson's death, which roughly coincided with an air show and a stopwork meeting by traffic controllers. But that's all it was: coincidence.

'So, likely cause of death,' Argent resumed, 'Based on enlargement of the heart, damage to the lungs and the presence of foreign matter in the airways, it has to be asphyxiation.' Though the result was not unexpected, it still prompted murmurs of surprise.

'Clarkson was buried alive, then?' asked Palmeira.

'Yes. All the indications are that he would've been unconscious, but still breathing when he was placed in the sand.'

Koslowksi: 'What about the head injuries, then?'

'There were lacerations to the scalp, consistent with the head having been struck — perhaps with nothing more than a glancing blow — by something. A sword? More likely, the leading edge of a spade or a shovel, perhaps.

'And, as some of you will have noticed, the deceased had suffered several more serious blows to the head, with a heavy instrument. No murder weapon has been found yet…?'

He turned to Palmeira for confirmation.

'… so what are we looking for? A bar. A baseball bat. An old-fashioned cosh. Something like that. Probably metal: no wood splinters were found. Uniform surface. Heavy enough to have caused depressed fractures of the skull and brain haemorrhaging.

'These were severe injuries but, as I say, they weren't what killed him. Nor did drowning. Though the victim had ingested some sand as he struggled for breath, his lungs were virtually clear of water.'

'Would he've regained consciousness?' Palmeira turned. It was Danniher, who had slipped into the back of the room.

'Unlikely. There's no evidence — in terms of accelerated post-mortem lividity, damage to the hands and nails, and so on — to suggest that any violent muscular struggle took place. I'd estimate it took him two or three minutes to die. But he would've gone quietly.'

'We can be sure, can we sir, that the body was put into the sand?' It was Danniher again. 'I don't know what the tide was doing at that time, but Clarkson couldn't have been just dumped and covered with sand by the water or wind or whatever?'

Good point. Palmeira made a mental note to have the high and low tides checked for that night. He should have thought of it before.

'No. Not possible,' replied Argent. 'The depth and the odd angle at which the body was found, pushed head-first into the sand with the legs sticking up at the back — couldn't have been natural. Or accidental. In fact, I'd say it was almost as if someone wanted to make it look like he'd dived into the sand. That, or perhaps the gravediggers were interrupted.'

Palmeira swapped glances with Danniher. ' Interesting.'

'Indeed. We did some cross-sectional analysis of the sand as it was being excavated at the scene. We may know more later. Forensics are still working on it. But I can tell you now that things seem to point to physical disturbance consistent with some serious spadework.'

Palmeira frowned. 'Correct me if I'm wrong, Bill, but what you're saying then is, we know how and where he died, but we can't say definitely where he was attacked and knocked out.'

'That's right, sir. The physical evidence obtained at the scene is not a lot of help, I'm afraid. Nothing was found that linked the body with another site. But at the same time nothing was found that proved that the injuries occurred on the site where the body was disposed of... if you follow me.'

Sedgwick did. 'So it's likely that Clarkson was attacked elsewhere, at his home, in the city, among the dunes, wherever...and, err, carried unconscious to the beach and buried?'

'Yes. Perfectly possible. Crime scene did a complete grid search of the roadside and dunes area and found nothing that could be linked to Clarkson. That's not altogether surprising. The roadside had been heavily disturbed by the time they arrived and the dunes are always being rearranged one way or another.'

'Thanks,' said Sedgwick, who was taking far too much interest in the case for comfort, thought Palmeira.

Argent went on. 'It might be worth asking the people who found the body if they noticed anything in the fresh sand. It's pretty isolated where Clarkson was. Someone might have noticed tracks. Assuming, of course, there were any.'

'Good idea,' replied Palmeira.

'Any luck with other witnesses yet, inspector?' Sedgwick again.

'Not yet, sir. Still working on it.' Palmeira suddenly felt clammy. He needed no reminding that he still had no witnesses, no murder weapon, no dead man's clothing, no dead man's car. 'We could use a breakthrough,' he conceded.

'Ms Prior's thoughts about time of death may help there, then,' said Argent, coming to his rescue. 'She calculates that Clarkson died only several hours before the discovery. What's that make it? Early hours of Sunday morning? The head injuries, though, appear to have been sustained some hours earlier.

'I don't know how that fits in with your thoughts so far, but it does suggest that the body was brought, possibly some distance, to the beach.'

'That helps,' said Palmeira, his hopes rising again.

'But again, look, sorry, but I have to stress the unusual effects of sand and water at the crime scene make it more difficult than usual to be more precise about these times.'

Palmeira looked at Danniher, who had a sceptical look on his face. Danniher, who was old-fashioned enough to believe that cases were more likely to be solved by hard-won witness testimonies than physical evidence, often scoffed at 'the boffins', as he termed them.

'Any signs of an earlier struggle?' he now asked.

'Some scuff marks on the man's nice new boots. May have been caused when he was dragged. But nothing under the nails to suggest he'd fought with his attacker. No blood. No fibres. And nothing near or on the body, as I say, to link it specifically to another site away from the beach.

'In fact, just the usual rubbish you'd expect to find on that stretch of beach. Bits of plastic, cigarette butts, discarded fishing line, used condoms.'

'Recently used?' asked Danniher, hopefully.

'I'm afraid not.'

Palmeira pondered. Did the lack of any signs of a struggle mean that Clarkson knew his attackers? Or merely that he was surprised by them, and unable to defend himself?

He was just about to thank Argent, who appeared from his long silence to have finished, when the crime-scene officer began again.

'I knew I'd forgotten something. On the subject of condoms — given the absence of the deceased's pants and jocks, and his discovery near an area of some local notoriety, we obviously made a point of testing for evidence of sexual assault.'

Again, Danniher leaned forward expectantly.

'There was no physical evidence that the deceased had engaged in sexual activity, of any sort, in the hours before his death. Of course, that does not mean he wasn't seeking some at the time.'

Agent still hadn't finished. 'Oh, and one last thing that might interest you. Stomach content.'

Ah-hah, thought Palmeira. Finally, the 'dog vomit factor'.

'Full stomach analysis takes a bit longer, but right now I can say it looks like the deceased hadn't eaten for several hours. Probably not since Saturday lunch-time. That may strike you as a little odd, given that he looked like a man who enjoyed his food.'

Palmeira nodded gratefully. Quite a lot to be going on with, there. 'Good on you, Bill.'

ဆဝဆဝဆဝ

Time for a feed, thought Danniher. No amount of grisly details, not even dead bodies could turn his stomach. The question was: could he elude Palmeira? No doubt, he'd still want a word about his non-appearance on Sunday. Oh, and the reckless driving. Sooner or later. Danniher preferred later. Right now he wanted lunch.

Too late. Once he'd finished shaking Argent's hand, Palmeira turned round, the expression on his face changing in an instant. 'Danniher. My office. Now, if you can spare the time.'

Palmeira followed him, shutting the door noiselessly. 'Have a seat.'

That sounded ominous. It's always the same, thought Danniher. If a small bloke wanted to give a big bloke a bollocking, he always got him to sit down first. A face-to-face talk never went so well if it was face to chest.

He sat. 'Look, Mario, mate, I'm sorry about the other day… and the business on the road… and just now. Honest, the traffic…' He shut up, belatedly realising he'd only been making matters worse by giving the DI a list of offences.

Palmeira raised a hand. 'Stop right there.' Danniher stopped and braced himself. Here we go. Assume the crash position. Quit whingeing and take your punishment like a man.

'We really haven't got time to discuss all that stuff now.'

ဆဝဆဝဆဝ

On the way into work, Palmeira had turned off the radio and rehearsed what he would say to Danniher. How he'd let the team down. How he let himself down. How he, Palmeira, couldn't go on protecting him from the trumps at HQ. How he, Palmeira, knew he'd had a few problems recently but really had to pull himself together now. Really get a grip. Danniher deserved it. He was increasingly erratic and impulsive. No, worse, he was unreliable.

-76-

But something had made Palmeira change his mind. Sympathy? Perhaps. The painful truth was that he really needed someone like Wayne Danniher who, when he was pointed in the right direction, was a tenacious, tireless, old-style detective. What's more, Danniher was well liked by the others. He would be a useful ally against people such as Jonno Sedgwick who, he suspected, was just waiting to pounce on him if the Birdman Case inquiries did not produce a quick result.

'Look, Wayne,' he said looking out of the window. 'I know we haven't always seen eye-to-eye. I doubt whether we'll be great drinking buddies...'

'Or jogging partners,' Danniher interjected.

'No,' Palmeira smiled. 'But I really need your total cooperation on this one, especially if HQ turn up the heat.' As they would, Palmeira thought.

ॐॐॐ

For a few seconds, Danniher did not quite know what to say. 'Well, no worries, sir,' he said eventually. 'I'm with you. 100 per cent.'

'Thanks. I appreciate that.'

'Go grab some lunch then. But no hanging around. Tell the guys I want them back here no later than 2.30.'

'Good as gold, sir.' Bloody hell, thought Danniher. Better get going, before we both burst into tears. 'Don't fancy a bite yourself?'

'Another time, perhaps,' Palmeira replied. 'But thanks for asking.'

Danniher stood, opened the door. 'By the way, sir,' he said, turning. 'It wasn't strictly true what I said just now.'

'What wasn't?' Palmeira asked sharply.

'The bit about being stuck in traffic this morning. To be honest, I thought I'd have time to drop in and have a chat to another of the birders. That bloke Waddell? Wife and kid, as well. It was on my way back.'

'And?' said Palmeira, shaking his head wearily.

'Found the street, no bother. But the number of the house doesn't exist. And I checked: no one there's heard of the family Waddell. Another name for the big whiteboard, if you ask me.'

ॐॐॐ

For the next ten minutes or more Palmeira sat, virtually immobile, staring out of his first-floor window. Beyond the supermarket car park, which filled much of his view, he could see Berwick going about its daily business. It all looked so normal. Shoppers struggling with white, plastic bags that seemed to sprout from their arms like bunches of balloons. Schoolchildren, most wearing the dark-blue uniform of the local high school, hanging out, talking, laughing, harmlessly roughing each other up. And office-workers heading off for a late lunch in the park.

Somewhere down there, among them, would be Danniher on his way to the pub — no doubt dying to entertain his mates with an account of his bizarre confrontation with the boss. Palmeira could just imagine the laughs.

Momentarily, he envied those people out there. Of course, everyone had problems: how to pay the bills, how to pass the Higher School Certificate exams, how to solve celebrity murder cases. But somehow they seemed better able than him to enjoy themselves. They knew how to compartmentalise different parts of their lives, the good from the bad, and even to let go occasionally.

Here he was just a few minutes ago thinking that Danniher really must get a grip and now he was resolving that he himself should loosen up. Who knows, it might even improve his productivity.

Fleetingly, he wondered if he should ask Prior or young McCrimond if they fancied sharing a sandwich with him. On second thoughts, that was too dangerous. Maybe it was a sign of getting old. Or the pressure of being involved in such a high-profile case. Or the deterioration in his relationship with Jenny. But getting too close to a young female colleague seemed like asking for trouble.

Then he wondered if should go for a jog. It always cleared his head and there were showers in the basement for when he returned hot and sweaty. He dithered. Should he or shouldn't he? Perhaps later.

He rang home. There was no reply. Presumably Jenny was out working. He took off his jacket, loosened his tie and went for a walk down into the crowded shopping precinct, where he stopped and bought a tuna and tomato baguette and a tub of fresh fruit salad from a self-serve sandwich shop.

He returned and ate them at his desk, reading the morning newspaper.

The arts pages. If the news pages contained anything, good or bad, about the Birdman Case, someone would have let him know by now.

Twenty minutes later he got up, walked into the outer office and wiped clean the whiteboard. He felt looser, fresher, and sharper as he set to work covering the board with what was meant to be a simple, diagrammatic statement of current thinking, missing links, future lines of inquiry and job allocations in the Birdman Case.

Just as the team started rolling back, bang on 2.30, he stood back to admire his work. It looked like...well, what? A map of the London Underground. A wiring diagram for a Ford Falcon? An organisational chart for the New South Wales police force? Or perhaps one of those awful street maps that have a big arrow advising 'You Are Here'? Except Palmeira suspected that, as far as inquiries went, he was all over the place.

'Believe me, it's really not that complicated,' he joked, as he grabbed a pointer and started leading his team through a maze of arrows, asterisks, flow lines and question marks by which several boxes of information were linked.

By the time Palmeira had explored several dead-ends, backtracked through the maze, tapped each box in turn and brainstormed its contents, the afternoon was virtually over.

'We'd be better off out on the streets asking questions than stuck in here,' Danniher grumbled to Koslowski at one point.

Palmeira heard the remark, but ignored it. He talked at length about the information contained in one box labelled 'timing': an, elongated box in which he had tried to produce a timeline representation of the last 24 hours of Phillip Charles Clarkson's life.

'We've got to fill in the gaps,' he said, pointing to some dotted lines.

Post-mortem findings suggested that Clarkson had first been attacked some time between 8 and 10 on Saturday evening. Burial and with it, death, followed four or five hours later.

'Say, within one hour either side of one o'clock on Sunday morning,' repeated Palmeira, recalling the briefing. This was consistent with tides that night, which the diligent McCrimond had checked during lunch, at Palmeira's request.

'If they — and I'm assuming that the way the body was disposed of means that one person was involved — if they had left it much later the site would have been covered by the incoming tide.'

Quite why they had chosen that place, below the high-water mark, to bury Clarkson, and why he had been buried with his feet pointing skywards, still puzzled him. But he still tended to think the 'crazy thing with the feet' was accidental, not deliberate.

Burying Birdman, he calculated, would've taken anything up to half an hour. It would've been a rush. Even at that time of night, on a section of the beach rarely visited, there was a risk of being spotted. Most probably from the nearby dunes.

Perhaps the gravediggers had been interrupted. By the incoming tide? Or, a witness? Perhaps someone who was too scared to admit they were in the dunes at night? One thing was certain, there were far too many perhapses.

Palmeira pointed back to the start of his timeline. 'Look,' he pointed out, 'Clarkson's movements in the 24 hours up to his death still haven't been established. Mrs Clarkson had spoken to her son at home, from Coffs Harbour, late Friday. But what did he do, where did he go on Saturday? Who, apart from his killers, last saw him alive? And when? And where?'

Palmeira paused and looked round the room at the alert faces. He picked up the pointer again and went to the next box, labelled 'motives'.

It was big, and contained all sorts of theories. Gay bashing? Blackmail that went wrong (because he was gay, because of his murky business past)? Professional jealousy (unlikely, but couldn't be ruled out)? Revenge (Clarkson had been disliked by employees and work colleagues)? Crime of passion (possibly gay lover)?

Or, the most difficult scenario to investigate, was he a victim of circumstance? Was it a thrill-kill, or a mistaken identity? Had he been an inadvertent witness to some other crime? This was the 'wrong place, at the wrong time' theory. According to Palmeira, the only motive that seemed safe to rule out was theft.

Tap, tap. Palmeira moved to the box of 'suspects'. It contained a daunting list.

Was it Clarkson's former personal assistant or her boyfriend? A member of Clarkson's film crew (hadn't Danniher said they hated the Birdman)? A rival birder, possibly even a member of the famous 750 Club? Or one of the nine birders who discovered the body? Well, why not? They all seemed to know Clarkson. And what better way to throw off suspicion than to return so soon to the scene of the crime? He ran down the list.

The teenage girl and the two older women could, surely, be excluded. But what about the sleazy journo Workman? He'd clashed with Clarkson before. Or Finch? Mrs Clarkson said he'd once been a visitor to her son's home. Or Waddell? He'd given a false address. Why? Or maybe it was even one of the others on the list: Morris, Clifford or Mrs Waddell. Could they be linked in some way with the dead man?

Then there were the nameless unknowns. A man who presumably hated gays. A jilted lover. A complete stranger.

As team members canvassed each suspect, Palmeira added two more. Margaret Clarkson and Paul Clarkson. Was she really in Coffs Harbour when her son was killed, wondered Koslowski? Was Paul really on such good terms with his brother?

And then there were the physical elements of the case that were still missing. Where was the murder weapon? The implement with which the grave was dug? The dead man's car? His missing clothing?

Palmeira stopped, allowing the questions to dangle in the silent room. So many questions, so few answers.

Had he forgotten anything? Almost certainly. But that was enough to be going on with. Leading his team from the maze, he started handing out tasks.

Danniher, he decided, should continue working through the list of birders, with the exception of Waddell whom he asked Munro to track down.

'I was looking forward to having a go at Waddell, sir,' said Danniher.

'He might take a while to locate. Meanwhile, I want you here helping me. Please? Have a go at Finch, if you like. Followed by...what was his name?'

'Morris.'

'Right. And I don't think we can strike Workman off the list yet. Make a few inquiries about him. Go back and talk to his girlfriend. Maybe then lean on him some more.'

The room laughed, knowing the sergeant's reputation. 'But not too hard,' added Palmeira.

'Understood, sir.' It would be a pleasure. He'd liked Jane Clifford almost as much as he had disliked Chris Workman.

'You should also check with the local council and developers about any dealings with Clarkson. Your man Workman seemed to think there'd been something dodgy going on there in the past.'

That should keep Danniher out of mischief, thought Palmeira.

That should keep me out of Palmeira's way, thought Danniher.

'Koslowski. You talk to Christine Withers. The "disaffected former employee". And anyone else who worked closely with Clarkson on TV or films.'

The gay link was a tricky one. Even in these more enlightened times, of Mardi Gras, gay pride and anti-vilification laws, some people still wanted to keep their sex lives private. Fair enough. But if they were in the dunes on Saturday night, they had to be found and interviewed. A sensitive task.

Only the previous weekend, Palmeira had read of a British police commander who'd admitted being gay and smoking cannabis at the home of his lover. The revelation had prompted a huge row. One MP had even joked that the traditional good cop, bad cop routine had been replaced by a straight cop, gay cop pairing.

As far as he knew, Palmeira had no such choice. He was left with two officers, Russell Park and Melissa Holmes: young, attractive, intelligent and, as far as he knew, straight. 'Park, Holmes, I've got a lovely little job for you two.'

Palmeira had thought of ending the whiteboard session with a brief pep talk, an exhortation to his team to 'get out and kick some ass,' but now he thought better of it. It'd be out of character and wouldn't impress anyone.

'Thanks everyone.'

As they trooped out, chatting animatedly, he checked his watch. Five-thirty. All bases covered. Nothing much else he could do right now. Just time to go for a run. And still be home at a reasonable time.

7

Birds in their little nests agree…
— Isaac Watts, *Love Between Brothers and Sisters*

'Mrs Palmeira?'

'Speaking.'

'Hello, it's PC McCrimond here from Berwick.'

'Oh?' Mario's going to be late and is scared to tell me himself, Jenny thought.

'Sorry to bother you, but it's about your husband.'

'Let me guess. He's been delayed.'

'Sort of. Nothing really to worry about. But he's had a bit of an accident and been taken to hospital. The poor wee thing's feeling not so bad now. But it looks like he'll be kept in overnight.'

A mix of emotions washed over Jenny Palmeira. There was fear: was this really an accident or had Mario been attacked? It was an occupational hazard. Guilt: only a few minutes earlier she had been silently cursing him for being late home, again, for not letting her know, again, for leaving her to feed the girls, listen to their stories about school and put them to bed. Again. And, finally, she felt relief.

'So what's he done now?'

'Broken his ankle. Fell over, running on the dunes.'

Jenny sighed. Hadn't she warned him repeatedly about the dangers of running at his age? It had taken her years to stop him playing football, a sport that seemed compulsory for South Americans, especially Brazilians. He was always getting injured.

Before what turned out to be his last game, he'd joked that he'd meet her afterwards in Berwick Hospital. In the event, when he'd tripped badly and broken a collarbone, he'd been taken to nearby Sutherland, from where he'd rung, pathetically asking to be collected.

It wasn't until an hour or so after McCrimond's call —after she'd bribed a neighbour's teenage daughter to baby-sit the girls — that Jenny was able to drive to the hospital and hear first hand the full story of this latest misadventure.

She had half-expected him to be enjoying the attention, revelling in the role of wounded hero. Instead, she found him, sitting up in bed in a side ward with three other men, looking very sorry for himself.

Jenny shook her head in resignation. She loved and supported her husband. Of course, she did. But, goodness knows, he could be infuriating. And selfish. His job seemed to take priority over everything. He hadn't wanted to discuss her job offer at all. Sometimes she felt like hitting him. She was, then, rather surprised by the surge of sympathy she felt as she gave him a hug.

'Sorry, I didn't have time to stop for any grapes.'

'That's OK. Not much of an appetite,' he replied with a sad attempt at a smile.

Already, his injury had been examined and immediate surgery recommended. All the same, Palmeira admitted to Jenny, he felt like any other ageing weekend warrior, especially after the doctor made the mistake of trying to console him with a reminder that such injuries must be expected by men of his age.

As Jenny knew, Mario simply wouldn't accept that he was a man of his age. Perhaps it was the pain or the painkillers, but he looked his age now.

'Poor you. So, what happened?'

೫೦೫೦೫೦

Palmeira winced as he tried to get his leg into a more comfortable position. Four or five years ago he'd torn a muscle in his calf, playing squash. He would never forget its name — the gastrocnemius, or monkey muscle — or the misery it caused him, and therefore his family. Then, he had thought he'd go mad. Or at least start serious drinking, binge eating or chasing other women. Indeed, it was while feeling sorry for himself that he had become perilously close to a policewoman who had shown considerably more sympathy than Jenny had.

This injury, he knew, was far more serious. Not a break, as a McCrimond had said, but a ruptured Achilles tendon.

Drowsily, Palmeira now explained the sequence of events to Jenny. His escape from Berwick police station hadn't been as simple as he'd planned...

First, he was intercepted by Sedgwick. The commander had been dragged off to a meeting with local community leaders over what they described as 'gang warfare' and so had missed the whiteboard session. Now, he demanded a quick update. That took 15 minutes because Sedgwick had been in a filthy mood and had found several ways to remind Palmeira that he, the press and the public demanded an early result in the Birder Murder Case.

'You've got to remember, there's an awful lot of interest out there in this one.' As if Palmeira forgot for a single waking moment. He even dreamt of dead bodies.

'This chap Clarkson was very popular,' Sedgwick had told him, 'enormously popular.' Except among those who knew him, thought Palmeira, as Jonno stomped away, looking to make someone else's life a misery.

No sooner had Palmeira seen the broad back of Sedgwick than he was buttonholed by a contrite Danniher. He explained that he'd arranged to see Simon Finch at his home first thing the following morning, and asked now to be excused for the rest of the day.

He had a date that evening. A hot date, he indicated with a suggestive lift of the eyebrows.

'Lucky you.'

'Yeah. You might know her, sir. Sandy Prior? Just bumped into her in the pub. She'd arranged to pick up Bill Argent. Promised to give him a lift back to the city.'

'Really.'

'Anyhow, we got talking again about this and that... and, well, there you go.'

Lucky Wayne, thought Palmeira again. He was young. Well, youngish. Single. No ties. Suddenly depressed, he had decided to phone Jenny. Let her know he'd be home early for a change. Again there was no reply.

Odd. She must be away collecting the two children from the day-care centre they went to after school, he'd supposed.

'That's right,' said Jenny. Even in his confusion, Palmeira could sense she was growing impatient, was willing him to cut to the chase.

Anyway, by the time he had been able to sneak down to the locker rooms, change into his running gear, and get going, it was past six o'clock. He knew it was because he'd paused in the car park to start his stopwatch.

Jenny rolled her eyes upwards. 'OK, you're right, Jenny. Most of my recreations have to be quantified and recorded if they are to be properly enjoyed. Bit like birding in a way,' he added.

He'd started out running fast, without a warm-up, anxious to put some space between himself and his fellow human beings. He didn't want to stop again and, anyway, he didn't like being seen all hot and sweaty.

Not that he was running away from work. Running provided excellent thinking time and, anyway, he'd chosen a circular route, about ten kilometres, that took him by quiet back streets on to Bayside Drive and, thereby, to the scene of the crime.

'Mario, why on earth did you do that?' asked Jenny, interrupting his woozy account. 'The traffic's awful and there's no proper foot path.'

'I know. But I thought, I might see something, be struck by something out there.'

'What, like a semi-trailer?'

'You know what I mean. A clue. A thought. A flash of inspiration. Believe me, Jen, I could really do with a break on this case. Jonno's really on my back.' Palmeira sighed deeply before resuming his account.

After about 30 minutes, he'd turned down the track running off Bayside Drive into the dunes. Now, he'd allowed himself to walk slowly, closely inspecting the soft sand, looking for clues that Crime Scene may have missed, seeking inspiration.

For the first time it had struck him just what an effort it must have taken to cart Clarkson's body across the dunes and down on to the beach. Yet whoever did it appeared to have left no track, no trace.

The tide appeared to be neither in nor out. There were some birds — seagulls as far as he was concerned — pottering around at the water's edge. Otherwise, the site had returned to normal, covered with man-made rubbish. Palmeira couldn't even point with any certainty to the exact spot where Clarkson had died.

What had he expected to see, though? A small shrine, topped with a cross and banked with flowers, like those you see on roadsides? A blood-stained bar poking conveniently out of the sand? A pair of tangled hiking shorts floating in the shallow water? Such good fortune was only to be found in cheap crime fiction.

At the end of the beach, near where sludge was once again spewing from the concrete pipe, Palmeira gave up. He touched the pipe, turned and started back running this time along the beach and into the dunes.

It was just as he neared the top of the first hillock that it happened.

There was a sudden 'crack!' — loud enough, he imagined, to have been heard above the noise of the traffic clattering along Bayside Drive — followed by a sharp pain in the back of the leg.

'Aaargh!' he cried. I've been hit with a stick, or a bat, or been shot, he thought.

It was just as though something or someone had switched off the power in his left leg. Briefly, the pain was so intense, the disablement so complete, that he fell, rolling in the sand, clutching his calf. It was like tearing the gastrocnemius. Only worse. And what's more, there was no squash opponent, in fact no one at all, near to help him.

Unable to put weight on the leg, he'd spent about 30 minutes, shouting and crawling towards help in the semi-darkness, before a man who had been walking through the dunes found him.

'You were lucky,' said Jenny. 'You could've been there ages.'

'I suppose so. Odd place for someone to be walking, really. But apparently he'd stopped to check directions on a map. Said he'd just popped in to take a leak. A likely story.'

'Must have been a bit of a surprise for him.'

'And me,' said Palmeira stoically. 'To be honest, when I think back it all seems a bit suspicious. Still, what's it matter? I'd still be in there if he hadn't found me. Didn't even have a chance to thank him properly.'

'Didn't get his name, then?'

'No. I wasn't thinking, I'm afraid. But I'd certainly recognise him if I bumped into again. Not much chance of that, I guess. Big fat man. Drives one of those huge four-wheel-drives.' Palmeira's words tailed away.

'Pity,' said Jenny. Palmeira eyes drooped. 'Poor old thing.'

Palmeira's eyes opened again. 'You've said that before,' he mumbled, glancing down the bed to where his damaged leg lay, immobilised, protected from the weight of the bed-clothes by a cage. 'What a disaster.'

'Sorry.'

'That's all right.' At least they'd slotted him in for surgery the following afternoon. Then the repaired leg would be put in a special, wired boot and a brace for several weeks.

'Oh well, the girls will be pleased. They'll get to see a bit more of you at home.'

Palmeira jerked to attention. 'You must be joking. I can't take time off work.'

'But Mario...'

'No, I'm sorry, I'm sorry. But I've already worked it out. I'll be on crutches. I'll be tied to a desk. I won't be able to drive. But so long as I feel OK and don't put weight on the leg, the doctor says I should be able to go back to work on...whatever it is, the day after tomorrow. Or, at worst, the day after that.'

'Please, Mario, you've got to...'

'No. No. I've already told them at Berwick. They're going to get a car to pick me up and take me home every day. They're setting up an office for me on the ground floor. Look, they've already sent my clothes and shoes round.'

෨෭ඁ෨෭ඁ෨෭ඁ

Earlier that same evening, when Palmeira and Danniher were both out — the one on a run, the other on a hot date — Margaret Clarkson rang asking to speak to the officer investigating her son's murder. So it was Koslowski who, by default, picked up her re-routed call.

He'd almost missed it. For more than an hour, he'd been on the line. First he'd tried to arrange to talk to Clarkson's former personal assistant, Christine Withers. A man had answered. The stroppy boyfriend, he presumed. He was wrong.

'Can I speak to Ms Withers, please?'

'No, mate, she's not here any more.'

'Since when?'

'Since just before I moved in I guess. About three months ago.'

'I suppose she didn't leave a new number?'

'Nah, sorry. It'd be somewhere in Melbourne. Can't imagine myself why anyone would want to leave Sydney for that bloody miserable place. But there you go. Apparently, her boyfriend was from down that way. Wanted to move back.'

'OK. Thanks.' Koslowski couldn't be absolutely positive, but the news pretty much put Withers and Mr Stroppy in the clear.

After eliminating Withers, he'd then spent another 30 minutes trying to track down, as instructed by Palmeira, Phillip Clarkson's producer on the bird documentaries. A call to the TV media relations department — on a number left by Danniher — had produced another number and a name. Marcy Roy. She'd agreed to see him at nine o'clock the following day.

Koslowski was preparing to leave when Mrs Clarkson's call was transferred to him. He wondered for a second whether to ignore it, to let whatever it was wait until tomorrow. But duty called.

'Hello, DC Koslowski.'

'Is that you, constable? You're the young man who came here the other night, aren't you?' She sounded distraught.

'Oh, Mrs Clarkson. That's right. How're you going? I'm sorry, it must be tough for you...not having your son around any more,' he said clumsily.

'It is. It's horrible. I still can't get used to the idea that he's dead. And then there's the not knowing what...'

'No.' She had struck Koslowski as intelligent and sensible. In his experience, the two qualities didn't necessarily come together. 'I hope you've got someone to talk to about it all.'

'Yes, I have. Paul. You remember, Phillip's brother? He's driven down for a few days to keep me company.'

'That's good, said Koslowski, wondering what Mrs Clarkson wanted.

'Yes. It's a long way to come. In fact, it's because he's here that I'm ringing.'

'Oh.' Thank goodness for that. At least, she wasn't demanding to know what progress had been made towards finding whoever killed her son.

'This is awkward.'

Koslowski waited silently.

'It's just that Paul and I have been going through some of Phillip's papers. Invoices, contracts, bank statements. Financial and legal stuff.'

'Oh, yes. From the boxes we found on the bed.'

'Yes. Well, I know you or that other man said the police would probably want to look at them eventually.'

'That's right. Just haven't quite got round to it yet.'

'The thing is we thought it might be a good idea if someone popped round while Paul's here. Just so, he can explain a couple of things. It's nothing complicated. More a family arrangement. I was wondering if perhaps you...'

Koslowski hesitated. The Clarkson house was on the way home. Then again, he'd already told his wife that he'd be home at the normal time. Then again, he'd banked brownie points with her by surprisingly turning up on time for the school concert. A few minutes late wouldn't make that much difference.

'How about if I see you both in, say, 30 minutes? Depending on traffic.'

'Perfect.'

In fact, traffic on the Eastern Distributor proved unexpectedly light. Koslowski was travelling against the commuter tide and the usual, early evening rush into the city from the airport had been postponed as traffic controllers staged another stopwork meeting.

For once, he found a parking place almost immediately and almost directly outside the Clarkson's house, next to a battered yellow Ford Telstar. It seemed so out of place in posh Paddington that he imagined it might have strayed there by mistake and died of embarrassment.

Barely 20 minutes after putting the telephone down, Koslowski was being welcomed into her lounge room. 'Come on in. You know the way,' she said.

Mrs Clarkson's face looked puffed, her eyes blotchy, but she seemed calm, in control.

'Paul,' she shouted. 'Detective Constable Koslowski's here.'

Down the stairs, which had effectively separated Phillip Clarkson's home from his mother's, came a man whom Koslowski would never have picked as being a member of the same family.

On television, in the photographs, and from what Koslowski had seen at the crime scene, brother Phillip had looked bulky and a little above average height. Paul was thinner and shorter. Phillip had fair, curly, untamed hair. Paul's hair was darker, longer and slicked back, and he had an unconvincing beard.

Phillip's complexion was ruddy; Paul's sallow. Phillip, Koslowski imagined, had dressed, probably even at home, in trendy, outdoor gear. Paul wore black. Altogether, he looked older and, to Koslowski, distinctly less wholesome than his younger brother.

'Hi, I'm the little brother,' said Paul, using one hand to rub his beard, the other hand to shake Koslowski's. 'The black sheep of the family, I'm afraid.' He laughed. He did not appear to be devastated by bereavement. Or perhaps he was just good at concealing it.

'Pleased to meet you, sir,' Koslowski replied, with rare formality. 'It must be a very upsetting time for you both.'

'Yes. Especially mother.'

Though Mrs Clarkson and her son had asked to speak to him, it was important to remember that both appeared in Palmeira's whiteboard box labelled 'suspects'.

'So, tell me about yourself, sir. What is it exactly you do up at Coffs Harbour?' He took out his notebook. A notebook always made things look more official, though it certainly didn't put people at their ease.

Paul Clarkson frowned and exchanged nervous glances with his mother before answering.

'To be honest not a lot right now.' Koslowski's eyebrows rose, involuntarily. What was it they said? You can always tell when politicians are lying because their lips move. And you can always tell when criminals are lying because their lips move and they use words like 'honest'.

Paul Clarkson stumbled on. 'It's a long story. Pretty boring, even for me. But, here goes.'

In short sentences, punctuated with occasional nods of encouragement from his mother, he told how he'd gone through school in the shadow of his older brother, how he'd scraped into university to do engineering but had dropped out after only nine months and headed overseas.

'Running away, you could call it.'

For more than three years, he'd bummed around, latterly in southeast Asia, making or scrounging money wherever he could, playing a lot of guitar and smoking 'a tonne of dope,' he explained, stretching out his hands.

Honest officer, I couldn't help myself, he seemed to Koslowski to be saying. A weak character.

'Anyway, I met this girl, Louise, an English backpacker, in Thailand. Chiang Mai, actually. She was on her way to Oz, so I came back with her. We travelled around some more. Became long-term items. Eventually, we decided to stay. Lou and me have got a couple of kids now. Though we've never found time to actually get married. One day, perhaps.'

Just where is all this leading? Koslowski was beginning to wonder. It was like he'd stumbled on to the set of 'This is Your Life'.

Perhaps sensing his impatience, Paul Clarkson fast-forwarded.

'But the point is, I couldn't settle. I've tried. It's not as though I haven't got a brain...'

Mrs Clarkson explained. 'It's more you don't like working for other people, isn't it dear?'

'Not if they're dickheads. Anyway, I even set up a few little businesses: office-cleaning, mobile discos, desk-top publishing. But they didn't last.'

'And all this time, you were living with your mother, here?'

'No, no, we had a place. But that's the other thing. I couldn't survive in Sydney. Too expensive, unless you're happy to live in one of those hell-hole suburbs out west.' Koslowski, who contentedly lived 'out west', let the remark pass.

'Actually, it was Phillip's idea that we should move north, start again. And, you see, this is the tricky part...it was his money that made it possible. He gave us the cash to put a deposit on a new unit up in Coffs and to buy the business.'

'What sort?'

'Holiday place. Motel and caravan site, with a pub and a disco. Fantasy Island Resort, it was called.'

'Fantasy Island?'

Paul Clarkson winced. 'Too bloody right it was a fantasy. You name it, it went wrong. We'd been ripped off on the price. The manager had his hands in the till. The police were trying to take away the liquor licence.'

'Why?'

'Complaints from the bloody neighbours. Said the place was too noisy. Even complained people used their backyards as a dunny.'

'And was it true?'

Paul Clarkson laughed. 'Too right. I did it myself sometimes.' Couldn't help himself, thought Koslowski.

'Sounds like you've been a bit unlucky.'

'Yes. On top of everything else the tourists stopped coming.'

'I'm not surprised,' said Koslowski.

Mrs Clarkson moved to defend her son. 'To be fair, it was a bad time all round. After the terrorist attacks, people didn't want to travel. Even if they had the money.'

Paul nodded and continued. 'We poured money in to get it right, but...basically, no go. It's in receivership now. Been up for sale for a year. As I said, inspector, I'm the underachiever of the family.'

Mrs Clarkson coughed. 'Why we're telling you all this is that Phillip put up most of the money for the scheme.'

'I see,' said Koslowski, suddenly taking an interest. 'As an investor or a lender?'

'Both, you'd have to say. That's the trouble with these family arrangements. They get terribly complicated. You'll see. It's all in the accounts,' said Mrs Clarkson.

'Well, most of it,' added her son.

'You can see why we wanted to tell you. It might look bad but apart from all the money he put into the business, poor Phillip is still having to support Paul and his family financially.'

'How so?'

'Standing orders. Direct debits. We'd starve without them.' Paul Clarkson seemed to think it was a huge joke. 'Anyway, feel free. Take a look,' he added, nodding towards a pile of boxes. 'It's all there.'

'Thanks.' So despite his huge popularity, big income and relatively modest lifestyle, Phillip Clarkson may have had financial problems of his own. 'How much do you reckon your brother has given you?'

Paul looked away, guiltily. 'Oh, a million or so.'

'Paul! Nearer two million, we worked it out.'

'Sounds like an awful lot of money,' said Koslowski, suspecting he could more accurately double the figure again. 'What did Phillip think about it?'

'He wasn't amused.' It sounded like another massive understatement.

Koslowski looked severe. 'So, how had you been getting on with your brother recently?'

'Good. Honest.' That word again. 'I saw him at Christmas. Four or five weeks back. OK, he was bloody angry with me that I'd lost a stack of his money and got him involved in a whole lot of hassle with banks and things. But we'd grown up together. Looked out for each other. We loved each other. It wasn't all one-way. He needed me, in a funny way. Even as a kid, he didn't have a lot of other friends, you know.'

To his side, his mother took out a handkerchief and blew her nose. She was, Koslowski could see, close to tears. It was an appropriate time to stop.

'We may need you to come down to the station and make a full statement, Mr Clarkson.'

'Sure. Though I was planning to drive back straight after the funeral.'

Koslowski had forgotten. Phillip Clarkson's body had now been released by the coroner. 'Oh, when's that?'

'Thursday afternoon. Three o'clock. St Mary's Anglican Church. Just round the corner.'

Mrs Clarkson seemed to have recovered. 'You or your colleagues are welcome to come along, officer. It may help you to understand a bit better who Phillip was and what he achieved in his… life.'

ಬಂಬಂ

When Wayne Danniher arrived back at his Brighton unit late that night with a tipsy Path Prior still, surprisingly, in tow, he found the red light on his telephone answering machine flashing urgently.

There were one, two, three, four messages, he noticed, as he dashed round trying to tidy up. Things had gone much better than he had expected.

'Do you mind if I . . .'

'No, go ahead. Which way's the bathroom?'

He pointed her to one of only two doors and pressed the play button on his answer machine.

The first message was from Sedgwick, who sounded chillingly cheerful. He was just ringing to let him know that DI Palmeira had had 'a minor sporting accident'. He was in hospital and was likely to be 'incapacitated' for a few days. Therefore he was instructing Danniher to take charge of the Birdman Case. Sedgwick was confident that he could cope, but would be around to 'give a hand'. Danniher sighed.

Shit! He could think of nothing worse than being given a hand by Sedgwick. What on earth had Pamela gone and done now? Whatever it was, he wished him a speedy recovery.

The second call was from Simon Finch. It was 'no longer convenient' to meet at his home. He now proposed Danniher meet him downstairs in the foyer of the city-centre tower where he worked. They would find somewhere more private to talk.

Danniher sighed again. He much preferred to speak to people in their homes. They were always so much more revealing than neutral venues.

The third was from Koslowski. Just letting him know about Palmeira's accident — 'always said he was getting too old for that sort of thing' — and his unexpected chat with Mrs Clarkson and son Paul. 'A dead-set loser.' Oh, and he'd fixed to go straight from home in the morning to see Clarkson's film producer. 'Sounds Indian or something.'

Oh, and one last thing. 'Hope it went all right tonight, Wayne.' Obviously, the news about him and Prior was all over the office.

The fourth and final message was from DC Park, who had some good news. Phillip Clarkson's car had been found in a multi-storey car park in Miranda only a 15-minute drive from the murder scene. It had been reported by a part-time attendant who'd heard the police appeal on the telly and immediately remembered a green Volkswagen he'd seen parked in the same place on consecutive nights.

Prior returned. 'Anything interesting?'

'Yeah. Palmeira's in hospital. He's had an accident.'

'How?'

'Don't know. Running, I bet. Always said jogging was bad for you.'

Sandy Prior punched him playfully in the guts. 'It'd do you a bit of good.'

'Hey, that's muscle.'

'Sure.'

'Mario'll be gutted.'

'I know. He's obsessed with this fitness thing.'

'He'll have to make do with his lettuce leaves.'

'Hmm. How're you guys getting along, anyhow? Not your type I wouldn't have thought.'

'Pretty good. He takes life too damn seriously. And he can be a bit sort of picky... but, no, not bad.'

'Good, because I like him. He's different.'

Danniher started to tell Prior about some of his other calls. Finch, the film-producer, the car...his promotion. Wouldn't that blow her away. But he was interrupted.

'All very interesting. But I think it can wait,' said Prior, leading him away to what, by a very simple process of elimination, she correctly assumed to be the bedroom.

8

Old is the love in his music, and cool to the ear
His joy is the width of a sorrow, the weight of a tear.
— John Shaw Neilson, *The Magpie in the Moonlight*

Koslowski was right. Film producer Marcy Roy was Indian. At least, she'd been born in India, in the teeming, movies-mad city of Bombay, capital of 'Bollywood'. She'd moved with her family to Melbourne as a 15-year-old and had studied biology at university, followed by a Master of Arts degree in film and television at the Australian Film Television and Radio School.

As she explained, it was a choice that surprised her father, a leading orthopaedic surgeon, and her mother. Not only did it involve a move to Sydney, but they'd assumed she'd go on to study for a doctorate. They'd not counted on her passion for the wildlife and wild areas of her new homeland.

Marcy — she'd quickly adopted an anglicised form of her longer, more lyrical, Hindi name — could remember as a child going with her uncle and aunt on a train to Sanjay Gandhi National Park.

Koslowski sat transfixed, staring into Marcy's big, brown eyes, as she explained how the park, supposedly famous for its birds, butterflies and small population of tigers, proved a big disappointment. Despite efforts by conservationists, the park was strewn with rubbish, especially plastic bags. Its outskirts had been invaded by desperate families spilling in from the nearby slums, who had brought in recycled junk to build new hovels, chopped down trees for firewood and started new rubbish dumps.

But what could you expect? Roy demanded. So ferocious was the press of people, so extreme their poverty, that it was difficult to assert the claims of wildlife over human life in her native India.

Koslowski found himself nodding in agreement as Roy explained how India was so unlike Australia, with its small population (not that much bigger than Bombay's!), widespread prosperity and wide-open spaces.

There would always be case-by-case arguments, but basically Australia could afford both to feed its people and to protect its wildlife.

'And what exotic wildlife!' exclaimed Marcy delightedly. Like the children of most migrant families, she'd been shown pictures of the animals she could expect to find in Australia: cute koalas and kangaroos, exotic frill-necked lizards and emus, and the scary stuff, snakes, spiders, sharks and jellyfish.

'Imagine my disappointment when I looked round our backyard in Newtown and found none of these things.'

Fortunately, there was the Australian bush. The English writer D. H. Lawrence, she told Koslowski, was terrorised by it, finding it 'so phantom-like, so ghostly...so deathly still'. Despite coming from one of the world's most densely populated cities, Marcy was enthralled by it.

Now, six years out of film school, she had never regretted turning her back on academic life and going bush. She loved her life making nature documentaries, but as she explained to Koslowski, it was neither easy nor lucrative.

Koslowski hadn't been looking forward to the meeting. A late finish, after interviewing the Clarksons, had been followed by yet another early start: his fourth in a row.

And for what? For all their frantic activity, searching for clues, looking for witnesses, interviewing people connected one way or another with Phillip Clarkson, and writing up reports, the Birdman Case team seemed no closer to finding his killer.

After five days, the newspapers were becoming impatient at the lack of progress. Starved of any new information, they had started manufacturing it, speculating wildly about what might have happened.

'Seen this?' Koslowski's wife, Marianne, had said at breakfast, tossing a paper across the table to him. It was an 'exclusive' — weren't they all? — story that police were now working on a theory that Phillip Clarkson was 'whacked' by double-crossed business partners. This was news to Koslowski.

It was also nonsense, of course. But the sort of nonsense that annoyed police top brass and added to the pressure on the team of detectives, already weakened by the loss of Mario Palmeira. The Birder Murder Case was beginning to look like a long slog. Sooner or later heads would roll.

Much to his surprise, though, Koslowski was enjoying the interview with Marcy Roy. Her drab, tomboyish dungarees and army sweatshirt could not disguise the fact that she was drop-dead gorgeous.

She was interesting and passionate about her work. And, to his delight, she'd agreed to meet him at film studios in Lindfield, a leafy suburb to the north of Sydney, where she was editing a short documentary.

'Nothing exotic this time. Suburban spiders,' she explained.

He'd been given a quick tour of the editing suites with their picture synchronisers, trim bins, splicers and the rest, been bought a plastic cup of coffee and installed in a large, empty presentation theatre.

It could have been perfect: him and an attractive girl in the back row of the movies, again. Pity, he was here to collect a character reference for a man who'd just been savagely bashed and buried alive in dirty sand.

'I could not believe my ears when I heard the news,' said Roy, sadly. 'It was a tragedy. He always seemed so full of life.'

Koslowski enjoyed listening to her. To his ears, she spoke an old-fashioned, formal sort of English. 'Did you work with him much?'

'On and off for the past five years. One overseas trip, to the Okavango, but mostly here in Australia. Lake Eyre, Kakadu, the Riverina, looking for the Mallee fowl…Where else? Mmm, Flinders Island.'

'Where's that?'

'Bass Strait. Half-way to Tasmania. It's famous for its mutton birds. They were the basis for a big industry once upon a time.'

'Tourism?'

'Goodness, no. People used to hunt them, then boil them up, pull them apart. Not just for eating, either. You can use their oil, their feathers…there's 101 things you can do with a mutton bird.'

'Doesn't sound very environmentally friendly.'

'I suppose not. Made an interesting film, though.'

'One hundred and two things, then.' Roy and Koslowski laughed.

'The thing is,' Roy resumed, serious once more, 'nature docos are very expensive to make. They involve a lot of time and, often, a lot of travel. They can also make high returns, but it depends very much on finding the right subject. The foreign cable networks just love big animals that eat stuff. Like crocodiles.'

'And birds?'

'Not really. They're more difficult to sell. And more expensive. Certainly not the sort of films you can go out and shoot on…what is it Aussies say? About a smelly rag?'

'The smell of an oily rag?'

'Yes, that's it. Phillip wasn't quite that stretched. But all that publicity stuff about him being Australia's David Attenborough made him laugh. Or cry.'

'Oh.'

'I'm not talking about talent, I'm talking about resources.'

'How do you mean?'

'Well, take Attenborough's series *The Life of Birds*. Very famous.'

Koslowski remembered it. He hadn't been interested enough to watch all ten episodes and he couldn't remember any of the bird names, but he did recall some highlights. There was that a flashy looking thing with a long tail that could make a sound like the motor drive on a camera, some dull little bird that had the most amazing sex life and, oh yeah, the film they got from strapping a camera to a flying duck.

'It was great.'

'Yes. Brilliant. Work of genius. But hugely expensive.' Attenborough's series, she explained, had taken more than three years to make, used 48 camera operators, involved visits to 42 countries on five continents and gobbled up more than 300 kilometres of film.

'Attenborough himself travelled more than 400,000 kilometres. That's about ten times round the earth.'

Koslowski was impressed. 'You know the figures off by heart.'

'I do. They make me so envious. But the main figure I remember is seven-point-five. As in seven-point-five million pounds. More than 20 million Aussie dollars. That's roughly what it cost to make *The Life of Birds*.'

'Wow!'

'Absolutely. Phillip would've killed for that sort of money.'

Koslowski looked up from his notebook.

Roy backtracked. 'Sorry, I didn't mean literally.'

'I hope not.'

'The thing is, that sort of money buys you months of research and reconnaissance trips, before a centimetre of film is shot. It buys you the latest technology. Low-light cameras, cameras so small they can film inside nests. Best of all, it buys you the freedom to be adventurous, to try new things.'

For one episode, a camera crew had travelled to the Himalayas to film the mating behaviour of a rare Nepalese bird. Forty porters were needed to carry the film gear, provisions and combs of dripping honey, which they needed to attract the birds.

'Can you imagine that?'

Koslowski couldn't.

'What's more, it didn't work out. The birds didn't turn up. But you see you can afford to stuff up if you've got millions of dollars to play with. Attenborough averaged more than two million dollars per hour of program. Aussie doco-makers are lucky if they can get a third of that. Many do it on far less. And they have to do all their own fund-raising, planning, filming, editing and — if they've got anything worthwhile at the end of all that — their own marketing.'

It was clearly a touchy subject. 'Did Clarkson resent this at all?'

Roy thought. 'I think he did. Especially, all the comparisons with Attenborough. Most times he laughed them off. But yes, I think they did upset him. I'm sure he thought he was as good as Attenborough.'

'Just not as flush with cash?'

'Right. He was better off than many. He was able to hire a producer, like me, and a camera crew. But it took him several years to make a name for himself. To establish some relationship with the TV people who commission docos here, and to crack a couple of cable networks. Like *National Geographic*. Or *Discovery*.'

'They must have rated his material highly, though?'

'Yes. But it still meant every project involved a battle to raise cash. You know, boring stuff like pitching proposals to backers, trying to pre-sell to networks, tapping potential sponsors, organising contra deals.'

'Sounds like hard work.'

'That part of it is. Film-makers want to get out and make films not mess around with money men. It can be soul-destroying. It drove Phillip mad at times.'

'He was difficult to work with, then?'

Roy paused, as if wary of being led into a trap. 'Who told you that?'

'I don't remember. Honest. I thought he was famous in the industry for being "difficult", for falling out with people all the time?'

'I think that's over the top. It's a difficult business. Long hours. Tough conditions. Tight budgets. Especially for people like Phillip. Creative types. With strong opinions. Principles. You're bound to have bust-ups.'

Roy had suddenly become protective about her former employer. Had her relationship been anything other than professional, Koslowski wondered. 'Tell me, how did you get on with him?'

'Well enough to keep going back for more — at least, when he could afford me. Look, he could be awkward. "Difficult" if you like. He worked people hard. He tried not to pay them much. He had high standards. He'd have firm ideas about what shot, what effect, he wanted and he would insist that we kept going until he got it.'

'I see.'

'Don't say it like that. That's what made him good at what he did.'

Koslowski still looked unconvinced. Roy tried again. 'Personally, I'd say he was no worse than any other television personality.' The way Roy pronounced it, the word 'personality' sounded like an insult.

'Ask other crews. They'll tell you that most times the friendly, happy, wise-cracking personality you see on the screen is a miserable, irritable, insecure creep off it.'

'Did he mix much with his crews?'

'Not if he could help it. He wasn't sociable at all, really. I'd say a bit of a loner. That didn't help matters, of course.'

'How do you mean?'

'Well, it wasn't just a case of not having a drink or palling around with the boys and girls after a hard day's shooting. He would often travel separately. You know, go business class, while the rest of us went cattle; get a hotel room to himself, while the rest of us would have to share.'

'I thought you said he was tight with budgets.'

'Yes. But, then, he raised the money. He was responsible for not wasting it. He said he couldn't function properly if he arrived half-dead from the flight, if he didn't get a proper night's sleep. After all, he was television's Mr Birdman.' She laughed.

'Can you think of anyone who hated him enough to have killed him?'

'Of course not.'

'Do you know if he was gay?'

'No, I don't know. I don't think he was, but I don't really know.'

'One final thing.'

'Yes?'

'When did you last see Phillip Clarkson?'

She thought. 'Month or so ago. I bumped into him at the movies in town actually. Some grimy, English film. Can't think of its name, but you know the type: cast of working-class heroes wriggling under the Thatcherite jackboot.'

'Was he alone?'

'Yeah. We didn't have much time to speak, but he was still moaning about having a hard time raising cash for his next project.'

'Any idea what it was?'

'Yes. He had this off-beat idea — a cheap idea, I remember he said — not about birds but bird-watchers…the twitchers, the twitchathoners who race each other to see who can spot the most in 24 hours, the real hard-core types, who'll go to any extreme, pay any price to see that one rare species.'

'Sounds a lot of fun.'

'Yes. Plenty of human drama there. They may look harmless, but they're a very competitive breed, birders.'

ଓଛଓଛ

Overnight, Danniher had had a change of mind. After providing Path Prior with bed and breakfast and a lift back home, he decided that as he was temporarily in charge of inquiries he wouldn't waste time driving into the central business district to interview Simon Finch. His home in the affluent eastern suburb of Double Bay was much closer.

He'd arrived at Berwick police station to be told by PC McCrimond that forensics had just rung. They should have something for him on Phillip Clarkson's car that afternoon. Good. Something good to tell Sedgwick. Meanwhile, he sat at Palmeira's desk and looked through the in-tray.

There was a report from DCs Park and Holmes. The previous night they'd been successful in speaking to no fewer than five men. Each admitted — three of them only after getting guarantees of strict confidence — that they'd been in the dunes at Bayside Drive at different times on the night of Phillip Clarkson's murder.

Each insisted that he'd seen nothing suspicious. Each was positive there had not been a green Volkswagen in the area. It was bad news.

He read a note from Koslowski, telling him about the funeral. 'You? Me? Or not worth it?' Kiwi had scrawled across the top.

He read an unsigned letter from something called the Make Australia Decent campaign — MAD, presumably. Clarkson's death, he read, was proof that God punished homosexuals. Nutters!

Danniher screwed up the note and chucked it across the room, where it rimmed the bin and dropped in. He punched the air in delight. Yes!

He scanned the newspapers which, finding little new to say or to speculate, had now relegated brief stories about the Birdman Case deep inside their pages. That reminded him to call the media unit, where he told someone whose name he didn't quite catch, that the dead man's car had been found. It might make a media release later in the day.

And he telephoned Finch to insist that they reschedule their meeting again, for his place, the following morning. The foreign exchange dealer was not impressed with the demand.

'But it's the funeral tomorrow afternoon,' he moaned.

'So I hear.'

'I've promised to go. Dammit, I'm going to waste a whole day.'

'Waste, Mr Finch? I wouldn't call helping the police with murder inquiries a waste.'

'This is not fair. Can I speak to your boss?'

'I am my boss. See you tomorrow.' Creep. Danniher slammed Palmeira's phone down, cracking the mouthpiece.

He looked at his watch and thought. No point just sitting here waiting for something to happen, someone to call. For one thing, he'd only get cornered by Sedgwick. Better to get out and talk to someone.

He got up and went to consult the famous whiteboard. What a work of art it was. Poor old Palmeira. Perhaps he'd have made a better draughtsman than a detective.

One or two names in the 'suspects' box had been ticked as having been interviewed; others, such as those of Christine Withers and her boyfriend had been struck through as having been cleared of involvement. But several others remained, including a few of the birdwatchers.

Danniher looked at his watch again. Plenty of time to knock over one of these. He checked the address list. Warnock? Too far. Griffiths? Too far. Waddell? Address still unknown! Must get Kos on to that ASAP. Morris? Ah, lives in Kurnell. Only a few kilometres away.

Derek Morris sounded distinctly nervous on the telephone. In fact, a worrier, a bit of an old woman, thought Danniher.

'I'm afraid you've rather caught me on the, the, err, hop. I really can't believe I'd be able to, to help you.' However, he agreed to meet, almost immediately, adding, 'Get it over with, eh, sergeant?'

Odd place, Kurnell, thought Danniher as he looked for Morris's address. One of those sleepy, out of the way places that looked like it had been trapped in a time warp. Not that the local residents, who seemed to spend most of their time fishing, pottering around in boats or fighting to be left alone, much cared. And good luck to them.

Kurnell was, of course, old. Danniher knew that. Some called it the birthplace of modern Australia because it was close to the point where Captain James Cook landed in 1770. Somehow, though, it had still not become part of modern Australia but remained, quite literally, out on a limb, at the end of its own little peninsula.

It wouldn't be a bad place to live, thought Danniher, as he checked the map again. These days Kurnell had a large oil refinery on its backdoorstep and many times its residents must have felt that it was being squeezed into the sea by onrushing development. But somehow it survived: a community more than a suburb. A village of small, cheapish homes with big, million-dollar views across the bay to the city. Yes, an odd place, with more than its fair share of odd people.

Derek Morris, Danniher quickly discovered, was one of them.

He arrived to find a neat, brick, two-bedroom bungalow with what estate agents would call 'sea glimpses'. A small, upturned dinghy sat in the drive, but there was no sign of a car. Morris was standing in his porch, waiting for him, watching a couple of magpies. Even Danniher could identify them.

Morris looked much as Danniher had expected from his brief telephone conversation: small, not much hair, spectacles that in one place were held together with what appeared to be a bent paper-clip, baggy shorts and a thin, but woolly jumper. In short, Danniher's idea of the stereotypical, middle-aged Englishman.

'Fascinating bird, the err, magpie, you know,' said Morris, without introduction. 'People don't realise. But they've excellent hearing and are capable of learning new songs — often from other species, like the kookaburra — in a matter of minutes.'

'That right?'

'Oh, yes. People talk about "birdbrains". But it's really is m-m-most unfair. There's a bird in Japan — in fact, a crow, I think — that's even worked out an ingenious way to crack umm, walnuts. They drop them in front of cars when they stop at red lights. The cars run over the nuts and, when the coast is clear again, the birds pop down and pick up the pieces. Quite remarkable.'

'Fascinating,' said Danniher, not too enthusiastically, he hoped. 'Anyway, about Phillip Clarkson...'

'Dreadful business, that. I suppose the police don't know, umm, yet, who, err...' Morris, Danniher noted, tended to become flustered and tongue-tied except when he was talking about his feathered friends. Then he became articulate, passionate even.

'No. Not yet. But we will, sir. Don't worry,' he said, as he was led into a lounge room. It was large and evidently lived-in. Like its occupant, it showed signs of neglect: there was dust, an indefinable musty smell, and a muddle of books, old papers, and newspaper cuttings, piled up on every available flat surface, including the floor. The curtains were still drawn. Perhaps they always were.

In the dim half-light, Danniher paused to look at some framed photographs, propped up on a dusty mantelpiece. He picked up a black and white shot of a couple of young boys. They were laughing and seemed to be fighting for the controls of a pedal car.

After studying it for a few seconds, Danniher waved the picture gently at Morris, who recognised it without even coming forward to squint at it. 'Me when I was still alive, sergeant.'

Danniher stared at him.

'Sorry. That sounds b-b-bitter. I'm only joking. It's me as a boy, in the umm, garden back in England. A long time ago now.'

'And the other boy?'

'Oh, my umm, brother.'

'Looks a bit of a tearaway.'

'Yes. I suppose he was.'

Still, Danniher didn't know quite what to make of Morris. He seemed harmless enough, but within minutes he felt a strong urge to strangle him. The long, rambling sentences. The woofy, Pommy accent. The umming and erring. The silly jokes. They made Danniher want to shake the words out of him.

Instead, he sat silently, taking the odd note, listening to Morris's life story, calculating how soon he could get back to some serious police work.

He'd been born in England — no surprises there — in Guildford, Surrey, to be exact, and had emigrated to Australia in the late 1950s with his mum, dad, sister and brother.

'Back home they used to call us Morris Major and Morris Minor.'

Danniher smiled.

'We were, err, ten-pound Poms, whingeing Poms,' he said. 'Before your time, I expect, officer. But believe it or not, Australia actually bribed people to come here in those days.'

Morris had left school in his late teens. The timing of his family's move, he later felt, had disrupted his education at a crucial point. For no other reason than that he was considered by his mother to be good with figures, he was persuaded to apply for a job with a local biscuits manufacturer.

'Not making b-b-biscuits. In the finance department. Cooking the umm, books.'

Unfortunately, he sometimes thought, he had got the job. It proved undemanding and unexciting, but secure...until, that is, the company was taken over by an American food conglomerate. It retrenched him, after 32 years' service, at the age of 50.

Since then, he'd been doing, well, not much at all. Just bits and pieces of financial consultancy. Most recently with the local council.

'That's pretty well, you know, it. My life story. Not v-v-very impressive, eh?'

Danniher ignored the question. 'You live alone, Mr Morris?'

'Err, yes.' Only 18 months after he lost his job, his wife, Margaret, had died from cancer. 'Possibly stress-related, the doctors said,' Morris explained pensively.

He brightened. 'By coincidence, she was another English migrant.' The couple had met at the biscuit factory and married after three years going out together. They hadn't had children, but were happy, very happy, together and, because Morris was good with figures, comfortably off.

'And how long have you lived here?'

'Seventeen years.' At first, the Morrises had rented property, then taken out a mortgage on a noisy bungalow near the airport, and from there moved to Balaclava Parade, Kurnell. 'To be near the water and to, well, watch the birds.'

Birdwatching, Morris explained, had become a binding passion for the couple. 'Look, here's M...M...Margaret,' he said, reaching across to the mantelpiece.

Danniher stood and took an ornate frame from Morris. It held a faded colour photograph of a man and a woman, holding hands, standing on what appeared to be spectacular cliffs, overlooking the sea. They were smiling up into the camera, which was presumably being held by a friend.

'Ah, me and my, err, late wife. Happy days. Many years ago, now, I'm afraid.'

'Looks like a nice spot.'

'It is. Top of the cliffs, near Magic Point, at Maroubra. Do you know it officer?'

'I know the cliffs.'

'Margaret and I used to go there regularly. It was our favourite place for sea birds, especially in winter, when you could see the albatrosses. Amazing birds.'

It took a few seconds for Morris to return from the distant past. 'How is it I can help you?'

Danniher sat down again. This really shouldn't take too long, he thought, anxious to bring Morris straight to the point. 'Obviously, we're trying to build up a picture of Phillip Clarkson, who his friends were, whether he had enemies, that sort of thing.'

'I understand.'

He prompted him again. 'So, did you know him well, sir?'

'Yes. Well, no, not really. Umm...I'd met him on several occasions. I'm a member of a few of the same bird groups, so our paths, err, crossed there. I've been on a few tours, guided by him.'

'I see.'

'He could be very informative and, umm, I'd have to say he was jolly good at identifying birds. Even us experts have difficulty telling some of those little waders apart, you know. There's one, looks like a...'

Danniher didn't have time to sit through another lecture. 'Mr Morris, you were saying. About Phillip Clarkson?'

'Sorry. I, umm, also came across him when I was doing some financial work for the council. I was a bit surprised to find him there, but he said he was doing some sort of, err consultancy for them. Like me, I suppose.'

'I see.'

More silence. Then, 'Oh and, of course, I knew him from his work on television.'

'How did you rate him?'

'Oh, awfully good. I know some people criticised him for, umm...dumbing-down, I think they call it. But that's what happens if you make something popular and you become rich and famous.'

'It's the same with those academics who go on television and make history interesting: their colleagues get all huffy. It was rather like that with Clarkson. I must admit his TV, umm, persona did sometimes make me squirm.'

'Really?'

'I'm sure others will have told you that the real Phillip Clarkson could be, err, rather more, err, prickly, shall we say.'

'Would you say that, Mr Morris?'

'My view is that it doesn't much matter. What matters is: whose side is someone on? The birds? Or the people who are destroying their habitats? The birds? Or the people who see them only as inconveniences standing in the way of profits?'

Danniher could hear a lecture coming. 'By the way, where were you last Saturday night, sir?'

'I err, well, here watching television, I believe. N-n-not much of one for going out at night, you see. Anyway, I always like to watch *The Bill*. Not what it, err, used to be — too much sex and violence now for my taste — but still watchable.'

'I suppose there was no one who could confirm that for us?'

'No. I was on my own. Let me think, though. Err, I expect Mrs Carroll next door may have seen the, umm, light on. You could ask her.'

'OK. I may need to speak to you again, sir,' he said, standing. Morris led him to the door and out on to the driveway.

'No car then, Mr Morris?'

'No. I sold it when my wife died. I never learnt to drive myself.'

'That can't be very convenient?'

'Not really. I have a, umm, bicycle. Public transport's not too bad, considering. And if I am going on a bird outing, there's usually, err, one of the members who can pick me up.'

'At least you don't have to go far for a bit of fishing, eh? Just over the road,' Danniher said, nodding at the dinghy.

'Sorry? Oh, the boat…no, it's not mine. I just look after it for my…err, err, my, somebody. To be honest, I don't like fishing. Personally, I think it's cruel, you know…and the, err, people, the fishers, they can be so bloody thoughtless.'

Danniher moved away. Morris followed him. 'Do you know how many birds are strangled by monofilament line carelessly chucked away by some selfish…' His words trailed off as Danniher jumped into his car, slammed the door and drove off.

He did not go far, just round the corner, where he parked. After allowing five minutes for Mr Morris to disappear indoors, he walked back and did, as suggested, check with the neighbour. Just to be on the safe side.

Mrs Carroll, a small, inscrutable woman about Mr Morris's age, stared at him suspiciously. Just when Danniher was beginning to wonder whether she spoke English, she replied. She hadn't actually seen **Mr Morris** that night — 'I don't spy on people, you know' — but, yes, she remembered seeing his light on. And, no, she hadn't been aware of any unusual comings and goings.

'Just a few cars. It's very quiet around here, you know,' she said proudly, before slamming the door in the policeman's face.

ᏁᏫᏂᏫᏂ

Danniher had wasted, or so he thought, more than hour in the land that time forgot, alternately being ear-bashed by Derek Morris and waiting for him to get the next word out. Now, he rushed back to Berwick police station, praying. Please, god, let there be some good news from forensics about Clarkson's beetle.

He was not optimistic. Too often these boffins reminded him of that old riddle. Question: How do you keep a bastard in suspense? Answer: I'll tell you tomorrow.

For one thing, they were ultra-cautious, almost invariably refusing to speculate on any subject until it had been taken away, cut up, put under an electron microscope and infra-red spectrometer and examined from every angle. And for another, when they did have something useful to say, they deliberately prevaricated.

Thus it was that Danniher spent ten minutes on the telephone becoming increasingly despondent as Stephen Erskine explained at some length precisely what they hadn't found in Phillip Clarkson's Volkswagen.

They hadn't found any fingerprints: 'clean as a nice, new pair of gloves, I'm afraid, sir,' said Erskine.

They hadn't found anything for DNA matching: 'I know it's a wonderful thing, but you can't expect it to work in every case.'

And they hadn't found a murder weapon, although they did carefully examine a car-jack, a wrench and 'that L-shaped thing you use to remove nuts and hub caps'. There were no prints on any of them. Indeed, they appeared never to have been touched before, let alone used to beat someone's head to a pulp.

They had found, in the foot-wells on both the driver and passenger sides of the car, plenty of sand, which probably matched that found at the crime scene. Analysis of partial footprints suggested they did not come from Clarkson's own brand of boots.

Interesting, but apart from suggesting that more than one person was probably involved in the birder's murder, what use was it?

It was then, just as Danniher's patience was nearing exhaustion, that Erskine dropped his only real piece of positive news. Apart from a few innocuous personal items, including some CDs, a bird guide and a pop-up umbrella, he had found....'

This was worse than waiting for Morris to finish a sentence, thought Danniher.

'...what looks like Clarkson's diary.'

'What!'

'Don't get too excited. It may not even be his main diary. I don't know. It's one of those little, pocket-sized things that are given away by companies, organisations. Or you can buy them in the shops for a few dollars.'

'All the same...'

'It was slotted in the back of the sun-visor on the driver's side. Stroke of luck finding it in a way. The visor was folded back and we missed it on the first run through. If I hadn't clipped it with my head getting out...'

'Never mind. You got it.'

'True. But as I say, don't get your hopes up too high. We're not into February yet so as far as I could see it only covers one month and, even then, Clarkson doesn't look like he's been having a very busy time of it.'

'Damn.' It was like being on an emotional roller coaster, one moment plunged to deep despair, the next raised to high delight.

'No dabs, apart from the dead man's. But there may be a few entries you'll find useful and there's a few other bits of paper tucked inside. Anyway, I've sent the lot 'round. I'm surprised you haven't already got it.'

'Thanks.'

A brown envelope containing the diary arrived ten minutes later. Danniher took the diary out. On its cover was the logo of a building materials company. Tucked inside the cover were some pieces of paper: petrol receipts, a few of his own business cards and a list of names.

Danniher recognised them immediately: they were the birding party for the tour that never happened. A checklist, he supposed.

He checked the diary. Erskine had been right. There were remarkably few entries for a supposedly busy man: just initials, times, and occasional, cryptic squiggles. It looked like Clarkson had a personal code to denote certain things were due to happen on certain days. Or had happened, possibly.

But what? Payments? Deliveries? Sexual encounters? Business appointments? He couldn't work them out.

He looked again at the initials. Who or what was 'BC'? Or 'PE'? Each appeared several times in January.

Or 'CW'? Now, that must be Christopher Workman. His initials, followed by three exclamation marks, had been pencilled in for the first Tuesday in February.

And 'SF'. Simon Finch! According to the diary, 'SF' had been due to meet Clarkson on the Saturday afternoon. Only hours before the discovery of the Birdman's body! Danniher could hardly believe his eyes. But there it was: 'SF 4 pm'. Let's see Finch talk his way out of this one.

He snapped the diary closed, rolled the envelope up into a ball and tossed it across the room, where it rimmed the wastepaper bin before dropping in, again. Yes! It was true, he was on a roll. He couldn't wait to tell Palmeira.

9

The flight of the Wild Goose is heavy and laborious, generally in a straight line, or in two lines approximating to a point...
— Alexander Wilson, *An Ornithology*

In the good old, bad old days, only a week ago, thought Danniher, he would've gone down the pub for a drink with his mates to celebrate his success. After four days off the grog — 'an Australian all-comers' record,' he told Koslowski — he certainly deserved a night out. But he didn't go.

He could've taken Sandy Prior out again. He quite fancied that. But he couldn't: she'd promised to visit her parents that night. 'A Prior engagement?' he'd joked. Her expression told him she'd heard that one a few times before.

Or, he supposed, he could reschedule his meeting with Finch yet again. Hit him with the discovery of the incriminating diary entry. But it'd wait until tomorrow. Finch clearly wasn't planning to disappear and, as Sedgwick had said, it didn't exactly look as though the Birder Murder was the start of a serial-killing rampage.

Quite the reverse, in fact, thought Danniher, as he stayed back at the station, back-tracking through reports to see if Palmeira had missed anything. He didn't tell Sedgwick, of course, but he worried increasingly that Clarkson's murder was a one-off, random killing, or had been executed by killers who'd vanished without trace.

He had moved several reports from Palmeira's in-tray to his out-tray. And had just come off the phone to Koslowski, who was slowly working his way through Clarkson's papers, when he was interrupted by Russell Park.

'How's it going, Russ? Good news I hope.'

'Afraid not, sir.'

'What d'you mean?'

'Sedgwick, sir.'

'Let me worry about him.'

'Thanks. But the thing is he's dragging me off the Birdman Case.'

'What? You must be joking,' Danniher exploded.

'Sorry, sir. He said to tell you he needs me to work with Jim Munro on an outbreak of muggings.' The young officer made it sound like a bad case of measles.

'When?'

'Straightaway. Says there's just too many other things happening locally to have me cruising round gay bars.'

'Brilliant! I suppose he does remember that Clarkson was murdered locally? Like on a local beach?'

'I dunno. Sorry. He didn't give me much chance to ask questions.'

'Sure.' No point taking it out on Park, thought Danniher. He couldn't have been in the job more than a couple of years. 'Thanks Russ. I'll have a word with him. Hang around until it's sorted out, will you?'

'No problem, sarge,' said Park, wandering off.

Danniher took a deep breath and weighed up the situation. Stomping off down the corridor and having a flaming row with Sedgwick might not be the smartest career move. But what the hell, he was in the mood for one!

Moments later he was in Sedgwick's office. 'Thought you might pop in, Danniher. Sit down. And calm down.' Danniher sat and seethed. 'I don't have to explain anything to you, but I will.'

Danniher held his tongue as Sedgwick explained. 'You won't have noticed because you're all too busy with the birders, but Berwick has been hit by a mini-crime-wave. At least that's what the local rag's calling it.'

'Really?' It was the first Danniher had heard of it.

'Yes, really. Cars being stolen and vandalised. Homes being broken into. And now the good people of Berwick being bashed as they go about their business.' But not actually murdered, thought Danniher sullenly.

Sedgwick was getting up a head of steam. 'Some really nasty attacks. Many of them on Asians. An old man even got bashed in his shop near the station the other day. In broad daylight. Point is, now I've got the bloody

Berwick Chamber of Commerce on my back.'

So that was it. For once it was Sedgwick who was feeling the blowtorch of others' expectations. 'But, sir...'

'But nothing, Danniher. I've got to show we mean business — that we're protecting the man and woman in the street. Not just throwing resources at the big-name cases.'

Danniher clenched his teeth. Keep calm. Keep calm. He tried again. 'But, sir, with the DI out of action...'

'I'm well aware of that. How could he do such a stupid thing?'

'No, no. The thing is, sir, I think we've made a breakthrough on the Birdman.'

Sedgwick snapped to attention. 'Are you saying there's a possibility of an early arrest?'

Danniher hesitated. No, he wasn't saying that at all. 'Yes, sir,' he replied nevertheless.

Sedgwick listened as Danniher explained how Clarkson's car had been found and how it had produced a clue to the dead man's final hours and, he hoped, to his murderer.

Eventually, Sedgwick relented. 'Sounds bloody thin to me, but OK. You can keep Park and Holmes...'

'Thanks.'

'... but only for now. Shall we say 48 hours?'

Either I'm a better liar than I knew or Jonno's going soft in his old age, thought Danniher as he returned to his desk. So, 48 hours and counting down. Bet Palmeira wouldn't have stuck his neck out like that.

Palmeira! He suddenly remembered: he'd promised to go and visit him. Why not now? A quick call to the hospital confirmed that the patient was still woozy after his operation but would, no doubt, welcome visitors.

಄಄಄

Danniher arrived to find someone already sitting at Palmeira's bedside: his wife Jenny. He'd met her several times before. She seemed more friendly, less intense than her husband. Attractive, too. Some sort of designer, he seemed to remember.

'G'day, Jenny.'

'Wayne.' She jumped up. It looked like she was pleased to share, or even pass on, the burden of entertaining her morose husband.

'So, how's the patient?' Maybe it was effects of the operation, or the size of the big, white bed, or his sorry, unshaven appearance, but Palmeira looked diminished, vulnerable.

It was Jenny who answered. 'Oh, impossible.'

'No change there then, eh.' The pair laughed, liked conspirators.

'Very funny,' said Palmeira, with an exaggerated grimace. He was only a few hours out of theatre and already he was plunged into despair by the thought of six months of slow repair and rehabilitation. No doubt it worried his family, but it depressed the hell out of him.

'Actually, I was just about to go. New babysitter,' Jenny said. 'I'll leave you to it.'

Danniher felt awkward. 'Sorry. Didn't mean to interrupt, you guys.'

'No, I've got to collect the girls. He's all yours.' Jenny looked at the two men and, not for the first time, was struck by how different they were: her husband, small and dark, and Danniher, big and reddish-fair. They made an ill-matched couple.

She lent over and kissed Mario quickly on the cheek, blushed and looked back to Danniher. 'You do know he's talking of going back to work before the end of the week.'

'No.'

'Perhaps you can talk some sense into him.'

'I'll do my best.' Danniher turned back to Palmeira. 'So, how's the leg?'

'Fine. How's the case?'

'Oh, fine.'

'What's that mean?'

Here we go again, thought Danniher, as he gave his boss — or was it his former boss? — a quick update. How Clarkson's car had been located. How a diary had been found. How it named Workman and Finch. 'Here, take a look,' said Danniher, handing over the little black book.

And how Jonno Sedgwick had tried to pull the pin on the whole Birder Murder investigations.

'He did what?' said Palmeira, twisting and wincing as a shock of pain ran up his leg.

'Don't worry, I managed to talk him out of it,' said Danniher, explaining how he'd kept the team intact.

'Well done,' said Palmeira, relieved now.

'Only thing is, I had to tell him we're about to make an arrest.'

'And are we?'

'No idea, sir.'

Palmeira shook his head in disbelief. Danniher had been in charge for less than 24 hours and already he'd committed professional suicide.

'But Workman and Finch...'

'Mmm. I don't know. Finch could be involved. Didn't Mrs Clarkson say he used to come round and see her son regularly? And now you say they met on the day of the murder...'

'That's got to be suspicious.' Danniher could see Palmeira was not impressed. 'At least, it'd be interesting to find out what their relationship was. Business? Friendship? Sex?'

'Birds?'

'You mean, something perfectly innocent?'

'I hope not. For your sake.'

The two men sat in silence for a while, before Palmeira spoke again. 'It's odd, isn't it? No one we've talked to so far seems to have liked Clarkson. They all say he could be difficult — even his own brother.'

'But...?'

'Well, I don't feel we've met anyone yet who hated Clarkson enough to kill him.'

'Or have him killed.'

'No. And yet, the lack of any evidence suggests that the killers knew what they were doing.'

'And who they were killing?'

Palmeira was silent for a moment. 'Probably. But it could still have been random, I suppose: a killer who didn't know his victim's name, didn't recognise him, didn't know he was something big on television.'

'Makes it difficult,' conceded Danniher.

'Yes. But you see what I'm saying. We've got no option but to assume that the killer, or killers, was known to the victim...'

'All the crime stats point that way, anyway.'

'... and that they had a motive that made some sort of sense.'

Palmeira winced as if he was getting a headache. 'So, what next?'

'Well, Finch, of course. Then, tomorrow afternoon, there's the funeral. I thought I'd go along. Koslowski's still going through Clarkson's finances — they're a right mess, he says. And the guys are still out there looking for witnesses.'

'No sign yet of our friend Waddell?'

'Still looking, sir. We're a bit stretched, I'm afraid.'

'Sorry. I know. It's my fault.'

'Nah, nah. I didn't mean that.' Danniher was running out of ideas and conversation. 'Oh, almost forgot. There's a couple of things in the diary you might be able to help with.'

Palmeira handed it back and Danniher opened it and pointed. 'This, and this.'

'Let's see,' said Palmeira, who despite the painkillers obviously still fancied he could solve cryptic clues. 'What we want is "BC" and "PE"'

'Right. "CW" and "SF" must be Chris Workman and Simon Finch. Just too much of a coincidence, otherwise. But these others...well, they may be people we don't even know about. A banker, a cameraman, an investor, a PR...you never know, may be even a friend. Who knows?'

'We could ask Mrs Clarkson.'

'OK.'

'Of course, they may not be people at all,' said Palmeira. 'Could be organisations. Or companies. Thought about that? "BC"? How about Berwick Council? Didn't Clarkson work for them?'

'I think he did,' confirmed Danniher, recalling his conversation with Morris. 'Anyway, they don't correspond to any other names we've got on the board.' He looked at the list of birders again, wondering how many more he or Koslowski had still to interview. 'At least one bloke didn't have his Sunday wasted.'

Palmeira was still trying to work out what "PE" could be, when the words sank in. 'Sorry. What was that you said?'

'Nothing really. Just saying somebody's day wasn't wasted. There was a no-show on Sunday.'

'You sure?

'Yes. Ten names on the list but only nine turned up. One bloke…Enderby. He was a no-show. Hope he didn't pay his 50 bucks.'

Palmeira's second double take caused him to shift painfully in bed. 'What was that name, again?'

'Enderby.' He checked again the typed list. 'Yes. Ellis Enderby. Do you know him?'

'No. But I've heard of him all right. Another one of those birding types. Had a huge falling out with Clarkson over who'd seen what.'

'Another name for the "suspects list"?'

'Absolutely.' For the first time that day, Palmeira's face brightened. 'Look, I want you to get McCrimond to give me a call first thing tomorrow.'

'Righto, sir.'

'Tell her we're going to play hunt the dead parrot. If she doesn't know what I'm talking about, tell her to get Koslowski to explain.'

'Anything you say, boss.' Must be the drugs kicking in, thought Danniher.

ಬಂಬಂಬ

Double Bay. A swanky area, full of dress shops and restaurants and expensive hotels, thought Danniher as he looked for Finch's address. You'd need a fortune to live here. Double Bay? More like double the price of almost anywhere else in Sydney.

He put his car on a three-hour meter down by the sea, and walked around for several minutes, smelling the sea air, watching the windsurfers on the harbour, and perving on the girls in their designer-label mini-dresses. Psyching himself up.

Finch's street turned out to be a steep, winding cul-de-sac, which because of a shortage of off-street parking, was clogged with cars. No. 46 Gresham Gardens was at the very bottom.

The block itself wasn't very impressive from outside either. Circa 1930s, Danniher guessed. Boxy. Redbrick. Still carrying an old nameplate. Point Jackson. Full of elderly residents, he suspected, who still used the old name rather than the new number, even if it meant their mail went missing occasionally.

At the front door, he checked a panel of buttons, and pressed the bottom one labelled 'S. and C. Finch'. 'S' was clearly Simon, but who was the 'C' Finch, Danniher wondered as he waited.

There was no reply. He pressed the button again and looked round anxiously. OK, he wasn't expecting to find a murder weapon or a killer waiting to confess, but what if 'SF' wasn't Simon Finch? What if this visit turned out to be, to put it in birder terms, another wild goose chase? Worse, what if Finch had stood him up? Or fled?

Just then, the intercom crackled and a man's voice was heard. 'Good morning, officer Danniher, is it? Bang on time. Come on down.'

The door suddenly flew open and a young woman, smartly dressed in a grey business suit, came running out. Danniher stood back to let her pass and went down some stairs.

Finch was waiting, and ushered him through a double front door. Danniher was surprised to find that instead of opening into a dingy basement, it led to a large, light-filled home with a long balcony that hung, breathtakingly, over the harbour's silver waters.

'What d'you reckon, eh?' said Finch, who clearly delighted in the surprised reaction of first-time visitors.

Danniher grunted non-committedly, stepping forward on to a carpet so gleamy-creamy coloured that he wondered if he was expected to remove his shoes. Screw that. Dragging his eyes away from the harbour, he looked quickly round a large, open-plan room.

It was expensively furnished and seemed to be littered with all the latest electronic gizmos: plasma television, DVD player, flat-screen computer, Palm Pilot, digital camera, MP3 player and, Danniher was surprised to see, a robotic dog. He'd stumbled into yuppie heaven.

No doubt Finch had a Beemer or maybe even a Merc parked close by, somewhere safe where it couldn't be scratched by some anti-yuppie anarchist or, more likely, by a Point Jackson resident trying to park a Volvo.

Simon Finch inclined his head, as if to ask, impressed? Seen enough?

Now that you ask, no, thought Danniher, wandering over to a side-table covered with framed photographs. He picked up one, showing a familiar-looking man in some sort of uniform. He was carrying a gun and smiling.

'You?'

'Yes.'

'Like guns do you?'

'Not particular,' replied Finch, explaining that, apart from birds, oh and rugby union, his other big interest was the American Civil War. 'I'm a re-enactor.'

'Playing at soldiers?' The closest Danniher had got to doing that was a paintball session out in the bush.

'I wouldn't call it "playing". That's me as Thomas Wentworth Higginson.'

'And who's he?'

'An amazing man, sergeant. A soldier-scholar, you might say. Supported women getting the vote. Commanded the first black regiment in the Union Army. And, would you believe, wrote books on birds in his spare time. If only he'd played rugby. Still, can't have everything.'

'Looks like you have.' Danniher had picked Finch's type as soon as he met him. A material boy. What had the judge said about that university lecturer they'd done for peddling drugs? 'A man with means, but no meaning.' Probably a troubled soul, who had everything and nothing.

He was disappointed to find that he'd been wrong. Simon Finch was healthy (no tell-tale signs of trading-room coke sessions), handsome (in a slicked-back, singles-bar sort of way) and happily married, unless the wedding photographs on the table were way out of date.

Unless Finch was bisexual — always a possibility these days — Danniher could discard the theory that Finch had fallen out with Clarkson and killed him in a crime of passion. But he had plenty of other theories involving Finch.

Danniher replaced the Civil War photograph. He sensed that, despite his big boy's toys and boastfulness, Finch was nervous. Certainly, he talked too much.

'And what is it exactly you do when you're not fighting wars, Mr Finch?'

'Buy and sell foreign currencies,' Finch explained.

'Must pay well?'

Finch quoted an 'industry average'. It was ten times as much as a detective sergeant made. 'All you need is a modicum of financial ability, a strong nerve, a loud voice and a rat-like cunning.'

'You've got rat-like cunning, have you Mr Finch?'

'You need it when dealing with other rats, sergeant.' He grinned.

Danniher felt he was getting nowhere. Without being asked, he took a seat. Finch took one opposite. They eyed each other with mutual distaste.

'Why did you fall out with Phillip Clarkson?'

'I didn't.'

'Mrs Clarkson said you did.'

For the first time, it seemed, Finch was temporarily lost for words. 'Well she's wrong.'

'Let's go back to the start, then. How did you first meet Clarkson?'

Suddenly, Finch seemed more cooperative.

'Through the local bird club. He came along and gave a talk. We got chatting afterwards and he told me about the tours.'

'A bit expensive I heard.'

'I don't mind paying for the best.'

'And he was?'

'Best in Australia, you'd have to say.'

'You must've found the pace slow. All those old folk?'

'I don't follow.'

'I thought you lived life in the fast lane.'

'I see. Boy soldier. Boy racer. In fact, that's why I got interested in birding in the first place. Chloe — my wife — thought it might slow me down.'

'Did it?'

'Not really. All a bit slow, really. But the twitchathons can be a real blast.'

'The what?'

'Twitchathons. High-speed birding. Birding by numbers. You get 24 hours to spot as many species as you can. Prize for the winner.'

'Sounds just your sort of thing,' said Danniher with what he hoped sounded like contempt.

'Absolutely,' replied Finch, ignoring the slight. 'All you need is a game plan: how to see as many different habitats — seaside, forest, wetlands and the rest. And a good map.'

'And, presumably, a fast car.'

'Essential,' replied Finch, adding with a provocative grin, 'All within the speed limits of course.'

Danniher frowned, but pressed on.

'Anyway, you got to know Clarkson well?'

'I wouldn't say that. I don't think anyone got to know him well. He was — how'd you put it? — aloof. He could be bloody arrogant at times.'

'But you got on well with him?'

'At first,' said Finch. A pained expression flickered over his face, suggesting that he had immediately regretted his words.

'But not later, obviously?'

'I suppose not.'

'Mrs Clarkson said you were a regular visitor to their home.'

'More like occasional.'

'She said three or four times a week.'

Finch frowned. 'Possibly. At first. Does it really matter, sergeant?'

'Possibly. She said you had some sort of bust-up and stopped coming. Must have been pretty serious.'

'Look…' Finch stood up and walked around. He seemed agitated. 'I don't see what this has got to do with Phillip's death, but it's all perfectly straightforward. I've got nothing to hide.'

'So just answer the questions.'

'Phillip and I were working on a business deal together. When it didn't work out we stopped seeing each other. Simple as that.'

'But you still went on his tours?'

'Not until last Saturday…and then of course, he didn't turn up. Good job he gave me a freebie.'

'That was generous of him.'

'He owed me.'

'Money?'

'Yes.'

'How come? The business thing?'

'Sort of. Look, Phillip always needed money for the next project. When he heard I was in the finance game, he asked if I knew anyone who'd be interested in investing in his documentaries.'

'And did you?'

'I was quite interested myself, actually.'

'You would be if you were interested in birds, wouldn't you,' said Danniher, encouraging him to continue.

'Yes, but it wasn't just a matter of raising funds. Phillip promised he'd use me in his docos.'

'Why would he do that?'

'He said he was going to do this program on birdwatchers. About how it attracted all sorts. Even people like me, sergeant. Anyway, I suppose he wanted to keep me sweet so as I'd go on helping him.'

'What happened?'

'It didn't work out.'

'Fail the screen test, did you?'

'Very funny. No, he dropped the idea. Decided there wouldn't be a market for something like that.'

'Disappointing.'

'Very. But not all that surprising. You ask anyone who makes nature films: it's dead risky putting people in them.'

'I don't get it.'

'He explained it to me. People limit your market, don't they? Unlike animals, people can look dated and, depending on their shape, colour and size, they may not cross cultural barriers. Like, Asian countries may not want to buy a doco featuring a westerner in a safari suit.'

Danniher nodded. 'I see. Interesting. But that isn't why you and Clarkson fell out?'

'I didn't say we fell out.'

'Stopped meeting then.'

'It was just that the fund-raising thing didn't work out. There were no hard feelings.'

'I see. So when did you last see Phillip Clarkson?'

'Let me think... just before Christmas, it would've been. I bumped into him at a talk in the city. A British academic trying to get governments to use bird numbers as environmental indicators. You know, to monitor pollution levels. Very interesting.'

'Are you sure?'

'About using birds?'

'No. The timing.'

'I think so. Why?'

Danniher pulled out the little black book. He opened it slowly. 'It's just that according to Clarkson's diary he met you last Saturday afternoon. Four o'clock. The day Phillip Clarkson was murdered, if you recall.'

Finch looked like he'd been punched in the guts.

'Ring any bells?' asked Danniher, mentally preparing to move in for the kill.

'The thing is we were supposed to meet. But it didn't happen.' He could see Danniher didn't believe him.

'Phillip rang me and said, sorry, something urgent had cropped up. He was going to have to rush out...'

'What time would that've been?'

'Oh, I'm not sure. Threeish? Anyway, I was bloody annoyed, being let down. It wasn't the first time. He could be very selfish. So typical of him to stuff people around like that.'

He could see Danniher still didn't believe him.

'It's the truth,' he shouted.

Danniher's expression was unchanged. 'But not the whole truth.'

Finch tried again. 'No,' he said slowly. 'OK. Clarkson and me did have a falling out, if that's what you want to call it. He was becoming impossible. I lent him money. And then I got mates to lend him money.

'And then mates of mates...it all just disappeared, like sand through his fingers.'

'Go on.'

'Looking back, I don't think he was ever straight with us. I'm sure he was using the money we raised for his so-called "next project" to pay off debts from the previous ones.'

'You must have been furious.'

'Yes. I admit it. Yes. I was. Because somewhere along the line the money I raised for films was being syphoned off to sort out some family problem. It got really nasty. A lot of people got very angry.'

Danniher did not speak.

'I know what you're thinking, sergeant. But it wasn't me. Phillip Clarkson ...he was getting into some really heavy stuff. That's why I got out when I did.'

'Like what?'

'Who knows? You might want to ask that reporter-guy — the birder — Chris Workman. He was always banging on about writing an exposé for his paper. Said he was going to 'clip the birdman's wings'.'

'I'll speak to him. But what sort of heavy stuff? You must have some idea. Drugs…?'

'No, no. OK, one night I went round to his place in Paddo and he's talking about getting into bird smuggling.'

Danniher turned away. 'Big deal!'

'It is. Believe me. I remember, one night Clarkson pulled out this article and started reading. Wildlife smuggling was now worth — what did he say? — five billion dollars a year. Bigger than illegal arms. Second only to drugs.'

'Keep going.'

'He'd obviously done his research. Apparently, you drug the birds and pack them into plastic tubes, like for paintings. Or you could just take the eggs. Either way, there was a big demand for Australian things like parrots and cockatoos in the United States, Japan, the Middle East.'

'Sounds risky.'

'You don't say. But he said the way to go was to launder them through New Zealand.'

'Why's that?'

'The wildlife export laws there are much laxer than in Oz.'

'Do you think he was serious?'

'At first I thought he was joking. But he was desperate and the thing is, he had it all worked out. Even talked about contacts up in Queensland — bird poachers — who could get him the birds.'

Danniher shook his head. 'I don't believe you.'

'It's the truth.'

'You know what I think? Smuggling was your idea. It was Clarkson who didn't want a part of it.'

'That's not true!'

'Well, we can't get his side of the story now, can we?'

Did Finch smirk? Danniher thought he did. 'Where were you on Saturday night?'

'Here. With my wife. Chloe.'

'And where is she right now?'

'Unless she's stuck in traffic, at the airport waiting to get on a plane to New York. You must have missed her by seconds. She's off to a buyers' meeting. She's in the rag trade.'

'Convenient.'

Danniher had been hoping that Finch's self-control would snap and, now, suddenly it did.

'This is ridiculous!' he yelled. 'Why would I want to kill Clarkson? The bloody man owed me hundreds of thousands of dollars.'

ဆဝဆဝဆဝ

Why me? thought Koslowski, half-hidden behind a wall of boxes containing the Birdman's papers. He'd never been good with figures. In fact, it was a joke between him and Marianne: he had only the sketchiest idea about how much money he had and almost no idea where it was to be found.

In short, he had, as his wife lovingly put it, 'the financial acumen of a mole'.

He hated going into banks. 'Not as a matter of principle — they make me feel sick,' he would explain. And when once he'd tried to use an automatic teller, the machine had chomped up his credit card after three unsuccessful attempts to input the correct key number.

Marianne had insisted he get a new card, but he used it only for the occasional purchases. All you had to do was answer a simple question — cheque, savings or credit? After some coaching, he could come up with the correct answer: 'credit'.

His wife did the rest. All she asked in return was that he put the 'yellow pieces of paper' called customer receipts — in a special envelope, so that they could be checked later against a statement.

For day-to-day cash Koslowski depended upon the $70 allowance his Marianne left on the table every Wednesday night. Why it should be Wednesday or why it should be $70 he never thought to ask.

Danniher had told him to yell out if the going got too tough: real financial experts would be called in. For now, Koslowski's orders were just to go through the papers and look out for anything unusual. So far, he had found no will (presumably Clarkson was not expecting to die so soon), no other diary and no revealing letters from family members or from lovers, male or female.

To Koslowski's untutored eye, the Birdman's business empire appeared chaotic, especially in the past few months, it seemed, after his PA Christine Withers had left in a hurry.

There were half-finished proposals to potential financial backers. There were hand-written copies of talks to be given to audiences that ranged from local government officials to countrywomen's groups to conservationists.

In many cases, Koslowski noticed, the same speech was delivered several times over, with one or two topical, or politic, changes to suit the audience. And there were lists of names signed up for guided tours going back a couple of years.

Koslowski recognised some names, including those of the two women Warnock and Griffiths, and Morris. They were each listed several times, for outings to different destinations.

He also found a duplicate of the list for the trip that never was. It showed that of the ten five had paid in advance, five hadn't. They were Morris, Enderby and the Waddells, although Clarkson, he noticed, had generously made a note to charge 14-year-old Emma Waddell only half price.

More revealing were Phillip Clarkson's bank statements, which looked much like those he'd seen his wife checking each month. Like she did, he ran his finger up and down the columns, for credits and debits, checking the incomings and outgoings for two accounts.

One was in the name of Phillip C. Clarkson, the other in his company name, Clarkson Eco-consult. Clecon, for short.

There were gaps: perhaps Clarkson had put them aside to query, perhaps with an impatient bank manager, or to show to someone else. Maybe he had simply mislaid them. However, even a financial mole such as Koslowski was not blind to the pattern of payments revealed in the statements.

Most outgoings were for regular, running expenses — things such as the mortgage, which he may have shared with his mother, repayments on the car, food, drink, petrol, water, electricity and telephone, meals out, membership subscriptions and, only rarely, entertainments. Some hefty tax bills had been paid, though Koslowski had no way of telling whether much, if any, back-tax was still owing.

What he could see was that Clarkson had been slipping into debt for some time.

For, superimposed on these 'household expenses' were a series of irregular but substantial payments. Some were to companies whose names suggested they'd supplied equipment, booked travel or accommodation. Some were familiar names, including Fantasy Island Inc and S. Finch. Others were to individuals whose names Koslowski did not recognise. Possibly crew. Investors. Blackmailers. They would have to be checked.

The incomings, at least until the last few months, had been even more erratic. Three years earlier, Koslowski noted, there'd been a credit for almost $80,000 from a television network, presumably for the sale — or pre-sale — of one of the Birdman documentaries.

There'd been a regular trickle of small payments, usually of $50 or multiples thereof, from birders going on tours, and larger payments for up to $2,000, from what sounded like tour groups, organisations and companies. For speaking engagements, Koslowski guessed. And there were credits for middling amounts from what looked like newspapers and magazines, who evidently paid generous freelance rates for authoritative pieces by one of Australia's leading naturalists.

Nothing out of the ordinary there, thought Koslowski. However, as he worked through the more recent statements he was surprised to see two names repeated with increasing regularity in the credit column: Berwick Shire Council and Pelican Industrial Estates.

Interesting. PIE. Could this be the mysterious 'PE' found in the dead man's diary? He would check with Danniher. Meanwhile, one thing was obvious: for several months up to his death, only payments by these two bodies had enabled the Birdman to defy financial gravity.

The amounts involved had been increasingly gradually, had been suddenly switched to monthly basis and, he now noticed, had, for a long time, been identical. As if some total payment was being shared. So, why were BC and PE each paying Clecon $2,500 a month?

'You still here then, Kiwi?' Sergeant Adamovitch's gruff voice shook

Koslowski out of his trance.

'Obviously,' he replied, shaking his head.

'Well, you shouldn't be.'

'Day off?'

'Haven't you heard? Jonno's abolished them. No, Clarkson's funeral. Two-thirty. You promised Danniher you'd be there.'

Koslowski was already rushing from the room.

10

Sunday Night: Cigar Night Parrot Club 363 Calle Fortaleza San Juan, Puerto Rico.
—- Ask Jeeves Internet search engine in answer to the question 'Where can I find a night parrot?'

A dark suit, a white shirt and a black tie couldn't disguise the fact that Kiwi Koslowski hated going to funerals — and especially going to funerals for the victims of unsolved murders. It wasn't that he was unmoved by the tears of the bereaved. Or that he resented the accusing looks they shot at the bungling police who'd failed to find whoever killed their loved one.

No, what he hated most about funerals such as Phillip Clarkson's was that they were almost always a waste of valuable police time. Take this afternoon, for instance. Koslowski just knew that the bereaved would be better served if he worked on solving a murder case instead of going to the church to share their sorrow. Certainly, Jonno Sedgwick would have preferred it.

As he had tried to explain to when he was being briefed by Danniher earlier, Jonno was now 'going troppo' over the lack of bodies to throw at the Berwick crime wave. But Danniher had been so insistent on mixing with people at the funeral, 'showing them we care', that Koslowski wondered if the big man was morphing into Palmeira. Next thing, he'd be drinking mineral water and getting Path Prior to pack him a salad for lunch.

'Mate,' he'd said. 'I want you to go.'

'But, Wayne, both of us? Jonno'll freak, if he finds out.'

'He won't. Point is, Kiwi, you never know who else might turn up.'

Koslowski shook his head. In his book, funerals only produced results in crime movies. He could just picture the typical cemetery scene: tearful women, wearing veils to hide their tears; vengeful men, wearing black, ill-fitting suits to hide muscles that were fast turning to fat; a minister going through his 'ashes to ashes' routine as they all stood, heads bowed, staring into a hole in the ground.

And, just out of frame, the police, hovering respectfully in the background, hoping that the murderer would turn up to pay his last respects. Or, if he or she was already present, that they'd break down at the graveside and confess.

The scene at St Mary's Church could scarcely have been more different, thought Koslowski, as he and Danniher arrived to find more than 100 people standing in the churchyard, chattering noisily, waiting 'to farewell and to celebrate the life of Phillip Clarkson', as the program put it.

Far from being an intimate family funeral of the kind featured in movies, this seemed to be a celebrity bash: somewhere to see and be seen, and to swap gossip with showbiz cronies on why a man known to millions for his love of birds was found dead, butt-naked, on a gay beach.

Pooling their limited knowledge of prime-time TV, the two men could pick out several famous faces, and some of their names.

There was the celebrity-pet vet, famous for being savaged on live TV by a gerbil; a team of TV angels who gave fifty-something women make-overs, and the married couple who had re-located from their inner-city apartment to live in the bush as simple, 19th-century Australian settlers. They had survived for 12 weeks and scored top ratings but, according to the gossip columnists, had separated immediately after the series. Must tell Marianne, thought Koslowski. Despite her high-powered teaching job, she loved all that sort of soapie stuff.

Four television networks, several women's magazines — one of which had tried to buy exclusive rights to the event — and the three newspapers had reporters on the spot. The funeral was a great opportunity to reopen speculation about the grisly murder and to crucify the police for failing to solve the crime.

Almost immediately, Danniher was accosted by a young woman. He recognised her as one of Palmeira's media pals, Karen Chan.

'Sir, sir, I know now's not the best time to ask, but is it true the Birdman investigations are already being scaled down?'

'No,' he replied exasperatedly.

'Sorry. No, as in, they're not being scaled down? That's what we heard. Or…'

'No. No as in, no, now's not a good time to ask. If you'll excuse me…'

Danniher moved quickly away with Koslowski, who was already itching uncomfortably inside his collar and tie. A little further on, they saw Clarkson's mother and his brother, who acknowledged them with a nod. Paul's attempts to smarten himself for the occasion had only made him look sleazier, shiftier, more menacing, like a reject from a Tarantino movie, thought Koslowski, nodding back.

Koslowski introduced his colleague to Marcy Roy who, he was disappointed to see, was with several scruffy, 'creative'-looking types. She had just started to explain that they were members of Clarkson's old film crews when the gathering began moving into the church for the service.

On their way to their seats, the two police officers noticed other familiar faces. Derek Morris, dithering over where to sit. Simon Finch nervously checking his watch, probably to see how much money this time was costing him. Christopher Workman, not with Jane but another equally attractive woman, Danniher noted. And the two older ladies, sitting together.

With the help of family and friends, the Reverend Tony Birmingham had produced a service that was designed to capture the mood of the moment and the audience. There were readings that reflected the dead man's supposed anti-materialism. 'Consider the lilies of the field, how they grow; they toil not, neither do they spin. And yet I say unto you, that even Solomon in all his glory was not arrayed like one of these.'

There were hymns, such as *All Creatures Great and Small*, that lauded the ornithologist's love of nature. And there was a eulogy that skilfully celebrated his achievements while avoiding any mention of the squalid circumstances in which he had shuffled, in signature boots, from the mortal coil.

More than once Danniher and Koslowski exchanged meaningful glances. Who did these people think they were kidding? But then this was showbiz. And by the time the body was carried away for private cremation, many of those left behind in the church were left wondering whether, perhaps, they'd been harsh on poor old Phillip. Perhaps he hadn't been such a bastard after all.

ဢဢဢ

Back in the churchyard, Danniher and Koslowski caught up with the small group of birders, who were discussing plans to get together for another outing. 'As soon as all this, mmm, unpleasantness is over,' Derek Morris explained.

'Mr Workman!' Danniher said. 'Sad Jane couldn't be with you today.'

The PR man seemed unfazed by the jibe. 'Ah, constable. So nice to see you, again. This is Emily, my researcher,' he said without a blush.

'Of course, pleased to meet you, Emily.' Danniher turned back to Workman. 'And how's the research going?'

'Good. Good. Thanks. Just a few loose ends for Emily and me to tie up, but I hope to have a couple of pieces, maybe even a three-part series, ready for publication soon.'

'I'll look forward to reading that,' said Danniher amicably.

'You will?'

'Yes,' replied Danniher, his tone turning hostile. 'I'll be checking every word to see if you've obstructed police inquiries by withholding evidence.'

Without another word, Workman mumbled some goodbyes, grabbed Emily by the hand and dragged her away. Danniher turned to the other birders, who had been standing expectantly, waiting to see what, if anything, the police would require of them.

'So, Mr Morris. You made it all right then?'

Morris seemed puzzled. 'Sorry, sergeant, I d-d-don't understand.'

'Transport. I thought you had a problem with transport.'

'Oh, I see. Yes. Thank you. I, umm, took a taxi.'

Danniher nodded. He changed the subject. 'Good turn out.'

'I suppose so,' replied Morris. He seemed to regard the people leaving with distaste.

'You didn't see Ellis Enderby among them, by any chance?'

Again Morris looked surprised.

'You do know Mr Enderby?'

'Yes. Dear me, no. I err, err, I don't think he'd come.'

'Really?' said Koslowski.

'No. No.'

'Why not? I thought he was a fellow birder.'

'I suppose so. But, you see, Ellis and Phillip didn't, umm, get along at all. They had this silly, err — what would you all it? — contretemps some years ago. A big slanging match. They stormed off in opposite directions and never, err, spoke to each other again. As far as I know.'

'Any idea what it was all about?' Danniher asked, as casually as he could. It did not work: Morris now seemed spooked by the line of questioning.

'Oh dear, sergeant. I don't know what to do. You know what they say, m-m-mustn't speak ill of the dead. Ah, not that Ellis Enderby is dead, of course. Far from it, I...'

'But Clarkson is.'

'Yes, well, Phillip was much, err, younger that Ellis...'

'And how old is Enderby?' Danniher demanded.

'Late fifties, early sixties, I'd say. He was a trained umm, naturalist, respected expert on birds and things. He made lots of wildlife documentaries himself, you know. Well respected. Not that he ever became a "personality" like Clarkson.'

A personality. Like Roy, Morris seemed to spit the word out as if he strongly disapproved of the concept.

'Go on,' prompted Danniher.

Morris exhaled noisily and tried to compose himself. 'I think Ellis was happy to help someone like Phillip when he err, err, arrived on the scene. But, as I say, they had this umm, umm, bust-up eventually.'

Danniher tried his question again. 'Yes, but what about?'

'This was all a very long time ago. Water under the bridge...'

'I know. But what?'

'Err, err, something about who'd spotted some special bird or other. There was all this "oh yes I did, oh no you didn't" business between the two of them. All very childish. It all got quite out of hand. They were at it for m-m-months — bickering, making threats, writing letters to the journals.'

'It sounds serious,' said Koslowski.

'More like unseemly, I'd say,' said Morris, picking his word carefully. 'And deeply regrettable. You see it didn't do much for the reputation of birding to have two of its best-known proponents, you know, s-s-slogging it out in public. Hammer and tongs.'

'I see.'

'To be honest, I could see it coming. It was inevitable that sooner or later they would come to blows... not literally, of course.'

'Why?'

'The old story, two big f-f-fish in a small pond. Australia is, you know?'

'What?'

'A small pond. Experts, sergeant, are a bit like birds, I suppose. They tend to be territorial. You know, this is my patch, stay out. Perhaps Australia was err, err, too small a patch for more than one Birdman.'

'So Clarkson chased Enderby away,' Koslowski suggested.

'Exactly,' said Morris. 'Another thing. Despite the age difference, Phillip and Ellis were very much alike. You know: didn't suffer fools, tended to ride roughshod over others, et cetera, et cetera. Big egos, short tempers, I suppose.'

Morris fell silent, and stared down intently at his scuffed, black shoes. Obviously he felt he had said enough. Or too much.

'Do you know Enderby well?' asked Koslowski.

'Actually, I did. He was more my g-g-generation,' replied Morris. Koslowski suppressed a smile. The stutter made the sentence sound like a line from an old pop song. 'Hope I die before I get old', eh? Who was it? The Who.

Danniher hadn't even noticed. 'You say "did," Mr Morris?'

'D-d-did I? Well, yes. I did. We met through bird groups, went to the same meetings and for a while my wife and I were good friends with Ellis and...well, whoever he was living with at the time...'

The two policemen looked baffled.

'Sorry, you know, of course, he was, err...?'

Koslowski nodded. 'Oh I see.' Gay.

'But then something, umm, happened. He seemed to change, became bitter. He had this row with Phillip Clarkson, lost his regular slot on the, err, television and...I don't know, started drinking m-m-more. He always did like a drink.'

'Terrible,' said Danniher, with the clarity of one who had not touched a drop for several days.

'After a while, he, he, decided to move out of the city... got this big new place up at Palm Beach, where the rich and famous live. Sort of faded from the scene. We went up there a few times to see him — Margaret and I — but it was, err, a long way from Kurnell.'

Out of the corner of his eye, Danniher could see the other birders were becoming restless, but he sensed Morris was running out of steam.

'And anyway, as I say, the row with Clarkson — the young l-l-lion as it were — seemed to change him. At first we kept in touch telephoning and writing to each other every now and then…but, umm, umm, I suppose he lost interest in birds. Or at least in birders.'

'So when did you last see him?'

'Three or four years ago, it must be.'

'And you say he isn't here today.'

'No. I d-d-don't think I'd miss him. Tall chap, big beard, red face — from the whisky, he always said. Very distinguished-looking in his day, of course.'

Morris had said enough. He looked at is watch.

'Sorry. I must be going. Err, err I have a taxi picking me up.'

'So must I,' said Simon Finch, hovering on the edge of the group. 'I've wasted enough of today already,' he told Danniher accusingly.

Only the two women, Maddy Warnock and Libby Griffiths, remained. They seemed in no rush to leave and now stood smiling inscrutably at the two policemen.

'I thought you or that other nice officer, the small man, I can't remember his name, would have come to take our statements by now,' said Warnock. 'It was me who first spotted the legs you know.'

'Yes, I know. I'm sorry, ladies. We've been a bit busy. Unfortunately, the little man — that's Detective Inspector Palmeira — had a little accident in the dunes himself and is out of action. So we've been stretched.'

'Nothing too serious, I hope,' said Griffiths.

'Not at all,' Danniher assured them. 'He'll be back on the case in next to no time.'

'Time we made a move, boss,' Koslowski whispered under his breath, before speaking aloud. 'So if there nothing else, ladies?'

'I don't think so,' said Warnock.

Griffiths still wanted to talk. 'Do you think one of us is involved in the murder, officer?'

Danniher looked at her sternly. 'We have to consider every possibility.' The warning seemed to excite the women.

Warnock brightened. 'Did you know, we're going to go on another walk together?'

'Sounds fun,' said Koslowski, anxious now to get back to the office.

'Yes. They're such lovely people. I can't believe that one of them would...'

Griffiths corrected her. 'Most of them are lovely. That young man, Simon, he can be a bit pushy.'

'But he's harmless, I think,' said Warnock. 'And of course we don't really know that family.'

'The Waddells,' Danniher prompted.

'That's right. The mother and girl never said a word and the man... well, a rough diamond.'

'Not the sort to turn up to a funeral, you'd have thought,' added Griffiths.

'What!' Both men spoke almost simultaneously. 'You mean he was here?'

'Oh, yes. He was on his own, I think, but he said hello,' said Griffiths. 'He was telling me that only th...'

Danniher interrupted her. 'Is he here now?' This is just like in the movies, thought Koslowski.

'Let's see,' said Warnock looking round. 'You can't really miss him. He really is very f...'

'...big,' Griffiths interjected.

'There he is, over there,' Warnock announced, before shouting after the big man, 'Mr Waddell...'

Her words tailed off, as the man turned round, saw the women in conversation with two official-looking men in suits and started running through the churchyard gate and down the street. For a big man, he had an unexpected turn of speed.

Danniher and Koslowski set off in pursuit, snaking through the funeral stragglers. Sorry... Excuse me... Let us through... Police... police.

It was too late. With some 30 metres start, Waddell outpaced the two policemen. In the distance they could see him pull up and jump in a maroon Land Cruiser, parked in a side-street. Like its owner, the heavy vehicle proved surprisingly quick off the mark, twisting in its parking place and turning into a line of traffic. There was a head-turning screech of tyres, as other cars were forced to brake to make room.

Koslowski watched the Land Cruiser disappear. 'What kept you, mate?' he said when, a few seconds later, Danniher arrived, puffing.

'Old football injury. The point is, did you get the rego?'

'Enough of it, I reckon. NH something 0 something 1. I think. Can't be that many maroon Land Cruisers around.'

'No. Thank goodness. I'll get it checked out.'

'I'll do it. You better have a sit down, mate. You're getting too old for this sort of thing. For one moment back there, I thought you'd end up with Pamela in hospital.'

⳥⳥⳥

In fact, Palmeira had already left hospital. Against the advice of his doctor, his wife and his colleagues, who'd said they could easily cope without him, he had already shaved, dressed, collected a pair of crutches, arranged transport and gone straight to Berwick police station.

He now sat, dressed like a canary in a yellow and green Brazil soccer shirt, a gift from colleagues and a pair of neatly pressed blue shorts, with his plaster-encased leg on a second chair, alongside PC Helen McCrimond at a computer. As promised, they were playing hunt the parrot.

For more than two hours they'd been searching through the Internet for the elusive night parrot — the bird that seemed to have triggered the feud between Phillip Clarkson and Ellis Enderby. Now they were closing on it.

To Palmeira and McCrimond, it was difficult at first to see what all the fuss had been about. An old picture of the night parrot showed a very ordinary-looking bird of subdued green, yellow and black colouring, peering quizzically out from behind a clump of grass. To their untrained eyes, it looked like what McCrimond called an overweight budgerigar.

'A bit like my dad used to keep in his loft back in Glasgow,' McCrimond explained. But as Palmeira explained, *pezoporus occidentalis* — he read out its scientific name — was no ordinary bird.

'From what it says here it's a sort of feathered version of the Tasmanian tiger.' The legendary — and almost certainly extinct — thylacine.

Was the night parrot extinct? The subject, Palmeira learned, had divided experts for decades. There'd been half a dozen full-scale searches and two big publicity campaigns to find the bird. One Australian businessman had even offered a big cash prize to anyone able to prove the bird's existence.

The bird had inspired novels, newsreels and even poems. 'Hey listen to this,' announced Palmeira. 'It's about our bird.' He read from a poem by someone called John Kinsella.

> If at all, then fringe dwellers
> of the centre.
> Ghosts of samphire, navigators
> of the star-clustered tussocks.
> Of salty marsh, limestone niches
> and acrid airs.
>
> If at all, then flitting obscurely
> the rims of water tanks, the outlands
> of spotlights and filaments of powerlines…
> in brief nocturnal flight, with long
> drawn out mournful whistle
>
> If at all, then moths in a paper lantern.

McCrimond seemed moved. 'How romantic.'

But it was a romance that appeared to have an unhappy ending. After being spotted in and around Central Australia through the second half of the 19th century, the bird appeared suddenly to disappear. As early as 1915, it was reported to have been exterminated. By the mid-20th century, it was being written off as, in Koslowski's words, a dead parrot.

So who killed it, DI Palmeira wanted to know. Experts, he discovered, came up with a list of suspects: feral cats and foxes, who preyed on the parrot; humans, whose changed fire and farming regimes helped to destroy its traditional habitat; and rabbits, cattle and even camels, who stole its food and water.

Birders had not given up all hope of finding a night parrot, however. Like a lost gold reef or a lost city the mysterious disappearance of the bird had captured people's imagination. They lived in hope, eagerly devouring reports of any sighting, however unreliable.

In the 1970s, a camel expedition from Adelaide to the Cooper Creek area flushed out four birds, believed to be night parrots, from the undergrowth. Even a brief glimpse was sufficient to reduce the leader of the expedition, a South Australian museum director, to a state of shock. A fellow explorer later described him as 'frozen on the rear camel, one arm pointing and his face looking whiter than his pith helmet'.

Then, in 1990, McCrimond was delighted to read, an actual night parrot was found. Sadly, a dead one. Its corpse was found purely by chance. A member of an Australian Museum team, which had spent six weeks criss-crossing the northern half of the continent looking for the bird, had stopped by the side of the road in a remote part of western Queensland.

He looked down and there it was. The bird had been killed by a car or a truck. Its head had become detached, much of its tail was missing and its plumage was faded. A vet said it'd probably been dead for between three and 12 months. But it was, unmistakably, a night parrot.

'Poor wee thing.'

'Died in a hit and run accident as well,' added Palmeira. He was enjoying researching the subject with McCrimond. 'What happened next, then?' he asked her.

Not much it appeared. A Sydney newspaper had reported that a German scientist was convinced he'd seen a pair of birds at a water hole one night somewhere out in the Northern Territory, in the back of beyond.

'Did he get a photo?' asked Palmeira.

'It seems not. Though from what it says here he seems to be regarded as an excellent witness,' said McCrimond, scrolling the newspaper article on the screen.

Palmeira was intrigued. 'So what was a German doing out in the Australian bush at night?'

'Mmm.' McCrimond read on. 'Here it is. Studying the sex life of feral camels.'

She burst out laughing. A very attractive laugh, thought Palmeira.

'You're joking.'

'No, sir, honest. Look.' Together, their heads almost touching, they read to the end of the article. There had been talk of using dogs, specially trained to locate threatened wildlife by scent, to search for the blessed parrot. And satellite tracking to monitor rainfall, which seemed to have an effect on the vegetation where the bird had been spotted. And 24-hour video surveillance of water holes. The bird seemed about as elusive as the Birdman's murderer, thought Palmeira. At least the parrot was not officially dead, just 'critically endangered'.

'Fascinating story, eh sir?'

'A real mystery. Next they'll be cloning the poor thing,' he replied, recalling the work being done with Tasmanian tiger DNA. 'Hey presto! A back from the dead parrot.'

McCrimond laughed.

Palmeira now felt he knew why the night parrot meant so much to birders. In a funny way it had come to represent other Australian birds threatened with extinction. It had assumed an almost mystical quality. He could also understand the thrill of the chase. He could appreciate how the report of a new sighting would cause enormous excitement and pride. Not to mention suspicion and controversy.

But really! At the end of the day, it was still only a flaming parrot. What did McCrimond call it? 'An overweight budgie.' Hardly worth coming to blows over — let alone fatal blows — thought Palmeira. Hardly a motive for murder.

With Clarkson now dead and buried, there was only one man left alive who could confirm that. As McCrimond ran to the canteen to fetch him an orange juice — after all he was incapacitated — he picked up the phone and tapped out a number.

'Hello, is Mr Ellis Enderby there please?'

ಐಐಐ

Not far away, DCs Park and Holmes were standing, waiting on the doorstep of prime suspect Gordon Waddell. Park rang the bell for a third time and, finally, the door was opened, by a young girl. In her early teens, they guessed.

She was wearing a pair of tight low-slung jeans and a short T-shirt, between which bulged a generous roll of white flesh. The girl was carrying an open packet of chips. From the familiar theme music coming from inside the fibro bungalow, Park guessed she'd been vegging out in front of an American soap-opera.

'Hello, is your father in?' he asked.

'No,' she said, without further explanation.

A bigger, adult version of the girl now appeared in the doorway. 'Who is it, Em?'

'Two people looking for dad.'

Park tried again. 'Hello Mrs Waddell. Remember me?'

She looked at him and Holmes blankly. 'Oh, you're the cop from the murder,' she said eventually.

'Correct. And this is DC Holmes. A colleague.'

'How youse both going?'

'We're after your husband, Mrs Waddell.'

'Well, you've come to the wrong place. For one thing, I'm not Mrs Waddell.'

'You are not the wife of Gordon Anthony Waddell?'

'Certainly not. I'm Mrs Flett. Geraldine Flett. And that's my daughter Emma,' she added, pointing back into the house where the bored teenager had already retreated to watch television.

'So Waddell, Mr Waddell, isn't here?'

'No.'

Park and Holmes looked at each other, confused. Suddenly, what should have been the successful conclusion to a good day's work was turning into a horrible mess. Sedgwick would be really furious this time.

It was Jonno Sedgwick who, three hours earlier, had sent the two officers off in search of Waddell. Park and Holmes had just come on duty that afternoon, after another long night trawling city clubs for witnesses, when Sedgwick marched in.

'You know where I've just been?' he yelled, spotting them.

'No sir,' replied Park, already fearing the worse.

'I'll tell you: a meeting of the neighbourhood watch coordinating committee.' Evidently it had not gone well. 'For 90 minutes I've had my ears hammered by people wanting to know when the police are going to anything about these bashings, thefts and such like.'

'Sorry, sir.'

'They're getting out of hand.'

Park and Holmes started to back off.

'Where are you two going?'

'A tour of the local pubs, sir,' said Park.

'Still chasing up witnesses,' Holmes added, just in time to head off an explosion.

'Where is everyone?'

Park explained.

'This can't go on. I just can't afford to have you lot going off to funerals, cruising round pubs and clubs and lying about in hospital.' Clearly, Sedgwick hadn't heard that Palmeira was back in the office.

'I told Danniher we needed some quick results — or you're both going to be back here clearing up all this local crime.'

'I thought we'd been given 48 hours, sir.'

'Don't be smart with me, son. Anyway, I thought Danniher said he was close to an arrest. This man, what's his name...?'

'Waddell?'

'Yes. So why isn't he in the cells having the truth beaten out of him with a house brick?'

Park hesitated before telling Sedgwick. 'We can't find him, sir. I believe he gave a false address last time.'

'What! I want this man brought in this afternoon. Not tomorrow, not tonight. Now. Understand?'

Sedgwick stomped off, leaving Park and Holmes wondering what to do.

'Could try the telephone directory,' suggested Holmes. 'The other guys may have missed that — I mean, they thought they'd already got the address.'

Reluctantly, Park had checked. To his surprise, she was right. There was a listing for a Gordon A. Waddell. Within 15 minutes, he and Holmes were at the address in Mascot — only to discover that once again the address was wrong.

'How do you mean, he's not here?' Holmes asked Mrs Flett.

'He's gone.'

'What, to work?'

'No, I told you, didn't I? He doesn't live here any more. You can check if you like.'

Holmes tried again. 'Look, Mrs Waddell…'

'Flett.'

'Sorry. Flett…'

'He did live here. Up until a month ago. Then he shot through. Glad to see the back of him, to be honest. Though he does come back every so often.'

'But I thought you and…Emma were with him on Sunday? You remember, when you found the body?' said Park. Was she being deliberately obstructive or just routinely stupid? he wondered.

'Yes, that's right. Awful it was.'

'Well, we want to talk to Gordon about it.'

'I see.' She sounded disappointed that the police did not have questions for her.

'And talk to you, of course,' Park started to explain, when his mobile rang. 'Excuse me.' It was McCrimond. Waddell had been spotted a couple of hours earlier driving a maroon Land Cruiser. The owner and the address were now being checked.

A bit late, thought Park, turning back to Mrs Flett. 'Sorry. Yes, we'll talk to you, but first it's very important we find Gordon. You know he gave us a false address?'

'Two false addresses,' added Holmes.

'No. But it doesn't surprise me. He's an odd sort of bloke. You better come in.' Mrs Flett took the two officers through to the kitchen, leaving Emma to watch television.

'Gordy's not her father, you know,' she explained in a low, conspiratorial voice.

'No?'

'No. That was Dougie Flett.'

'Oh.'

'Yes. My de facto.'

'What happened?

'He shot through as well. But that was years ago, like.'

'And Gordon?'

'Me and him have been an item, like on and off, for about four years.'

'But now "off"?'

'Yes. As I say, he does come back to collect his mail now and then. I thought this one would stay, but a few weeks back, he announces he's off. Said he was bored living with me and Em. Can you believe it?'

Park ignored the question. 'Can we have a look 'round?'

'If you want. But you won't find anything. He took all his stuff. Or I chucked it out.'

While Holmes took a look around inside, Park pressed on. 'Any idea where he is now?'

'Not really. He said he was going to crash at a mate's place until he found a unit.'

'Do you know the mate?'

'Only met him once. Somebody Kenworth? Kenning? Something like that. Works at the council. Something to do with garbage collection, I think Gordy said.'

'Same line of business as Mr Waddell.'

'How do you mean?'

'Waste disposal.'

Mrs Flett looked perplexed.

Park tried again. 'Waste disposal. Mr Waddell is the boss of a waste disposal company, isn't he?'

Mrs Flett laughed, wobbling alarmingly. 'Only in his dreams, love.'

'So what does he do?'

The question made Mrs Flett frown. 'You know, I was never really sure. Bit of a mystery man was Gordon. Always a bit vague. Always up to something. "This and that", he'd say. Or, "Doing a job for a mate". Always popping out suddenly, even in the evenings. "Something's cropped up", he'd say. And he'd be out of here.'

'But he must have had some money coming in,' said Park. 'That's an expensive vehicle he's driving.'

'Oh, it isn't his. I think he was, like, borrowing it. For his jobs.'

'Sounds a real loser,' said Park, sensing Mrs Flett had long ago reached the same conclusion.

'Yeah. He did have a company, into recycling and things, he told me once. But it went bust, I think. He said he hadn't come out of it too badly. But he never seemed to have a couple of cents to rub together. Always tapping me for a loan, he was.'

'What do you do, Mrs Flett?'

'Check-out at the local supermarket.'

'I don't know how you all managed.'

'No...he wasn't a bad man. He had a temper on him, but he never took it out on me or Emma.'

'Pleased to hear it. Big man like that could cause a lot of damage,' said Park. He wondered whether Mrs Flett knew Waddell had a criminal record. 'From what you say, he doesn't sound like your average bird enthusiast.'

'Not the feathered sort, anyway, eh? I don't think he gave a rats about them.'

'So why did the three of you go along on the outing?'

'No idea. Me and Em didn't really want to. But he said he wanted to get close to Clarkson. Those were his very words — "I've got to get close to Mr Birdman". And he was on telly. Em thought she might get his autograph.'

'Did Mr Waddell tell you why he wanted to get close to Clarkson?'

'No. Something to do with the deal he was planning, to do with the bay, I think. Turned out to be a wasted day, didn't it?'

'I suppose so.'

Holmes emerged, blinking into the sunlight. 'Nothing sarge though we could get forensics to take a look.' She turned to Mrs Flett. 'You don't have a photo of Mr Waddell by any chance?'

'No, love. He hated having his picture taken.'

Park and Holmes looked at each other. Yes, they agreed tacitly, they'd come to a dead end. 'Jonno's not going to like this,' said Holmes.

Just then Park's mobile rang. McCrimond again.

'That rego check on the maroon Land Cruiser.'

'Don't tell me. Gordon A.Waddell, 14 Lilac Drive, Mascot. Right?'

'Wrong. Michael M. Kenyon, 2/17, Ocean Street, Berwick.'

11

Establishing a territory can be hard work, requiring continuous vigilance to defend and maintain it. There may be a different set of problems in the centre of a territory as against the fringe of it, called the centre-edge effect, and the territory may never be secure from takeover by intruder.
— Gisela Kaplan & Lesley J. Rogers, *Birds, Their Habits and Skills*

Sparkling waters. Shimmering, impossibly blue skies. And temperatures tipped to peak in the high-20s. You've got to love this city, Wayne Danniher thought, not for the first time, as he navigated a police-issue Ford Falcon from the strip-lit blackness of the Harbour Tunnel and set sail, as it were, for the northernmost of Sydney's ocean beaches.

It'd been many months since he'd crossed the harbour on to the North Shore in pursuit of criminals. Not that its affluent suburbs were free from murder and mayhem. Indeed Mosman, the most affluent of them all, had an infamous history of crime that included a serial granny-killer, the kerbside murder of a world-famous heart surgeon and, in more distant times, an assassination attempt on a leading federal politician at the local Town Hall.

It was because Danniher knew the southern suburbs, their people and their police officers intimately, in a way only a long-time resident could, that he tended to be directed to jobs on the south side by his bosses at the Homicide HQ at Strawberry Hills.

Now, he was looking forward to the 45-minute trip through 'God's own country', up the peninsula to Palm Beach. It would take him along Military Road, where they used to roll out the gun-barrels for the harbour defences built on Middle Head, down through the snaky S-bends leading to the Spit Bridge, and out past world-famous surf beaches such as Curl Curl, Collaroy and Narrabeen. According to the locals, it was on such beaches that the Lucky Country's dole-bludgers queued to catch waves.

It would have been nice to stop for a bite of lunch on the way back, he thought, preferably at one of those waterside restaurants looking back across Pittwater, with its windsurfers, sail boats and sleek cruisers. Danniher felt he deserved some downtime. After his late start on the Birdman inquiry, he'd been working up to 15 hours a day. Detectives were used to such long hours, especially in big, fast-moving murder hunts. On countless occasions he had slept on the office floor, too tired to drive himself home safely.

He'd managed to grab a few hours' sleep in his own bed, but the case was playing havoc with his social life. Thank goodness, Sandy Prior knew the demands of the job, knew what she was letting herself in for. Pity he couldn't have taken her along. Instead he had Mario Palmeira as a passenger. He was now stretched out across the back seat, the seam of his trousers unstitched on one side, his exposed injured leg supported on a couple of cushions.

Much to Homicide HQ's amusement, the two men had been rubbing along smoothly, but in the 15 minutes since Danniher had picked up Palmeira from his home, they had barely exchanged a word.

If he'd been on his own, Danniher would have selected a rock music channel on the car radio, set the volume too loud, wound down the window, and driven with his elbow out of the window, crooning loudly to some old seventies hits.

Now, he pressed the pre-set button for the rolling news station and politely asked, 'All right by you, sir?'

'Fine, just so long as it's not one of those talkback programs,' came the reply from the rear.

Both men agreed: one reason police work had become far more difficult in recent years was because it had become far more politicised. Governments today made knee-jerk reactions to whatever the radio shock-jocks were saying on any particular morning.

The two men fell back into silent thought, staring out at a sun-blessed world of people contentedly going about their business and pleasure. It seemed strangely at odds with the widespread doom and gloom and violent crime being described on the radio.

ഇൻഇൻഇൻ

Unlike Danniher, Palmeira had found it difficult to adopt a sunny disposition. The prospect of enforced inactivity still filled him gloom: after only a couple of days, he was feeling claustrophobic. Though Jenny and the girls had provided lashings of love and sympathy, and even a packed lunch for the Palm Beach trip, he feared he'd quickly exhaust their patience.

Jenny had shaken her head in dismay at his decision to return to work and, he guessed, she'd only postponed her plans to return to full-time work. Now he felt that the issue lay, like a stick of dynamite, waiting to blow them apart. Of course, they needed the extra money her job would bring in. And of course, he recognised that she needed to work to feel truly fulfilled. She was a bright, attractive woman and he was proud of her. Hey, he didn't want to be old-fashioned, but he could not see how he could do his job and shoulder more of the domestic chores of shopping, cleaning and being around for the girls. Perhaps in a few more years…

Then there was the Birdman inquiry. The butterfly-brained media had temporarily moved on to some other passing fancy, but Sedgwick was ropeable. In his view, the case was gobbling up resources, desperately needed to deal with his crime wave. And, worse, it seemed to be going nowhere.

What if today's expedition to see Ellis Enderby turn out to be just another futile expedition? The possibility already made him feel sick in the stomach.

Perhaps he should have stayed back at the office, overseeing the others and organising. He could have staged something new for the media: a tearful plea by Mrs Clarkson for information leading to the arrest of her son's killer. Or the release of the pictures of the two vehicles that featured in the crime: Clarkson's Volkswagen and Waddell's Land Cruiser.

Still, he could do that later, while Park and Holmes continued to hunt Waddell. For the time being, he should concentrate on Enderby. By all accounts, he was, like the elusive night parrot, an odd bird. He was now in his mid-sixties, looking back on a life that seemed best summed up in a series of those awful old newspaper euphemisms.

He was 'a confirmed bachelor'. In his heyday, long before gays gained the self-confidence and pride on display in the annual Sydney Mardi Gras, he'd become a fixture at the Oxford Street clubs. He was 'a colourful identity', a man who'd surrounded himself with people who had police records: associates, contacts, friends, lovers, whatever. He was a man prone to becoming 'tired and emotional'. He was, by all accounts, irascible.

But was he, by his own hands or those of another, a killer? And why on earth did he book to go on a bird tour with a man he had first fought with and then shunned for years? And why, after booking, had he not turned up? Palmeira was just beginning to drown in self-doubt when he was thrown a lifeline by Danniher.

'Almost there sir,' he said, nodding ahead towards the landmark white lighthouse standing atop Barrenjoey Head. 'Feeling OK?'

♊♊♊

The door to Ellis Enderby's home was opened by a middle-aged woman who wearily introduced herself as his housekeeper. She made it sound like a job she'd endured without enjoyment for centuries.

'Come in. He's expecting you.' She was as brusque as her employer was reputed to be and seemed to ignore the fact that one of the two visitors was struggling to cope with crutches. Perhaps she was used to people turning up with broken limbs, thought Danniher, recalling rumours that Enderby had once been close mates with a notorious Kings Cross debt-collector known as The Knee-capper.

'I'll warn you now, though. He's in a cranky mood this morning.'

'Thanks,' said Palmeira, gingerly negotiating an archipelago of small rugs and pieces of carpet thrown haphazardly across a slippery-looking sea of shiny pine flooring.

Even from outside, the two policemen could hear the old man shouting, presumably into a telephone, giving someone — a neighbour, a council official or a local politician, they guessed — an angry lecture on the subjects of noise, nuisance, sea-planes and helicopters. He did not stop to acknowledge their arrival.

'Sit down,' the housekeeper said with a sigh, herding them through a large living room to a balcony almost as big. 'He may be some time.'

The two men shrugged and followed orders. A cup of something would go down great, thought Danniher. But the housekeeper walked away to tackle chores elsewhere in the house, leaving the men to amuse themselves.

While Palmeira tried to make his leg comfortable, Danniher stood and crossed to the low stainless steel railings running round the edge of the balcony, a cantilevered construction that seemed to reach with outstretched arms into the wide blue yonder. The drop to the cliffs below was dizzying.

'Mate, you wouldn't want to come sleep-walking out here in the middle of the night,' said Danniher, lifting his eyes to take in the view across the ocean. It was spectacular and seemed to go on forever. 'Wow!' Danniher whistled.

Palmeira wasn't listening. He was far more interested in the living room. Though the cliff-top house itself was modern, the interior decoration was incongruously old-fashioned — as though the contents of a 1920s Federation-style home had, several years ago, been unloaded into a new, futuristic house. In fact, they had.

The promise of a light, clean, uncluttered look suggested by the stainless steel, white walls and pine flooring had been ignored in favour of décor that was heavier, darker, smokier and dirtier. Although the sliding windows to the balcony had been thrown open, a smell of stale tobacco smoke still hung in the air, and closer inspection of the ceilings would have shown that the same smoke was slowly turning the bright white décor to brown. Little wonder the housekeeper was so stroppy. The house must have been impossible to keep clean and tidy.

The room was crammed with furniture: oriental rugs, drapes, lamp-standards, oil-paintings with thick wooden frames, a bulging, floral-design three-piece suite, an ancient dining table and chairs and, in one corner, pointed away from the ten-million-dollar view, a finicky, roll-down office desk, loaded with papers, pens, ink-wells, ash-trays, and old whisky bottles. Clearly, Morris had been right about the old man's drinking.

There was a telephone nearby. Otherwise, the only concession to 20th-century technology appeared to be a clumsy wooden radio and an old Remington typewriter.

Suddenly, the harangue stopped, a handset was slapped hard down on a holder, an f-word curse was uttered, and into the living room stalked a man, angrily slapping a rolled-up newspaper against his thigh. He looked completely in keeping with his furnishings.

Ellis Enderby was a tall man. He'd probably been as tall as Danniher once, but with age he'd developed a pronounced stoop, as though his body was bending itself into a shape that offered comfort against some back problem. He must also have been a well-built man, but, Palmeira imagined, his advancing years, too many cigarettes, the booze and a long, briefly newsworthy battle against colon cancer had left him looking lanky and hollow-cheeked.

He had a dirty, grey-brown beard, with wild, wire-like, matching hair that had long ago retreated from the top of his head while simultaneously advancing down his neck and across into his eyebrows, and into ears and nostrils, where it now flourished.

Those parts of his face not covered by hair were florid. His eyes, hidden behind heavy, brown-rimmed spectacles were red and rheumy, and his nose was a swollen blob of broken veins. These were the features of a committed drinker.

In careless disregard for the day's fine weather, he was dressed in clothes more suited to tackling a Tasmanian mountain than a New South Wales beach: a thick, checked, cotton shirt, tweed trousers, and brown leather brogues.

Perhaps, these were all props to support the slightly eccentric, superficially English persona that had made Enderby such a popular figure for a decade or so. But Danniher and Palmeira, who'd painfully tried to jump to attention at Enderby's entrance, now found it difficult to believe that here was a man who once boasted one of Australian television's best-loved faces and best-known voices.

'Bloody bastards,' Enderby growled, throwing the newspaper down on the table, raising puffs of ash and dust. 'They've been denying it for months. But there it is, in black and white. Bastards. All those helicopters. Dropping in at all times of day and night. Ever since they built the helipad this bloody place has been busier than Sydney airport on a holiday weekend.'

Enderby lit a cigarette, sat down, stretched out and, slowly, his temper subsided. Only then did he acknowledge the two men's presence. 'So, farewell, intrepid Birdman, eh?' He chuckled maliciously before being overcome with a coughing fit. 'I always knew he'd come crashing down one day. Surprised he got away it for so long. Bloody charlatan.'

Palmeira was taken aback. Most murder suspects — and that was how he considered Enderby — affected some sympathy or respect for the dear departed, or were, at least, diplomatic and evasive.

Not so the cranky Enderby. Though he had not yet been asked a question, he pressed on energetically. 'Do you know, when I first met Phillip Clarkson he seemed a very presentable young man. Not my type, to be frank. I've always preferred something, how shall I put it, rather more rough trade.' He smiled lasciviously, perhaps at the recollection of some especially unsavoury encounter, before getting back to Phillip Clarkson.

'Still I have to admit he was quite attractive in a jolly, schoolboyish way, with all those curls and chubby cheeks. How absolutely delicious that he should be found, stuck in the sand with his bare bum waving in the air. Ready and waiting, as it were, eh? How the mighty are fallen, eh? I don't mind admitting it made my day, when I read it in the rag.' Once again, Enderby laughed until he coughed.

'Right,' interjected Palmeira. Whatever happened to the old system whereby the police asked questions and the suspect provided answers, he wondered. Enderby continued as though he had not heard.

'I went out of my way to help him. Introduced him to some absolutely top people in the birding business. Put in a good word for him with the networks. Bloody helped him raise money for his rotten documentaries. Even put some tasty consultancy work his way. Very lucrative. And very easy. Just a matter of putting the right word in with the right people, every now and then. Money. For. Old. Rope.'

'I see.'

'Little bastard. After all I'd done for him.'

'Can we just stop there Mr Enderby?' Danniher said firmly. 'What exactly did he do to you?'

Enderby lurched forward, spluttering, spilling more ash on the carpet. 'Only destroyed my career. The bloody bastard.' He threw himself back into his seat at the memory of a humiliating reverse of fortunes.

'But how?' Palmeira asked neutrally. He'd already concluded that whatever Phillip Clarkson had done, the tedious Enderby had almost certainly been the co-author of his own destruction.

'Long story,' replied Enderby, temporarily subdued, suddenly uncommunicative.

The two policemen waited patiently for the story to begin. Instead, Enderby now launched himself to his feet.

'Need a drink. Can I, err, offer you gentlemen anything?'

Neither Danniher nor Palmeira accepted. It was not yet ten o'clock.

'Mary! Mary!' Enderby shouted. His housekeeper did not respond. With another muttered curse, he stomped off into an adjacent room, returning after a few minutes with a tumbler three-quarters full of what looked like straight Scotch. No doubt, the other quarter had been consumed on his return trip from the bottle.

'Been in the wars, old son,' he said, lurching into the outstretched leg of Palmeira who flinched at the contact.

'You were saying, Mr Enderby?' Danniher asked.

'Was I?'

The pugnacity seemed to have drained from him, to be replaced by something even less attractive, self-pity. 'Sorry, the old memory seems to come and go, these days...'

'Clarkson?'

'Let me see. I can't even remember when it started, but one day I think I must've woken up and realised that Clarkson was no longer a friend, a "protégé", as someone once put it. Protégé! He was a bloody rival, who'd been...'

He stopped, as if searching for the foulest curse.

'...who'd been white-anting me all along. That was it. I'd been helping him get his career off the ground and all the time he was white-anting me. Undermining me. Telling people that I was past it. Had lost the plot. Had started talking rubbish...'

Ellis Enderby now seemed to turn an even deeper shade of puce. '... had even starting seeing things!'

'Like the night parrot?'

Though Palmeira's words fluttered down softly, Enderby seemed to react as if a long-concealed bomb had gone off in his brain, or some clumsy idiot had just kicked his injured leg, instead of Palmeira's.

First, there was a wince of pain, then stunned silence, before, as the smoke cleared, he made a confused attempt to find his bearings again.

'All a very, very long time ago now. Got very nasty. Swore I'd never talk about it again. No point re-opening old wounds now.' The words came tumbling out, before collapsing in a sorry heap.

Mercifully, Palmeira did not press the old man for more details. He knew most of them anyway, thanks to Helen McCrimond's research.

He knew how, back in the early nineties, when Enderby was the nation's most popular commentator on all things avian, he'd joined the hunt for the elusive, 'if at all', parrot of the inland plains. With a wide, empty area to choose from, he'd based himself at what he calculated, from a reading of all the night parrot literature, was a potential hot spot: Cloncurry, close to the Queensland mining town of Mt Isa.

Professional reputations, financial rewards, sensitive egos were at stake. For more than a month, he and a camera team zigzagged back and forth, targeting the areas of dense saltbush and spinifex where the parrot was believed to hide by day, and the waterholes, where it was thought to emerge under cover of darkness.

Eventually, his backers had run out of money and patience. Like Clarkson, Enderby had proved a prickly, not to say sexually predatory, person to be cooped up with for long periods. His camera crew and most of his support team deserted him. Even then the dogged Enderby persisted in his search.

He had to. The stakes were too high not to. By then, his reputation and career were on the line.

What happened next was to be the subject of acrimonious controversy. But the way Enderby subsequently told it, one evening, about a week later, he was out with a local driver, poking around an area close to a little place called Duchess.

It was then that he — and he alone, for the driver was sitting in a pick-up truck, listening to the radio, many metres away — heard the tell-tale 'low, drawn-out, double-noted whistle' made by the night parrot as it approached water.

At first he couldn't believe his ears. But before he could properly check with his eyes, he explained, he inadvertently disturbed the bird. To his amazement it rose in textbook 'quail-like' flight for a short distance, before running for cover. Just like a night parrot.

Ellis Enderby had rubbed his eyes. Shaken his head. He had. He had seen a night parrot. He was convinced of that. The trouble was that he was unable to convince anyone else that mattered. Despite many attempts — one of which had ended in a birder having to be rescued by air after going missing for days on a remote stock route in Western Australia — none of the other members of the 750 Club members had seen a night parrot. Most had pronounced it dead. Almost all were suspicious of Enderby's claim.

Enderby continued to press his claim forcefully, citing his public reputation, his long experience, his proven expertise at spotting and identifying rarities. Ultimately, however, the claim was unanimously rejected by a committee of experts, among them the one person he counted as a friend and protégé. The one person he thought he could rely on. The youthful Phillip Clarkson.

For whatever reason, they decided that the ears, the eyes and — most hurtful — the word of Ellis Enderby, leading ornithologist, leading member of the 750 Club, simply could not be trusted. Publicly, it was reported simply that the claim had been rejected for lack of sufficient substantiation: no disrespect or discredit to Enderby was intended or should be taken, said the report. Privately, though, the unsuccessful claimant quickly learned that there'd been allegations that his evidence was tainted — by competitive pressures, by greed for fame and fortune, even by excessive alcohol consumption.

Rightly or wrongly — who would ever know? — Enderby had blamed Clarkson. He threatened the younger man, first with legal action, then with physical violence. Both men had been dragged into a long, increasingly public brawl. Clarkson had emerged a clear winner.

Palmeira imagined that Enderby would've survived with his reputation and lucrative career intact had he taken this reverse philosophically, quietly. After all, maybe on this occasion he had been wrong. Maybe he had not seen a night parrot. Certainly, he could produce not a shred of evidence. All he could do was remind doubters of his expertise. Instead of letting the matter die, he appealed and pursued the claim long after it had been finally rejected, prosecuting the feud with his friend, alienating his allies, embarrassing the birding community and the records committee.

He protested too much. And, increasingly, he drank too much.

From being entertainingly outspoken, Enderby became tediously repetitive. He became bitter and twisted — feelings that were only intensified by the discovery soon after of the corpse of a night parrot close to his sighting.

Now they'll believe me, he'd exclaimed on hearing the news. They hadn't.

Nursing another large whisky, Enderby told Palmeira and Danniher, in a rambling, roundabout way, how things were never quite the same after that, how he had subsequently decided to 'cash in his chips' and go into semi-retirement in Palm Beach, from where he now made only occasional forays into the city.

'Too damned expensive these days,' he said. He'd lost his driving licence and loathed public transport, and was increasingly forced to rely on taxis. 'And anyway, it's not as though there's anyone left in Sydney who wants to sit down with an old bugger like me and talk over the good old days.'

'How about Phillip Clarkson?' asked Danniher.

Far from exploding at the suggestion, Enderby gave it serious thought. 'Funny thing is, I was thinking about him only a few days before…he got whacked. I read in the paper somewhere about his next film — all about crazy birders. The stupid things they'll do to see the rare stuff, the wild claims they make…'

'Yeah, we heard.'

'…and I thought, that young bastard, he's at it again. He's going to rake up all the old dirt about the night parrot again. I'm going to have to go through it all over again. The ridicule. The humiliation. The bloody jokes about the old bloke who was so pissed he started seeing imaginary parrots.'

Enderby slumped back in his chair, cradling his glass. 'I won't have to go through all that again now, will I?' he said, with a weak smile.

'No, I guess you won't.' Palmeira paused. 'So, when did you last see Phillip Clarkson?'

'Can't even remember. Awful long time ago, anyhow. To be honest, after what happened, I never wanted to see the little bastard again.' He relaxed and took another big swig of whisky. But Palmeira wasn't finished.

'In that case, why did you book to go on one his tours?'

It seemed to take several seconds for Enderby's boozy brain to decode the simple sentence. 'Come again?'

'Mr Enderby, you booked to go on to Clarkson's bird outing last Sunday. The day he probably died.'

'I bloody didn't,' he said, with a confused look that suggested fleetingly that he was wondering whether he might, indeed, have done such a thing in a moment of extreme drunkenness. 'I'm sure I didn't. I mean, who says I did?'

'You were on a list of names we found in Clarkson's diary.'

Over the years, Enderby had come to terms with the fact that the world did not take his word for things, but now he straightened his seat, composed himself and spoke, very clearly, very soberly.

'Constable, inspector, whatever you are. I can assure you I never booked to go on any such trip…I wouldn't be seen dead with the man.'

It may not have been the most sensible way of putting it, but the categorical denial left Palmeira and Danniher confused. Nothing they subsequently asked could shake the old man's insistence that he had not planned another meeting with Clarkson.

'OK, that's all for now,' said Palmeira, finally, as he painfully got to his feet.

Danniher, though, had one more question. 'What's your feeling about the night parrot now, sir?'

'I wish I'd never seen the bloody bird.'

'So you did see it?'

Enderby shrugged. 'You know, I'm not sure any more.'

Leaving the old birdman slumped in his chair, seemingly lost in thought, the two officers made their way out. Mary, the cantankerous housekeeper, caught them just as they were opening the front door.

'All done, then, gentlemen?'

'Yes, thanks,' said Palmeira, turning painfully to speak. Yeah, thanks for nothing, thought Danniher.

'I hope you weren't too hard on Mr Enderby?'

'Not at all.'

'Good. I suppose he didn't tell you he's very ill?'

'No.'

'Dying, in fact. He got the tests back yesterday. He's got cancer again.

But now it's spread.'

Before they could even express any sympathy, Mary had slammed the door behind them.

ೞೞೞೞ

Palmeira waited until they were a few kilometres down Barrenjoey Road before he asked the question on the minds of both men.

'What did you make of all that then?'

'All pretty pathetic,' said Danniher. 'Well, pathetic and sad, if what that bitch of a housekeeper said was correct.'

In the rear-view mirror, he could see the DI nodding in agreement. 'I wonder whether the old queen fancied Clarkson at some point.'

'I'm sure he did.'

'Still, doesn't much matter, now. The point is that, for whatever reason, he hated him, had threatened him with violence…'

'… and he was a big man before…' said Danniher, picking up the line of thought, 'who could call on some real thugs if he needed to teach someone a lesson…'

'…someone like Clarkson…'

'Sure.'

'… and he was obviously worried that Clarkson might be about to take another pop at him in his new video…'

'I don't know. Somehow it just doesn't seem to add up again,' Palmeira conceded.

'And then there's all that funny business about the booking. I don't know about you, sir, but I reckon the old bloke probably rang up one night when he was well into the turps. Maybe as a prank. Give young Clarkson a bit of a wind-up, a bit of a scare.'

'You're probably right.'

Leaving the riddle of the warring birdmen up in the air, the two men lapsed into silence once more, as the road south widened to dual carriageway and the Falcon picked up speed.

To Danniher's surprise, they did not drive straight back to Berwick police station, however. As they were driving through the surf-beach community of Collaroy, Palmeira suggested they turn at the next left. Danniher could pick up some food at the corner takeaway. They could then drive on another few hundred metres to Long Reef to eat their respective lunches.

'Top idea, sir.'

Clearly, Palmeira wasn't going to make it up the long escarpment on crutches. So the two men found a patch of grass overlooking the rock platform and the ocean beyond. For more than an hour, they ate their lunches and talked, awkwardly at first, but then more amicably, and watched the hang-gliders soaring, like birds, high in the sky above them.

'Never get me up in one of those things,' said Danniher.

'Getting up's OK. It's the coming down bit that's the problem,' replied Palmeira. Both men couldn't help thinking of the Birdman's death.

It was mid-afternoon by the time the pair arrived back at the station. Sedgwick was waiting for them.

'Didn't realise it was that late,' he said, exaggeratedly checking his watch. 'Long lunch?'

'Not at all, sir, we …'

'I see Mr Enderby isn't with you.'

'No.'

'Nor Mr Waddell.'

'No. Still looking, I think.'

Sedgwick came closer, towering over Palmeira. 'I'm running out of patience, detective inspector.' Palmeira could smell his hot breath. 'And you are running out of time.'

He returned to his lair, leaving the two men standing, dejected, in front of the crowded whiteboard. Danniher knew it. Palmeira knew it. And they suspected Sedgwick knew it. They had no arrest in sight.

Despite all their efforts, no witnesses had come forward; no weapons had been found. Though several suspects had been eliminated, and prime suspect Waddell was still on the run, none had firmed as the likely murderer.

The inquiry hadn't come to complete full stop. Not quite. They had been to see Ellis Enderby, Park and Holmes were still chasing Waddell, and Koslowksi had been out all morning talking to the local council about its relationship with Phillip Clarkson.

That, at least, was encouraging. Before leaving for home the previous night, Koslowski had left a cryptic note. 'Still not got to bottom of last couple boxes. One thing clear: Berwick Council and Pelican paying him a lot of money. Should know more tomorrow.'

12

The early bird catches the worm.

— William Camden, *Remains*

It was just past eight o'clock in the morning. Somewhere across the city, Danniher would be collecting Palmeira for their trip up to Palm Beach and Koslowski would be preparing to interview Keith Medlicott, general manager of Berwick Council.

With a start, Detective Constable Russell Park shifted, stretched his arms and legs as far as he could in the cramped space, yawned, rubbed his eyes, yawned again and looked at his watch.

'Sorry, have I been snoring?' Park asked rotating his neck stiffly.

'Not much,' came the weary reply from beside him. 'Have I?'

'I don't think so, Sherl,' said Park, worried that both had fallen asleep.

'Russ?'

'Yes?'

'Don't call me "Sherl", eh?' Long ago, Melissa Holmes had realised that her surname was no asset for a detective.

'Sorry.'

'And stop saying sorry.'

'Sor... right.'

Though he'd never admit it, especially to his sensitive, new age mates outside the police force, Park had sometimes wondered what it'd be like to spend the night with colleague Melissa 'Sherlock' Holmes.

Now he knew. It was, by turns, exhausting, frustrating, boring and surprisingly uncomfortable and uneventful. Then again, he'd not envisaged that the night would be spent on a quiet, suburban street in Berwick, sitting in a small beaten-up Toyota, waiting for a fat man with an attitude problem to turn up.

For all but a few hours either side of midnight, when two uniformed officers relieved them, Park and Holmes had been driving around looking for — or, worse, sitting around waiting for — Gordon Waddell. Both were now tired and irritable and ready to kill Sedgwick for telling them to get Waddell, or else.

Their vigil had effectively started the previous evening shortly after they returned from interviewing the Waddell Fletts. Armed with the name and address of Michael Kenyon produced by the rego check, they'd then rushed round to the Ocean Street unit.

Neighbours confirmed that it was shared, at one time or another, by the two men, but there had been no sign of the maroon Land Cruiser, nor of its two drivers. They'd then driven the short distance to the council offices, where they were told by a security man on the front desk — who rang upstairs to find out — that Michael Kenyon had already left for the day. He was not due back in until Monday.

So they shuttled back to Ocean Street, again. They'd been sitting around for another hour or so when an observant neighbour living on the same floor of the unit emerged to ask, suspiciously, what they wanted. Told that she was talking to the police, the elderly woman became terribly excited. Clearly, this was one of the most interesting things that'd ever happened to her.

The neighbour confirmed that the unit usually contained 'Mikie' and another, bigger man, though she hadn't seen him much lately. She suggested that, if it was urgent, they should try Mikie down at the Berwick Council offices, where he was 'something to with the garbos'.

Just as the two officers thanked her and turned to go, she asked, 'Are they in some sort of trouble then?'

'Could be,' Park replied, vaguely. 'I'm afraid I can't go into details right now.'

'Oooh, I understand. Can't say I'd be surprised, though.'

'Why's that then, Mrs…?' asked Holmes, who was reminded of her grandmother by the woman.

'Corless, dear. Franny Corless. No, it's just that they were always going in and out at odd times, especially the other one. Mikie was nice enough — helped me put the bins out for the garbos and that — but the big one… he was a shocker.'

'Mmm.'

'They used to fight you know? You'd hear them banging around, shouting at each other. Sounded like they were having an argument. Especially when they came in late. It kept me awake.'

'You didn't hear what about?' asked Holmes. She could just see Mrs Corless excitedly climbing out of bed and holding a glass to the dividing wall. It would have beaten anything on television.

'Sorry. But you know what I think?'

'Tell me.'

'They'd been out drinking. You know, heavy drinking. They shouldn't be out driving that jeep thing if they've been drinking, should they?'

It was not the most stunning insight they'd heard that day, but now, bleary-eyed and fuzzy-headed, the two officers thought it might explain why neither of the men had returned overnight. That or they'd taken fright.

Time seemed to have passed twice as slowly as normal — like being trapped in economy class on a long-haul jet, a fidgety Holmes told Park.

'Except the food's better.'

'How about the company?' asked Park.

'Not too bad, I suppose,' she said, smiling palely. At least they hadn't got on each other's nerves too much.

However, the toilets were non-existent and the entertainment negligible and the pair had quickly tired of each other's conversation and the quizzes, inane chatterings and easy-listening music that seemed to be the staples of radio for insomniacs. Worse, unlike a flight, their long wait had not got them anywhere: unless they'd missed something while dozing on duty, it'd been a wasted night. Neither the Land Cruiser nor its crew had returned.

'What now?' said Park, desperately hoping that Holmes might suggest they go home to bed, separately if necessary.

She hesitated. 'Sorry. I think we should give it another hour or so. If Kenyon isn't back by then, we'll try him at work again. If he's not there… well, I don't know. Report back in, I suppose.'

'And face Jonno. No thanks.'

Knowing Sedgwick, they'd be bawled out for wasting their time, dragged off the depleted Birdman team and assigned to his new unit set up — no doubt, as a sop to local politicians and ratepayers — to fight crime in Berwick.

'Operation Kookaburra' was to be run by the unit headed by Jim Munro and, Sedgwick insisted, was to include fellow Berwick officers Park and Holmes.

With muggers and thieves 'on a rampage', he couldn't spare them for the Birdman inquiry, he'd told Palmeira and Danniher, waving sheets of paper under their noses. 'Know what these are? More crime reports.'

When Palmeira objected, Sedgwick had given him and his sergeant a lecture on crime-fighting. Describing himself as 'an old-school cop with old-school methods', he accused them of ignoring the obvious.

'Think about it,' he had told the two men from HQ. 'One, Waddell's got a record. Two, his wife or whatever she calls herself says he's got a foul temper. Three, he runs away from the police. He must be your man. Whether he is or he isn't he must be found.'

When Palmeira had tried to explain, Sedgwick shouted him down. 'I'd venture to say that finding a convicted thug is more important than swanning up to Whale Beach, or wherever it is, to talk to an old man about parrots.'

Under the threat of losing two officers, Palmeira had been forced to comply. Details of the missing maroon Land Cruiser had been circulated to all police in the greater metropolitan area, and Park and Holmes had been dispatched to find an unmarked car and stake-out Ocean Street.

Since then, more than 12 hours had passed and the only threats Melissa Holmes had faced were cramp, hunger and boredom. Now, sitting in the warm, pink light of another fine summer's day, they wondered what to do next.

Eventually, it was Park who came up with a mutually acceptable suggestion. 'Let's give it another hour or so and then grab a late breakfast. It'll only take a few minutes. I don't think we're going to miss much.'

ଓଃଓଃ

Later that morning, at about the same time as Park and Holmes were driving off to grab some breakfast at a café, Koslowski arrived at the offices of Berwick Shire Council, only a few streets away.

The Town Hall must have been an imposing building once, he thought. It seemed to cast a superior eye over Berwick citizens moving up and down the main street. But the clean, neo-classical lines of what had originally been a bank office had been spoiled. In the 1970s, an inexpensive extension had been added, before heritage listing could intervene.

Even Koslowski could see the ill-fitting blockhouse addition was a monstrosity. It stuck out like a boil on a beautiful face, or a car jutting out of a bank after a ram-raid. The symmetry of the building had been destroyed. Still, cheap space had to be found somewhere to house the 300 or more staff now employed to service a municipality whose population had grown in just ten years from barely 100,000 to more than 140,000.

Of these, some 45 per cent were from non-English speaking backgrounds, though Danniher would never have guessed it, looking down a main street plastered with American brand names — McDonald's, KFC, Coca-Cola, Starbucks and so on.

And to think that 200 years ago the area would have been roamed by Aboriginals. Apart from some rock carvings down on the bay, no trace remained of their 40,000-year stay. However, that of the shire's earliest European settler, a Scottish farmer called Alexander Berwick, was commemorated, not just on all council signs and pieces of stationery, but in the form of a bronze bust placed at the entrance to the Town Hall.

Early for his appointment and anxious to gather his thoughts, Koslowski stopped to look at it. The gimlet-eyes of the pinched, curmudgeonly looking Scots lowlander seemed to pick him out and follow him with a scowl of disapproval through the large, open foyer.

Already, the officer was feeling uncomfortably out of place, possibly out of his depth. For the second time in a week, he was wearing a suit, collar and tie — funereal black had been swapped for business-like blue — and he was carrying a briefcase.

As Marianne had told him, even if you don't feel the part, you can look it.

The case contained several pens, a few of Phillip Clarkson's papers and a list of questions compiled quickly, with his wife's help, the evening before. But basically it was a prop to support his sagging confidence.

Koslowski had a low opinion of local councillors. He still recalled the night he'd been forced to sit through a council meeting, waiting for an item on local policing. For more than an hour he'd listened, with growing disbelief, to councillors discussing the pros and cons of purchasing a set of what one referred to as 'those chairs with the tubercular legs'.

The debate seemed typical of small-minded, meddlesome councillors: men and women who were charged with overseeing millions — a whopping $50 million a year in the case of Berwick Shire — yet were obsessed with minutiae.

Eventually, he expected, he might have to talk to the mayor. This morning, however, he'd be facing only officials. He was determined not to be intimidated by them, though he rather wished Marianne could have come with him. Koslowski was prepared, if necessary, to bully the council into an immediate meeting to discuss Clarkson's role. Instead, he was surprised at the speed with which they agreed to a meeting to 'put the record straight'.

Far from being fobbed off with some acting assistant deputy to the council flak-catcher, or other such minion, he was to meet the top man, Jeffrey Medlicott.

All the same, he wasn't expecting to be shown, not into the office of the general manager, but into a first-floor conference room, which overlooked the council car park. Not one but four people were already seated at a large, oval table.

'Good morning, officer,' said a tall, gaunt man, who looked uncannily like a younger version of Alexander Berwick. He extended a thin, mottled hand. 'Christian Koslowski, isn't it?'

'Oh, yes,' said the officer, momentarily failing to recognise his real name. Even Marianne and his seven-year-old son called him 'Kiwi' or 'Kos' these days.

Medlicott introduced his colleagues. 'Clive Partridge, planning and environment officer. Miranda Franklin, public affairs. And Thomas Atkinson, the council's legal adviser.' In turn, each rose, beamed and shook hands with Koslowski.

The young officer was put on his guard. Why the show of strength, he wondered. It looked suspiciously like overkill. Why all the smiles? The council had plenty to hide, he suspected.

'Right,' he said, sitting. He took some papers from the briefcase and arranged them on the table in front of him, just like Marianne had suggested. 'No doubt, you'll all have read about the murder of Phillip Clarkson…'

From around the table came expressions of regret and shuffles of feet. Koslowski waited for them to subside before continuing. 'Well, I'm here to clear up a few questions about the council's precise relationship with the dead man.'

It was Atkinson, the legal eagle, who spoke first. 'Just before we start, I must point out a couple of things, officer.' Here we go, thought Koslowski, more evasion.

'One, that the relationship between the council's officers and Mr Clarkson was never anything less than cordial and constructive. And, two, that some of the issues likely to be covered this morning must be treated as commercial in confidence.'

'Kept secret, you mean.'

'Well, yes.'

'I see.'

Medlicott now intervened. 'We have nothing to hide…' Like hell, thought Koslowski. '…but there are some sensitive issues whose disclosure could jeopardise on-going negotiations.'

'That was the basis on which Mr Clarkson worked,' added Ms Franklin.

'But he's dead.'

'Yes, but I'm sure it would have been his wish…'

Already, Koslowski was losing patience.

'What exactly did he do for you?'

'His role changed over the years,' volunteered Medlicott, measuring his words.

'How?'

Medlicott nodded to Partridge, who took up the story. 'Originally, he was used, on a one-off basis, to carry out specific tasks.'

'Such as?'

'To carry out an audit of bird life. To let us know what we'd got here and — how can I put it — what it was worth.'

Ms Franklin intervened. 'You know officer, that Berwick is very proud of its wildlife.'

Receiving no response from Koslowski, Partridge continued. 'We also used Mr Clarkson's considerable talents to brief our staff, to keep them informed on environmental issues. Sensitive issues, you know?'

'You paid him for this?'

'Of course.'

'Didn't this put him a difficult position?'

'I don't think so,' said Partridge.

'But surely he was speaking on behalf of the bird groups and such-like?'

'Well, yes he was.'

'I'm just surprised that he was being paid if he was representing bird groups anyway.'

'He continued to do so. But in the case of some proposed developments, we felt it was important that council be kept fully informed on an ongoing basis of the thinking of groups which might raise objections.'

'So, essentially, you were paying for his name, his reputation.'

'You could put it like that. Yes. It was a perfectly normal business relationship.' The planning officer looked to the legal adviser for help.

'There is nothing wrong, illegal or unethical about that, I can assure you officer,' said Atkinson.

'It sounds like a conflict of interest to me,' Koslowski replied after a short pause.

'Not for us. For Phillip Clarkson? That's not for the council to speculate. All I can say is that Phillip never raised any objections with us about his role. In fact, quite the reverse. At the time of his death, Mr Clarkson was talking about expanding it.'

Koslowski shook his head and looked down at the papers in front of him. 'It seems that his role had increased already in the last six months or so.'

'That is correct,' Medlicott replied.

'Please explain.'

'Council thought that Mr Clarkson's expertise would be especially valuable in connection with a specific development proposal...'

'Which is?'

Medlicott again looked to his legal adviser before answering. 'Is that OK?' Atkinson nodded.

'The application by Pelican Estates to extend its business park. You may have heard about it?'

Of course Koslowski had heard about it. Pelican Estates. PIE. Before the meeting he'd even popped into the local newspaper office to read through the back numbers. 'Yes. What's it worth? One hundred fifty million in investment? A couple of hundred new jobs? Big boost for the area...'

'That's it, officer,' said Ms Franklin. 'It is very good news for all ratepayers.' She smiled proudly.

'Not according to the environmentalists,' the policeman pointed out. 'You know and I know that there's been a huge fight over the development. It's been in the papers for months.'

'A small minority oppose it,' Ms Franklin corrected him.

Koslowski pulled out a piece of paper. 'Council meetings disrupted. Demonstrations on the beach. Even opposition from your local MP...more than a small minority, I'd have thought.'

'Well, maybe...'

'Plus the birders fighting to save habitats which....'

'Be fair, officer. Highly degraded habitats,' Ms Franklin insisted, reminding Koslowski that the development only affected the dirty, polluted, fag-end of Moreton Bay, exactly where the Birdman's body had been found.

'With the rates we receive from the new business park we can clean up the remaining stretches of harbour foreshore and upgrade Berwick's parks.'

Medlicott reinforced the point. 'Unfortunately, in all such cases, some compromise has to be struck between the loss of natural amenity and the gains in terms of investment and jobs. Mr Clarkson was being paid to assist us in coming to a wise decision on how best to strike the right balance.'

'But I thought he was also being paid by Pelican Estates?'

To Koslowski such an arrangement seemed extraordinary, but no one round the table registered surprise. Atkinson answered the question. 'You would have to speak to them about that.'

'Don't worry. I will.'

'Good. But any financial arrangement the late Mr Clarkson had with anyone else has absolutely nothing to do with Berwick Shire Council.'

'But the birder groups clearly thought he was representing them,' said Koslowski, instantly realising how naïve he must sound.

'Possibly. But as I explained, that has nothing to do with us.'

Koslowski tried again. 'But he seems to have been playing both ends against each other?'

'It might seem like that to you,' said Atkinson. 'As I keep saying, it's not really our problem. But I would suggest that if someone, in this case Mr Clarkson, could help broker an acceptable solution to a tricky development it is to the benefit of all parties. A win-win situation if you like.'

Koslowski consulted his papers again. 'Why were payments to Mr Clarkson put on a regular, monthly basis?'

'The new arrangements reflected an envisaged expansion in the role for him in the future.'

'Which was?'

'More of a public, educational role,' explained Medlicott.

'In connection with the Pelican Estate scheme?'

'Yes.'

'You mean, lobbying for its approval.'

'I still prefer the phrase "educational role".'

'Did the Berwick rate-payers know about all this?'

'As I explained at the outset, officer, the retention of Phillip Clarkson and related issues were treated by council as commercial in confidence.'

'But they did go through council?'

Again, Medlicott considered his reply carefully. 'At an early stage in the negotiations with Pelican Estates it was decided by council to give its officers a certain flexibility and autonomy in its handling of some of the more sensitive issues.'

'Discretionary powers,' Atkinson added.

Koslowski felt flummoxed, unsure what line of inquiry to pursue next. Was the council in the clear? Or had it committed some crime that could, perhaps, be referred to the statewide corruption commission? Either way it didn't seem to get him any closer to finding whoever murdered Clarkson. He looked down at his papers for inspiration and found a few names that had been belatedly added to his list for checking.

'Morris. Let's see…Derek Morris? He used to work with the council, I believe.'

The four officials frowned in ignorance, until Partridge remembered. 'I think we had someone in the finance department of that name once. It would've been a while back.'

He thought some more. 'Checking contract work, I think. I guess the work ran out and he left. I can check. Bit of a moaner, if it's the same man — but I suppose that's what these accountants are paid to do.'

'What's this Morris character got to do with it anyway?' asked Medlicott, evidently anxious to bring the meeting to a close.

'Probably nothing. I was just wondering if he'd ever been involved with Phillip Clarkson or the Pelican Estates project while he was here.'

'I wouldn't have thought so. Different departments altogether. Personnel might be able to tell you.'

Koslowski tried another name. 'Have you had any dealings with a Mr Waddell? Gordon Waddell?'

All four faces turned blank. 'I think you can take that as a "no", officer,' said Medlicott. Koslowski could almost touch the sense of relief felt by the general manager as the line of questioning had veered away from Phillip Clarkson.

Koslowski tried again. 'Michael Kenyon?'

This time, three faces registered blank, but Ms Franklin knew the name. 'I know Mike Kenyon. Hunky guy. In waste disposal. We — public relations, that is — used him recently in one of their community awareness campaigns.'

She turned to the others. 'You remember, the one to encourage people to recycle more household garbage?'

To her disappointment, no one round the table did seem to remember. Ms Franklin shrugged. 'Never mind. Anyway, surely, he hasn't got anyth…'

Koslowski did not hear the end of the sentence. At that moment the PR woman's words were cut off by a long screech of skidding tyres followed, almost inevitably, by the sickening crunch of sheet metal upon sheet metal, a rush of what sounded like escaping steam, and raised voices.

'What the hell was that?'

In an instant, Koslowski was up, out of his seat and over to the window. The scene below him was a blur of action: four figures, slamming doors, flailing arms and pumping legs.

Two of those involved he recognised at once: DCs Park and Holmes. By the time he'd rushed from the room, down the flight of stairs, across the foyer, and out through the back entrance into the car park, he'd also worked out the likely identities of the other two.

Gordon Waddell and Michael Kenyon.

ఴఴఴఴ

Russell Park and Melissa Holmes had lingered over a leisurely breakfast, returned to the council offices to confirm that Michael Kenyon was definitely not there and was still not expected until Monday, and were actually heading back to his home when the call from the Berwick police control room came through.

'I thought you guys were waiting outside Ocean Street for our elusive Mr Waddell?' said Robert Adamovitch.

'Just a couple of minutes away, sarge,' said Park.

'Well I'd get a wriggle on. We've just had a call from some woman there, a Mrs…' The line went quiet while he checked. '…Corless, saying that there's two men outside loading up a maroon Land Cruiser…'

'Oh my God. Does Sedgwick know about this?'

'Not yet, he's away, up in the city. Another brain-storming session about police reorganisation, I bet.'

'Bob.'

'I know. If he asks, I'll have to tell him. But if he doesn't, I see no reason why he should find out.'

'Thanks, sarge. We owe you.'

'Too right, you do. Just make sure you get him this time.'

'We're on to it right now, Bob.'

When they arrived at No. 17, Ocean Street, the Land Cruiser was gone, but Franny Corless was still there. She was standing outside on the footpath, with a frown on her face and her hands on her hips, like a nagging wife waiting for her husband to return home from the pub.

'I don't believe it,' said Melissa Holmes, shaking her head in disbelief as she climbed from the car.

'You two took your time, didn't you?' said Mrs Corless. 'You've missed them again.'

'So it seems.'

'I told them the police were after them.'

'I wish you hadn't done that, Mrs Corless. It wasn't very helpful,' said Park.

'Sorry. I asked them where they were going. They told me to "get effed". Pardon the French.'

In fact, it was not much later, as Kowslowski's meeting with the council officials was coming to a frustrating close, that the two detectives finally spotted the maroon Land Cruiser.

It was slotted into a line of vehicles parked outside the rear entrance of the offices. The engine was still running. The passenger-side door was open. And a man, evidently Michael Kenyon, was climbing out, evidently heading inside.

'There, quick,' shouted Park, swinging the beaten-up Toyota, borrowed from a friend especially for the stake-out, in a circle and accelerating hard towards the far heavier Land Cruiser.

For a couple of seconds it appeared to Holmes that he planned to ram it from the side: a small family car taking on a two-tonne monster in an uneven contest that could kill them both.

'No!' she screamed.

At the last moment, Park pulled the steering wheel over, causing the smaller car to swerve suddenly, side-swiping the bigger one. Now, just as suddenly, he stopped, slammed the gear into reverse and backed the car up, leaving its passenger side hard up against the driver-side door of the Land Cruiser.

Holmes was whiplashed violently forwards, sideways, and backwards again, her head rebounding painfully from the windscreen. She sat, slumped in her seat, moaning with pain. Park flung open his door and jumped out. 'Police! Stop!' he shouted.

Waddell suddenly realised what was happening. He yanked the steering wheel round, revved the engine furiously in an attempted to drive the

Land Cruiser away.

When it became obvious that he was hopelessly hemmed in — by parked cars on three sides and a high kerb on the fourth — he tried several times to slam open his driver's side door. When that failed, he unbuckled himself and started clambering feverishly across to the passenger side.

Now Kenyon, who'd been making his way into the council offices, turned back. Briefly, he stood there, confused, a witness to what seemed at first to be an extreme case of road rage.

'Police!' yelled Park. 'Stay where you are!'

Like Melissa Holmes, still strapped inside the small car, bleeding profusely from a head wound, Gordon Waddell had no alternative. Briefly, he managed to squeeze the door open a little and to land a couple of blows on Park, but after a few seconds he was forced to face facts: he was trapped, by his bulk and by his ungainliness, inside the Land Cruiser.

Michael Kenyon, as tall as Waddell, but leaner and fitter, made a run for it. Guessing that Park wouldn't risk losing Waddell by abandoning the Land Cruiser, he turned once more and dashed back into the Town Hall.

He hoped to run straight through and out on to the busy main street on the other side. Instead, he found himself almost face to face with another obstacle: Koslowski, who'd come hurtling down the stairs into the foyer.

The two men confronted each other, crouching forward like sumo wrestlers, trying to anticipate each other's next move.

It was Kenyon who moved first. Instead of turning on his heels and heading back towards the car park, he dashed almost straight at Koslowski, like a rugby three-quarter hoping to sidestep or simply run over the top of a defender.

The detective was ready for him, though, throwing himself forward and tackling him round the waist. For several seconds, the two men wrestled on the tiled floor, this way and that, as an audience of fascinated council officials gathered on the first floor balcony.

Finally the writhing bodies smacked against something solid. There was a mighty bang, and the sneering bust of Alexander Berwick came crashing down off its wooden base, bouncing heavily on Kenyon's shoulder before rolling harmlessly away.

'Aaargh,' screamed the star of Berwick Council's recycling videos. As

Koslowski later explained to his mates, the old Scotsman had knocked all the fight out of Kenyon, who now lay passively beneath Koslowski, moaning quietly.

From the balcony above came a smattering of applause. Koslowski could not help himself: he turned and waved a clenched first in acknowledgment. After a mind-numbing morning spent talking to the council officials he'd rather enjoyed the short physical encounter.

Slowly, order was restored to the chaotic scene. Uniformed police were summoned to extract Waddell, breathing heavily and swearing loudly, from his vehicle, and to take statements from several witnesses. Waddell was now subdued.

An ambulance was called for DC Holmes and Michael Kenyon. Both were taken away separately to Berwick hospital for treatment. A tow-truck came and took the two vehicles away, the Land Cruiser for examination, the borrowed Toyota for repair.

Park and Koslowski returned to the station with Waddell. There he was charged with assault. In addition, the media would later be told, he was 'helping the police with inquiries into a suspicious death'. It took no great imagination to work out what that was.

It was then, as Waddell was being taken to the cells that he bumped into Palmeira.

'You?'

'You!'

After the initial shock of recognition passed between the big man and the small man, Koslowski introduced them to each other with comic formality.

'Detective Inspector Mario Palmeira, Gordon Waddell. Gordon Waddell, Detective Inspector Mario Palmeira. I see you've met before.'

The two nodded and parted without exchanging words: that could wait until the formal interviews began.

As the one lumbered away to his cell and the other hobbled away to his desk, it was difficult to know who was the more surprised: Waddell, to learn that the jogger he'd found crawling in the dunes was a top cop, or Palmeira, to discover that his Good Samaritan was a well-known thug and, he sincerely hoped, the man who murdered Phillip Clarkson.

13

The bird that can sing and won't sing, must be made to sing.
— John Ray, *English Proverbs*

It hadn't taken long for Danniher, Palmeira, and Jim Munro of Operation Kookaburra to understand why Waddell was so keen to avoid them.

Found under the front seat of the maroon Land Cruiser was a crowbar — exactly the type used by burglars to break into homes. On the back seat were more than a dozen DVD players. A quick check showed they'd been stolen three weeks earlier from a Berwick electrical appliances warehouse. And in the driver's wallet were credit cards bearing the names of six different people.

Gordon Waddell knew he was in big trouble even before he assaulted DC Park, whom he only belatedly recognised as the policeman who spoke to him at Moreton Bay on the very day when Phillip Clarkson's body was discovered.

What worried him was: big trouble over what, precisely? His muggings? His break-ins? His occasional gay-bashings? Or his part in the discovery of a dead body? Or all of the above? Just how much did the police know?

Normally, he was a sound sleeper, especially after a gutful of grog, but these worries had kept him awake, tossing and turning in his cell all night.

ജ്ഞൽ

In fact, Palmeira and Danniher had also been worrying: worrying that the big man would be difficult to crack. When he'd been brought in the previous afternoon, they'd failed to extract much from him beyond his name.

At first, he'd refused to supply even an address. When he finally responded to Danniher's threats and Palmeira's reasoning, he'd given the one in Mascot. When Danniher had smashed his fist so hard down on the table that it spilled three glasses of water, and yelled, 'You're lying,' he gave that of Michael Kenyon.

This was accepted — but only until Kenyon was brought back from the hospital, where he'd been treated for a badly bruised shoulder, to be charged with assault, and questioned further along with Waddell.

On being booked in, Kenyon had confirmed his own Ocean Street address. But when Palmeira suggested he'd shared the address with Waddell, he denied it furiously. Maybe for a couple of weeks over Christmas, Kenyon explained, he'd allowed Waddell to sleep on his floor. It had been like living in an effing pigsty.

Now, he insisted, the porker had found a place of his own. 'Where?' Danniher demanded, making the table jump again. This time it was no act: he was really losing patience with the man.

Typically, Palmeira had taken a different approach. 'We're not just talking about assault here, Mr Kenyon,' he explained quietly. 'We're talking murder.'

The news seemed to come as a genuine shock to Kenyon, who amid a rush of denials, oaths and threats quickly provided an address for Waddell in Napier Street, Botany. Only about 15 minutes away.

'Number?'

'I can't remember. Honest. But you can't miss it. Ground floor. Right on the corner, opposite a Chinese restaurant. Gordon doesn't like to go too far for a feed.'

Dobbed in by his mate, Waddell grunted, then with a deep sigh, resigned himself to having the police turn over his latest home. 'Help yourself. Number one, at number one. It's your lucky day,' he said grimly.

He was right. It was their lucky day. The officers from Operation Kookaburra couldn't believe their eyes when they opened the door of the unit. Inside was what the media was later to describe as an 'Aladdin's cave of stolen goods'.

Among the empty beer bottles, discarded fast-food cartons and unwashed crockery were boxes, most of them not even opened, containing television sets, personal computers, electronic game stations, video cameras and more DVD players.

Lying on the unmade bed, as if thrown there in haste, were wallets, handbags and purses, most of them still containing coins and banknotes. Unless he was holding them in safekeeping for their owners, it was safe to assume they were the ill-gotten gains from muggings.

Elsewhere in the plain, partly furnished unit, the officers found other sums of money, bits of jewellery, several small, easily carried household gadgets — Walkmans, Game Boys and the like — and stacks of pornographic videos. Far too many for Waddell's personal consumption.

Munro whistled. 'Mate, what we're looking at here is the result of a flaming one-man crime wave. Jonno's going to just love this.'

Even as they spoke, DCs Park and Koslowski had just finished searching Kenyon's unit and were moving to the rear of the block to open his lock-up garage, helpfully pointed out to them by the neighbour, Mrs Corless. To their disappointment, the garage contained nothing out of the ordinary — at least, nothing obviously belonging to someone else, nothing incriminating.

Inside the unit, however, they'd found several boxes containing electrical appliances. The way they'd been stacked neatly near the front door suggested the boxes had just been delivered or were awaiting collection.

Of more interest to Palmeira and Danniher, Kenyon's maroon Land Cruiser had produced more evidence: a significant quantity of sand. Forensic experts were examining it now.

'It may or may not be interesting, but we'll give it a go,' said a man from crime-scene, as he took the Land Cruiser away.

⁖⁖⁖

When he heard this, Palmeira's spirits rose. After a frustrating week spent searching unsuccessfully for witnesses and weapons, pursuing false leads and 'pussy-footing around with the airy-fairy, birdie brigade,' as Danniher put it, the Birdman Inquiry finally seemed to be heading somewhere. What's more, Sedgwick would be off their backs for a while.

Even the injuries to Melissa Holmes hadn't been as serious as they'd feared, though she'd been detained for observation overnight. She was suffering from concussion, bruised ribs, a sore neck and a gash to the head that had required 12 stitches.

When Park and Koslowski visited her that evening, she was sitting up in bed, talking about returning to work the next day. As they reported back to Danniher, she seemed more concerned about the damage to the stake-out car than her own injuries.

Now all that was required was to link Waddell to the crime scene and persuade him — if needs be, force him — to confess to the murder of Phillip Clarkson.

ೞೞೞ

Palmeira had arranged to be picked-up by Danniher early the next morning and had dashed into work, wrecking any hopes his wife may have entertained that he'd use the weekend to recuperate.

'Sorry, Jen. Not now.'

'But Mario…'

'This won't take long. Promise.'

For a couple of hours, the two men discussed possible lines of questioning, reviewed aspects of the Birdman case and listened as Jim Munro listed the number of crimes — muggings, break-ins and such-like — that could be pinned on Waddell and/or Kenyon. There were more than 20, which Munro had helpfully listed — with times and places — on a sheet of foolscap paper. 'Looks like they've been shuttling back and forward, moving the gear from Ocean Street to Botany.'

Waddell was brought from his cell. The prisoner had eaten a hearty breakfast but he'd not slept well and he looked decidedly nervous for someone who, as Sergeant Adamovitch had told Palmeira a week earlier, was no stranger to prison cells and police interviews.

Defence papers submitted at previous court appearances briefly told his life story. It did not make pleasant reading.

The only son of a violent, alcoholic father and a doting mother, he'd apparently left school at the first opportunity. He'd spent the next ten years moving from one poorly paid menial job to another, supplementing his income with minor crimes, for which he was infrequently caught and still more rarely properly punished.

His first marriage, to a young woman whom he'd met and made pregnant while working as a shelf-stacker at a Berwick supermarket, lasted only three years. Working less, eating and drinking more, Waddell had then drifted in and out of several more unsuccessful relationships.

One resulted in a second marriage, at the age of 32, to a barmaid. One day he lost his temper and beat the woman severely. She complained to police, but when it came to pressing charges and appearing in court, she ran away.

Waddell was soon in trouble again, though. He bashed a man, whom he'd met and gone home with while drunk. The man had made sexual advances, he claimed, in his defence. Waddell was still found guilty of assault and jailed for 18 months.

A pattern was beginning to emerge, Palmeira noticed. Waddell was in — and just as quickly out — of employment, as a labourer, scaffolder, courier, nightclub bouncer, and collector and disposer of noxious waste.

Geraldine Flett had been able to bring the Waddell story almost up to date. As she'd explained to Holmes, woman to woman, while Park had answered his mobile phone, they'd met in a pub.

She'd always liked a man around the house and, foolishly, she thought she could get Waddell to mend his ways. Quite what Waddell could see in her, she couldn't quite remember. 'I'm not a bad cook, and I did give him lots of money,' she suggested. Anyway, the arrangement had not worked for long.

When Waddell had shot through he'd gone to live with Michael Kenyon, with whom he had resumed a life of crime. Bashings. Break-ins. And now, Danniher and Palmeira were sure, murder. Given that sort of past, it seemed strange to Palmeira that Waddell had not immediately asked for a lawyer. Perhaps he was even more stupid than he looked.

Palmeira's opening question hit Waddell like a left-hook to the temple. It was not so much the strength of the punch but its unexpectedness. 'Why did you kill Phillip Clarkson?'

'You what?' Waddell looked, first at Palmeira, then at Danniher. He seemed to be seeking confirmation that this was somebody's idea of a joke.

Both men sat stone-faced. 'Why did you kill Phillip Clarkson?' Palmeira repeated.

Waddell had still not recovered. 'That's bloody ridiculous,' he blustered. 'I thought I was here to...'

'Don't start raising your voice with me,' said Palmeira, almost inaudibly.

'But...'

'Why did you kill Phillip Clarkson?'

'I didn't.'

Like the other half of a tag-team, Danniher took up the fight. 'You did. You're a loser. You're a bully. You're a violent man. You have a history of bashing people. You obviously know your way around the dunes where he was found...'

'I saw you there myself,' Palmeira put in.

'And you were found in possession of a crowbar, which matches the description of the murder weapon. It's being tested by forensics right now. We expect them to show that it was the weapon used to attack Phillip Clarkson.'

Danniher stared fixedly ahead, his face betraying none of the doubts he and Palmeira shared about the 'evidence' being hurled now at the Waddell.

Compelling or not, though, it seemed to be working. Patches of sweat were beginning to darken the dirty, open-necked shirt of the big man, as he squirmed in his seat. Behind panicky eyes, Waddell's mind seemed to be struggling. Where had he been on the Saturday night the Birdman was murdered?

Waddell shook his head as if trying to shake himself out of a bad dream. 'I didn't even know the bloody man.'

'That's not what Geraldine Flett told us,' said Palmeira, unsure whether this was strictly true.

'What do you mean?'

'She said you'd got some business deal going with Phillip Clarkson.'

Waddell hesitated — for far too long — before limply denying it.

'She said you had dragged her and the kid along on Sunday morning because you said it was a chance to get alongside Clarkson again.'

'No.'

It was an answer Danniher 'would not accept'. He shouted so loud even Palmeira winced before resuming.

'You don't seem to me to be the type who'd spring out of bed on Sunday morning to go bird watching. So what was it then?'

'What was what?'

'What was the idea? A chance to show you hadn't killed Clarkson?'
Waddell looked baffled.

'After all, who'd suspect someone would turn up to meet the man he'd killed only hours earlier? Very clever.' Probably too clever for Waddell, thought Danniher. Still, it was worth a try.

By now Waddell seemed thoroughly confused.

'Hang on, hang on,' he said, seeking time to think.

'And why did you run away when you saw my guys at the funeral?' asked Palmeira, pressing home his advantage.

'I just saw these two blokes coming at me. I didn't know they were cops.'

ༀༀༀ

So it continued, like an uneven boxing match, with Palmeira and Danniher probing and pressing and Waddell soaking up punishment without ever being knocked out for the count. After another 45 minutes, the detectives decided to call a temporary halt.

For all his confusion and sweaty discomfort, Waddell had still not admitted anything. Not even knocking people over and stealing their credit cards.

Not to worry, thought Palmeira. It was only a matter of time. Only a matter of playing Waddell and his partner in crime off against each other.

'Think about it, Mr Waddell,' urged Palmeira. 'It'll be better for you if you co-operate.'

'Tell your side of the story,' added Danniher. 'I mean, what happened: did you fall out with Clarkson? Have an argument? Hit him harder than you should? Perhaps you can convince us it was an accident. That you didn't mean to kill him.'

Waddell was returned to his cell and Michael Kenyon brought in. A quick check had already established that he was single, aged 33, had been employed by Berwick Shire Council for eight years and had no police record.

Apparently, he'd met his new best mate at a council tip. Waddell had been trying to dispose illegally of toxic waste. The two men had come to an 'arrangement'. Their partnership had kicked on from there.

To Palmeira and Danniher, the inexperienced Kenyon appeared to be the weaker link. The one more likely to crack, to break down, to dob in a mate to save his own skin. Certainly, he looked weak after spending his first night in a cell. He emerged tired, dirty and dishevelled, complaining of pain in his injured shoulder.

Yet, the cockiness had still not been knocked totally out of him, Palmeira was surprised to see.

'Look,' he started confidently. 'I'm sorry about yesterday.'

The two policeman did not speak.

'I didn't know what was happening. I never thought it was police. I thought it was one of those car jackings. You read about these things...'

Danniher stopped him in mid-sentence. 'We're not here to talk about you assaulting a police officer, Mr Kenyon,' he shouted 'We're here to talk about the murder of Phillip Clarkson.'

Kenyon's mouth dropped open.

Danniher bent aggressively forward. 'You did know Mr Clarkson, of course?'

'Yes...well...sort of...Through the work he did for the council. But you don't think I had anything to do with his, you know...'

'We've had a long chat with your good mate Gordon,' explained Danniher, leaving Kenyon to fill in the detail. 'We're all agreed that killing Phillip Clarkson and burying him in the sand was a two-man job...'

He left the damaging allegation to dangle invitingly in the air.

Kenyon glanced hurriedly round the room, as if searching it for something convincing to say. For what seemed like a minute, the two detectives patiently waited until he started again.

'Look, guys...this thing's becoming a flaming nightmare. Can we start again, please?'

Palmeira and Danniher did not speak.

'I think I'm going to need a solicitor. But I want it written down now that I helped you guys. I'll tell you what you want to know, but the main thing I want to say is I had nothing to do with Clarkson's murder.'

'No?'

'No. And I'll tell you something else for free, neither did the Fat Man. And that's the truth.'

'Really?'

'Yeah. God knows how I got involved in all this…the buzz more than the money, I suppose…anyway, the point is, we couldn't have done it. We were nowhere near the area on Saturday night.'

'Who said anything about Saturday night?'

'Come on. It was all over the papers.'

'Where were you, then?' Danniher sounded apprehensive. He didn't want to be convinced that the two men had been elsewhere.

Kenyon hesitated. Palmeira had seen it all before: another loser wondering whether he could get away with another lie, or whether it was time to start telling the truth and face its consequences.

'We were doing over this warehouse. Live-wire Electronics or something it was called. Up past the airport.'

'We don't believe you.'

'I'm sure you can check it out,' Kenyon replied, coolly. 'Your blokes would have found some of their gear at Gordy's house, I bet.'

Palmeira and Danniher would check it out. Time, place, goods reported missing. But they knew it had to be true. They felt deflated.

For the next hour, they listened despondently as Kenyon twisted and turned, doing his utmost to incriminate his former house-guest, while admitting only that he'd helped Waddell on some, though not all, of the break-ins on the Operation Kookaburra list.

His recall of times and places, they found, was almost faultless, even on jobs going back several weeks. He tried to convince them that he'd stupidly allowed his unit to be used to store the stolen gear. But he vigorously denied being involved with Waddell in any of the muggings. 'You know, sometimes I think the guy's a psycho.'

It was difficult now to shut Kenyon up. 'He enjoys having a go at Asians and gays and that. He's proud of it. Thinks he's doing Aussies a big favour. You ask him, I bet he'll be pleased to tell you. He should be locked up.'

So he will be, for a very long time, thought Palmeira. But, unfortunately, not for the murder of Phillip Clarkson.

Where the hell did that leave the inquiry? Palmeira was reminded how, only a week earlier, Bob Adamovitch had picked Waddell's name out of the list of birders. He'd said he'd been involved in race attacks. Who else had the old cop mentioned? Finch? Certainly. Morris? No, it was the wrong Morris. Workman? Yes.

As a list of suspects, it was painfully thin.

'Shut up will you please, Mr Kenyon,' said Palmeira. He was anxious now to hand him over to Munro, whose Operation Kookaburra team could sort out precisely who did what.

If Kenyon could prove he wasn't involved in any of the bashings, he'd probably escape jail, he thought. Meanwhile Palmeira tried again.

'Now, just to get back to Clarkson...'

Kenyon's body stiffened again. 'Not that again. I've told you. I bumped into him a few times at the council. Mainly over the Pelican Estates development. Waste disposal was a big issue. I gave him some advice. But that was it. Honest.'

Kenyon had little more to add. He was sent back to his cell. Waddell was brought back in.

The two officers were surprised by how easy it'd been to persuade each man to incriminate the other, and how effectively they'd been able to bounce one man's testimony off the other's.

Now, they hit Waddell hard with Kenyon's latest allegations and the evidence collected from his new home. Waddell shrugged. He seemed relieved to go through the Operation Kookaburra list, admitting some items, even muggings. Just so long as he wasn't fitted up for murder.

Palmeira had not finished with it, though. 'So, back to Phillip Clarkson...'

Waddell sighed wearily.

Palmeira ignored him. 'Michael Kenyon said all that stuff with Clarkson was your idea.' He fully expected Waddell to ask, what 'Clarkson business'?

Instead, he replied, 'Well, he's a bloody liar.'

'What a surprise,' said Palmeira, looking bored.

'Really. I don't know what he's been telling you...'

Nothing, really, thought Danniher. He had to admire the ability of his boss to finesse information from suspects.

'…but it was his idea. You know me. I'm the big, fat bloke with the muscles. He's the brains.'

'Sure,' said Palmeira, still waiting patiently for Waddell to tell him what the 'Clarkson business' was.

'The thing is he was on the inside, right? He knew what this Clarkson character was up to.'

'And what was that then?'

'You know.'

'Remind us.'

'Taking backhanders from all sides, he was. According to Mikie, he said it'd be dead easy for us to get a slice of the action.'

'And if Clarkson didn't give you one?'

'He had to. Any problems and he knew we'd telephone the local rag. Tell everyone about his dirty little games.'

'It sounds like blackmail to me.'

Waddell again wobbled at the suggestion. 'No way. We were not after cash, just one of those nice juicy contracts up for grabs. We had it all worked out. We'd get the contract for shifting all the waste from the new estate. That's my trade.'

'So what happened?'

'Nothing really. Mikie spoke to him just the once. Told him what we had in mind, like. Clarkson told him to get nicked.'

'And you decided to get rough with him?'

'Nah. Never got the chance. Mikie got me to go along on Saturday, nice and friendly like with the family in tow, to give our friend the birdman a bit of a scare. Show him we were still on his case.'

Waddell paused, before spreading his arms, and adding, with a look of sublime innocence, 'Too late. Someone else had got there before us.'

ജ്ഞോജ്ഞ

Jonno Sedgwick was overjoyed. The arrest of Waddell and Kenyon enabled him to wipe out a big backlog of unsolved crime. He was also happy to take personal credit for having pressed the Birdman team to pursue the big man.

'I won't say I told you so, but…dammit, I did tell you so, didn't I?' he goaded Palmeira and Danniher, as soon as the two men responsible for Berwick's crime wave had been formally charged and returned to the cells.

'A triumph for good old-fashioned policing, eh?' he added, before marching off to tell the media unit to set up a press conference, at which stolen property retrieved from the 'Aladdin's Cave' could be proudly displayed.

Palmeira and Danniher were left to ponder another disappointment.

'So what did we get out of that that we didn't already know?' asked Palmeira. His leg was throbbing. He was tired. He feared he was already putting on weight. Suddenly, this felt like the longest week of his life.

Danniher recognised the symptoms and tried to think positively about the day's events.

'Not a lot, I'm afraid, sir,' he said, at last. 'Forensics may come up with something next week on the crowbar. But my bet is it was just used by Waddell for breaking into places, not bashing up people.' Nor clubbing Clarkson senseless.

'I think you're right.'

'I suppose we got it loud and clear from these guys that Phillip Clarkson was up to some pretty dirty tricks.'

'Yes. But that isn't much. Koslowski got pretty much the same message from the council. Still, it explains why some one, one of the birders for example, might have a grudge against Clarkson.'

Danniher had almost exhausted his powers of positive thinking. 'I suppose we now have one less suspect to worry about?' he suggested.

'So, who's left? There's always Workman. And, I don't know, Enderby? But you saw him: you'd have to say he's almost physically incapable of getting to the toilet on his own let alone carting bodies about in the night.'

'I think we can rule him out,' conceded Danniher. 'Though how he came to be on the list of birders is still a bit of a mystery.'

Palmeira sighed. 'My big worry is that the murderer simply isn't on the list of suspects. It's someone we haven't thought of.'

'Or we simply don't know the existence of,' added Danniher.

'Thanks for that piece of encouragement.' Palmeira said, hanging downcast, limp-armed, on his crutches.

'Sorry.'

Palmeira pulled himself up and smiled. 'You're right,' he announced. 'Let's call it a day. We've been going pretty much flat out all week. Unless there's some new development, let's look at it again on Monday.'

Danniher could hardly believe it. 'Good idea. Maybe think about getting Mrs Clarkson to do a stand-up for the TV boys, eh? You know, "tearful mother pleads for information about dead son"?'

'Not a bad idea,' conceded Palmeira, though he did wonder whether it was wise to alert the dozy, distracted media to the fact that the police were no closer to finding the Birdman murderer.

'Right,' said Danniher, anxious to close the conversation before the detective inspector changed his mind. Already, he was planning to call Path Prior and see if she had anything on at the weekend, or what was left of it. 'Do you need a lift home, sir?'

'No, I'll be right. I'll get one of the others.'

'See you Monday, then.'

'Sure. See you.' Palmeira was already worrying about how difficult he would find slotting back into domestic life with Jenny and the girls. One thing was certain: with his leg in plaster, there'd be no escape from enforced rest and relaxation.

❦❧❦

Crime does not pay. Mario Palmeira had always found the old adage amusing. Of course, it's wrong. It would be more accurate, he thought, to say that crime 'does not play'. It does not take a relaxing day or two off. There really was no rest for the wicked.

It came as no surprise to him, then, to learn that while he and his team had been resting, crime was still going about its dirty business.

On Sunday, just as he had half-expected, there was a development — one that did not require the urgent attention of either Palmeira or Danniher, but was serious enough to rule Mrs Clarkson out of any staged media event.

By a bizarre coincidence, it occurred, just like the Birdman murder, early on Sunday morning. It was just before 6 o'clock that Inspector Clive Leyton, back on duty at Berwick station, received the call from police at Coffs Harbour.

A man taking his dog for an early morning walk along cliffs north of the city had spotted something odd on a beach. On closer inspection it was found to be the body of a man. He was still alive, but unconscious, and clearly had been bashed and kicked about the head and stomach.

'Oh, and another thing,' said the Coffs Harbour detective, 'he was naked from the waist down. When I heard that I immediately thought of you blokes. I know you love that sort of thing.'

'Very funny,' said Leyton.

'We thought so,' the detective laughed down the line. 'Anyway, he's been taken to hospital. Doctors say he should be OK — but the thing is we didn't need to wait for him to come round to tell us who he is. We've had a few dealings with him before. Nothing too serious. Drunk and disorderly. Some soft drugs...'

'I think I can guess,' said Leyton.

'Thought you might.'

'Paul Clarkson.'

'Got it in one, mate. The bare bum's a dead giveaway, isn't it? Must run in the family.'

'Thanks for letting us know.'

'No worries. We could hardly miss the connection. It's been all over the papers up here. "Local man's grief over murdered brother". All that sort of stuff. Question is, do you want to leave it to us, or send your own man up?'

'I'll have to get back to you. But thanks again for thinking of us.'

'Any more naked men — you'll be the first to know.'

Immediately after he'd put the phone down, Leyton called Palmeira. No reply. Odd. He always seemed to be on duty, even at some ungodly hour on a Sunday, even when he was on crutches. Disappointed, Leyton then rang Danniher who, after listening yawned and said, 'Thanks Clive. Leave it to me.'

If Danniher did not seem particularly unhappy at being disturbed it was because he immediately passed the buck to someone else.

'What was all that about then?' asked a sleepy voice, when Danniher had put the phone down.

'Nothing that can't be flick-passed to someone else, Sandy.'

Thus it was that Kiwi Koslowski found himself taking a 75-minute flight to Coffs Harbour.

He did not enjoy having his weekend messed up, though in other circumstances he'd have quite enjoyed spending a few days in the city. It was a pleasant, sub-tropical holiday resort, famous for its local industry variation on the Big Australian Things theme: in the case of Coffs, a huge, concrete landmark celebrating the 'Big Banana'.

But this was a rush job. Another bashing. Another Clarkson. Was someone working their way through the Clarkson family? Surely, it couldn't be a coincidence?

By the time Koslowski arrived at the local hospital, Paul Clarkson had been moved from intensive care into a general ward and was sitting up in bed, with his wife, Louise, beside him.

'Oh god, not you again,' he said through swollen lips, on seeing Koslowski. Swathed in bandages, covered in cuts and bruises, and nursing two cracked ribs, he looked an even sorrier sight than when Koslowski had interviewed him in Paddington.

Koslowski shrugged. 'Sorry, I need to have a few words. It shouldn't take too long,' he explained to a pretty woman, dressed in hippy backpacker gear.

'You're wasting your time,' she said in a soft, English voice. 'He won't tell you anything.'

That was not entirely true. It was like pulling teeth, but Koslowski extracted some basic facts. How three men in a car had picked up Clarkson near his home late the previous night. How they'd taken him for a 'short drive' to a secluded spot, near the nudist beach, where all four had got out for a 'quiet talk'.

'What about?'

'What do you think? Money,' Paul Clarkson answered.

'Money you owe them?'

'Obviously.'

'Getting behind on the payments?'

'You could say that. I'd already missed a couple of payments and then, Phillip...' Paul Clarkson's voice trailed off. 'Things have got messy.'

'A cash-flow problem?'

'Yes.'

'So what happened?'

'These guys aren't like your local bank managers. They're mean. They don't like being messed around.'

'Go on.'

'I told them, you know, the cheque's in the mail,' Clarkson smiled weakly. 'Guess what? They didn't believe me. Decided to give me a taste of what happens next.'

'So what was the deal with the trousers?'

Clarkson snorted through his bloodied, though unbroken, nose. 'They read the papers, too. Just their sick joke. "Birdman's brother in copycat attack". Funny, eh?'

'OK, thanks.' Koslowski had heard enough. 'No doubt you've passed on the names of these three jokers to the cops here,' he said, ironically.

'Now you're joking,' replied Clarkson, closing his eyes.

As he sat in the terminal at Coffs, waiting for his return flight, Koslowski spotted Mrs Clarkson, arriving from Sydney. She looked haggard, as though she'd aged a decade in a week.

She did not see Koslowski and he made no attempt to speak to her. He wouldn't have known what to say. Except perhaps 'sorry'.

14

You're about as cheerful as a Mallee hen with a toothache.
— Arthur Russell, *Bungoona*

Not even in their worst nightmares could Palmeira and Danniher have imagined that there would be two more violent deaths before the murderer of Phillip Clarkson was found.

But each felt a strange sense of foreboding as they returned to work on Monday morning. If picking up the pieces of the Birdman Case wasn't dispiriting enough, each felt distracted by domestic worries.

Wayne Danniher had had a wonderful, if short, weekend, spent getting to know Sandy Prior better. And, he slowly realised, getting to know himself. To his surprise, the junk-food-eating, beer-drinking, footy-watching stereotype Australian male had been replaced by a man who went shopping in a supermarket, cooked meals for two in his cramped kitchen, and took in French movies — with sub-titles, even — in the city.

They'd had a great time. But now he worried. Where was all this leading? This relationship with Prior was getting serious. Perhaps too serious. Someone could get hurt. Probably him.

By contrast, Mario Palmeira had had a wretched time and so, inevitably, had Jenny and the girls. After the previous week's dramas, he knew they'd been looking forward to a quiet family Sunday at home and, predictably, he'd ruined it.

For one thing, Jenny needed some 'quantity time', as she put it, with her husband to discuss a backlog of issues: the girls' schooling, a family holiday and, top of her list, her plan to go back to work full-time.

And that meant extracting a pledge from Mario that he'd do his fair share of household duties. Not an easy thing to do. The last time they'd discussed the subject, she'd lost her temper with him.

'You're always talking about getting "balance" in your life,' she'd shouted at him. 'But what you mean is that family life has to be organised round one thing. The only thing, you really care about. Your bloody work.' Mario had sulked for days.

This weekend had not been much different. Unable to move far on his crutches, Palmeira had moped around the house, fretting about the Birdman Case, dipping into newspapers, surfing the TV channels. Trying to find something to take his mind off his work and his aching ankle.

Even Claire and Preya, whom he loved dearly, couldn't shake him out of his bad mood, though they did their best. Asked to fetch a couple of paracetamols to ease the pain, they returned instead with aspirins.

The other tablets had all gone, they giggled, because 'the parrots eat 'em all'. It was an old family joke. Palmeira laughed, but really he'd had quite enough of parrots for one week.

Detecting the warning signs, Jenny hadn't dared to raise the subject of her job. Whatever his strengths and weaknesses as a husband and father, Mario was a bad patient and increasingly a reluctant listener — except when the speaker was another policeman.

Even her plan to stop him being bothered by work by muting the telephones did not work. Spotting a missed call on his answer machine, he'd checked into work to see if there'd been any developments. She could hear him chatting animatedly: about Clarkson, about 'another body on the beach', about Koslowski catching a plane somewhere. It was the only time he'd perked up.

The day had been ruined. Jenny knew it. Mario knew it. And, as he shuffled back into Berwick police station, he too wondered, guiltily in his case, where his marriage was going.

He was surprised to find Danniher already at his desk.

'G'day, sir, good weekend?'

'Great, thanks,' said Palmeira, cheerfully. 'How was yours?'

'Great.'

That Monday morning ritual out of the way, the two officers sat down in front of computer screens and started the painful task of sifting through the wreckage of the Birdman inquiry.

ೞೞೞೞ

Even the 'Ploddites' — cop-shop slang for Luddite officers who hate new technology — conceded that in the good old, bad old days before computers, police investigations could be haphazard, hit-and-miss operations.

In those days police struggled to cope with the huge amounts of information generated by a big case: written statements, photographs, forensic reports, videos, maps, diagrams and so on, usually stored in boxes. It meant they often failed to make the connections between pieces of information needed to solve crimes speedily.

Even the appointment of a senior officer as a full-time 'reader' to sift through all the boxes of case-material, was limited by his or her powers of concentration and comprehension.

Palmeira recalled how the 20-month investigation into the infamous 'Backpacker Murders' of the early 1990s had been hindered by precisely this problem. There'd been seven bodies and seven discrete investigations, each with its own team, each with its own silo of evidence. Altogether, the inquiries produced more than one million pieces of information from the public alone.

In addition, detectives were faced with massive tasks, such as checking some 50,000 registered owners of Ruger .22 rifles and investigating potential suspects among long lists of known sex offenders and wife-batterers.

Eventually, it was only by sheer chance that a vital piece of information was found and a crucial link made between other incidents involving backpackers, hitchhikers and disappearances.

Since then, things had changed. Palmeira and his fellow detectives still took notes, still wrote reports, still collected photographs and still employed whiteboards to analyse cases. But now they also used a wonderful new intranet system of investigation management.

It was called *E@gle-i* and it promised a 'truly bird's eye view of crime' enabling detectives to review information from several angles, search for new information, alert investigators when it became available, search through lists, make connections, manage tasks, analyse scanned fingerprints.

There was only one snag. As Berwick's resident computer whizz Helen

McCrimond explained, the all-singing, all-dancing *E@gle-i* system had a limited imagination. 'Put it this way, sir: it can't see outside its own computer box. It can only work with the information it's given.'

Palmeira and Danniher reflected gloomily, as they sat in front of their terminals, that it hadn't been given much at all. It was up to them to think outside the box.

What had they missed? Who had they overlooked? What could they do, apart from waiting for something to turn up, someone to make a mistake, someone else to be killed?

Despite the bizarre, copycat attack on Paul Clarkson — a whodunnit more easily explained than solved — all the signs were that his brother's murder was a one-off. But had it been random? Or planned? Had Clarkson known his killer? Or was he, or she, a stranger?

'I still think we don't know who we're looking for. If you get my meaning,' said Danniher after several minutes' thought.

'No, I get you. What you're saying is that it's someone not on any of the lists. Someone we haven't thought of.'

'Possibly, someone we couldn't even link to Clarkson. Someone he'd never seen before.'

Palmeira grimaced. 'We're just going round in circles here.' The statistics, he reminded himself, showed that the vast majority of murders were committed by people known to their victims. In many cases, they were family.

Now, there's a thought. Clarkson's mother and brother relied on each other for an alibi. But what had they to gain by Phillip's death?

Then again, there was the motley collection of birders. What if the murder was the work of a conspiracy among the people who found the body? It seemed far-fetched, but just such a crime had happened in an Agatha Christie novel, Palmeira seemed to recall.

'So, what next?' Palmeira tried to sound purposeful.

Danniher frowned. 'Sorry, sir.'

'Don't worry,' Palmeira replied. 'I know how you feel.' He pulled himself to his feet and went outside to scrutinise the whiteboard.

'Look,' said Danniher, joining him. 'It seems to me we've got to cover both possibilities. One, the name of our killer's up here staring us in the face. So we work through the names. Some we still haven't even interviewed.'

'Like the two women.'

'Yes. Others, like Finch and Workman, we go back on.'

'And, two?'

'He's not on the list. In which case our only hope of catching him is to find a witness. Someone must have seen something. You've got to believe that.'

Palmeira nodded. 'We could use Mrs Clarkson. Media conference. Mother's plea for help to catch her son's murderer. That sort of thing.'

'Is she up to it?'

'Doesn't really matter, does it? The media won't want self-control. They'll want grief, bloodshot eyes, a flood of tears.'

'Sounds good.' Danniher almost sounded like he meant it.

'At least we've got Jonno off our backs for a few days.'

'Yeah. Haven't seen him today.'

'In town with the top brass, apparently.'

'Thought it was quiet.'

ജന്ധ

The two women, whom Palmeira always thought of as a pair, couldn't have been more cooperative. They'd been waiting eagerly to be interviewed and offered to meet up at Maddy Warnock's house.

'You can kill two birdwatchers with one stone,' she joked. If the two women had been traumatised by the gruesome discovery of Phillip Clarkson's corpse they were disguising it remarkably well.

They made an odd-looking group. Palmeira and Warnock were short; Griffiths and Danniher tall. In fact, looking at Libby Griffiths now, Palmeira could quite easily imagine her dragging Clarkson's body across the dunes.

'You poor man,' said Libby, giving Palmeira a helping hand with his crutches and guiding him to the sofa. 'Make yourself comfortable. I'll fetch you a cushion.' Maddy produced tea and cake.

It was more like a social get-together than a police interview, thought Danniher, as he juggled plate, cup and notebook. Tea was followed by a tour of Maddy's leafy suburban garden and a ten-minute lecture on the birds to be found there: miners, magpies and currawongs — 'bully birds' as Libby called them — but also cockatoos, lorikeets, kookaburras and even the occasional king parrot.

The women described once again how they found the body of the Birdman. They volunteered, without being asked, alibis for the night he was murdered. And they invited the two policemen — and their families — to join the birding group on its next outing.

'It was Mr Finch's idea,' explained Libby. 'He wants to organise a count of the birds still on the bay. So we can monitor what happens to them over the next few years.'

'Come along. Next Sunday it is,' said Maddy. 'Ten o'clock.' Two weeks almost to the hour since Clarkson's body was found, thought Palmeira.

'Same little group,' Maddy commented.

'Not quite,' said Danniher. He explained to her that Mr Waddell was now in jail, facing serious charges.

'Did he do it, then? Kill Phillip Clarkson?'

'We don't think so.'

'Oh dear. Perhaps his wife…'

After two hours, Palmeira and Danniher left, little wiser.

ର୍ଷ୍ଠ୍ୟ

It was a suitably tearful, distraught-looking Margaret Clarkson who appeared at the media conference appealing for public help to solve the mystery of her son's murder.

Paul had made a quick recovery and been released, sore and somewhat scared, from hospital on the Monday evening. Local police had called Koslowski to say he refused to name the loan sharks who'd bashed him, insisting that he'd 'sort things out' himself.

Meanwhile, Koslowski learned later, his mother had given him enough money to make two months' repayments.

Margaret Clarkson had flown back to Sydney on the Tuesday morning. To Palmeira's surprise she readily agreed to do the media conference. When he'd offered some coaching, she turned him down.

'I'm quite used to appearing before big audiences, thank you.' He had forgotten she was a university lecturer. He still worried that she would freeze when confronted with a bank of cameras and microphones. But she turned out to be a natural. Her tears, when they came, were real.

The media conference was packed. Fortunately, it was a 'slow' news day when human-interest stories were in short supply. Among the familiar, reptilian faces of the press, Palmeira spotted Chris Workman, grinning smugly, and his media mate, Karen Chan, who gave a friendly nod.

Palmeira's hands were clammy and shaking as he stood to give a brief outline of the case, so far. Surely someone would ask him why the police hadn't made more progress. And, as he knew to his cost from previous conferences, it only took one nasty question to set off a media feeding frenzy. He half-expected to be savaged.

Instead, the press pack heard him out politely. Maybe even the media thought it unfair to accuse a man prepared to come to work on crutches of sitting back and doing nothing. Palmeira moved quickly on.

Photographs both of Phillip Clarkson and of his green Volkswagen were flashed up on to a big screen. Copies of the pictures and maps of the crime area were distributed. Palmeira appealed for anyone who'd seen either man or vehicle on that Saturday to come forward.

Only then did he introduce his star turn. Mrs Clarkson emerged theatrically from behind a screen, on the arm of Wayne Danniher. For a moment, she stopped and blinked, her vulnerability exposed — as Palmeira intended — by a burst of flashbulbs and a rattle of camera shutters.

On the advice of Palmeira and Danniher, Mrs Clarkson declined to answer questions. They didn't want her harassed. And, more important, they didn't want to give the media an opportunity to raise other distressing issues, such as the Birdman's sexual preferences and his business dealings.

What they wanted was five minutes of raw, wet emotion from a grief-stricken mother. Mrs Clarkson gave it to them.

With Palmeira and Danniher sitting either side of her, she delivered a simple, tearful, four-minute statement. It was part scripted, part spontaneous; part a heartfelt expression of genuine pain, part a clear-headed appeal for information.

'Nothing will ever bring my son back,' she concluded. 'All I seek now is closure to my suffering. Please help me find it.' She then stood and, as Danniher leapt to his feet to help, walked off.

Everyone agreed, it was a compelling performance. 'Almost made me cry,' Danniher admitted later.

The coverage on television and radio that evening and in the newspapers the next morning exceeded the expectations of even the media unit. As far as Palmeira could see, all the reports had concentrated on Mrs Clarkson's impassioned plea; none had thought to question why, after more than a week, the police had made such little progress. Good.

࿋࿋࿋

Palmeira's day had started well. It did not last. Around mid-morning, as the first reports of public offers of help in the Birdman case began to trickle through, Palmeira and Danniher were interrupted by Clive Leyton. He had a strange look on his face.

'Hi. Heard the news about Jonno, then?'

The two detectives snapped round. 'No,' said Danniher. 'Don't tell me, he's fallen under a squad car?'

Leyton laughed. 'Almost as good. He's leaving. In fact, he's left.'

Palmeira felt like clapping. Or cheering. Instead, he asked the obvious question. 'Where's he going?'

Leyton smiled. 'It's just come through. Homicide HQ. Part of the reorganisation. Apparently, they were impressed with his recent clear-up rate here.' He left the news sink in, before adding, 'I think that means you will still be reporting to him.'

Even from across the city, Palmeira could feel Sedgwick applying the pressure to make an arrest. Turning the screws at least to come up with some new leads. Or else.

'Knew you'd be pleased,' said Leyton, his laughter echoing down the corridor.

࿋࿋࿋

Poor Koslowski, meanwhile, was on his way to the headquarters of Pelican Estates in the city to question Hugh Boswell-Smith, its English-born chief executive about payments to Phillip Clarkson.

Some quick research had revealed that Pelican was a mid-size development company, owned by a mix of Australian, Malaysian and Singaporean investors. It specialised in city-centre office blocks and out-of-town business parks. The expanded estate at Berwick would be far and away its biggest.

Koslowski wondered what other payments Pelican was making to guarantee it went ahead. Bribes? Kickbacks to council officials? 'Donations' to political parties?

He arrived at Boswell-Smith's offices on the 27th floor of a soaring tower of concrete and reflective glass to find himself confronted by several men, representing the executive, legal, financial, media relations and corporate secretarial arms of the Pelican empire.

'Here we go again,' he thought, recalling his reception at Berwick Town Hall.

It was immediately obvious to the detective that PE chiefs had been tipped off by their council mates. Getting their stories straight, no doubt.

Yes, Boswell-Smith and his team of advisers agreed, they'd used Phillip Clarkson, as a well-known and respected authority on conservation matters, on an occasional basis, to brief Pelican staff on sensitive issues, such as the protection of bird habitats.

Why? Such briefings were an 'important part of ongoing staff education aimed at ensuring the company fulfilled its social and environmental obligations'. Yes, they agreed, he had then been employed on a more regular basis. What for? To help create an 'informal forum' where developers and conservers could 'constructively exchange views and establish a mutual understanding'.

Yes, they confirmed, in recent months Clarkson had been paid according to a new contract, which 'reflected his increased public education responsibilities' as the Berwick business park project advanced.

No, Pelican had nothing to say about any similar arrangement struck between Berwick council and Mr Clarkson. And, no, it could see nothing wrong with him being paid to act as what the company described as, an 'honest broker', bringing together the various interest groups involved in a complex multi-million dollar project such as the business park.

An honest broker! You had to laugh, thought Koslowski, gratefully emerging into the fresh air. He felt like he'd been repeatedly hit over the head for two hours with several four-by-two pieces of foam rubber.

ເວເວເວ

If Wednesday had been bad for poor Palmeira, Thursday was worse.

First there was a note saying Jonno Sedgwick had already called. He was on his way to a meeting, but would ring back later. It could only mean more bad news.

Then there was the feedback from Mrs Clarkson's media appearance. Palmeira had come in expecting to find the office swamped with new information, but there had been barely a trickle to add to the drops on Wednesday.

No one, it seemed, had seen Phillip Clarkson anywhere near the crime scene. Even the number of crank callers, who could always be relied upon to respond to appeals for information about the whereabouts of anyone, from Elvis Presley to E.T., was small.

Several members of the public telephoned in to say they'd seen a green Volkswagen. Two had spotted the car in the area of Miranda, near to where it had eventually been found, early on Sunday morning. Neither remembered anything about the driver.

Of more interest, three callers — who sounded sensible to Helen McCrimond — claimed to have seen the car on Saturday night. All three placed it not on Bayside Drive, near the dunes, but on the other side of the bay, in the car park, right where Clarkson was supposed to rendezvous with his group of birders.

Palmeira was still puzzling over what this meant, when Danniher came in with the morning paper.

'Seen this?' he said. His tone suggested it was not good news.

The newspaper was folded open at a full-broadsheet-page feature-length article, boldly headlined 'The Birdman Unmasked'. It was written by someone who now styled himself Christopher Robin Workman.

It was all there in Workman's self-styled 'exposé': all the lucrative deceptions, all the double-dealings, all the cash-for-comments dirty deals by which one of Australia's leading avian experts had tried to 'dig his family and himself out from beneath a mountain of debts'.

Palmeira winced at some of the writing. At one point, Workman accused Clarkson of having 'betrayed not just the nation's bird-lovers, but its birds as well'. The illustration, too, was preposterous: a cartoon showed a big, parrot-like bird with Phillip Clarkson's head looking through binoculars at piles of money.

All the same, it was powerful, emotive stuff. Workman concluded that Phillip Clarkson was a cheat, a traitor, and a hypocrite.

'Pity dead men can't sue,' said Palmeira.

'I warned him what would happen if we found he was withholding information.'

'We should pay him another visit. Remember he's got a history of taking the law into his own hands. And of bashing people who get in his way.'

'There's more,' said Danniher. 'Front page.'

Strung straight across all eight columns, at the top of the page, was another article by Christopher Robin Workman. 'Revealed: How Australia's "Birdman" Feathered His Own Nest'.

Palmeira read it with mounting anger. Much of the article was a preview of the material inside. What was new were comments from a man described by Workman as a former friend.

'One really doesn't like to speak ill of the dead,' the quote ominously began. 'but I'd always had my doubts about Phillip. He was always very commercially minded. Not that there's anything wrong with that. But, yes, I was surprised to learn of some of his business arrangements. No doubt he thought he was doing the right thing.'

The former friend had gone on: 'His death was a terrible, terrible shock. It's impossible to imagine who could've done such an awful thing. But to be honest, no one who worked with the young Phillip would deny he made enemies easily. As some people may know, he and I had a falling out some years ago.'

The journalist explained briefly the background to the row over the parrot, before quoting from the former friend again.

'By an odd coincidence, Phillip came to my house only a few weeks before his untimely accident. Or, rather, death. I fondly thought for a moment that the dear boy had come to say sorry. Sadly, that wasn't the case.'

The meeting had ended 'in raised voices, shaken fists and the Birdman flying off in a huff'. The former friend had been terribly upset. 'I've always said you should never walk out of a door in anger, slamming it behind you — you may never have the chance to go back'.

Palmeira slammed the newspaper down. His eyes were blazing with anger: not at the story, not at its author, but at the so-called former friend.

Ellis Enderby. The devious old bugger! He'd told them he hadn't seen Clarkson in years. Now, he was saying he had a fight with him only a couple of weeks before his death.

15

Nowhere to fall but off…

— Benjamin King, *The Pessimist*

Palmeira's telephone call to Jonno Sedgwick was short and to the point — Sedgwick's point being that the detective inspector had precisely one more week to make an arrest, or at least come up with a credible suspect. Otherwise, he would be dropped from the Birdman Case and forced to take leave.

'Nothing personal, but you're tired. You're incapacitated. You need a break.' Sedgwick told him. 'And I'm afraid we need some fresh thinking about Birdman.'

Palmeira had been expecting the worst: he knew when he rang Sedgwick that it wasn't going to be for a cosy chat about how sad Jonno was to be leaving all his old mates at Berwick behind. But this was personal. Of course, it was. Jonno had never liked him. Had always thought he was too smart, too reliant on new-fangled technology. It was humiliating. And worst of all it was unfair. He was devastated.

What else was he supposed to have done? What mistakes had he made? Could anyone else have done better, or worked harder, he demanded to know from Jonno, as he struggled to retain some dignity and self-control.

'Waddell. You lost him. You let him get away for too long. If I hadn't got on to this case, he'd still be out there mugging folk. Breaking into their homes.'

'But…'

'Look, I haven't got time to argue, detective inspector. The Birdman inquiries have been going nowhere. You have one week to prove me wrong.' There was a deathly rattle and the line went dead.

For several minutes, Palmeira sat there, shaking. Who else knew? Had Danniher been told? Should he tell Danniher? What would Jenny say? How on earth could he go on leave like this?

Not surprisingly, Palmeira was in a subdued mood as he and Danniher set off to interview first Workman and then Enderby. One — or possibly even both of them — had been making up stories. Telling lies to the police. Why was that?

'Did you have a yarn with Jonno?' asked Danniher, as they walked to the car. Clearly, he hadn't heard anything.

'A quick one.'

'So?'

Palmeira shrugged. 'The usual stuff. How he's got his eye on us. How he's looking for a quick result on the Birdman.'

'Huh. Easy for him to say.'

'That's what I told him.'

'You didn't?'

'You're right. I didn't.'

Danniher laughed and glanced sideways to share the joke. Palmeira looked grim. Perhaps his ankle was giving him pain. Perhaps he was just feeling tired after another long, eventful day.

It had taken a few hours to track down Workman to a radio station, where he was being interviewed by a fellow journalist. His articles had reignited public interest and, no doubt, made him the leading expert on the life and times of Phillip Clarkson, Palmeira thought bitterly.

Workman had arranged to meet them back at his home, at seven pm, but when the two detectives arrived it was immediately obvious he wasn't there. The door was opened instead by yet another young woman, probably in her mid-20s.

'Police?' she said, after briefly registering surprise at seeing a big man, with fair hair and ruddy complexion and a short, dark man on crutches. They reminded her vaguely of characters in a film she'd once seen. *Midnight Cowboy*. Jon Voigt had played the strapping country boy and Dustin Hoffman the short guy with a bad limp.

The Voigt character flashed his ID card. 'Wayne Danniher. And this is DI Mario Palmeira.'

'Pleased to meet you both.'

Danniher checked out the woman. She had dark-brown hair, cut boyishly short, and matching, brown eyes that seemed to be magnified by heavy black-framed spectacles. She wore a long-sleeve jumper, short skirt and tights, all black.

'And you are?'

'Sorry. Kath McCann. I'm a freelance writer. Chris is helping me. He's, like, my mentor.'

First, Clifford. Then, that 'research assistant' at the funeral. And now this Kath woman. Danniher shook his head in disbelief. What was Workman's secret?

For the first time, Palmeira spoke. His voice seemed to Danniher to tremble with emotion. 'So, where's Workman?'

'He said to tell you he's running late. More TV interviews, I bet.' She smiled proudly. The detectives looked at their watches and fumed.

'We'll wait,' said Danniher. Fair enough, Workman was an arrogant, annoying creep, but he was surprised to see how he'd got to Palmeira. Danniher had never seen his boss in such a morose mood.

Kath McCann stood aside and beckoned them inside the tiny house. Nice to be back, thought Danniher, pulling a stool from the breakfast bar. Palmeira sat uneasily on the edge of the bed, stretching his leg out in front of him.

'Want something to read?' called McCann, from the kitchenette, where she'd resumed chopping some vegetables.

'Thanks,' said Danniher. This was like being in a dentist's waiting room, he thought, as he started to leaf through back copies of magazines: *Private Eye*, *The Big Issue*, *Australian Geographic* and *Wingspan*.

Palmeira, he noticed, just sat and stared into the middle distance.

'Want the news on, then?' the young woman asked.

Danniher was just about to say yes, when Palmeira answered curtly. 'No.'

It was just after eight o'clock when Workman breezed in. 'How can I help you gentlemen?' he said with exaggerated politeness, after patting McCann ostentatiously on the backside and climbing out of his suit jacket, collar and tie. 'Just give us a couple of minutes, will you?'

'No,' said Palmeira. 'You just sit down and listen, or sort this out down at the police station.'

'You can't do that.'

'Yes we can. You'll be charged. Wasting police time. Obstructing a murder inquiry.'

Immediately, Palmeira regretted the words. Perhaps Workman would call his bluff. No doubt he'd like nothing better than to be charged, beaten up and thrown in a cell. What a story that'd make for his paper!

'I don't think that'd look very smart, would it, inspector?'

'What do you mean?'

Workman seemed to have regained his confidence. 'For one thing, you'd have to admit that one journo armed with a little tape-recorder — and a lot of enthusiasm — managed to ferret out more about the Birdman Case that you lot with your teams of detectives, your clever computers and whatever.'

'That's garbage,' said Danniher.

'No it's not. I happen to know one of your clowns went and talked to the council and the developers. Koslowski, wasn't it? The council told me he'd got into a fight and broken a bust of some local bigwig. It's going to make another ripper story.'

'You wouldn't dare.'

'Wouldn't I?'

'Anyhow, who did you speak to at the council?'

Workman straightened himself. 'You don't expect a journalist to divulge his sources, do you officer?'

'You still don't get it, do you, you grub.' Danniher was shouting. 'Withholding information. It's a serious crime.'

Workman ignored the threat. 'And all the stuff I got from that old boozer Enderby…'

Palmeira didn't let him finish the sentence. This was getting the police nowhere. And time was short. 'Look, Mr Workman, this isn't a game, it's a murder inquiry…'

'Oh really — and I suppose I'm a suspect, am I?'

'Too right you are,' said Danniher, turning to Palmeira for confirmation. 'It's not looking good for you, Mr Workman. You've had a run-in with Phillip Clarkson before. According to police records, you're a violent man. And as your article this morning proved, you've got a pile of dirt on him.'

If Workman was rattled, he did not show it. 'But I still don't have a motive, do I?'

'Blackmail,' said Palmeira. It was a long shot, he realised, as he started to lay out a murder scenario. 'You'd been blackmailing Clarkson. He'd had enough. Said — I don't know — that he was going to go to the police. You arranged a meeting. Saturday night. There was a fight and, well, you ended up killing him. How's that?'

'Total fantasy.'

'Then you tried to pin the blame on Ellis Enderby.'

'I don't believe what I'm hearing,' said Workman, turning to McCann for support.

Danniher jumped in. 'You made that stuff up about Enderby fighting with Clarkson again, didn't you? We spoke to him. He hasn't even spoken to him for years.'

'Not true. Clarkson came round to see him. About three weeks ago. Enderby told me himself.'

'You're lying.'

'That's ridiculous. Why would I do that?'

'To protect yourself. To get a good story.'

'I don't need protection and it's more than my job's worth to fabricate information.' Workman could see Palmeira and Danniher weren't impressed. He tried again.

'OK, maybe he'd had a few and I had to, how shall I say, edit some of his quotes, but I couldn't shut him up. Honest. He rambled on and on about Clarkson. How he'd done everything to help him. How he'd been stabbed in the back by him. How it was all down to this parrot that he'd seen in the desert. Et cetera. Et cetera.'

'You're still lying.'

'I'm not. If you don't believe me you can always go and ask him yourself.'

'Don't worry,' said Palmeira. 'We will.'

'I'd go in the morning. Might even catch him sober.' That, at least, made sense, agreed the two detectives as they decided to call it a day. Another frustrating day.

It was some time after seven o'clock the following morning, while he was having a shower, that Danniher took the call.

The body of a man had been found. On a rock platform at Palm Beach. According to police at Dee Why, some 20 minutes drive away, it had been reported almost simultaneously by a couple of people.

Danniher wrapped himself in a towel as the young officer explained that a fisherman had been walking across the rocks to a favourite fishing spot when he spotted what looked from a distance like a bundle of clothes. He had discovered it was a body and rang the local police.

At almost exactly the same time, a housekeeper, a Mary Jeffries, had turned up at the home above the platform to prepare breakfast for its elderly resident.

She'd opened the door with her own key, called out to wake him, as usual. There was no reply, as usual. After all, he was a heavy sleeper. When she called again and there was still no answer, she'd gone into the bedroom to rouse him.

The bed was empty. Indeed, the house was empty. She'd noticed the curtains flapping gently in the open french windows, and gone out on to the balcony, looked down and seen a body.

The arms and legs were almost spreadeagled, the head surrounded by a dark patch that proved to be a halo of dried blood.

Luckily she had been spared the pain of seeing the mutilated face, but guessed from the clothes — blue, winceyette pyjamas, fluffy slippers and heavy tartan dressing gown — that the body must be that of her employer.

Danniher did not need to be told the name. At the first mention of Palm Beach, he knew what was coming. Ellis Enderby was dead.

'Poor old bugger,' he said, as the young officer finished his account. 'Thanks for letting us know so soon. Detective Inspector Palmeira and me'll get up there straight away. Say, 45 minutes or so.'

'Righto. I know someone was talking to your DI a few minutes ago. Anyway, crime scene are already on the spot, sarge. And I was just trying to track down the pathologist.'

'Sandy Prior?'

'Yes.'

'Don't worry. I'll do it.'

Danniher switched off the phone, grabbed a towel and turned. 'Job for you,' he said to a wet body emerging from the shower behind him. Before he had time to explain, the telephone rang again.

It was Palmeira. 'You've heard, then?'

'Yes sir. Just come off the phone. Bloody awful isn't it?'

'Yes. We'd better get up there soon as possible. I'd better let Jonno know.'

'Good thinking.'

'I suppose so. All depends whether Enderby jumped or was pushed.'

'Hang on, sir,' said Danniher. 'It could have been an accident. He could've just fallen. Long session on the grog. Bit unsteady on his feet. Last look at the sea from the balcony before he goes to bed. And off he falls. Remember, that railing was very low.'

Palmeira grunted. 'Jonno'll blame me whatever happened. Still, better get going. Wayne, do you think you can give me a lift?'

Danniher had hoped he wouldn't ask. It involved a detour across town and he rather fancied driving up the coast with Prior.

'Sure. No worries.' At least Prior had her car parked outside.

❦❦❦❦

By the time the two detectives arrived at Enderby's house they could see from the balcony that the pathologist had completed preliminary investigations. The body was now inside a bag, ready to be lifted on to a litter.

'Want a look before we pop him away, sir?' shouted Prior, looking up.

Danniher glanced at Palmeira, who nodded. 'You do it. I can't do much rock-climbing with these,' he said, waving a crutch. 'I'll talk to her,' he added, motioning towards Mary Jeffries.

She was in a sorry state. Gone was the cranky old woman who'd intimidated them only a few days back. In her place was a sad, distraught woman, who'd shrunk into one of Enderby's deep chintzy chairs and seemed not to have spoken a word, nor barely moved, for more than an hour.

She seemed to be in shock and completely oblivious to the crime-scene officers working around her, methodically examining the damaged balcony railings and checking among the clutter of the dead man's belongings for signs of a suspicious death.

It was an almost impossible task. Despite Jeffries' attempts to impose order, Ellis Enderby remained chaotic in his personal habits. Who could tell what, if anything, was out of place among the piles of books and bottles, papers and plates scattered about the room.

'We've sent for her doctor, sir,' whispered one of the officers, who'd been taking fingerprints from bottles, glasses, cups, door-handles, even the old typewriter. 'I don't think you'll get much sense out of her for a while.'

'Thanks.' He had to have a go, though.

Palmeira tried. 'Miss Jeffries?' He placed a hand gently on her shoulder. There was no response. He tried again, a little louder now. 'Mary?'

Like someone emerging from a deep sleep, she turned her head, just a few degrees, and blinked. There was no hint of recognition in the eyes, but almost imperceptibly the lips moved.

'The silly old fool.' Tears welled in her eyes.

Palmeira did not rush her and it was several seconds before she spoke again.

'I knew something like this would happen.'

Over the next hour, Palmeira was able to piece together, painstakingly, from fragments of speech, a rough idea of the role played by Miss Jeffries in the life and death of Ellis Enderby.

A local woman who'd never married, she'd nursed her mother through the last ten years of life. After that she'd lived on her own. She'd started working for Enderby almost as soon as he moved to Palm Beach: first as a cleaner, coming in twice a week to tidy up.

But over the years, as Enderby's health deteriorated and his drinking increased, her work and her hours had expanded to the point where she came in every day to run errands, organise his precious papers and prepare meals, starting with a little breakfast each morning. She urged him to eat the meals, tried to ensure he took his medication, and occasionally nagged him about his smoking and his drinking.

Palmeira could see it would have been an odd, bickering, belligerent relationship. Though neither was likely ever to have admitted it, he suspected Enderby and Jeffries had grown to need each other.

It must have been painful witnessing his decline. First cancer. Then violent death. She'd miss the 'old fool' terribly.

'Mary, are you feeling up to talking about what happened now?'

She was, though her words came in fits and starts. Enderby, she recalled, had been especially difficult the previous day. The last day of his life. 'Something in the newspapers upset him…but then it usually did.' She smiled briefly at the memory.

Workman's articles, thought Palmeira, that's what upset him.

'I just stayed out of his way. His bad moods usually blew over once he'd had a drink.'

'Did this one?' Palmeira could almost hear Miss Jeffries trying to concentrate.

'Not really. He stomped around for a few hours like a bear with a sore head. Tried to phone someone. Had a drink. Had a few more drinks. Wouldn't eat any lunch.'

'When did you leave?'

'About five o'clock. He still didn't want anything to eat, but I made him some sandwiches, anyway. They're still there. He hadn't touched them.'

'Do you know if he was expecting visitors?'

'He didn't say. But it's most unlikely. Apart from you and that other policeman, I thought I was the only person he's spoken to in weeks…'

Palmeira was puzzled. Obviously, Miss Jeffries hadn't seen Enderby's comments in the newspaper. Or maybe she was right: he hadn't seen anyone and the story about a meeting with Clarkson and an interview with Workman had been fabricated. If she had seen the story, she presumably did not consider it her job to ask him about it.

'Oh my God. You don't think someone killed…' She dropped her head into her hands.

'I honestly don't know what to think, Miss Jeffries.' It was true. Murder? Suicide? Accidental death? He simply didn't know. Yet.

As Miss Jeffries sobbed again, Palmeira went over the permutations again.

The brutal murder of a man by someone who wanted Ellis Enderby dead? Perhaps so he couldn't speak to the police again?

The suicide of a man stricken by remorse at his own misdeeds, possibly even the murder of Phillip Clarkson, or depressed by the prospect of a painful death by cancer?

Or the accidental death of a sad old man who was probably so drunk he couldn't stand up straight? A tragedy waiting to happen.

One thing was certain: the death was suspicious, deeply suspicious — and he would say so to Sedgwick and to the media in the press release he was already preparing in his mind.

Miss Jeffries' doctor arrived. Palmeira took the opportunity to excuse himself and join Danniher, Prior and the others in the kitchen where they'd now gathered to swap notes. They seemed surprised to see him, falling silent as if they'd been sharing some secret, some joke, at his expense. Perhaps they knew about the ultimatum he'd been given. Surely not?

'Right. What've we got, then?' he said, banishing the thought.

Prior spoke first. 'Multiple fractures, including of the skull. Instant death, I'd say. It's a big drop. Fair to assume the deceased had consumed a considerable amount of alcohol. The smell — whisky, I guess — was still quite overwhelming.'

'Time of death?' Palmeira asked, avoiding eye contact. As so often happened with office romances, somehow her closeness with Danniher had complicated things, put distance between her and other colleagues.

For once, Prior did not hedge. 'An hour or two before midnight, I'd say.'

'Thanks.' Palmeira nodded at the crime-scene officer.

'Well,' he said, 'the railings where he went off the balcony are obviously a mess. But there are no obvious signs of a violent struggle, not on the body, nor upstairs here. The place is a tip, but if you look around there's no furniture overturned, bottles knocked over, that sort of thing.'

'Fingerprints?' demanded Palmeira, worried by the apparent lack of useful evidence — just like in the Birdman Case. Or, more accurately, he reflected gloomily, the first Birdman Case. He could already see the headline: 'New Birder Murder'.

'No good dabs so far, but we're still looking, sir.'

'OK. While I remember, can we check, see who Enderby was phoning? Danniher?'

'Sure. Will do. Another interesting thing, sir. Two of the uniformeds have already been out talking to neighbours.'

'And?'

'Well, we could have a lead. The houses are pretty big and set apart. People don't tend to see or hear a lot...'

'But?'

'...but the people at the end of the road were coming back about half eleven last night. I've just been round to have another word with them...' He took out a notebook.

'They'd come back from a night in town...anyhow, near the turn on to the main road they almost collided with a car coming from the other direction. The funny thing was apart from going pretty fast, it had no lights on...'

Palmeira leapt on the scrap of information like a starving man. 'Any details? Rego? Make?'

'Some. Odd really. They thought it might have been a cab. Metallic grey, silvery coloured, the man said. They knew old Enderby and thought it must have been bringing him back after one of his sessions in a pub.'

'Odd. Miss Jeffries here says he didn't get out any more. I mean you saw him the other time. Too sozzled by tea-time to go far I'd have thought.'

'I know.'

'Anyway, what do you mean they "thought" it was a cab? It'd be pretty obvious even without lights, I'd have thought.'

'The thing is, they said it didn't have one of those big taxi boxes strapped to its roof, or advertising on the back.'

'Sorry. So how did they know?'

'They were pretty sure there was writing on the side.'

'Did they get a name?'

'Nah. Couldn't make it out properly and...' He checked his notes again. '...they said they thought it might even have been covered over. Like it was disguised.'

'Well that's something,' said Palmeira, enthusiastically. Whoever was killing the birdmen of Australia may have just made their first mistake.

Danniher was less optimistic. 'I did wonder if it could have been one of those cars that sponsors give to sports people, or something.'

Palmeira shrugged. 'Never mind. Get someone — Koslowski or McCrimond — to check with the taxi companies. There's only four big ones in the city. It shouldn't be too hard to find out who took fares to Palm Beach late last night.'

'Kiwi's already on the case, sir. Of course, the taxi needn't have been on duty. Or the owner could have lent it to a mate. Or the mate of a mate. You now what those cabbies are like.'

'True,' said Palmeira. He refused to be downcast. 'Still, it's our best shot at the moment. Koslowski should also check if any of the companies have cabbies living up round this area.'

Suddenly, he sensed a breakthrough. Two birdmen dead. It couldn't be a coincidence. With any luck — and even the most meticulous detectives needed help from Lady Luck — he could get still get a quick result.

ଔଇଔଇ

As Danniher had anticipated, Koslowski quickly discovered that checking out the cabs was a slow job. Though Sydneysiders always whinged that you couldn't get a cab, when you wanted, there were, in fact, more than 4,000 working in the city. Roughly one for every 1,000 people.

According to the companies' records, none of them had been picking or setting down in Palm Beach between, say, nine and midnight, that Thursday night.

However, that wasn't to say, Koslowski was told, that an off-duty taxi couldn't have been in the area. Indeed, that could've explained why the rooftop box hadn't been displayed. Mates and relatives also drove taxis illegally, he was also reminded. Still, Koslowski was cheered to learned that only one of the four companies used grey-silver vehicles. It would email him a list of its licensed drivers, for what it was worth.

ଔଇଔଇ

Meanwhile, Palmeira had other pressing matters to occupy him. The media, the media unit, the acting chief at Berwick and, of course, Jonno Sedgwick all wanted to know what he was doing. With a sudden insight that sent a chill racing up his spine, Palmeira realised that his rush of confidence may have been premature.

Already, some people seemed to be blaming him for the death of a second birdman in disturbingly similar circumstances. The only difference was that while Clarkson only appeared to have fallen from the sky, Enderby actually had.

Inexplicably, Palmeira was reminded of Oscar Wilde, himself an old jailbird. What would he have said? To lose one birdman may be regarded as misfortune. To lose two looks like carelessness. Or incompetence.

His phone rang. It was journalist Karen Chan, wanting some inside info on Enderby's death. Was it being treated as murder? Palmeira cut her short. 'Sorry, no comment. No. I've got to go.' Where'd she got his direct number from? he wondered.

His phone rang again. It was the switchboard. There was a Mr Simon Finch on the line, asking for Danniher or him. And Danniher had slipped out.

'OK,' said Palmeira. 'Better put him through.' What did he want? Unless he was ringing to confess…

'Ah inspector,' came a voice down the line. 'I hear on the radio that you've lost another birdman.'

'Don't be stupid, Mr Finch,' said Palmeira. 'Look, I'm very busy. So…'

'All right, only joking. Whatever, they seem to be dropping like flies. Or shot pigeons, or…'

'Mr Finch. Stop wasting my time. Did you have something important to tell me? If not, I'll…'

'Hold on. Yes, I did. It was about our little reunion, wake, or whatever you want to call it. The ladies said they'd mentioned it?'

'Yes, but…'

'It's been cancelled. Or rather rearranged.'

'Oh,' said Palmeira, looking up as an envelope was dropped in his in-tray. It was marked urgent. 'Thanks.'

Finch was still talking. 'The thing is, suddenly there doesn't seem much point now.'

'Right.'

'For one thing, the others have gone off the idea of honouring Clarkson in some way. All that stuff in the papers by Chris has been a real eye-opener…'

'That's fine then…' Palmeira slapped the envelope rhythmically on the desk, waiting for Finch to finish.

'… and when you think about it there's only five of us left.'

Palmeira had stopped listening. Odd, he thought, looking more closely at the envelope. By the number of misprints and overtypes, he guessed the address had been typed not on a word processor but an old-fashioned typewriter.

Not many of those around these days. He opened his penknife and carefully slit open the envelope.

'Workman says it will be worth your while coming. Sorry, are you still there, inspector?'

'Sure,' said Palmeira absent-mindedly as he used the point of the knife to extricate the contents of the envelope.

'So, we're going to meet tomorrow, late afternoon, in the middle of Centennial Park. Near the concrete lake. Got that?'

'I'm sorry, Mr Finch. I'm really going to have to go. Something important's cropped up.' He put the phone down.

Laid out on Palmeira's desk was a single sheet of paper. On one side was a photocopied picture of a night parrot. On the other, were six words. They, too, were typewritten, in capital letters.

'SORRY. IT'S JUST ALL TOO MUCH.'

Beneath, was a signature. Ellis Enderby's.

ಜಐಜಐಜಐ

It took the Birdman team — or Birdmen team, as Danniher had amended it — less than three hours to answer Palmeira's questions about the suicide note.

When had it been posted? About six o'clock on Thursday evening.

Where was it posted? It had been sorted at the Northern Suburbs office at St Leonards, so probably somewhere on the North Shore.

Where had the picture of the parrot come from? A book called *Australian Parrots* by Joseph M. Forshaw.

Where was the typewriter on which the letter had been written? No doubt about that. At the home of the late Ellis Enderby.

Who signed the letter? Ellis Enderby, according to his housekeeper Miss Mary Jeffries. She'd seen his signature many times before.

However, no satisfactory answer had been found to the first question Palmeira asked himself on unfolding the letter: what did the six words mean?

'Pretty obvious. The old bloke topped himself,' said Danniher.

Palmeira was not so sure. It all depended, you see. On who the author was: it may not have been Enderby. On what he — assuming it was a he — meant by 'sorry'. And on what he meant by including a picture of the night parrot.

Was Enderby apologising for killing himself? Heavens, the old Birdman may have had good reason for contemplating suicide. He knew he was dying of cancer. He feared fresh scandal over his birding exploits. And, who knows, he may belatedly have felt remorse over the death of an old friend.

Was the apology for lying about ever having seen a night parrot? That might explain the accompanying illustration. Or was Enderby apologising for killing, by his own hand or the hired hands of others, Phillip Clarkson? It would be nice to believe that, thought Palmeira.

Then again, perhaps, it was wrong to read too much into the late-night words of a confused, drunken old man.

'Mate, I think you're over-complicating things. I still say he topped himself,' said Danniher.

'So what you're saying is that his death had nothing to do with Clarkson's?'

Danniher thought. 'I don't know whether I'd go that far.'

'Brilliant,' replied Palmeira. 'But I disagree. I've got to believe the two deaths are linked.'

It was past midnight when the two detectives decided to give their aching minds and bodies a rest.

'By the way, Simon Finch — remember, Mr Moneybags — rang while you were out,' said Palmeira, as he waited for a lift home.

'Oh, yeah. What'd he want?'

'That do, on Sunday, wasn't it? Been cancelled. Not enough birders left to make it worthwhile, he said.'

'I'm not surprised. Waste of time.'

'Anyway,' his chief continued. 'It's now just drinks, apparently. A time for the birders to catch up and talk things through. I guess they may be feeling a little lonely these days. Four o'clock. Tomorrow. Centennial Park. Finch said Workman thought it was important we come along.'

'Stuff him. It sounds grim to me. More like some group therapy deal. Thanks, anyway. I'll think about it.'

'Please yourself,' said Palmeira. 'I think I'll have more important things to do.' Like book a holiday, he reflected gloomily.

16

Colonial, aggressive, with noisy group displays... outer suburbs, parks, gardens.
— Graham Pizzey & Frank Knight, on the noisy miner, in *The Field Guide to the Birds of Australia*

Centennial Park is to Sydney what Central Park is to New York and Hyde Park is to London. It stands on what was once called the Second Sydney Common, a reserve created in 1811 by an early governor of the colony of New South Wales, Lachlan Macquarie, to provide pasture for grazing and water for drinking.

However, it wasn't until the 1880s, when the colony was looking for ways to commemorate the centenary of the arrival of the first boatload of convicts, that the uninspiring patchwork of swamp, scrub and rock of the original reserve was transformed — by hundreds of unemployed men — into a grand, picturesque, solidly European, eminently Victorian park.

Premier Sir Henry Parkes urged his fellow colonists to cherish it. 'You must always take as much interest in it as if by your own hands you had planted the flowers.' And so they did. Today, the park attracts thousands of people each day, some 3.6 million each year, who come to take the air, just as they did a century or more ago.

Then, they strolled or circled the Grand Drive in their carriages. Today, they come to walk, jog, cycle, roller-blade and even ride horses. They come to practise tai chi, throw Frisbees, have picnics, make love in the long grass, play several forms of football and, though it is not strictly allowed, to sleep for the night.

And some come to look for birds. Not the intrusive, increasingly aggressive ibis, who strut around the park poking their long, curved black beaks into everybody's business, but the ducks and the darters. The coots and the kingfishers. The pelicans and the pigeons. The wrens and the ravens.

They're still to be spotted, amid the hurly-burly of humans, among the trees, in the gardens and the froggy hollows, and on remnants of the Lachlan Swamps: Busby's Pond, Willow Pond, Duck Pond and the more prosaically-named One More Shot Pond.

What more appropriate spot could the dwindling band of birders have chosen to meet than outside the sturdy sandstone pavilion that stands at the centre of the park? Simon Finch could safely park his BMW nearby. Chris Workman and his protégé could spread their newspapers on the tables provided. Maddy Warnock and Libby Griffiths could buy tea from the refreshment vans that turned up every Saturday. And Derek Morris could go looking for birds, while staying in range of the gents' toilets.

As he led Sandy Prior across the grass to join them shortly after four o'clock, Danniher couldn't help wondering, for the umpteenth time, what on earth he was doing here on a Saturday with a bunch of people he did not even understand, let alone like. Like Palmeira, he'd originally decided not to come along. 'I really can't face that mob again,' he'd told Prior.

For one thing, he needed a break. It had been one hell of a week. Far from throwing in the towel, Palmeira had worked himself and the Birdman team until nearly midnight on Friday, chasing taxi-drivers, talking again to Enderby's neighbours, going back, again and again, through the Clarkson files looking for any person, anything, to link the deaths of the two birdmen. He'd never seen Mario so motivated, so driven, dashing here and there, as fast as his crutches would carry him, pointing out new lines of inquiry, checking progress, praying for a break, desperately seeking a breakthrough. As if he was facing some sort of deadline.

Sadly, it had turned out to be a frustrating experience. Apart from the discovery of some interesting clothing fibres at the Palm Beach house late on Friday, the team had come up with no encouraging new leads. The newspapers — first one, then all of them, in a typical display of feeding frenzy — demanded to know why Clarkson's killer, let alone Enderby's, had still not been found.

This morning, the racier tabloid paper went further. According to inside sources, it claimed, police were now working on the theory that a serial killer was stalking the nation's leading ornithologists.

Very soon, it warned, they would be as rare as dodos. Or night parrots, Danniher thought. And then, on Friday night, came the bombshell: the shock news that Palmeira was standing down from the case. At least that's how he put it.

The DI had called them together in his office, late on Friday night, just as they were breaking up. He looked exhausted. Dejected. Defeated. His voice broke occasionally as he thanked them for their efforts and explained that he'd been told to take a few days off. There were no prizes for guessing who'd told him. Sedgwick.

Danniher would be taking over. He wished him well. Then, with barely another word, he was gone, dragging himself outside to where Jenny was waiting with a car to take him home. Danniher had tried to ring him this morning, but there was no reply. Clearly, Palmeira didn't want to talk about it. Not yet, anyway.

෨෨෨෨

In the end, it was Prior who suggested he dropped in on the reunion. She could do some shopping beforehand. They could grab a meal and a movie afterwards. And anyway, she knew that, despite himself, Danniher was intrigued by Workman's promise to make it worth his while coming along.

So here they were, wasting a fine late summer's afternoon. For a while Danniher wondered if he'd be able to the spot the birders among all the lycra-clad cyclists, joggers and roller-bladers. But they'd been looking out for him with their binoculars.

'Over here, sergeant.' He recognised the crowing voice of Christopher Robin Workman and turned round to see the birders at one of the tables. It was already covered with crumpled newspapers, bird books, binoculars, teacups, water bottles and soft-drink cans and empty sandwich cartons.

'Sorry, we started without you,' said Maddy Warnock.

Danniher sat down awkwardly. 'Seen any good birds, then?' he asked politely.

'There's no such thing as a bad bird, sergeant,' said Warnock. The two women were looking past him, far more interested in his companion.

'Sorry. This is Sandy Prior, a colleague,' he said. It surprised him how proud it made him feel to say it. 'She's a pathologist.'

'That must be very interesting,' said Warnock.

'So are you here on pleasure or business, Sandy?' asked Workman, leaning towards her with what Danniher interpreted to be a predatory smile.

'That remains to be seen,' Prior warned him, with mock severity. She jumped involuntarily as under the table, Danniher gave her a heavy proprietorial squeeze just above the knee.

'Dear me, we'll have to be careful what we say,' said Morris. 'Are the police any closer to finding who, err…'

Danniher knew what he was going to ask, but before Morris could finish the question, hostile glances from the other birders shut him up. Perhaps they'd decided not to talk about the murder.

For the next ten minutes, the little party swapped small talk — about the long, hot summer, about the parched grasslands, about the possibility of bushfires, about blue-green algae in the ponds, about the tenacity of the city-dwelling birds, about the sweaty people constantly huffing and puffing round the Grand Drive. The sight of the joggers reminded Danniher uncomfortably of Mario. No doubt he'd be at home, sitting with his leg up, champing at the bit, getting on Jenny's nerves. He and Sandy would have to find some way of cheering him up.

He was just thinking how soon he and Sandy could politely leave, when suddenly the taboo subject was brought up by Libby Griffiths with a sudden laugh.

'What is it, dear?' asked Warnock.

'It's sad really. I was just thinking how angry Phillip used to get at all these… these people,' she replied, waving at passing squadron of cyclists.

'Oh yes. Do you remember that time he got so angry that he stopped a tour right here and stormed off home?'

'How could I forget?'

It had been several years ago, the two women told Danniher. Before Clarkson had become a television personality. A newspaper had published a piece about this young man's amazing ability to charm the birds from the trees — literally, it was reported — by mimicking their song.

The article had mentioned that he led regular birding tours of the park.

Predictably perhaps, the following Saturday, Maddy and Libby had turned up to find the young man surrounded by more than 50 people, including ten journalists and three camera crews. All expected him to do the bird trick, as advertised.

Not surprisingly, the outing had turned into what Clarkson had called a noisy 'circus,' as members of the media became entangled with early-morning cyclists and joggers.

'It was total chaos,' said Warnock.

'Poor old Phillip was terribly angry,' recalled Griffiths. 'But looking back it seems so very funny.'

The story seemed to disturb the birders, who sat solemnly in silence. It was Maddy who spoke first. 'You know,' she said, fondly. 'I liked Phillip. He could be awkward and impatient, but I still liked him. His heart was in the right place.'

'How on earth can you say that?' asked Workman. 'After all the stuff that there's been in the newspapers about him.'

'Oh, we don't read that rubbish,' said Maddy.

'That's all it is,' added Libby. 'Newspaper talk.'

'I don't believe I'm hearing this.' Workman shook his head and turned to Kath McCann. 'Can you?'

Danniher could sense the mood of the meeting was about to change.

'I have to say I think for once Mr Workman is right. Clarkson was a terrible hypocrite,' said Morris, so softly that Danniher thought at first that he must have misheard him.

'That's right, ladies,' said Finch joining in for the first time. 'He was a fraud.'

Maddy Warnock ignored the smear. 'I always say you take people as you find them. And I found him entertaining and, well, charming.'

'You must be joking,' said Finch. He rolled his eyes.

'No, I'm not.'

Libby Griffiths intervened. 'I think we should change the subject. Talk about something nice.'

Danniher was bracing himself for Workman to make some caustic comment when, to his surprise, Morris again spoke.

'I know we all want — what do they call it these, days? — closure on this issue. But just think back,' he said, looking round the table. 'That Sunday, he was taking us to see birds, all those wonderful waders...'

The two women nodded.

'...yes, well, we now know that for the rest of the week he'd probably been discussing with the council, the developers, ways of concreting over the birds' habitats.' He looked round the table again, to make sure everyone had fully understood.

'Bravo,' shouted Finch. 'Couldn't have put it better myself. And...and, we were effectively paying him to do it.'

Danniher could see that Maddy was close to tears. 'He must have had his reasons.'

As if cued by telepathy, the two women stood up. 'I'm going to fetch another cup of tea,' Maddy announced. 'Can I get anyone else one?'

'I'll come with you,' said Libby, following her friend.

'Typical,' snorted Workman. He seemed to be still upset that his meticulously researched, painstakingly written, in-depth exposé of Phillip Clarkson had been dismissed as 'newspaper talk'.

No one, not even Danniher, seemed to know what to say. Just when the silence threatened to become embarrassing, Morris stood up. 'Excuse me. I need to stretch my legs.' He wandered off in the direction of the toilet block.

For a few seconds, Danniher and Workman glared at each other. 'Sergeant, I wonder if I could have a word in private. You may...'

'Not now, Mr Workman.' He looked at Prior. 'I think I will get a drink. Want anything?'

She nodded. 'Anything cold.'

Leaving her to fend off Workman, Danniher joined the two women round the refreshment van.

'Sorry about that ladies. I know it must be very upsetting for you both.'

Maddy scrunched up her face. 'It was very rude. And unfair. We agreed at the start of the picnic that whatever we thought we wouldn't argue.'

'We want to have nice memories of Phillip Clarkson.'

'Yes, like when he lost his temper with those film crews.'

'I know,' said Danniher.

'And now it's all in the newspapers about poor Mr Enderby dying,' Maddy continued.

'Did you ladies know him as well?'

'Not really. Not like Phillip,' explained Libby.

'We remember when he was still famous.'

'He used to be on television as well, you know.'

Danniher nodded, gravely. 'Yes, so I've heard.'

'But then he just seemed to disappear. I don't know whether something happened.'

'No.'

'Poor man,' said Maddy. 'Things must have got very bad for him to kill himself.'

Danniher nodded. For a moment he wondered whether he should put the record straight. Clearly, the women hadn't caught up with the latest newspaper speculation.

'Actually,' he began tentatively, 'I'm afraid it looks like he didn't kill himself.'

The two women turned to him, clearly perplexed. 'Well, he said he did, didn't he?' said Libby.

Danniher was puzzled. 'What do you mean?'

'In his letter.'

Libby elaborated. 'In his suicide note.'

For a moment, the world about Danniher seemed to stand still. He was trapped in a bubble with a single thought. Round and round it went. Slowly. How could the women possibly know about this letter, let alone its contents?

Only a handful of police officers knew about it and they had told no one. He was positive of that. Palmeira, with typical caution, had wanted its authenticity checked before he even considered making public its existence.

'Of course, the note,' he said at last, trying to disguise his rising sense of apprehension. 'Who told you about that, then?'

The two women looked at each other, as if seeking in each other's faces permission to answer the question. They certainly didn't want to get into trouble with the police again for gossiping.

'The newspaperman, of course,' said Maddy.

'That horrid Workman,' her friend confirmed. 'He said tha…

Danniher did not wait to hear more. He was already running back towards the table.

'Got you,' he shouted as with one, two, three, strides he launched himself at the unsuspecting Workman's back, knocking him forward, head first on to hard wood, the impact softened by only an opened copy of the morning newspaper's colour magazine.

Elsewhere on the table, empty cups and cans and the contents of several bags went flying as Danniher banged Workman's head on the table.

Kath McCann screamed. 'What the hell…' shouted Finch, as the other people jumped away. 'Wayne, what…' yelled Sandy Prior in an instant, as she watched Danniher struggle to restrain Workman.

Not that he seemed to be offering any resistance. But Danniher seemed out of control, fired up by some pent-up anger. It was a side of him she had not seen before. And one she did not much like.

'Christopher Workman I'm arresting you for the murder …' Danniher shouted as a small crowd gathered round, drawn by the sudden explosion of noise. His head pressed hard into the table, Workman fought for breath.

Prior looked round at their faces, the birders' and the sticky beakers'. They were alarmed, excited, intrigued. 'It's OK. It's OK. Police. Police,' she moved to assure them, as Danniher strengthened his arm-lock round the journalist's neck while slowly allowing his head to rise from the table.

Workman's nose was bleeding badly — mostly over his own newspaper, Danniher noticed, his anger subsiding. It took several minutes for Danniher and Prior to restore some sort of order, and to walk Workman to Prior's car. Only after he was bundled into the back seat, with Danniher wedged in beside him, was he able to catch his breath, regain control of his mouth and say anything coherent. Even then the words came out mangled.

'Thish ish a mishtake,' the journalist said through his busted lips. The muddy results sounded almost comical. 'I've not murrerred anyone.'

'What?' Danniher asked, as Prior started the car and set off towards Berwick.

'Nah, nah. No murrerr…'

'What's that?' said Danniher. 'Oh, bloody hell.' He could see Workman was dropping blood on the upholstery.

'He's saying he didn't murder anyone,' Prior explained.

'Save it for later, mate.' Danniher pulled a handkerchief from his pocket and handed it to Workman. 'And for god's sake stop bleeding over the car, will you.'

'Itch true.'

'Then how come you knew about a suicide letter?'

'Doh understand.' Prior looked at the pair in the rear-view mirror. She wasn't sure she understood either.

If he was totally honest, Danniher didn't understand himself. But he was certain Workman was lying again. He tried to put the situation in terms so simple even a man who'd been badly bashed and was now probably in a state of shock could understand.

'You know damn well Enderby didn't commit suicide. He was murdered. By the person who faked his suicide letter,' he said, adding in voice that echoed round the car, 'You!'

Workman shook his head, trying to clear it, trying to wake up from a nightmare.

'You. You boasted to the two women about the letter. Didn't you?'

Maybe it was the blow on the head that slowed him, but it seemed to take Workman an age to understand Danniher's question. He was badly rattled, but slowly, he worked out what was going on.

'Shomeone toh me. I wash, aagh, pashing it on.' The words came out as a slobbery gurgle.

'Sure,' said Danniher, ironically.

'Nah, nah. Honesh.'

'Who then?' asked Danniher, shaking Workman violently. Prior glanced over her shoulder, and said, 'Wayne, please, that's enough.'

Workman seemed to be thinking. Or trying to think. Should he stay silent? Or should he break the first law of journalism and betray a source? It was time to save himself.

'It wash Morrish. Derek Morrish.'

'Bullshit.'

'Nah, nah. He tole me when we shpoke last night. Shaid not to worry, we're all in the clear. Ennerby hah written to you shaying he couldn't faysh any more.'

'You're lying again, Workman.'

'Nah, nah,' he screamed, swallowing hard, clearing his mouth. 'I believed him. I thought, he'sh killed himshelf becaush of what I wrote. I tried to tell you, but you wouldn't...'

Danniher watched as tears — of self-pity, he imagined — began to flow, mixing with the blood and running on to the upholstery again.

The detective was thinking hard now. What if, for once in his miserable life, Workman was telling the truth? What if Morris, the little man with the irritatingly disarming stutter, had known about the 'suicide note'? How had he known about it, unless...?

Danniher couldn't take the chance. 'Sandy, I'm sorry, but we're going to have to turn round, please.' As she slammed on the breaks and turned to double back, he could feel Workman's body go limp against his. At least he had stopped blubbing and bleeding.

As fast as they could in the late afternoon traffic, they retraced their route back through the gates, along Grand Drive and down the radial road to the pavilion.

The cyclists, joggers and roller-bladers had resumed their ceaseless lapping of the park. He was somewhat surprised to see that despite the afternoon's dramas, life was going on. Somehow, it always did.

There was no sign of Morris, or of the others.

After ten minutes of touring the park, Prior looked over her shoulder at Danniher. 'So, what now, boss? Personally, I think we should get him to a doctor.'

'Sure. Anyway, I think I know where I can find Mr Morris.'

ಚಿಚಿಚಿಚಿ

Within 20 minutes, a shivering, badly shaken Workman was receiving medical attention from a police doctor. Before being led off for treatment, he had offered the police full cooperation in their investigations into the murders of Birdman One and Birdman Two.

After telephoning the station to let his colleagues know where he was and what he was doing, Danniher had made Prior take a small detour and been dropped off near the surf club, south of Maroubra.

There, he squeezed through a hole in some wire-mesh fence, and started climbing up, and up, along the cliff-top path, past the army rifle range.

It was late afternoon now. Some of the heat had gone out of the sun and the higher the path rose the more it was exposed to the cooling southerly breeze. But it was still hard going, as Danniher tried unsuccessfully to sprint up a path that seemed to be alternately, gluey, dune sand and hard-baked concrete, strewn with gravel as slippery as ball-bearings.

It was hard work. He was sweating heavily beneath his light, open-necked summer shirt and khaki slacks by the time the bush died away, the shiny, bare cliffs flattened out and it was possible, for the first time, to see the depth of the drop to the churning sea below.

It was dizzying, and Danniher could hardly bring himself to look down to where gulls seemed to float in the air and terns launched their aerial assault into the waves. Several times he stopped and looked along the line of the cliffs for the figure of Derek Morris. He was sure that this was where he would find him, at his favourite place, at Magic Point, where he used to come with his wife — Margaret, wasn't it? — to sit and stare out at sea, sharing the moment, scanning the horizon for albatrosses, perhaps vicariously experiencing the adventure his mundane life lacked.

Just when he was beginning to fear that he had misread the man, he saw Morris, by the track, some 300 metres away, though far closer as the gulls flew.

He was sitting, as Danniher would tell Palmeira later, 'like the proverbial shag on a rock', on an open rock-shelf a little way out from the graffiti-daubed concrete remains of old, wartime gun emplacements and observation posts. Even from a short distance away, he seemed a small, lonely, insignificant-looking figure, caught between a rock and a hard, high summer sky, seemingly contemplating a wild blue yonder.

Already, Danniher could see an image of Morris leaping forward and plunging off the rock shelf to his certain death. He could not let that happen, even if Morris did turn out to be a murderer.

Unsure whether to shout and warn Morris of his approach, or to creep surreptitiously as close as he could unseen, Danniher continued to make his way at an even pace across the cliff-tops.

Suddenly, Morris moved, turned in his direction. He must have seen me, thought Danniher. But instead of jumping to his feet and running off,

Morris seemed to acknowledge his presence and resumed staring out to sea. Danniher stopped, raised a hand and, knowing now that he had been seen, continued walking slowly towards him.

Now, as he closed on Morris, another image flashed through Danniher's brain. It was that of the photograph he'd seen at Morris's untidy little home in Kurnell. Not the one of him with his wife up here on the rocks, but an older one showing him as a carefree little boy, playing with his brother in the garden of their old home back in England.

How sad, he thought, such pictures seem with the benefit of hindsight. How painfully, blissfully innocent the little boy appears when the tragic end of the middle-aged man is known. Today, Morris was even back in shirt and short trousers. Like the schoolboy in the photograph.

'Hello, Mr Morris. I thought I'd find you here.'

Morris did not move. 'And I thought you'd think you'd find me here.' The complicated sentence came out word-perfect. He sounded calm, controlled, so unlike on the first occasion, when such a sentence would have required several attempts.

'Are you feeling OK, Mr Morris?'

'Thank you, yes, sergeant.'

'Is it all right if I come over and have a quiet word?'

'Why not? It's about time.'

Soon, Danniher was sitting alongside Morris on the rock-shelf, more than 50 metres above the water, but no more than a couple of metres apart.

In that endless moment, it seemed to him a unreal, other-worldly scene. Just two men, police officer and murder suspect, sitting quietly together, watching the dying of the day.

17

O, that I had wings like a dove! For then I would fly away, and be at rest.

— Psalms 55, 6

For what seemed like a lifetime, neither man spoke. Danniher was thinking hard. How should he handle this situation? How sure was he that Morris wouldn't do something silly? How far could he push Morris to talk without unbalancing him? After all, at some point, Morris had to be forced to confront some disturbing facts.

Such as the fact that he had killed one, possibly two people.

Fortunately, Morris broke the deadlock.

'I suppose you'd like to know how I did it,' Morris began, casually removing his spectacles and rubbing them clean on his shorts. He paused to hold them up to the sky, to check no smears remained.

'Yes, I would,' said Danniher. Did what, precisely? He wondered.

'It's difficult to know where to start,' said Morris, dreamily. He seemed easily distracted by the birds swooping back and forth beneath him 'Crested tern,' he murmured. 'Pied cormorant,' he whispered, before returning to his story.

'Perhaps the day of the first, err, murder.' Now he seemed to stumble over the word.

So, too, did Danniher. First murder? So there was another, he thought, his face betraying no sign of his shock. He simply nodded, as if to reassure Morris than serial murder was the most natural thing on earth.

Morris, he resolved, must be allowed to talk at his own pace, and in his own direction. There'd be time later to backtrack and search for the missing pieces in his story.

'It's funny,' Morris reflected. 'Looking back, it seems unreal now. More like something out of a film. That's right, an old, black and white film, where the characters jerk along and everywhere looks like a cardboard set.'

Danniher waited patiently for him to cut to the action.

'Really, it was all remarkably simple. Well, terribly risky, I suppose, but still remarkably simple. Would you believe, the difficult thing was persuading Phillip Clarkson to come along and meet me.'

'You weren't the best of friends.'

'Gosh, no. He and I fell out a few years ago. I thought he was an arrogant, over-bearing, hypocrite. And I'm sure he considered me a miserable, sanctimonious little shit. Oh yes. That's what he called me, a little shit.'

He stopped again, as though still hurt, or angered, by the insult. 'Of course, I'd never made much secret of how much I disliked him…well, despised him actually. And several times I warned him I'd do anything to expose him…'

He smiled. 'Though I'm sure that never in a million years would the great Birdman have guessed I was capable of murder.' This time, the former accountant didn't flinch at the word. Quite the reverse. He seemed to grasp it and wave it proudly in front of Danniher.

'He knew I'd been watching him for years. Gathering evidence. Passing stuff to the media. He didn't trust me. So my biggest problem was to persuade him that he had nothing more to fear.'

'Not easy,' said Danniher.

'No. But Phillip was the sort of person that loved flattery.' Morris threw his head back. 'Ttch. He was so arrogant, he probably didn't even realise he was being flattered. Anyway, I did my best to patch things up between us over the last few months. You know, to put his mind at rest.'

'A few times I even spoke to him — quite reasonably I thought — on the phone about this wretched new Pelican development. Can you believe it? He actually thought he'd persuaded me that it was a good thing? The right thing to do? Judas! Sacrificing all those waders for a few pieces of silver!'

Danniher showed his indignation. 'Madness.'

Morris shot Danniher a glance. Was the policeman patronising him? No matter. He went on. 'I even booked in for one of his tours — well, what would have been his last tour but for his most untimely…But of course you know that.'

'Yes.'

Morris chuckled. 'A masterstroke, I thought at the time. Almost the perfect alibi. I mean, who'd suspect someone who discovered a dead man to be his murderer?'

'Very clever,' said Danniher, thinking, well, the possibility had been considered by him and Palmeira.

'But that wasn't all. I had it all worked out. Booking for his silly tour reassured Clarkson that he'd got nothing to fear from me.'

Suddenly, something made Morris smile. 'I almost forgot... and the best bit as it turned out, was that I actually got to see our famous birdman — television's Birdman —brought down to earth.'

'Exposed, as it were.'

Morris turned excitedly to Danniher, squinting as the setting sun bounced off his glasses.

'Exactly! You understand! I mean, literally exposed to the world. His bare bottom poking up in the air for all to see. Hah! How ridiculous he looked. Much more devastating than anything that pompous prick — sorry, I must be getting tired — Workman could achieve in his articles. Wouldn't you agree, sergeant?'

Danniher smiled, conspiratorially he hoped. For the first time, he feared that despite his meek exterior and his measured, English Home Counties diction, Morris had become seriously unhinged.

The memory of his rediscovery of Clarkson's half-buried body seemed to fill him not with horror, still less with remorse, but with manic glee.

'What was I saying?'

'Sorry...'

'I remember, the tricky bit. I meant to tell you. I had to get Clarkson out, at night, on his own. Defenceless. And that's where the Kentish plover came in,' he announced with a triumphant flourish.

Danniher was immediately lost. 'Sorry?'

'The Kentish plover. A rather pretty little bird, sergeant, but so easily confused with a red-capped plover.'

'Oh.'

'Oh yes. But that's because it also has a reddish cap and a white collar.'

'I see.'

'They're very rare, you know. I think I'm right in saying there's been only one sighting ever in New South Wales. Not so long ago, actually.'

'Very rare, then?'

'Oh, yes, very rare. But the point is, though, it wouldn't be totally out of the question to see a Kentish down on one of the tidal flats.'

'You mean on Moreton Bay?'

'Yes. So, when we rang Phillip and told him we were going to check out a possible sighting of a Kentish that Saturday afternoon he couldn't resist joining us. It would have been quite a coup for him.'

'You'd done your research, then?'

'Oh, yes. It would have been another nice little tick for him…'

'Sorry?'

'You don't know? I'm afraid Phillip Clarkson was another one of those birders who's obsessed with how many species they've seen. You know, tick, tick, tick, on their little lists, another name crossed off in their little black books.'

Morris's face showed utter disdain. 'I know, I know what you're thinking. And I agree it's really quite pathetic. Like they're collecting stamps or something. Of course, it's all about bragging rights, who's seen this, who's seen…'

'Clarkson turned up, though?' Danniher gently guided Morris and his hobby horse back on course.

For a moment, Morris seemed thrown by the interruption, but again he took a deep breath and continued.

'Yes. Just as arranged. He parked his car and we met…'

'Near the dunes?'

'Oh, no.' Morris looked puzzled. 'On the other side of the bay. In the car park. It's really the only place you can launch a boat. There's a ramp there. You couldn't take a boat through the dunes. And, anyway, it can be dangerous there at night.'

To Morris, mention of the meeting place seemed a mere detail. To Danniher, though, the revelation came as a shock, a most disturbing piece of news.

Now he saw it. Throughout the investigation, he gloomily reflected, the search for clues and for witnesses had been concentrated on the wrong side of the bay, in the dunes and along Bayside Drive. And what was this about launching a boat? The possibility of a boat being involved had not been raised let alone investigated, as far as he recalled.

'But you did know that that area of the beach had a bad reputation? You know, as a pick-up spot?'

At first, Morris looked mystified. Then embarrassed. 'No. Well, yes, I did know. But not really until that evening, when someone told me. But then it didn't seem to matter.'

The stream of contradictions confused Danniher. 'Sorry, Mr Morris, I don't follow.'

Morris looked at the detective severely, as if he was a simpleton.

'Don't you see? In the end it became part of the joke. Part of the deception. I mean, what could be better: "Birdman with bare bum found on gay beach"? The perfect headline. And more suspects for the police to worry about.'

Danniher rubbed his eyes. No wonder the police had struggled to nail Morris. Far from being an ineffectual, old bumbler, Morris was slowly revealing himself as a criminal mastermind.

'So dumping the body there…that was deliberate?'

'Sort of.'

Danniher let the answer pass. It was, after all, only one of several things in Morris's story so far that he didn't fully understand.

'By the way, Mr Morris, how did you get to the car park?'

Morris looked confused. It took him some time to answer. 'Taxi. I think.'

'Right.' Now Danniher remembered that Morris had told him he didn't drive.

The two men sat, staring silently out to sea. Behind them the sun was fast sinking out of sight. Danniher suddenly realised how thirsty and cold and tired he was. It had another long day.

'Where were we up to?' asked Morris, cheerfully. He didn't seem tired at all. He seemed to be having the time of his life.

'At the boat ramp?'

'Right. So we get in the boat and set off…' The words tailed away as Morris scanned the horizon as though searching for some childhood memory. '…like the owl and the pussycat, in search of a non-existent

Kentish plover. Number 563, or something, on Clarkson's list. As if it any of that really matters…'

He scrunched up his face in concentration. 'I know you probably won't believe me. But even at that point, out on the bay, things could have turned out differently.'

'Right.'

'It doesn't matter now whether or not you believe me, sergeant. But I swear it's true.'

'I believe you.'

'Good. Thanks. You see, over the years I'd collected some terribly damaging stuff about Clarkson. Stuff that would destroy his career if it ever got out. I sent it all to Workman. Chapter and verse. Page after page of photocopies. It was all there.'

'Right.'

'He promised to write a big story. But the big crusading journalist was always too busy. Or he had to go somewhere on another story. A more important story! Or his legal eagles — that's what he called them — had said it was all too libellous.'

Morris was almost shouting. Danniher looked round nervously, half-expecting to see someone coming to investigate what all the noise was about. But they were quite, quite alone.

'You've got to understand, Workman was getting nowhere.'

'So you had to do something.'

'Something, yes. The original plan was to confront Clarkson. To show him what we had on him.' Morris laughed.

Danniher didn't even register the laugh. Did Morris say 'we'? He decided not to interrupt.

'Then what?'

Morris considered the question. 'Well, we were giving him a last chance to, to come clean, to publicly admit what he'd been up to…' Morris was becoming increasingly agitated. His voice was soft, but he had resumed swaying, now more violently, from side to side.

Danniher noted it clearly this time. He *had* said 'we'.

Morris continued '…all the dirty deals he'd done. The double-talk. The compromises. The sell-outs. I assure you sergeant I had material that would ruin him completely, far worse than Workman's miserable rag saw fit to print...'

Slowly, he regained some composure. 'But would he listen? No way. He started to get angry. Demanded to know whether there was a bloody Kentish plover here or not. And, if there wasn't, how he insisted on me turning the boat round and taking him straight back. Pompous idiot!'

Don't stop now, thought Danniher. Not far to go. 'Do you think he suspected he'd been tricked by then?'

'That's a good question.' Morris thought. 'I honestly don't know. Maybe, he thought he'd been the victim of some cruel joke. Not that he was about to get... well, you know.'

'Killed?'

'Yes. But he just got angry so quickly. All at once, he's yelling, saying he thought we were friends, telling me what he'd do to me if I didn't go back.'

'But you didn't.'

'No. When I just sat there, sneering at him, he stood up and...' Mid-sentence, Morris decelerated, as if describing the action on a slow motion video playing in his mind.

'...he came at me. It all got very confused. I can see it now. We're out there on the water. The little boat's rocking. No one else seems to be around. It's getting very dark. And suddenly lots of things seemed to be happening at the same time. I didn't know whether he was trying to grab me or the oars or what. Then he goes flying. Like, like tumbles forward. His head bangs on the side of the boat. He screams and falls over. I can see blood on his head. And on his hands. But he pulls himself up again and I, I err...'

As he approached the defining moment, Danniher could see the old Derek Morris taking over, hesitating, stuttering, groping for the words.

'...I reach down into the boat and pick up this thing, like a metal bat or bar it was, and, well, smack him hard across the back of the head...' Morris shuffled nervously. '... and then I did it a few more times. Just to make sure.'

Danniher nodded as if to reassure Morris that he quite understood, that if ever he found himself confronted by a bleeding birdman, out in a boat on the harbour at night, he, too would've probably bludgeoned the man to death. It was one of those things that could happen to anyone.

Except, of course, according to the pathology report, Danniher knew that Clarkson was not dead.

Morris seemed to sense this. He turned, shrugged, and half-apologetically said, 'He looked dead to me at the time.'

Danniher prompted him gently again. 'You must've been worried, though? I mean, what if you were seen? In the boat? Covered in blood? With a dead man? How would you have explained that? An accident?'

Morris's head slumped forward. 'I honestly don't really remember. Things had happened very quickly. But, actually, no, I don't recall feeling worried. I felt…felt…well, strong. Perhaps that sort of thing concentrates the mind.'

'And then?'

'There was no one else around, as far as I could see. It was in a pretty remote part of the harbour, of course. I presume you were there, when the body was…'

'Dug up? Yes,' Danniher lied.

'Well you'd know that there's not much reason for anyone to go there now, of course. Full of rubbish, grossly polluted, no fish, very soon no birds…might just as well concrete it over now, in fact…'

'Sure. So…'

'Oh, I'm not stupid. I knew I'd have to dispose of the body.'

'You could've tipped it over the side, of course,' suggested Danniher.

'Yes, I suppose I could've.'

'But?'

'It seemed to make more sense to bury him.' He turned to look at the detective. 'I know what you must be thinking. And I agree. There was a degree of pre-meditation about all this.'

Danniher nodded.

'Good. But it really wasn't until we were sitting there in the boat that I realised, God, what do we do with one dead body. The problem doesn't crop up too often.' He gave a grim laugh.

There it was again. 'We'.

'Believe me, sergeant, I've come to terms with my crime pretty much now. I guess I always knew it would come to this, but at the time I really didn't want to get caught. I thought burying the body, hiding it for a few days perhaps, might give me a better chance.'

He turned back to the sea and laughed again. 'Anyway, when we got there we thought it might be more fun if we could bury him so it looked as though he had fallen from the sky.'

Danniher turned to look Morris in the face. Was he joking? How could anyone tell? 'I see.'

'So I waited a few hours, just floating about on the water. When it got really late, and we could be pretty sure no one else was around, we rowed back to the end of the bay. You know, near the dunes.'

'And?'

'And... let me think.' Morris was talking now in slow motion. 'I got out on to the wet sand. Dug a hole. Pushed Clarkson headfirst into it...'

'Took off his trousers?'

Morris seemed to have forgotten this detail. 'Yes. Took off his trousers. And started digging.'

This was becoming comical. Danniher dared not risk tipping Morris over the edge. Literally. But he had to get this right.

'You just happened to have a spade with you?'

Morris looked suspicious, then confused, as though trying to recall the details of some long-ago dream. 'Good point. I suppose I must have done.'

'And the bat, or the bar, or whatever it was you used to kill Clarkson. What happened to that?'

'I'm sorry. I don't remember.'

'Thrown into the harbour, perhaps.'

'Yes. That would have been it.' Morris seemed grateful to Danniher for helping to clear up this little mystery for him.

Unprompted, he now picked up the threads of his story and started quickly tying up some loose ends — like a man suddenly remembering that he had other places to go, more important things to do.

'It all became a bit of a rush, as I remember. I couldn't get Clarkson's legs to stand up straight, like I wanted them. The tide was coming in. And, yes, at one point, I thought I saw a figure standing in the dunes. I was sure we'd been seen. Yes, it was really all rather scary.'

Just like playing games in the garden with a younger brother, thought Danniher. Except this game had been for real. Though there were still far too many unanswered questions in Morris's account, he had heard enough for now. It was getting dark, and late, and unseasonably chilly.

It seemed an appropriate point to walk back. 'How are you feeling, now, Mr Morris?' he asked quietly.

'Fine. Thank you, sergeant. It's been a beautiful evening. One that I'm sure we'll both remember for the rest of our lives.'

'True.' Danniher sighed histrionically. 'Time to go, then?'

He waited nervously for Morris to make the first move. Instead, he shuffled his bottom back and forth across the hard rock shelf. For a moment, Danniher couldn't see what he intended to do: to stand, turn and walk back to the main road with him, or to jump forward, into the abyss.

Morris did neither. Instead, he made himself comfortable again and, in a soft old-world, English accent, said, 'Let's stay just a little while longer. It's such a lovely evening — and, anyway, I thought you might like to hear what happened to poor old Ellis Enderby.'

He turned to Danniher and smiled. 'I believe you and your colleague had the pleasure of visiting him before his nasty fall.'

ജ്ഞാന

Across Sydney, another perfectly ordinary, altogether spectacular, summer Saturday was drawing to a close. Cricket matches had been won and lost, family barbecues cooked and consumed and inexperienced swimmers plucked from the raging surf.

So little local news was there that the half-hour evening bulletins had to be padded out, with an analysis of celebrity divorces, amateur footage of a fatal crash at a German air show and more than 15 minutes of sports highlights.

Christopher Workman had returned home after being given a couple of aspirin and been treated for nothing worse than a sore head and a badly bruised and bloodied nose.

Now, he was cuddled up in front of the television with Kath McCann, explaining bravely to her how he planned to sue for police brutality.

Maddy Warnock and Libby Griffiths had travelled back across the Harbour Bridge together, chatting excitedly over the day's dramas. Who would have thought it! Mr Workman, a murderer!

Now, separated in their loneliness by only a few kilometres, they did their respective washings up before settling down in their respective comfy chairs to watch television. After what they'd witnessed in Centennial Park it seemed rather tame.

Simon Finch had also returned home, far too fast and had been booked for speeding. Damn! The fine was piffling, but if he incurred any more points he'd lose his licence.

He'd decided to stay in, and now sat, staring blankly at the television set, wondering why his wife spent so much time in the United States.

Sandy Prior was still at Berwick police station, waiting to hear from Wayne Danniher. She worried about whether he needed assistance and, after his outburst of anger in the park, whether he was really the right man for her.

Mario Palmeira was at home. He had pottered, as best he could, round his small backyard, helped the girls with their homework, went shopping with Jen and pulled together a salad for their dinner and then stretched out on the lounge, with his feet up, reading a book.

It was about the secret life of birds and had been borrowed by Jenny from the coffee table of a client whose house she was currently helping to redesign. 'Thought it might help you relax, give you a new interest,' she had said, dropping it on his lap.

He had started to read it, but after only a few pages was interrupted by a phone call. It was from Prior, who apologised for interrupting his holiday. She explained how Wayne had arrested Workman, how he'd had second thoughts and gone in pursuit of Derek Morris.

Now, the words and pictures of his bird book danced meaninglessly before his eyes. Workman? Morris? Murderers?

In Palm Beach, a lonely, grief-stricken housekeeper was writing a letter to an address in England — she hoped it was the right one — to let an old man know that his distant relation Ellis Enderby had died in an accident. As far as Mary Jeffries knew, he had no kin in Australia.

And in Kurnell, a part-time taxi driver was knocking on the door of Derek Morris's house in Balaclava Parade, just as he often did on Saturday evenings. He worked illegally, borrowing he cab from a mate under whose name the vehicle was registered. There was no reply. He knocked again, so loud this time that the square pain of patterned glass in the upper half of the door shook.

There was still no reply. Angrily, he cursed, kicked the door and stalked back to his silver-grey cab.

೫೫೫

High on the cliffs at Maroubra, the cabby's missing fare had fallen silent again — this time for so long that Danniher feared that he might have lost consciousness.

The detective gave him a quick, sideways glance. Morris, he could see, was smiling. It was eerie: some trick of the half-light cast a long shadow that transformed the curl of his mouth into a sneer and made his face look cadaverous, evil even.

At length, the thin lips moved. 'That was another master stroke, I thought.'

'Sorry, what was?' asked Danniher, thinking Morris meant pushing the old man off the balcony to his death.

'Signing Enderby up for an outing with his old enemy Phillip Clarkson.'

'You mean…'

'Oh yes. You know you really did underestimate me, sergeant.'

'So it seems.'

'Yes. I made the booking. He knew nothing about it. In one way, it was another of my little jokes. I mean, the very idea of him going on an "outing" — isn't that what they call it? — with his golden-haired boy. It would have been quite like old times.'

Morris turned serious again. 'But booking — I never did pay for it — was like taking out an extra piece of insurance.'

'How d'you mean?'

'Obviously. I thought it might confuse you people.'

Now, it was Morris's turn to look sideways at Danniher.

'It worked didn't it? Don't tell me the police weren't just the teeniest, weeniest bit intrigued when they discovered that Enderby didn't show up for a tour he'd booked himself in for. It must have looked horribly suspicious.'

Danniher didn't wish to be reminded that he and Palmeira had been sent on a wild goose chase up to Palm Beach to see Enderby. Unwittingly, perhaps, they may even have contributed to his death. 'Well, I suppose…'

'I thought as much,' Morris said, proudly.

'Don't look at me like that, sergeant. All right, with Clarkson it was personal. I'd been his friend and his supporter. I'd been working alongside him when he was fighting to save the birds and the habitats.'

'I thought he was on our side. Working against the greedy developers and the stupid councils. They were only interested in dollars. And then I discovered he was working with them. Against us.'

'Or on both sides.'

Morris scowled. 'No. Against us. I know. I was working at the council. I saw what he was up to. God, at one point, I was even signing off on some of the payments they were sending him.'

'That must have made you furious.'

Morris did not seem to hear. 'And then, when he found out I was gathering evidence and saw how difficult I could make life for him, he got his council mates to sack me.'

Morris paused to catch his breath.

'I can understand, just about, how you must have felt,' said Danniher. 'But Enderby? He was just a sick, old man.'

Morris looked at him and turned away, in disgust.

'You just don't get it, do you? You're just like the others. All those old birders. Always prepared to see the good in people.'

'But Enderby, he'd given up years ago.'

'Enderby and Clarkson were in the same line of business: they sold their high profiles, their reputations, their opinions to the highest bidders. They might just as well have killed thousands of birds with their bare hands.'

'Surely, not.'

'Believe me, Enderby would still've been doing it today — except he got greedy. Like Clarkson. He didn't like the youngster moving in on his patch, taking his clients.'

'But that business with the night parrot, didn't they…?'

'Don't even mention that bird to me. How can two grown men fight over a bird that may or may not exist? How can they spend thousands of dollars looking for it? What does the night parrot matter when the habitat, the very future, of dozens of other species is at stake?'

In his excitement, Morris leapt to his feet, like a politician rising to harangue a crowd. Danniher could only lean back, look up and listen.

'I've told you, sergeant, the night parrot is no more than a tick on a rich man's list, a paragraph in a tabloid newspaper, a total distraction.'

Danniher looked at him disbelief. 'But all this is ancient history, surely?'

Morris sat back down. 'True.' He gave what sounded like a snort of indignation. 'But just remember, but for the persistence of the police, he might still be alive.'

'Hang on, we…'

'No. Don't you see? Workman went to see Enderby for his story. He told me. Enderby told him that he was helping the police with their inquiries, that he'd told you he had a pretty good idea who killed Clarkson. He said he knew someone who had a big enough grudge to do it.'

Danniher was lost in the maze of Morris's logic. Either Enderby or Workman or Morris, or any combination of them, was lying. 'But…'

Morris pressed on. 'Then, that day, Enderby started ringing me, demanding to know what was going on, why the police were harassing him. That's when we decided it…'

Morris's voice turned cold, calculating. '…that he was becoming too dangerous. We had to… well, you know the rest.'

The man is a monster, thought Danniher. How on earth could we have missed him?

'In a way I was doing him a favour. I mean, what had Ellis Enderby got to live for? He was drunk all day. He was dying of cancer.'

'You knew about that?'

Morris nodded. 'I don't know whether it was his drugs or the drink — but he was so dead drunk when we arrived he probably didn't even know what was going on.'

'It must've been easy, then?'

Morris shook his head. 'You'd think so. A defenceless old man. In fact, it took some working out. A couple of visits, in fact.'

'Right.'

'One to do the letter and get it in the post.'

'You used his typewriter?'

'Yes.'

'What about the signature?'

'Simple. Didn't I tell you that after he moved up to Palm Beach, we swapped letters regularly? I had plenty of copies of his signature.'

'Yes. I remember.'

'Anyway, it's not that difficult to forge the shaky signature of a hopeless drunk.'

'Nor to push him over a balcony.'

'No. That was later.' Morris looked down. For the first time he seemed to Danniher to be showing some emotion. Remorse? He couldn't tell.

'You know the worst thing about it? Having to sit there for a couple of hours, listening to the drunken ramblings of the old fool, moaning about Clarkson, droning on about how he'd been misunderstood, how he really did see the night parrot... it was a relief to get away...'

'But you went back later and pushed him over the balcony?'

Morris looked at the detective, as if fearing some sort of trap. Danniher shook his head and shrugged.

'Didn't you say that's what you did?'

'Did I? Yes. It was something like that.'

The answer struck Danniher as being oddly inconclusive and vague, but it seemed that Morris had finally come to the end of his story.

Seconds began to stretch into minutes, until Danniher spoke. 'I'm curious, Mr Morris. I know you've been very frank and I appreciate that, but there are several things I still don't understand.'

'Oh really,' Morris replied, with the lightness of one who'd just made his confession to a priest. 'Needless to say, I'd be happy to help you.'

'Well,' started Danniher, planting one word cautiously in front of the other. One false step, he imagined, could still provoke panic in Morris.

'When you were talking about the fight in the boat, you kept talking about "we". You know, "we" did this and...'

Morris's face darkened. He thought carefully before replying, 'I meant me and Clarkson.'

Impossible, thought Danniher. Someone — Finch or Waddell or maybe even Workman — must have helped. He decided to nudge Morris towards the whole truth just once more.

'But, seriously, you must've had an accomplice. You couldn't have done these things on your own.'

Morris frowned, more deeply this time. 'What things?'

'Get a boat. Bury a body. Drive Phillip Clarkson's car away. To Miranda, wasn't it? Get back from Palm Beach. Mr Morris, you can't even drive. You told me so yourself.'

'I've told you what happened. That's it. There is no more.'

Danniher could see, even in the gloom, that Morris was becoming agitated again, removing his spectacles, pushing his face deep into his hands, shaking. Or was it shivering? Or even sobbing? The detective decided to back off.

'Never mind, Mr Morris,' he said, gently. 'We can talk about it later.'

Morris appeared to nod in agreement.

'OK. Come on, let's go back.' Danniher said, rising slowly. He extended a hand.

At first, the other man did not move.

'You do know, we're going to have to go back some time, don't you?' said Danniher.

Morris mumbled something, and slowly rose.

Both men now turned their backs on the silver sea, the wheeling, screeching gulls, and, together, took a step back from the edge, facing towards the track that led past the old gun emplacements.

Danniher took a second step. Suddenly, Morris was no longer alongside him. Instantly, Danniher turned... just in time to see Morris disappearing over the edge.

It was a split-second image that Danniher immediately knew would remain with him until his own dying day: Morris did not simply run over the edge like, say, a lemming.

Rather, he took two steps forward and launched himself from the shelf, with head held high, legs tucked under his body, and arms outstretched, spread-eagled.

Like a bird.

Epilogue

Wayne Danniher was heading north from Cairns with Sandy Prior on the fifth day of what was supposed to be a carefree, 'get away from it all' holiday deep in the Daintree rainforest when he received the news. Or, more accurately, spotted it by chance in a shop window.

It was, perhaps, a sign of how closely he'd become attached to 'Path' over the previous few weeks that, for the first time as far as he could remember, he was happy to hand over the responsibility for driving to a woman. Well, he had had a couple of cans of beer during a lunch-stop taken just north of Townsville and, anyway, it was a hire car.

While she sat rigidly behind the wheel, quietly concentrating on a road that seemed to change without warning from dual carriageway to single lane, or from freeway to fraught way (as she put it), he slouched in the passenger's seat, feet on the dashboard, elbow hanging out of the window, humming tunelessly to an old INXS tape.

'Way to go, eh, Path?' he said, reaching over and playfully pinching her above the knee. She flinched.

'Wayne! You'll have us both killed!'

In fact, Wayne Danniher had rarely felt more alive. More like living. When his girlfriend had first suggested they take a holiday, he had dismissed the idea. 'Nice idea, love. But too busy. You know how it is…'

Jeez, he'd thought at the time, he was beginning to sound like poor, old Palmeira, who he just knew would be sitting at home, with his foot up, seething with impotence after being sidelined by Jonno Sedgwick. But Danniher was nursing his own problems.

First thing, on the morning after Derek Morris had jumped from Magic Point to his death, he had gone round to see his old boss to explain what had happened. But as both men conceded, there were still gaps — big gaps — in the story. As Danniher went through it all— the meeting in the park, the arrest of Workman, the chase across the cliff-tops and Morris's final testimony, even Jenny was forced to admit that she couldn't imagine who felt worse. Mario or Wayne.

The two men sat for hours cursing their incompetence at not having picked Derek Morris earlier as a murderer. Belatedly, Palmeira had recalled the cynical advice of an old detective, now desk-bound at headquarters. 'Never trust anyone who's tricky with figures and wouldn't say boo to a goose.' Morris was both. Significantly, or at least it seemed so in retrospect, he'd also stuttered.

Meanwhile, Danniher had continued to blame himself for Morris's suicide. After Morris had jumped, Danniher hadn't left immediately. For several minutes, he'd sat on the cliff-top, shivering and shaking, replaying in his mind the final few seconds of Morris's life. By the time he'd recovered sufficiently to telephone Berwick police station for assistance, he'd convinced himself that he'd fatally mishandled the situation.

'I pushed him too hard,' he kept telling Sandy Prior later. 'I pushed him over the edge.' Nothing she or Palmeira could say — not even the sensible suggestion that Morris's suicide was obviously as pre-meditated as his killings and his confession — could persuade him otherwise.

'No, no, everything was OK,' Danniher had insisted. 'He was coming back with me, until I pressed him about an accomplice. I should've waited until we got back. Or grabbed him. Or...'

'Wayne...'

'No. Believe me. I was there. It needn't have ended like that.'

The media had not made things easier. Unaware that the police were still not convinced that Morris had operated alone, the newspapers especially were scathing of the police handling of the Birdman case. Or cases.

'Dead. Dead. Dead.' ran a particularly tasteless headline in the tabloid paper, above pictures of the three 'dead parrots' — that is Clarkson, Enderby and Morris — who, it tactlessly pointed out, had all, in their different ways, been pushed to their untimely deaths. The broadsheet was little better.

It spiced a fairly straightforward front-page news story with no fewer than four feature articles inside. There were potted biographies of the three dead birders, a timeline of events, which suggested graphically that the police were blundering about as the bodies piled up, and a long 'why, oh why' think-piece questioning the way the once-gentle pastime of bird watching could generate so much carnage.

And, there was a typically vicarious article examining how the mischievous foreign media had covered the story. One London tabloid, the Sydney paper had been thrilled to discover, still refused to drop the gay angle, outrageously regaling its readers with a racy, thrill-kill account of 'Aussie Horni-thologists in Sex Triangle Slayings'.

The only real surprise, Palmeira and Danniher had agreed, was that Christopher Robin Workman hadn't burst into print again. For a few days, at least, it seemed that he was prepared to let someone else have the last word for a change.

But just when it appeared Workman must have been chastened by his encounter with the police, a new piece by him duly appeared. Its author, Danniher noticed, was now being billed as the man on the inside of the birder-murders and the article was headlined, 'My Misunderstood Son by Birdman Mum'.

To their surprise, they found the story moving and quite unsettling, as Margaret Clarkson put the public record straight about her dead son. Though by far the most famous of the three birders, he'd slipped quietly from the public eye possibly because he'd been the first, as Koslowski had put it, to fall from the perch.

Now Mrs Clarkson, in words that really did read like her own, brought Phillip Clarkson a little way back to life, describing a human being who was flawed but whose good qualities, she believed, had been overlooked in the rush to judgment over his business activities.

Conjuring up kind memories of an earnest little boy looking for birds in bushland at the back of his childhood home, she described his lasting contribution, as a speaker, as a writer and, latterly as a television documentary-maker, to the nation's knowledge and appreciation of its native wildlife.

She reassured the public that finding, studying and filming birds had always been the driving passions of his life. Almost every cent he earned went back into making those documentaries we all loved so much. Apart from making films, his personal pleasures were simple and inexpensive.

Mrs Clarkson even addressed the unsavoury accusations made against her son. Bravely, she denied what she called rumours about her son's sexuality. 'We never discussed the matter, but I would've said, if asked, that Phillip was basically asexual: a loving son but a self-sufficient, probably lonely person who did not have a sex life.

'In any case,' she added, 'I would've assumed that in this day and age we're all mature enough to accept that whatever his sex life was or wasn't, it was nobody's business but his own.' Except that of the police, if they thought if was material to the case, Danniher had pointed out angrily on reading what he saw as a rebuke.

Without mentioning how he'd been bankrolling his younger brother Paul, Mrs Clarkson conceded that the financial demands placed on Phillip in the months before his death had increased, but added that he would have coped with them somehow. Given time. Although, she said, she'd been unaware of his precise relationship with Berwick Shire Council or the developers Pelican Estates, she still denied that he was either corrupt, or even hypocritical in his business dealings.

Rather, she suggested that unlike many of his critics, her son had always taken a commonsense, pragmatic view of bird habitats, recognising that it was not worth fighting to save each and every one. 'His motto, quite rightly, was "Live to fight another day".'

Phillip Clarkson, his mother agreed, was neither saint nor sinner beyond salvation. But whatever his flaws, whatever his faults, he did not deserve to die that awful death. Workman's article ended by quoting her voicing a short prayer that her son, along with his old friend, Ellis Enderby, and their alleged killer Derek Morris, would now each be allowed to rest in eternal peace.

That last sentence had puzzled Danniher and Palmeira, as they sat around later, consoling each other, picking up the pieces after Morris's death. What did Margaret Clarkson mean by 'alleged killer'? Or was that, in fact, the phrase of the writer Christopher Workman?

Did she, or he, still harbour doubts about Morris's guilt? Or had someone guessed that the police were still working on the theory that he had worked with an accomplice?

Either way, as far as Danniher and Palmeira were concerned, the case remained open. And would stay so for several more weeks. Over the next few weeks, possible accomplices — Workman, Finch, even Waddell were re-interviewed and eliminated. Fresh appeals for witnesses were issued and proved fruitless. Further searches for weapons were made and proved unsuccessful.

Other leads had been pursued. While Palmeira fretted at home, took a short break with his family, and came home to fret some more, Danniher returned to Kurnell to look for the boat in which Derek Morris said he'd attacked Clarkson and to search his house for, well, he didn't quite know what.

Though the sad, empty house yielded nothing, it appeared to have been visited recently — by Morris's neighbour, Danniher supposed. But she denied it, adding that she still couldn't believe he would have done such an awful thing. 'He was a very private person. Kept himself very much to himself.'

And the boat was gone. Indeed, none of the neighbours could recall seeing a boat in Morris's yard, even though Danniher himself had seen one there.

At the same time, Koslowski had continued working his way, meticulously, through a long list of names of people who were licensed drivers of grey taxis. The problem was that almost all were reluctant to say when and to whom they'd lent their taxis.

Inevitably, though, other crimes, other areas, had gradually assumed greater importance. Suddenly, it seemed a sex attacker — immediately dubbed by the media the 'Beast of Berwick' — was on the loose: people could no longer be spared for the birdman cases, especially as someone, Derek Morris, had confessed to the crimes, and the run of birder murders appeared to have halted.

And, when two labourers were found with their throats cut, in what appeared to have been a bizarre murder-suicide, on a remote property west of Dubbo, Jonno Sedgwick decided it was time to 'pull the pin' on the Birdman inquiry. It was a simple matter of matching bodies and priorities, he'd explained to a disappointed Danniher.

It was at that point that Sandra Prior had revived her suggestion that they 'get away for a few days'. This time, Danniher could find few excuses.

Even Jonno Sedgwick had grudgingly suggested he take some time off, 'to recharge the batteries'. And, anyway, he had grown very fond of Prior. In fact, he was beginning to wonder whether he was in love.

Whatever, he'd allowed Path to book the two of them into a remote bed and breakfast alongside the Daintree river. She'd also borrowed some fishing gear from a neighbour, bought him a selection of books, and packed an old pair of binoculars.

'You never know, you might want to look at some birds,' she'd explained. Away with the birds! Away from Berwick and dead birdmen! It hadn't been such a bad idea, Danniher was thinking, when he saw the poster in the display window of a newsagent's shop.

They were driving slowly through a smallish country town and he had no difficulty reading the words, unevenly thrown over four smudgy, black lines: SYDNEY BIRDER MURDERS: SECOND MAN HELD.

'Path,' he shouted. 'Pull over.'

છાઉજાઉજા

Though they carried handcuffs, had powers of arrest and had been given some basic instruction in self-defence in case anglers turned nasty, New South Wales fisheries officers Mick Matthews and Col Nevin were not expecting trouble. Indeed, they'd been having a relatively quiet day, patrolling the familiar harbour hot spots, checking anglers had licences, that they weren't using illegal gear and keeping undersized fish.

Then, just before going off-duty, they decided to make another swing past the boat ramp at Kyeemagh near where the Cooks River enters the bay. In the fast-fading light, two men, whom they'd spotted acting strangely earlier, were now loading catch bags from a small boat into the back of a rusty utility truck.

"Here we go,' said Matthews apprehensively, as they approached the men. One, they guessed, was in his mid-thirties, gangling, with long, straggly blond, beach-bum hair, and a cigarette dangling from his mouth. He was whistling contentedly, absorbed in the task of loading the catch into the ute.

Nine snapper, a nice yellowfin bream, more than a hundred blue-swimmer crabs, most of them with eggs: it was not a bad day's haul, and one that could be quickly and lucratively off-loaded down the pub that night.

The other man was older, probably in his fifties, a short, stocky, muscular man, whose bald head twisted repeatedly on his shoulders as he looked round for approaching danger with furtive, owl-like glances.

Despite the Owl's vigilance, it was Beach Bum who saw the fisheries officers first.

'Den,' he shouted. 'Let's get out of here.'

As Mick Matthews later explained to the police, suddenly, the two men started running this way and that, zig-zagging in what might from a distance have been mistaken for a pre-arranged football move, or an avant garde dance routine.

After a brief dummy run towards the road, Beach Bum doubled back to the ute, where he fumbled, trying to open the driver's side-door. It was still locked. Realising that he was stuck, he held his hands up in submission. The cigarette was still dangling from his mouth.

The Owl showed no such tactical sophistication but displayed far more determination. Feinting neither to left not right, he turned and, with a turn of speed unexpected from one so sturdy, ran straight down the ramp, splashing out to the boat.

Quickly, he bent over the side and from beneath a mass of illegal netting pulled out a weapon. To the non-expert it looked like a half-size baseball bat. But Matthews and Nevin recognised it immediately as a priest, or a donger, used to club fish and, now it seemed, fisheries officer Matthews.

For several seconds, he and the fisherman stood eyeing each other from a short distance. The Owl, standing calf-deep in water, swinging the club menacingly; officer Matthews standing on the ramp, looking down, waiting patiently. He knew that, unless the Owl had well-hidden talents as a long-distance swimmer, or rower, he was trapped.

Even Beach Bum could see that. 'Den. Come on, mate. Give it away,' he shouted, just as the Owl started wading away from the ramp, swinging the club above his head, yelling abuse.

For a few metres officer Matthews shadowed him along the shoreline. It was only a matter of time, he knew, before the man ran out of steam.

Sure enough, the more powerful Owl made one last bid for freedom, splashing out of the water, like some prehistoric sea monster, still swinging the club, still cursing incomprehensibly until, confronted by not one but two advancing officers, he lost his footing, and fell ignominiously backwards in the shallow water.

The two men dived on top of him. Still he refused to give in, thrashing in the shallow water like a beached kingfish for several more seconds, until his head was pressed under the water and into the soft sand long enough to drain from him the last air bubbles of belligerence. Handcuffed, he was dragged from the water.

Now, Matthews and Nevin seized the fish, the boat and a quantity of illegal netting and arrested the two men. They took them immediately to the St George local area command centre in nearby Kogarah to be charged with illegal fishing and resisting a fisheries officer in the exercise of his functions.

It had all looked pretty routine. Except that when police came to consider whether the older, more aggressive angler should be further charged with assault and checked his record on computer, they found he had a long history record of violent crime. As well as an oddly familiar name.

ഓയോയോ

Such was his shock at seeing the newspaper poster that Wayne Danniher had automatically jammed both feet hard down, forgetting in the instant that he could not operate the clutch and brake pedals from his passenger seat. For a moment, he thought that, like his old boss, he had snapped a tendon.

At the same time, Path had braked hard, as instructed, causing a car behind to make an emergency stop, and throwing her and Wayne forward. No one was hurt. No cars were damaged. But Prior was furious. 'What now?' she demanded, as Danniher flung open the door.

'Birdman Case,' he said, turning to her with wild, urgent eyes. 'There's been a development.' Prior shook her head. 'I don't believe this. You're worse than...' But it was too late. Danniher was already running back to the shop where he'd seen the poster. 'Won't take a moment.'

It was empty but for a bored-looking girl, sitting behind the counter, reading a magazine. 'Papers? Papers?' he demanded, looking round on the shop, thrusting a ten dollar note in her direction. 'Over there,' the girl said, as she shrank from the wild-eyed stranger.

He picked up a newspaper from a shallow pile. Where was it? Yes! There they were, at the foot of the front page, almost the identical words: BIRDER MURDERS: SECOND MAN HELD. Hastily, he scanned the story. Damnation. It told him nothing new, apart from what was in the poster.

The first paragraph revealed only that police in Berwick were now questioning a second man in connection with the murders of Phillip Clarkson and Ellis Enderby, the eminent bird experts. But most of the story, written by Karen Chan, was a restatement of recent history.

Danniher looked around frantically. 'Phone. Is there a phone here?' For a couple of seconds the girl behind the counter stared at him in alarm, as if desperately trying to think how her boss would expect her to handle a crazy customer.

'There's a blue box, outside,' she said, meekly, relieved to see him turn on his heels, come back, fumble in his pockets, and then rush out again.

'Your change, sir.'

Danniher did not hear. He was already through to Berwick police station. A familiar, Scottish voice answered. 'Berwick police. PC McCrimond speaking.'

He could barely hear above the noise of the traffic trundling through the town. 'McCrimond, is that you? It's Wayne. Wayne Danniher.'

'Thought it wouldn't be too long before you rang, sir. We tried to contact you a few days ago, but your mobile must be off. Aren't you supposed to be on holiday?'

'Yeah, yeah.' Much though he liked McCrimond, Danniher had no time, or change, for small talk. 'The Birdman Case. So, what's happened?'

'Another man's been charged. But you should speak to Mario. I'm sure he'd want to tell you himself.'

'Don't tell me he's at Berwick again?'

'No. He's back at home. I'll put you through if you like.'

'Don't worry, I'll do it. I'm running out of change.' Danniher slammed the phone down, ran back into the shop, picked up his change from the puzzled girl and dialled again. The phone range several times. Don't say Palmeira's out.

'Hello, Jenny Palmeira.'

'Jen. It's Wayne…'

'Hi. I'm just rushing out. I'll pass you on to Mario. He's right here beside me.'

Danniher could hear Jenny saying goodbye to her husband as she handed the phone over to him.

'Wayne. How's it going? Great result, eh?'

This was becoming infuriating. 'Mate, I dunno. I been out of touch for a few days…'

'I know. They tried to get you, before phoning me…'

'Stop messing about. So, who was it, then?'

'Morris. Dennis Morris.'

At first, Danniher thought he must have misheard. 'Derek Morris?'

'No. His younger brother. Dennis Morris.'

For several seconds, Danniher did not reply. Desperately, he tried to cast his mind back through his various meetings with Morris, on the cliff-ledge, at the park, at the funeral, at his little house in Kurnell.

'You still there, Wayne?' asked Palmeira.

Finally, Danniher spoke. 'Dennis Morris. So that was his name. The one in the photograph. Morris Minor.'

Now, it was Palmeira's turn to be confused. 'I don't understand.'

Danniher sighed deeply. 'Perhaps I didn't mention it at the time. But at Morris's house. Derek Morris's house. There was this old picture of him playing in the backyard with another little boy. Dennis.' He paused. 'Now we know what happened to him: he grew up big and ugly and violent.'

'I'm sorry, Mario. I should've made the connection.' He paused again. 'I remember, after Derek's death, we tried to turn up a next-of-kin. The nearest was a sister-in-law, or something. In Melbourne, I think.'

'Don't be too hard on yourself,' said Palmeira. 'This Dennis didn't live with Derek. Had a place over in Matraville. Seems to have a few mates he goes drinking and fishing with, drives a cab, but basically pretty much another lonely bachelor.'

'The cab? Then shouldn't Koslowski have…'

'No. I checked. It wasn't his. Seems he just borrowed it so it wasn't registered in his name.

'But still, I...'

Palmeira cut him short. 'It was just as much my fault, anyway.'

'Rubbish. You're just saying that.'

'I wish I was. But Bob Adamovitch — bless him — reminded me yesterday that he'd mentioned a Dennis when he checked Morris on that list of birders I gave him right at the start. I should have made the connection as well. One of those things I guess.'

'Ancient history,' suggested Danniher brightening slightly. 'So how did you get on to him?'

'I didn't. He was given to me. A couple of days ago. By the blokes down at St George. Stroke of luck really. They were running computer checks on a poacher-type who'd put up a bit of a fight, when one of them thought the name sounded familiar...'

'Another win for the Eagle Eye system, eh?'

'No, remembered reading it in the newspapers, I'm afraid.'

'Obviously have their uses after all.'

'I wouldn't go that far,' Palmeira laughed. 'Anyway, they checked the files and rang Berwick looking for you.'

'And I'd just left for the bloody rainforests.'

'Something like that. Anyway, instead of passing them up the line to one of Jonno's boys at HQ, McCrimond put them on to me. Said I deserved a change of luck.'

'Good on her.'

'Absolutely.' Even through the roar of passing traffic, Danniher could detect the joy in Palmeira's voice. It had been several weeks since he'd heard that. 'Even Jonno was forced to let me back in on the interviews.'

'Good on you. So, has Morris been charged yet?'

'No. But he will be. I've had a couple of chats with him. He's still denying everything, even the fish...'

'The fish?'

'I'll explain later. When you get back. But he'll be charged soon enough. When he was arrested he had the club used to bash Clarkson with him. And when we searched his garage we found a spade. He says it was for digging worms, but it looks the right shape to explain those other cuts on Clarkson's head.'

'Sounds pretty solid.'

'Sure. As usual, we're waiting on forensics, but it all fits. We even found an aluminium boat round the back of his house.'

Oh god, the boat. Briefly, Danniher wondered whether to tell Palmeira that it was probably the same boat that he'd seen, parked outside Derek Morris's home. Perhaps another time.

'Another thing, Wayne.'

'Yes?'

'Dennis the Menace iseems to have been a bit of a night owl altogether. Getting home in the early hours. Sleeping through the mornings. Bit of fishing in the arvos, then off in a cab.'

Danniher thought, and realised, so that explains how Derek got around town, how he got up to Palm Beach and back. His was the cab the neighbours spotted. 'I suppose Dennis would also have dropped Clarkson's car off after helping him dispose of the body?'

'It looks that way.'

'How did he get back then, if Derek couldn't drive?

'I don't know yet. Walked some ways and then caught a cab? It's a minor detail. I'm sure he'll tell us sooner or later.'

Danniher was running out of dollar coins. 'Any idea yet why Dennis did it?'

Back in Sydney, Palmeira stopped to think. In the rush to confirm the who and the how, he'd not really paused to consider the why.

'I give up. You tell me. He got off on the thrill? He had a record of violence. He was paid by Derek? Possibly. He had a thing against birdmen, as well? I doubt it. Maybe it was simply because they were brothers? They looked out for each other.'

'Like Phillip and Paul Clarkson?'

'Could be.'

Silence fell between the two men.

'Wayne? You still there?'

'Yeah.'

'I've got to go. Pick up the girls.'

'Oh?'

'Jenny's back working full-time now and…well, I'm off the crutches, but until the leg gets properly better, I'm sort of working round her.'

'Flexi-time, like?'

'I suppose so.' To Danniher, Palmeira sounded resigned rather than rapt with the arrangement. 'We'll see how it goes. Can't let this job ruin your whole life.'

'No.' Danniher sounded equally unconvinced. 'Do you need me to come back and…'

'No. Get off and enjoy your holiday. Give my love to Sandy. She's a good match for you.'

Briefly, Danniher considered pressing his case to return, but then thought better of it. 'OK, boss. Take care. See you around.'

Gently, he put the phone back on the hook and walked back to the car. Path Prior was leaning against the passenger-side door, eating a banana. To Danniher, she looked impatient, even angry, but undeniably sexy.

'Don't tell me, we're going back to Berwick.'

Danniher paused for dramatic effect, frowned apologetically, then smiled broadly. 'No. We're going on holiday. Get in.'

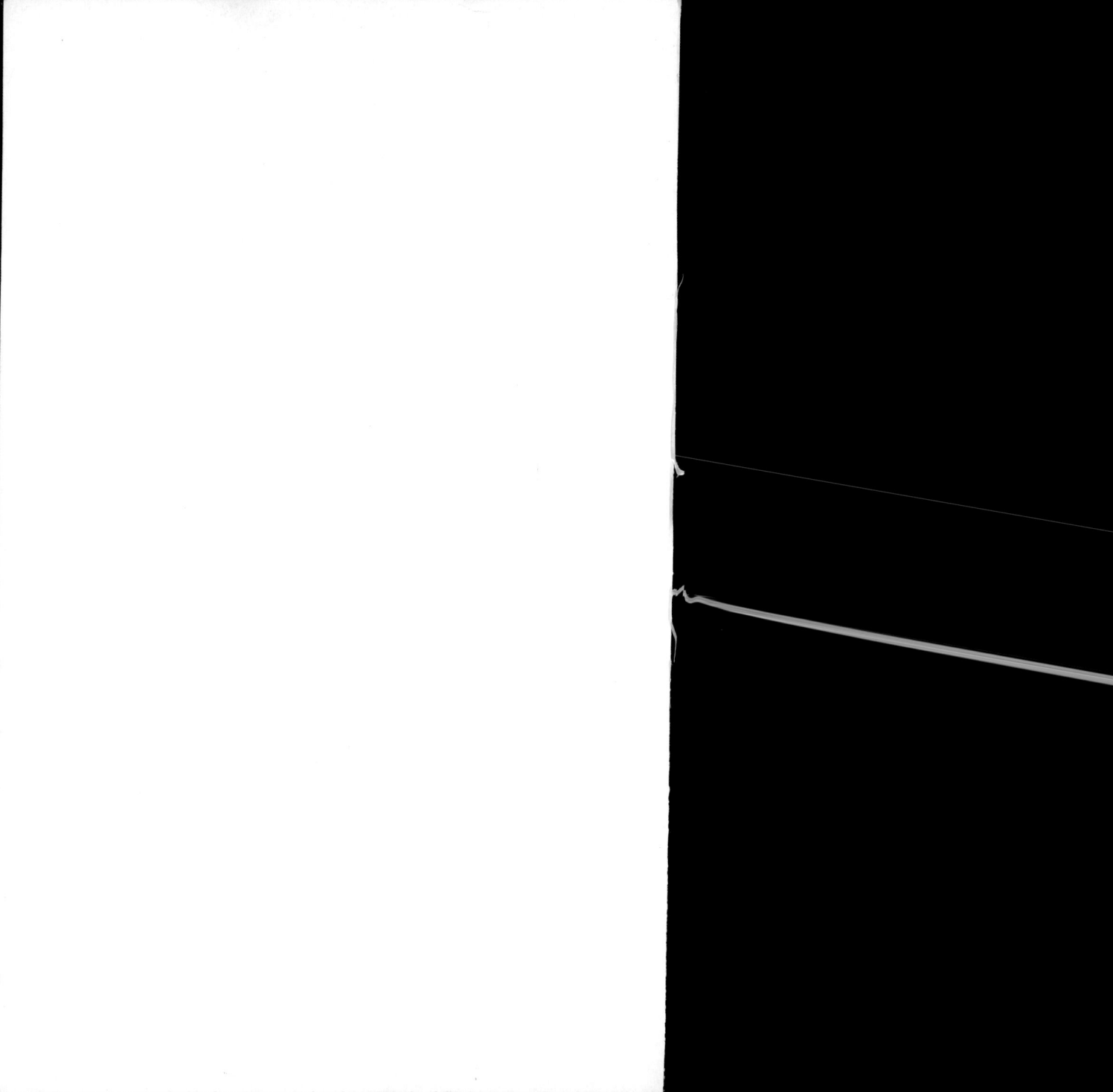